DUST OF LIFE

A Novel

By

Cameron Michaels

www.dustoflife.com
www.cameronmichaels.net

DUST OF LIFE

Copyright © 2003

Cameron Michaels

ISBN 0-9707600-3-5

First printing   May 2003
Bellwether Publishing

The content of this book is based on actual events and the people who endured them. Wherever possible, permission to include their personae was secured from those persons (or their estates) depicted in this novel. The events themselves were researched with meticulous care to insure authenticity. Otherwise, any similarities to any person, occurrence, or location is strictly coincidental and not to be interpreted by the reader as anything other than a work of fiction.

Visit the author's website at www.cameronmichaels.net
Or www.dustoflife.com

To my father: who served his country and
loved his family.
(US Navy: Oct. '56 – Oct. '58)

A book project doesn't just happen. It's the result of a collaboration of many people. I'd like to thank a few of them now.

Special thanks to my good friend and fellow author Robert 'Bert' Rooney. Without your help, this never would have come together. To my other author friends, Den Gleason, George Grace, and Bunkie Lynn, I say "Thank you for your support and the occasional kick in the ass." Thanks to the members of my focus groups, who got to see the unfinished and unpolished product and still offered their encouragement. My thanks to Chris Donegan with United Imaging, for his help with the cover design and artwork. Robert Dixson created the background image for the cover and graciously allowed me to use it. He is also the web master for The Wall USA web site. (www.theWall-USA.com) Christine Nguyen's lovely face is the one you see enlarged on the cover. Her interest and enthusiasm validated all of my efforts and allayed the doubts and insecurities I had amassed while writing this book. The photograph of the "Street Child" on the cover is courtesy of Dr. Kenneth Hoffman of Seton Hall University. My collective thanks to the countless people who helped me in researching the details so I could 'get it right'.

To anyone who has ever worn the uniform of any one of the United States armed forces, we all owe you a debt of gratitude. To my family I simply say this, "Thank you for your love and support." Most importantly, I thank God for all of His blessings.

Cameron Michaels

"Whatsoever you do to the least of my brethren, that you do unto me."

Matthew 25:40

Prologue

They were coming. Mai could hear them laughing as they approached. Standing shin-deep in trash in the mid-day heat, she hastened her search for just one scrap of something edible amidst the pungent smell of rotting garbage. She spat and blew at the flies buzzing her lips; a huge rat brushed her leg, en route to a nearby chicken carcass. Glancing over her shoulder at the approaching mob, Mai's heart pounded as she sifted through the squalor with her bare hands.

Half a world away, other eight-year-old girls played with dolls, sipped imaginary tea from tiny cups, and cuddled with their mothers at bedtime. In Mai's world, each day brought a new challenge in survival for a girl who had been "born of the enemy," born *bui doi.*

"*Nguoi lai!*" one of the approaching children called out to Mai. "Half-breed!"

"*My lai!*" another cried out with equal venom, launching something in Mai's direction.

Mai felt a heavy thud and her vision blurred as a half-rotten melon struck the side of her head. She tumbled forward, into the filth but did not cry out as the approaching horde of children pelted her with rotting fruit and decaying animal remains. Nor did she protest when the small mob pushed her down into the refuse and began kicking and hitting her. Blow after punishing blow landed on her back, ribs, and head. She curled into a ball face down in the putrid foulness and waited for it to end.

When the beating had stopped Mai crawled away, hungry and hurting, clutching a small piece of bread within the waste heap just a few miles north of Da Nang.

Chapter One

It was a simple wooden box, lying in ambush among the flotsam of their lives. Had she known the turmoil it would cause, Donna never would have opened it. Maybe the past was meant to stay where it belonged.

After watching the last of the mourners amble away along the sidewalk, Donna closed the front door. Leaning headfirst against it, she exhaled heavily: finally alone. The old house seemed to sigh along with her. The whole ordeal had been harder than she had ever imagined.

From behind her she felt the familiar beckoning that had started that morning. At first she tried ignoring it, hoping its lure was temporary. But its pull had only grown stronger as the day progressed. Donna turned and glanced up at the source, visible just off the kitchen beyond the small foyer. With her resistance a mere formality, it began dragging her like an unseen tether until she found herself slowly climbing the attic stairs.

It was the same standard footlocker issued to every soldier: that hideous olive green color, dull metal hinges, a common hasp for a lock, and rope handles. On the top, stenciled in three-inch white block letters, was U.S. ARMY, his name and service number.

Kneeling on the dusty planked floor in her black dress, Donna slowly ran her delicate fingers over the painted letters before lifting the cover, half-hoping there was nothing of interest inside. Memories, some fond, others painful, washed over her as the contents of the battered wooden box came into view.

"Donna?" a voice called from below. "You up there?"

The lid slammed shut. Startled, Donna turned toward the stairway leading down to the main floor of the modest one-story house. She made no reply.

With his feet landing heavily on the old steps, the top of Brad's head gradually rose into view through the skinny balusters. While he didn't have a Mister Universe physique, he was far from being out of shape; standing well over six feet in his socks and tipping the scales at better than two hundred and thirty pounds. He stopped partway up, looking like his head was perched on the floor. A pair of cool blue eyes greeted her, tucked under a canopy of thinning brown hair.

"You all right?" he asked, his head cocked slightly to one side.

"I'm fine." She was nodding, her eyes momentarily closed. "You just startled me. I thought you were still driving Wanda home."

"It was a quick trip." Brad climbed another step, his broad chest now in view. "She's quite a character," he added, his eyebrows rising.

"She's always been feisty."

"She thinks I'm too skinny." Brad laughed and patted his flat, hard stomach.

"She thinks everyone is too skinny."

"Said I should take you out to dinner more," he added, continuing up the steps. "Put some meat on your bones, too."

"Her home cooking would do that in no time." She took in a deep breath.

"You look tired," Brad offered, a note of concern in his

voice. "It's been a long couple of days. We need to go away somewhere together." He paused for a moment. "Get away from the world for a while."

"I used to come up *here* to get away from the world." Donna reached out to peel an errant fleck of green paint from the side of the locker.

"It's pretty secluded." He glanced around the room at the bare studs and rafters. "The décor could use some work, though."

"Things went well today."

Brad nodded. "It was a nice service," he said, reaching with a sturdy arm farther up the railing. "Reverend Patterson said some good things about your father."

"They were fishing buddies." Donna reached to the back of her head and untied her thick mane of auburn hair. "I think he'll miss him as much as I will," she said, letting loose her long, flowing locks. She felt them bounce back and forth with the shaking of her head like the rhythm of a pony's tail in full gallop.

"I never knew your dad had so many friends."

"He didn't always." She glanced, once again, down at the locker. "It took a while for this town to accept things."

"What things?"

Donna didn't answer but only looked around the small attic. It was mid-day and a shaft of sunlight shone through a small semi-circular window near the peak. On either side, stretching from the far end to the stairwell were stacks of various-sized cardboard boxes, all lined up like a company of good little soldiers. Even the attic was perfectly neat. She smiled at the thought. Specks of dust, floating in the light, danced in circles as she let out a burst of breath.

Brad climbed the last of the steps, his towering frame nearly reaching the low ceiling. He knelt beside her. "You gonna be okay?"

She took his hand in hers and nuzzled it to her cheek, ignoring the roughness of a workingman's calluses.

"This house seemed so big when I was a girl." Looking around the musty attic, Donna continued. "I used to sneak up here and read books I knew he didn't want me to read."

"Like what? I can't picture you as a renegade."

"All the good ones," she replied. "Books like *Looking for Mister Goodbar*." She looked off at the far wall. "*The Story of 'O'.*"

"Whoa, no wonder you're so twisted."

Donna looked up, rolling her eyes. "He is probably turning in his grave right now." She laughed slightly. "He was pretty conservative, if you couldn't tell."

"He must've known what he was doing." Brad placed his big hands on her delicate shoulders and began massaging them.

"Oh, please." Donna reared back, offering a look of mock disgust.

"You turned out pretty good."

"Give me a break." She playfully pushed his hands away.

"Hey, cut me some slack," Brad began. "I'm new at this support thing." Brad shrugged and smiled again from one side of his closed mouth, a dimple forming on his left cheek.

"Thank you for taking Wanda home," she said, and then motioned for him to continue massaging her shoulders.

"No problem," Brad replied, kneading the muscles near her neck. "She only lives a couple miles away," he continued, now plying his fingers to her upper arms. After a moment, he reached down and lifted her chin. "How 'bout you? Ready to go?"

Donna sat in silence for a moment, looking deep into his eyes, bright with sincerity. "I just want to be alone right now."

His eyes betrayed the hurt she knew he was feeling at the remark. "Don't make me worry about you," Brad said as he stood up.

"Why would you worry?"

"It's my job."

"To make sure I don't fall apart?"

Brad pursed his lips and looked off to his left. "You don't have to go through this alone." He looked back at her, his expression reflecting his insecurities.

She reached for his hand, hoping he would understand that sometimes alone is the only way to face certain things. It was alone that she had faced much of the pain in her life. Was there any other way?

"I'll see you at the motel." She nodded slowly then squeezed his hand. "I'll drive my father's car over. We can return it in the morning."

Brad smiled and gently stroked her hair before turning away. He stopped at the stairwell, his hand on the banister. "He didn't like me very much, did he?" Brad remarked, without turning around.

"It wasn't that he didn't like you," she continued. "He just didn't like you lusting after his daughter."

Brad chuckled before descending the last few steps. "Don't stay too long, okay?"

Donna stared at the empty stairway for several long moments before turning her attention once again to the foot-locker. She wondered if the answers were worth the pain they might inflict. But the pull on her conscience would not be denied. From somewhere within that plain, green chest a force stronger than her will beckoned her. She once again lifted the lid.

On the left side of the locker were several pairs of neatly pressed fatigues. Next to them lay a pair of shiny black combat boots and three pairs of tightly rolled dark green

socks. Farther to the right was a smaller wooden box, about
the size used for cigars. On the lid was a rough carving of
an elephant carrying a log with its trunk. Donna had seen it
before and knew that her father had kept it for years. It
reminded her of the little carved wooden boxes you see at
flea markets and import stores.

Inside she found his old service forty-five, a pair of dog
tags on a silver chain, and his rack of service ribbons and
medals from his dress uniform. Seeing the pistol again
reminded her of the times he tried, in spite of her reluctance,
to teach her to shoot. The gun was heavy and too big for her
small hand and she hated the noise it made. The explosion
from the shell hurt her ears and caused her to close her eyes.

With her heart beating heavily, she reached slowly into
the chest; daring to let her fingertips make contact with the
weapon. They recoiled from the cold smooth steel.
Withdrawing her hand, she inhaled deeply, trying to slow
her heart. Her hands were suddenly cold.

Donna turned her attention to another region of the old
chest. Stacked in the upper right corner were six leather-
bound books bundled together with heavy twine.

She closed the small, carved box and lifted the heavy
batch of journals, allowing her fingers to gently glide along
the soft surface of the leather. Bringing the packet to her
nose, she inhaled the comforting aroma. They even smelled
like him. The twine unraveled with one pull, the bowknot
yielding readily. Donna carefully opened each one, the
inside covers revealing the year they were written. She
picked one at random, opened it somewhere toward the
back and began reading.

Nov. 18th, 1971
*We got hit hard again today. What a goat fuck. Charlie
has been pretty quiet the last few days. I guess they got*

bored. Things around the camp had just settled down since the mortar attacks last week. That's how the little bastards work. They wait until the very moment we let our guard down. They always seem to know just when to hit us.

I saw her again. That little waif that comes around the camp every so often looking for food. (All these orphans are starting to get to me.) She comes and goes, like most of the kids. Most of them get taken to the orphanages in Da Nang, but it's strange that she's never around when the other kids get rounded up. It's like she knows when it's going to happen and doesn't want to go. Maybe she likes it here. I see some of the guys giving her food. I suppose that's OK.

Donna flipped ahead a few more pages.

Nov. 27th, 1971
We got mortared again today. Lost Miller and Gaines in the firefight. Gaines was new and nobody knew him well, but he was a good kid. Freddie Miller was short, only had two months left on his tour. He talked about becoming a stand-up comic when he got back to the World. He would have been a good one. He could make anyone laugh. He was a good soldier, too. I'll miss him.

She closed the journal.

It was late fall in Tennessee, yet the sunlight from the crisp day was beginning to bake the dark roof outside. After closing the lid on the locker, Donna scooped up the five leather-bound journals and left the attic that grew stuffier by the moment.

She descended the stairs to the first floor where she passed a row of pictures hanging on the wall just outside the kitchen. The first in the series had been snapped at his retirement party just one year earlier. Donna stared at herself in the snapshot, a lovely woman of thirty-four. Her long, thick hair had been tied in a ponytail, revealing a face that had turned many heads over the years. Her slender body filled her summer dress with a regal grace.

Donna ran her fingertips over his image. He never said anything directly, but she knew that he had mixed emotions about retiring. He was still a fairly young man, but the years were taking their toll on his health. Retirement was not what he wanted, but he knew it was inevitable.

The next shot was taken four years earlier, on his sixtieth birthday. He was still an imposing man, even at that age. How time had flown by. She felt a tear roll down her cheek. She would miss him more than she ever imagined.

The last picture was an eight-by-ten, showing a handsome man, in his late thirties, standing next to a gangly nine-year-old girl. His short-cropped hair made even more prominent his square jaw and high cheekbones. He stood a full head and shoulders above her in the picture. Donna gazed with contempt at the image of the little girl beside him.

"He gave you everything," she said, glaring at the image of the girl. Her hair looked black in the old photo, her Asian features pronounced. "And you only brought him shame."

"Was I the only one?" A woman's voice called to her from the kitchen doorway.

Donna recognized the voice instantly and turned toward the lovely mixed-race, half-Vietnamese woman dressed in a white *áu dài* –a traditional garment of loose fitting pants covered by a long, flowing top.

"Mai, what are you doing here?" Donna ran a glance up and down her body.

"I lived here, too," Mai said. "Remember?" she added, expressionless.

"I'd rather not," Donna replied, turning and walking slowly toward the kitchen.

"What are those?" Mai pointed a slender finger at the volumes in Donna's hands.

"None of your business." Donna pulled the journals close to her chest, unconsciously wrapping her arms around them.

"How can it be your business without it also being mine?"

Donna did not answer her but brushed past Mai, entered the kitchen, laid the journals on the tile counter and opened a cupboard door. Inside, the cups, glasses, and plates were arranged in perfect order.

"Why did you come here?" Donna said, dragging a coffee can across the counter.

"I think you know." Mai moved from the doorway into the kitchen.

"I didn't see you at the funeral." Donna pulled a package of coffee filters from the cupboard.

"I was there," Mai replied. "You chose not to see me."

"Don't be ridiculous." She filled the coffeemaker with water. "Why would I do that?"

Mai didn't answer.

Donna remained silent as she scooped coffee into the filter and flipped a switch. Turning toward Mai, she lowered her voice and slowly shook her head. "You don't belong here."

"He was my father, too," Mai replied, standing her ground.

"Yes, he was." Donna nodded at Mai. "But you were never his daughter." She struggled as the words caught in her throat. "You betrayed him."

Donna tried to sound menacing but she knew Mai would not take her seriously. The attempt would have been amusing, if the underlying problems between them weren't so serious. The two women stared at each other for a long moment before Mai broke the silence.

"You have no right to read those," Mai said, tipping her head toward the journals,

"He's gone now," Donna said. "What does it matter?"

"It was my life, not yours." Mai's face tightened. "You have no right to intrude."

"I have to know."

"You will never learn the truth until you are ready to face it," Mai said. "And you will not find it in those books alone."

Donna turned her back to Mai and stared out the kitchen window at the back yard. The old swing set she played on as a child had been replaced with a hammock on a metal frame. The tree house she and her father built in the large oak tree was still there but the knotted rope she used as a ladder was gone. He must have taken it down to keep the neighborhood kids out. She remembered when her tree house was a castle tower, she was the trapped princess, and Jimmy Tyler was her brave knight in shining armor. He would jump over the back fence with a beach towel tied around his neck like a cape, swinging his wooden sword, to kill the dreaded dragon and rescue his ladylove. A few years later, in that same castle tower, he had given the Princess her first kiss. Donna hadn't seen Jimmy since high school and hadn't thought about him in years. Now, she wondered what happened to him. He wasn't at the funeral so she assumed he moved away.

"Some things are better left alone," Mai said, her voice trailing off toward the front door.

Donna awoke from her thoughts and turned to reply but found Mai gone and the room empty.

A short time later, Donna stood in her father's bedroom and slowly slid his dresser drawer open. Reaching in, she closed her eyes and let her fingertips absorb the softness of his cable knit sweater. She slipped it over her head. It wrapped loosely around her waistline, falling below her hips, the sleeves swallowing her hands and arms.

Curled up in his favorite chair in the cozy living room, Donna took a final sip of the hot coffee in her hands. She set the cup on a nearby table and picked up the journal entitled '1972'. With her heart thumping, she hesitated a moment, unsure. Her hand moved with a will of its own, tentatively opening the old book.

Feb. 16th, 1972

This might be the hardest decision I will ever make. But, I've made up my mind. After last week, I can't do this any more. I'm going to see Turner tomorrow.

Chapter Two

Jack Roberts craned his neck to look out the window while straining to hear his thoughts over the white noise of the droning engines. Spreading out beneath him to the horizon was the flat, low-lying countryside; a random mosaic of lush green jungles and rice paddies. In the distance, nearly hidden under a gray-brown canopy of smog lay Saigon, a city slowly choking on its foul air and endless hordes of refugees seeking shelter from the war.

A case of beer traded to an opportunistic flight operations officer was all it had taken to get on the next transport. From this altitude he could not hear the gunfire. The distant screams of terror were stifled and the constant smell of death was held in check, if only for a short time. Cramped and noisy, the small cargo plane was his temporary haven, providing him a brief yet welcome respite from the suffocating heat below.

On the ground, Jack could hardly recognize the beautiful landscape he had first seen when he arrived in-country. How it had changed. The land itself was like a beautiful woman disfigured by some sadistic assailant, her wounds deep and her scars visible, perhaps permanent. He took another look out the window. From this distance he could barely see the scars, only the level expanse of the Mekong Delta sprawling through the haze toward the distant rolling hills.

He stared out the window for several minutes, thinking how distance was like alcohol; both distorting reality. The thought brought to mind a few women he had indulged because of distorted reality. He could barely recall their faces. Maybe that was a good thing.

There had been a woman once, a local girl from Saigon, a face he could recall. But, that was five years and several lifetimes ago. He hadn't been back since the night he broke her heart, deciding instead to stay married to the army. He wondered where she might be now and hoped the years had given her solace. Part of him really didn't want to know. It had taken every day and every shot of scotch since then to keep her memory expunged.

Thank God for distance.

Thank God for alcohol.

The plane landed at the Tan Son Nhut Air Base, just north of the city. Jack hailed a taxi outside the terminal.

The ride into town brought back memories of another city, a different Saigon. It had been only five years, but it may as well have been fifty. There to greet him were the same wide boulevards and narrow side streets, lined with tall, leafy trees, countless bicycles, and nearly as many lumbering water buffalo pulling rickety carts that threatened to collapse under their own weight.

The same one and two-story buildings, connected by low hung awnings covering street-side cafés, stood like spectators watching his return. In many ways it was the same old city. He could still taste the familiar sting of the bitter, fouled air. In the busy streets the heavy hum of the scooters, mopeds and motorcycles resonated through him like low voltage. Yet, some things were different: not at all as he had remembered them.

Gone were the young lovers strolling arm-in-arm along the handcrafted mosaic sidewalks. Missing were the elegant women browsing along the outdoor markets in their colorful *áo dàis*. In their place, the newly arrived refugees wore the drab pajama-like outfits of the peasant class, fleeing the countryside in droves. The streets were crowded with orphans begging for handouts, old men on crutches and old women with children in tow. Young men were only conspicuous in their absence.

Jack's khaki pants and the back of his heavily starched shirt clung to the vinyl seat as he climbed from the twenty-year-old taxi. The fabric pulled away with a steady hiss. He rubbed the back of his neck, moist and gritty from the short ride in the mid-day heat.

He walked along the narrow street, sidestepping piles of garbage, squinting at the white sheet of paper in his hand as he went. The scribbled note said 1265 *Pho Con Rùa*. The driver had assured him he was in the right place. Turtle Street. Jack shrugged. Every few steps he scanned the doorways and storefronts for an address. His foot slipped on something slick.

Jack stifled a cough, almost choking on the acrid exhaust fumes from the heavy traffic flowing noisily by on the busy street. Farther along, he saw a young woman carrying two buckets full of water, one on either end of a long pole slung across her shoulders. She startled a huge rat feasting on a rotting pile of entrails from some unidentified animal, while a toddler followed her close behind, his naked body caked with filth.

A few steps farther he nearly tripped over two men squatting in the middle of the sidewalk. Flanked by baskets and rows of produce, they were unaware that Jack had almost bowled them over. Having picked up a passing knowledge of the language, Jack was able to follow part of their conversation. He couldn't make out everything, but they seemed to be arguing over the best way to repair a disassembled bicycle.

Standing in front of a small restaurant, he fixed his gaze

on the sign hanging over the grimy windows. The pale layer of the stucco-like cement had pulled away from the exterior in many places, looking like the rough scales of some dormant beast. Several bullet holes formed a dotted line over the front doorway. A small window next to the door had been boarded up. He took a few tentative steps toward the entrance, pausing only briefly to notice the smell of something cooking inside mingled with the stench of stagnant garbage along the street.

Once inside, Jack strained to see his way in the dim light. He smiled, seeing his friend and mentor sitting at a booth at the far end of the restaurant. He was next to a window with his back to the wall, an old habit of his.

The noisy room, filled with the lunchtime crowd, was narrow and long. Two rows of wooden tables flanked his pathway. He removed his hat and waved at the man he had traveled so far to see. Jack's late night phone call, placed out of the blue it seemed, had set the stage for their meeting. Jack approached the table. The two men shook hands and sat down.

Across the table sat Brigadier General Turner "The Burner" O'Keefe, a barrel-chested, war-horse of a man, looking older than his fifty-three years. A red, bulbous nose anchored itself to the center of his wide face; streaks of his shiny scalp peeked through wiry strands of red and gray hair. His uniform, dotted with sweat, strained against his stocky frame; his thick arms filled the short sleeves of his neatly pressed shirt.

The tiny bar, located in a working class section of Saigon, smelled of stale beer and day-old puke. From the back of the room came the clatter of clanging pans and the staccato chatter of Vietnamese kitchen workers barking orders at each other in their native tongue.

"How was the flight down from Da Nang?" the general asked.

"I swear they have teams of dwarfs designing those planes," Jack replied, shifting in his seat.

"What'd you take, a C-119?"

Jack shook his head, his lips slightly pursed. "Caribou."

"I'm surprised you can still walk."

"Barely." Jack smiled as he nodded. "I don't know which was worse, the flying garbage can or the kamikaze taxi ride." But, he knew deep down that being tossed around in a transport and basting in the back of a cab was at least familiar to him. What he was about to do scared him half to death.

"Hungry?" Turner nodded toward his plate. "The fish head soup here will take your scalp off."

"No thanks." He waved a hand, looking sideways at the general's plate.

"Well, then," Turner continued. "How 'bout some of this *chò*?" He bit into a hunk of dark meat skewered with a small bamboo stick. The general licked his fingers. "Hard to believe this little guy was fetching sticks this morning."

"No. Thanks," Jack replied, shaking his head. "Really, I'm not hungry."

"So, what's so urgent," Turner said, "that I get a phone call from you in the middle of the night?"

"I'm sorry about that. I shouldn't have called so late."

"Don't worry about it." Turner waved his hand. "As I recall, I dragged your old man out of bed a time or two. What's on your mind?"

He stared at the general for what seemed like an eternity. The resolve that stood so firm only twelve hours earlier was quickly fading, replaced by an anxiety he didn't understand. Jack groped desperately for the words to begin, but was instead stifled by an inexplicable fear nibbling away at the fringes of his courage.

Jack's thoughts briefly flashed to his boyhood days,

growing up on one army base after another. "Where ya from, soldier?" Someone would now ask him. *Where am I from?* The thought of actually having a home to return to seemed suddenly amusing. His mother had died four years ago and his father's final days were spent in a VA hospital near Raleigh just one year ago. His closest blood relative was a cousin he hadn't seen since grade school, who might still live somewhere in South Carolina. This is crazy, he thought. *Where the hell am I going to go?*

With each passing day, it seemed, the war would claim one of the few friends he had left in the world. His life, the totality of his existence boiling down to the uniform he wore, hit him one day like a cold slap, and it had come at the hands of a terrified eight-year-old girl.

Jack searched the general's face, as if conducting critical reconnaissance for a mission that could not fail. A bead of sweat rolled down the middle of his arched back, riding his spine under his shirt.

"I need a favor."

"A favor?" The general pointed toward his beer while looking over Jack's shoulder, toward a waitress. He held up two fingers.

Jack looked down at the table for a moment before raising his eyes to meet the general's. "A big one."

Jack paused for a moment, thinking that this shouldn't be so goddamned difficult. The man before him had been more of a father to him than even his old man had been. In spite of that, he was still a general. Maybe that's why it was so hard. He could handle disappointing Turner, the man. The thought of disappointing Turner, the general, was more than he could bear.

Jack looked at him with sad eyes. "I want out."

"Out?" Turner took a bite of meat. "Are you crazy? How many years you got in?" he asked, his words garbled by a mouthful of food. "Seventeen? Eighteen?" A small chunk of dark meat flew from his mouth as he spoke. "What about your pension? You're up for lieutenant colonel. You've got a hell of a future, Jack. And having an old 'Ring Knocker'," he tapped his heavy West Point graduation ring on the table for emphasis, "like me in your corner certainly won't do your career any harm."

"I appreciate that," Jack replied. "More than you might know. But, I've made up my mind."

"No," Turner said, waving a hand in front of him. "I'm sorry Jack. But, I'm not going to be a party to ending the career of a damn good soldier."

"I used to be," Jack replied, looking down. "I'm not any more. I'm a liability to my men, Turner."

"Bullshit." Turner's face turned a darker shade of red. "What the hell are you talking about?"

Jack's gaze drifted once again out the window for a moment. "You always told me that I'd know when it was time." He looked the general in the eyes. "Well, it's time."

The general stopped chewing and swallowed. He sat with a pensive look for a moment before taking in a deep breath. "Have you really thought this through?"

"Yes, sir."

Turner nodded. "Jack Roberts not in the army." He shook his head and took a long drink of his beer, his shoulders shrugged slightly. "You'll hate civilian life," Turner added, setting his beer glass down. "There's no order."

"Order?" Jack motioned out the dirty window at the busy, sun-drenched street. "Like this?"

"Oh, hell," Turner replied. He glanced around the room before leaning toward Jack across the table. "Off the record, this whole mess was a SNAFU right from the beginning." He shook the stick full of meat at him. "It'll get better. It has to."

"Better? How?"

"This won't last forever." The general stopped chewing and looked off in the distance. "One way or another, this thing will get resolved and we'll move on to the next...whatever we call these things now." Turner smirked. "Maybe next time around we'll actually be allowed to win."

"That would help."

"Just give it some time, Jack. Things will be back to normal soon."

"I wish I could believe that."

The waitress arrived with two beer bottles and a glass.

Jack thought about his father who had served in the Second World War in Europe and the South Pacific, not far from where he was now. When he was a boy, Jack used to beg his father to tell him war stories. Always disappointed, it would be many years before he understood why his father wouldn't discuss it. It was only after his death, that Jack had found out about the horrors he had endured on the beaches of Normandy. Would he ever have a son from whom he would withhold his own experiences? Would anyone discover the secrets of his career when he was gone?

"This city used to be alive." Jack looked out the window, smudged with unwashed dirt blown from dusty streets. It hadn't been many years since the same streets were humming with merchants and travelers. Many of those same people were now either dead or taking flight. In their place was a new class of victim, walking, limping, even crawling in from the surrounding villages. Even the Americans were beginning to pull out, fearing the inevitable.

"Alive?" Turner swatted at the flies buzzing his plate of food. "Saigon's just another shit hole."

Jack glanced behind him, to the other side of the room where a waitress stood glaring at them, having overheard the remark.

"It wasn't always." Jack cocked his head, his thoughts wandering off to the local girls he had escorted down some of these same busy streets. "Now it's dying a slow death."

"No great loss."

"What are we doing here?" Jack ran his thumb over the opening of his beer bottle. "Are we saving these people?" He motioned with his head toward the crowded street. "Is anyone better off by our being here?"

"Defense contractors, for one."

"That's about it."

"We're soldiers, Jack. We do what we're told." Turner raised his glass, inspecting the last few ounces of the lukewarm liquid.

"Just like that?"

"At the end of the day, I can look myself in the mirror and know that I have a purpose." He accentuated his remark with a quick flick of his glass just before downing the last of his beer.

"And what's your purpose, Turner?"

"Like I said, I'm a soldier. Same as you."

"Is that all? You never wonder what your life might have been like if you'd taken a different road?"

Turner looked down at his hands, unconsciously rubbing his finger devoid of a wedding band. Jack was still an officer candidate when the general had made his choice.

"Hell," Turner looked up at Jack, the slightest hint of remorse in his eyes, "I'm too old to think about that now."

"Well, I'm not."

Turner O'Keefe sat looking at Jack for a long moment. Without looking away, he raised his empty glass, alerting the waitress that he was ready for a refill.

"So, what do you need from me?"

"The discharge paperwork can take up to three months."

"That's not so bad." Turner's brow furrowed. "What's the problem?"

"It's complicated."

The general cast Jack a wary look. "You want an immediate discharge. Is that it?"

"Would that be a problem?" Jack was scratching the label on the beer bottle with his thumbnail.

"A man with your record?" Turner shook his head. "If you're sure about this, I can push that through myself."

"That's only half of it." Jack set his beer down. He looked at his fingers, the tips meeting just above the table as if connecting five circuits. "I have to take a child with me."

Turner let go with a roaring belly laugh. The diminutive waitress, approaching with his beer, reared back slightly at the sudden outburst.

"That's what you get for foolin' around with a loaded gun," Turner said, taking the beer from the young woman. He ran his eyes up and down her shapely buttocks as she walked away. "Should've paid more attention to the hygiene films." He took a long drink.

"She's not mine."

The corners of Turner's face dropped, his thick teeth disappeared behind a curtain of pink lips curving into a frown. A set of bushy eyebrows contracted.

"Now *that*," Turner raised a finger, "is a problem."

"Why's that?"

"Washington's not in a big hurry to flood the states with orphans right now." He looked away. "Hell, Jack. This war isn't exactly going as planned. You know that. Those goddamned hippies," he waved his hand as if motioning toward a group of the unkempt radicals, "got everyone worked up. The public opinion's turning to shit and we can't be parading orphaned gooks around back home. It just doesn't look good."

Jack stared silently at Turner, wondering if he knew him anymore; wondering if he really knew himself.

"The word from the top brass on down is you gotta prove she's yours and then, maybe—"

"Well, I can't." Jack frowned and looked away momentarily. "I told you, she's not mine."

Jack stared at Turner. Another long moment passed between them.

"I don't know, Jack." The general looked down at the table, running his meaty hand over the expanse of his balding head. He pulled his hand away, inspecting the wetness in his palm. "The timing's all wrong. Maybe a few years ago… It's complicated right now. Nixon's got his hands full. There's pressure from the left to wrap this thing up over here. People back home are getting restless. Their boys are coming home in body bags and wheelchairs. They don't want to see more reminders of this place."

"So, we're just gonna sweep them under the rug?" Jack set his bottle down. He laid his hands palms up on the table. "What's gonna happen to these kids?"

"You can't help them," Turner replied. He pulled a handkerchief from his pocket and swabbed his brow. "Somebody will take her in."

"She's a half-breed, Turner," Jack said. "You know what happens to them. She'll be dead in two years. If not, she'll be a drug addict and a street whore by the time she's twelve."

Turner O'Keefe sucked in a long breath. He closed his eyes while wiping his mouth with a napkin.

"Who is she?" He looked Jack up and down. "Why this kid? Of all the poor little wretched bastards running around this country, why did you pick her?"

Jack's mind wandered to that place where the hurt, fear, shame and sorrow get piled up like so much dirty laundry. It's that place where you bury the really dirty clothes; truly believing that one day you will wash them, but knowing you never will. Just the same, you can't get rid of them. They haunt you as much as they define who you are. It was in this place where her memory dwelled, the dirty face of a child whose eyes stared up at him from the elephant grass while he waited for the medics to arrive. They were the same eyes he saw now, accusing and convicting him.

"I guess it was more like she picked me."

Turner O'Keefe sat looking at Jack for a long moment, no doubt deciding how much more he needed to know.

"How in the hell are you gonna take care of a child on your own?" Turner asked. "And a little girl at that."

Jack offered only a weak shrug. "I'll manage."

"Do you have any idea what you're getting into?"

They sat looking at each other until Jack broke the silence.

"Do you remember the first time we hooked up here in Saigon?" Jack nodded toward the entrance. "We were having dinner. Not far from here," he added, moving his head slightly. "You remember that?"

"How could I forget?" Turner answered. "I still can't hear much out of my left ear."

"That sapper who threw the satchel charge through the door," Jack continued. "He was just a damn kid, Turner."

The general wiped his mouth and leaned close to Jack. "That *kid* killed four people that night."

Jack looked away. "When the MPs found him a few hours later, he was already dead."

"Too good for him, if you ask me."

"He was ten." Jack turned his gaze back to the general. "It was a ten-year-old boy."

"Maybe so," Turner responded. "Those four people were just as dead."

Jack looked away, the image of a girl's frail little body slumped in the grass coming to mind. "The NVA strapped a

satchel to her and sent her toward the camp right in the middle of a damn firefight," Jack said. "She got hit." He closed
his eyes, trying to shake the memory of the young girl
writhing in her own blood. "I can't do it any more."

The general raised his eyebrows. "Jack," he said, setting
down a bamboo stick stuffed with meat. "A kid got shot. It's
a terrible thing. But it happens in war. It goes with the terri-
tory."

"Yeah, I know it happens in war," Jack replied. "But it
can happen to someone else from now on."

"You're throwing away one hell of a career."

"I know." Jack nodded. "I can't believe I'm doing this,
either," he added looking down. "But, something tells me
I'm supposed to take this kid. It doesn't make a damn bit of
sense, but I know I gotta do this." Jack looked him in the
eye. "Now."

"It's that important?"

"When's the last time I asked you for anything?"

The general nodded slowly. "I'll make a call to the
Pentagon," Turner offered. "A certain bureaucrat there owes
me a favor. They'll have to run it through the morons over
at State. Might take a couple of weeks."

Jack sat motionless; beads of sweat trickled down his
temples. He wasn't sure if he was more terrified or relieved.
"Thank you," he finally said.

"You may not thank me by the time this is over." Turner
cast Jack a concerned look, his lips pressed tightly together.
"I hope you know what the hell you're getting into."

Jack sat staring back at the general feeling like the floor
had just fallen away beneath his feet.

Chapter Three

"A few more miles and we'll set a new record." Brad smiled while glancing sideways at Donna from the driver's seat.

"A new record?" Donna turned to him, shaken from her daze. "For what?"

"Continuous silence on a trip." He glanced at the road ahead and then into the rearview mirror before changing lanes to pass a slow moving truck.

"You keep track of such things?"

"Yeah," Brad continued, slouching in his seat, his head half turned toward her. With one hand on the wheel, his other hand was resting on his left knee. "The old record was one hundred and thirty miles. 'Course, we were fighting then." He offered a mischievous smile. "Are we fighting now?"

"No." Donna shook her head and looked out the window, her thoughts as distant as the horizon. With her eyes fixed on the rugged countryside far beyond the highway, she foundered in a flood of memories, their rising current threatening to sweep her away.

It was nearly one hundred and ninety miles from her father's house in Middleton to her home in Oak Ridge. She knew every inch of it by heart, having traveled it so many times during the last year as her father's health deteriorated. The journey had never felt as lonely as it did at that very moment. Donna stared into the blur of dull, gray leafless trees and browned grass along the highway.

It was mid-morning on the Cumberland Plateau; the black Trans Am sped east down Interstate Forty toward Knoxville at eighty miles per hour. They rounded a sweeping bend and began their descent down a long escarpment. Off to her right the Tennessee River valley stretched out toward the distant foothills, looking like giant tree-covered stoops in front of the Smoky Mountains: rising like brownstones over the surrounding plain. Randomly spaced houses, scattered among the rolling countryside, were tiny dots on the gray-brown landscape. Donna wondered how many daughters lived in those houses and how many still had fathers to love them.

"I love being up high," Donna said, not fully cognizant that she had spoken out loud. "Looking out over the rest of the world, life seems so far away."

"You can come to work with me, then," Brad replied. "You'll have all the heights you can handle."

"So you can drop more things on my head?" She turned to face him. "No thanks."

"Oh, come on. One little mishap." Brad raised his index finger. "You still remember that?" He turned to her.

"Only by the grace of God." Donna smiled. "I'm lucky to remember anything, now."

"It wasn't that bad." Brad offered her a mock frown.

"I still have a bump." She touched the top of her head. "Feel it. Right there."

Brad reached across the front of the car, his big fingers landing on her scalp.

"No shit." He drew his hand back, his face revealing his surprise. "I thought you were just fooling around when you started staggering."

"No." She turned, again, toward the window. "It really hurt."

Donna watched the surrounding trees and countryside slowly rising up to meet them as they traveled down the long hill. She turned, stealing a look at Brad. He was staring out the windshield at the road, unaware.

While not terribly handsome, he had a boyish quality that immediately attracted her. Maybe because he hadn't tried to impress her like so many others had. It seemed to Donna that the better looking the man, the more complicated the agenda.

Brad's agenda was simple. He had none.

In fact, he would confess to her months later that dating her was the farthest thing from his mind. "What chance would a guy like me have with a girl like you?" he had said. "I had nothing to lose by being myself, I guess." She sat staring at the side of his face, drinking in his simple honesty.

"Thanksgiving's coming up," he blurted as he turned toward her.

Startled, she looked away, wondering if he had caught her staring at him.

"Mom's invited us up for dinner."

Donna felt a tightening in her stomach, but she didn't know why. "I guess that would be okay," she answered, squirming slightly in her seat.

"We've been dating for two years now." He hesitated for a second. "It might be a good idea for you to actually meet my parents."

"I'd like that."

Brad was silent for a minute. He cleared his throat while repositioning himself in his seat. "What about *your* mother," he asked.

"What about her?" Donna's eyebrows contracted at the abruptness of his question.

"You never talk about her."

"She died."

"Well, I know that." He glanced once again in his driver's side mirror before passing a slow moving car. Inside the car, an older couple sat staring straight ahead as they passed. "How did she die?"

"Can we talk about something else?" Donna reached for her bottled water. "Please."

"Sure." He shrugged and nodded. "What were you reading last night?" He continued a moment later. "I saw you flipping through some old books."

"My father's journals." She took a drink of water.

"Find anything interesting?"

Donna pulled the bottle from her lips and swallowed. "Not really," she said, once again looking off into the distance.

They continued their long descent from the plateau. The distant Smokies appeared to sink into the earth, the hungry hills and trees in the foreground now swallowing them whole.

Donna drifted off to visualize another mountain range, fifteen years and two thousand miles distant. The Santa Monica Mountains, visible from her dorm room, maintained their vigil above the UCLA campus through a translucent mask of heavy smog. Still cursing her father, a younger Donna had been desperately homesick in her room, trying not to hate him.

"But, it's so far away!" she had said to him just a few months before, the fellowship grant letter still in her hand.

"It'll be all right," her father had replied. "It's time you expanded your horizons a bit. There's a great big world out there."

"I've seen the world," she said, her tone somewhat condescending. "I didn't like it."

"Donna," he said to her in that way she knew meant the discussion was over. "You don't have to go to California if you don't want to."

"I don't?" She recalled how relieved she felt at hearing his words.

"Nope. But, you can't stay here, either. It's time to leave the nest, little girl."

Donna stared off into the trees, her father's face burned into the passing gray blur, wondering how she could have despised him for knowing what was best for her. At the time, she was so sure she understood his true motives. He had raised her alone and paid his debt to the world. It was time for his life to begin and his burden to end. In the years that followed she discovered just how wrong a person could be, even when she had all the answers.

A passing truck interrupted her thoughts. When Donna looked in Brad's direction, he was staring back at her.

"Watch the road," Donna said, motioning with her hand toward the front of the car. "We're going to wreck."

"What's wrong?" Brad answered, ignoring her admonishment.

"Do I have to drive us home?" Donna wasn't sure why she was getting angry.

"You're doing it and I told you not to."

"Doing what?" she asked, her open hand landing on her chest. "What am I doing?"

"Making me worry about you." Brad looked away.

Donna considered his statement for a moment while staring at the floor. "Worry about your driving," she finally said. She was spoiling for a fight but she didn't know why.

"My driving is fine," Brad replied, his tone turning sharp. He was silent for another moment before taking a deep breath. "I'm still worried about you."

"I am fine," Donna said, reaching up to rub her temple with her fingers. Deep inside her head a dull throbbing kept time with her heartbeat.

Ahead she saw the huge twin spires of the Kingston coal-fired power plant, its smokestacks towering above the pine trees in the foreground. As they rounded a long bend and dipped down the hill toward the Clinch River, the plant came into full view to their left as they crossed the bridge.

"You haven't been sleeping well," Brad said.

"My father just died."

"I meant before that." He reached to the dashboard and adjusted the heater setting. "You've been having those dreams again, haven't you?"

"Everyone has dreams."

"Not everyone wakes up screaming the way you did."

Donna's thoughts flashed to her sitting upright among sweaty sheets in the motel bed and sobbing in his arms in the middle of the night.

"It's getting worse, isn't it?" he added. "Maybe we can see some—"

"No!" Donna turned abruptly, glaring at Brad. "I'm fine."

He raised his hands in surrender. They both fell silent.

"Who is Mai?"

She felt an adrenaline surge. "How do you know about her?"

Brad shrugged, still looking straight ahead at the road while driving. "I don't really *know* about her. You kept saying her name last night."

"Someone I used to know."

"And..." Brad made a rolling motion with his right hand, prodding her to continue.

"And nothing." Donna folded her arms across her chest.

"Does everything have to be a mystery with you?"

"What do you mean?" Although she knew full well what he meant.

"When it comes right down to it, I don't really know much about you at all. You know that?"

"What do you want to know?" She offered him a sarcastic smile.

"I don't know." Brad shook his head, his face twisting into a frown. "Nothing specific, really. You never talk about yourself. Ya know? Like your past. Like, where you were born." He paused, and then shrugged his shoulders. "You see? I have no idea where you were even born. I should know that, right? I mean, shouldn't a guy at least know where the girl he's dating was born?"

"I don't know where you were born," Donna answered, turning again toward the window.

"Syracuse, New York," he replied without hesitation.

"Do you feel better now?" Donna maintained her vigil, watching the passing scenery.

"See," Brad said before letting loose an exasperated breath. "You do that."

"Do what?" She sneaked a look at him with a sideways glance.

"Right there." He pointed at her. "Just now."

"What are you babbling about?"

"Oh, hell. I don't know what they call it." Brad dropped his head back momentarily. "Deflection!" His head snapped forward. "Hah! That's it. You won't answer my question so you turn it around on me."

"All right, then." Donna set the hook. "You tell me. Where was I born?"

Brad let out a long sigh. "I'm gonna hurt you."

"Really, Brad. Something so trivial is not worth knowing."

Brad smirked and rolled his eyes. "That's not the point, Donna," he said, shaking his head. "I'm just saying that I feel like you're holding things back from me. There's a lot I don't really know about you."

The novelty of the banter was suddenly wearing thin. "Can we not do this right now?" she said, exhaling heavily.

Brad glanced over at her, his eyebrows drawn together. "Sure." He looked away. "No problem."

"I'm reeling just a little bit at the moment."

Brad returned his attention to the road. They were both silent for a few minutes.

"I'm sorry," he said. "I don't have a clue what you're going through. Both of my parents are still alive."

"I know I've been a little difficult lately." She reached for his hand. "I really need you to be patient with me right now."

Brad gently squeezed her fingers. "Okay." He nodded, his lips curled into pout. "I'll behave."

"When I'm ready," she added, pulling her hand away. "I'll tell you anything you want to know."

A few minutes later they took the Gallaher Road exit and left Interstate Forty. Donna stared out the window at the miles of forest along route fifty-eight heading into Oak Ridge. Passing the huge K-25 complex just south of town, Donna was reminded of her college intern days. As a young undergrad student at the University of Tennessee, she had spent many long hours assisting with research projects at the old plutonium enrichment plant: a sprawling campus of single and two-story buildings, relics of a cold war run amuck. It had since been converted to a high-tech business incubator by the county government.

They were soon driving down the wide boulevards of Oak Ridge. The tidy little city was a loosely packed collection of post-World War II era government buildings amidst the modern architecture of private engineering firms scooping up huge contracts to clean up the sins of the past.

Donna's home was a newly-built, two-story brick colonial tucked amidst a hillside community on the east end of town. After pulling into the driveway, Brad carried Donna's bags into the house while she raised the hatchback. She lifted a heavy box from the back of the car, made heavier by the last minute addition of five leather-bound journals.

After carrying the box into the kitchen and setting it on

the table, Donna looked up at the clock on the kitchen wall and reached for the phone.

"Thermal lab," a woman's voice greeted her on the line. "Valerie."

"Hello, Val. It's Donna."

"Donna! How are you doing? I'm so sorry about your father."

"Thank you." Donna nodded. "The last few months were terrible and I think he was ready to go."

"So sad."

Donna could hear a loud commotion in the background. "What is happening there?"

"Oh, Brandon and Suhail are installing the new infrared scanner. What a circus. We need you back here, like yesterday."

"I'll be back on Monday."

"Please. These guys are driving me nuts."

"I have to go back to Middleton this weekend and list my father's house."

"Oh, that must be hard for you, huh?" Valerie asked.

Donna tried to reply, but the words would not come.

"Donna…are you there?" Valerie's voice faded away as the phone slipped from Donna's fingers and bounced on the kitchen floor.

Brad was upstairs, in the bedroom when she felt the first wave. Her eyes blurred and her lids narrowed. For an instant she felt as if someone had suddenly spun her quickly in a circle. She grabbed for a nearby chair as her knees buckled.

Murky streaks of white light filtered through her barely-open eyelids. The jewel-cut, clear plastic lens of the fluorescent light fixture slowly came into focus as she strained to open her eyes. The linoleum felt cold on her back. Donna could scarcely recall where she was. She tried to move but could only manage a weak nod of her head. She tried calling out, but the only sound she heard was that of Brad flushing the toilet upstairs. Donna fought to regain her faculties as if she were in a deep sleep trying to awaken.

She had no idea how long she had been lying on the floor. Unable to move, her only option was to wait for Brad to come downstairs. After several grueling minutes she heard him calling.

"Donna?" His booming, yet gentle voice filled the house. "You down there? Did you drop something? I thought I heard something fall."

His summons was met with silence. He called again, in a more urgent tone. "Donna?"

She regained some movement in her arms and legs.

"Hey! What the hell's going on?"

More silence. She tried to speak, but could still not make a sound.

A few short moments later she heard his heavy footsteps coming down the stairs. She was just pulling herself into a chair when he entered the kitchen, his face fraught with concern.

"Baby, what happened?" He quickly knelt beside her; slipping an arm around her back. "Are you all right?"

The high-speed chase inside her head was beginning to subside. A stabbing pain gripped her, like a spike had been driven through her head. She took a few short, labored breaths and tried to speak, but nothing would come.

With her vision still blurred, she tried reaching for the table. The rumbling in her stomach became more intense. She tried to stand, her hand covering her mouth. With

Brad's help she made it into the small bathroom off the kitchen. After the retching and heaving subsided, Donna went limp, his thick arms still wrapped around her waist.

Chapter Four

Donna stopped the car on the quiet residential street and stared out the window. The old house looked sad. Its porch, spanning the front of the small white cottage, sagged at both ends in a slight frown. A small pile of newspapers had collected on the front steps.

She pulled the shiny silver Lexus into the narrow driveway, stopping in front of the tiny detached garage just to the rear of the house.

Standing at the driveway entrance, Donna peered into the kitchen through the side door window. It was just as she had left it a few days prior. She slid the old key into the lock and paused before entering, soaking in the sounds of her old neighborhood.

A block away a dog protested loudly. In the distance a whistle announced a locomotive about to rumble through the Becker Road crossing. A few doors down, the steady, hollow snap of a basketball butting heads with a driveway split the din of the busy Saturday afternoon.

A sudden icy gust snapped Donna's collar against her face, carrying with it the faint smell of melting plastic from the nearby molding plant: the sweatshop where he had spent the last twenty-four years of his working life, its menacing odor, wafting in on the chilly breeze, reminding her how much he had sacrificed for her over the years. She entered the house, the journals tucked under her arm.

It had been only five days since his funeral. The house stood cold and empty; the only sound, the constant tick-tock of a miniature grandfather clock on the fireplace mantle. Each step into the house brought Donna closer to the sorrow welling from somewhere inside her, refusing her any mercy.

She walked to the living room, dropped the journals into a chair and bumped up the thermostat. After a few moments she heard the faint clicking of the furnace firing, the gentle roar of the gas flames bursting to life. The blower kicked in shortly afterward. Waves of warm air began rushing through the rooms.

She looked at her watch. The realtor wasn't due for another ten minutes.

Donna walked slowly down the narrow hallway toward her father's bedroom. She looked in, half expecting to see him there.

A moment later she stood in a doorway across the hall, inspecting the contents of the room she had not slept in since she was twenty years old. Everything had been left the way it was on the day she left for California. A plain wooden cross still hung over the head of her old twin bed.

She entered the room, turning to look at the portrait of Martin Luther King Junior hung over her dresser. The skydiving poster, showing a single person from above with a checkerboard landscape of fields and farms below, still hung on the closet door. Donna was eighteen when her father had taken the picture of her from above on the occasion of her first and only sky dive.

A small object on her nightstand caught her eye. She picked it up. It was a simple brass bracelet, opened up enough for a man's wrist. Along the outside, tiny tribal engravings ringed the shiny metal. He must have placed it there for her before he died, knowing she would find it. Her throat tightened.

"Hello," a woman called to her from the kitchen. "Anyone here?"

Donna turned toward the voice, wiping the wet from her eyes. She slipped the bracelet into her coat pocket, left the room, and headed down the hall.

Through the small kitchen she could see her old schoolmate, Cindy Lewis, leaning halfway through the back doorway. Her pretty face, hidden behind untold strata of makeup, peeked out from underneath a tumbleweed of blonde hair. Her eyeliner and mascara, applied in generous amounts, made her eyes appear catlike.

"Donna Roberts!" Cindy blurted, holding out her hands. She wrapped her arms around Donna, patting her on the back. "Oh, look at you." She pulled back and held Donna at arm's length. "You're so pretty."

"Just lucky, that's all." Donna took a step back and turned away, glancing out the window.

"You were always so funny about your looks," Cindy offered. "No one could ever tell you how pretty you were. Why is that?"

"So many times," Donna began, letting her gaze travel to the floor. "I escaped being horribly disfigured by only a few steps or a few seconds." Images of roiling fireballs flashed through her mind. "It made me realize how much the way we look is random and subject to change without notice." Her thoughts turned to those who had not been as lucky as she had been.

Donna looked up and smiled at Cindy. "You look well." She ran a glance up and down Cindy's shapely body. "Fit and trim."

"Oh, honey," Cindy waved a hand in front of her. "Listen, this is all bought and paid for." She put her hands on her hips. "Lipo." She placed a hand under each breast and lifted. "Implants." She finally placed a flat hand across her stomach. "Tummy tuck."

"Beats going to the gym." Donna flashed another smile with a quick raise of her eyebrows.

"Yeah, I never did like to sweat much," Cindy said, smiling. The smile quickly left her face. "Except with Randy Dillard in the back of his Chevy." Her eyes widened. "Oh my gosh," she said, covering her mouth. "Listen to me going on like this. I heard about your daddy. I'm so sorry."

"Thank you."

"I was out of town and didn't have a clue until you called me for a listing," Cindy added. "I would have come to the funeral if I'd known. I'm so sorry. You must have thought I didn't care."

"Not at all," Donna replied, smiling at Cindy. "I would never think that."

"Was he sick long?"

"For about a year, I guess." Donna turned toward the refrigerator. "It was pretty rough. Toward the end he just wanted it to be over." Donna opened the door and held up a can of soda. "Diet Coke?"

"I'd love one, thanks." Cindy took the can. "The first year without them is the worst. I mean, you always miss them. But, that first year is so bad." She popped the top. "Every holiday is the first one without them. It's so sad. Momma's been gone for…well, going on four years now and I still miss her. It still hurts."

Donna nodded, a polite smile pressed into her closed lips.

Cindy brought her palm up to her forehead. It made a dull smack as they met. She dropped her hand down to her side and stared at Donna for a moment. "I'm such an ass sometimes."

"You're not an ass." Donna took a long sip of her Coke. "It's just been a long time."

"Oh, I know. But, how could I forget something like that?"

Donna cocked her head and smiled. "My mother would have liked you."

Cindy smiled. "God, how long has she been ... you know..." she motioned quickly with her head to the side. "Gone?"

"I hadn't really thought about it until now." Donna glanced upward. "But it's been almost twenty-six years."

"Oh, good God! That sounds so long ago when you say it out loud, doesn't it?" Cindy's eyes opened wide. "Don't hardly seem possible, does it?"

Donna looked down momentarily and shook her head, still smiling.

"I remember seeing you for the first time at school." Cindy looked off into a corner of the kitchen. "God, we were all so scared of you."

"Scared?" Donna glanced up at Cindy. "Of me?" She giggled. "Why?"

"Well, none of us had ever seen a... well, you know, an *Oriental* before."

Donna rolled her eyes.

"I know," Cindy replied, reaching out to touch Donna's arm. "That's not politically correct anymore. It's Asian. Or, I guess Amerasian in your case."

"I frightened you?"

"Well, not right away. I mean, we were all curious to see what you'd be like, of course." Cindy took a sip of her Coke. "But when Principal Martin told us you were... well..."

"Well, what? You can tell me. That was so long ago."

"Well, you know... retarded." Cindy tipped her head to the side. "He got us all freaked out over it."

"Why would it matter if I was retarded?"

"Oh, I don't know," Cindy continued. "You know how kids are. I guess we didn't know what to expect from you, that's all." Cindy smirked and rolled her eyes. "It's embarrassing to talk about it now." She covered her eyes with an open hand. "I think we were all afraid you were gonna pitch a fit in the class, you know? Or maybe throw up on us or pull our hair out or something."

"I think Mister Martin had his own agenda where I was concerned."

"Honey." Cindy waved a manicured hand. "That man had all kinds of agendas. Not the least of which was Miss Mavis."

"No!" Donna's index finger darted back and forth, as if connecting two unseen entities. "Principal Martin and the office lady?" She covered her mouth.

"Honestly, can you see that man jumping up and down on top of that poor woman?" Cindy puffed out her cheeks and rocked her hips back and forth. "Giddy up, ol' gal." She waved a hand as if using a riding crop. "I'm fixin' to take you to heaven, Mavis!"

Donna started laughing. Cindy stared in amazement and became infected. The two women stood in her father's kitchen howling like drunken sorority girls until their stomachs ached.

Their laughter subsided.

"But you weren't retarded." Cindy became solemn. "I think somehow I knew." She looked at Donna as if recalling a memory not quite in focus. "I don't know how. There was something in your eyes."

"I was determined not to fail."

"Well, I guess you showed them, huh?" Cindy nodded. "You showed them all."

"There were times when I wondered if it was all worth it."

"I was so proud of you on graduation day. The rest of us were getting our high school diplomas and there you were, getting your degree from UT."

"That was one of the few times I saw my father cry."

"We all cried, honey." Cindy smiled. "I never forgot your speech. To this day whenever I start feeling sorry for myself, I try to think about what you came through and what you accomplished."

"Not so much, really."

"So modest, too." Cindy smiled, one corner of her mouth turned up. "Now, look at you. Someone said you work at the National Labs."

"Yes." Donna nodded. "I do. In the thermal lab."

"God." Cindy shook her head. "That sounds so technical." She looked up at Donna. "I always knew you'd end up in a laboratory somewhere."

Donna glanced toward the hallway beyond the kitchen and then at Cindy. "Do you want to see the house?"

"Well, that's why I'm here," Cindy replied, pulling a note pad and tape measure from her bulky purse.

They walked down the hallway toward the bedrooms. Her father's room was their first stop. Cindy opened the closet double doors. Inside they found sweaters, jeans, and pull-over shirts folded and neatly placed on shelving on the right side of the closet. To the left were his dress pants and dress shirts, all meticulously pressed and hung on hangers at precise intervals. On the floor his shoes and work boots were lined up along the back wall, from tallest to lowest profile. On a shelf above their heads he had placed various hats, sweatshirts, and two black, heavy canvas ghis. Wound into a tight roll on top of the ghis was a two-inch wide black belt, the tip decorated with four strips of red tape.

"This is so like your daddy," Cindy said, motioning with an open hand into the closet.

"You can take the man out of the military..." Donna replied, staring blankly into the closet.

"Would you hold this for me, please?" She handed Donna one end of a tape measure.

After taking the room measurements, they walked past the neatly made bed and out into the hallway toward the only other bedroom. The door was already open. Cindy looked inside.

"Remember how we used to sneak Missus Calymour's cat into your room?" Cindy said, glancing around the small bedroom.

"My father would always know." Donna closed her eyes. A faint smile seized her face. "He would start sneezing the minute he got home and start yelling, 'Donna!'" Her tone dropped, imitating a man's voice. "'Get that cat out of the house!'"

"I know. He always knew."

Cindy carefully measured the room and jotted some notes on her pad.

"Hey," Cindy said, turning to face Donna. "I noticed you're not wearing a ring." She nodded toward Donna's left hand. "Did you ever marry? Was there anyone special? Seeing anyone now?"

"There was someone in college, but we went our separate ways. You know how that is."

Cindy nodded while leading them into the small living room. "Oh, I know how that goes."

"I'm seeing someone now."

"Anyone I know?"

"I doubt it." Donna shook her head. "I met him in Oak Ridge, at the labs. He was doing some work there and he dropped a brush on my head from three stories up."

"No!"

"Yes, he did." She held the tape as Cindy walked to the other end of the room. "He swears it was an accident. But, I'm not so sure."

"Oh my gosh," Cindy continued. "That is too funny."

"How about you? Did you marry?"

"For all the wrong reasons." Cindy glanced down at the bare skin of her left ring finger. She looked up at Donna, pausing for a moment. "Travis McCabe."

"You did not!"

"I sure did." Cindy's heavy mass of blonde hair bobbed up and down. "What that man lacked in brains he made up for in *other* ways."

"So what happened?"

"What else," Cindy replied. "He started drinking. He got fat, mean, and ugly. In that order. He 'bout beat me to death one night and momma told me if I didn't get out of that house she was gonna kill him. So, I packed up and never looked back."

"I'm so sorry, Cindy."

"Last I heard he was doing time for assaulting a police officer." She threw up her hands. "But, hey. Look at me now. I'm the number one agent," she bobbed her head back and forth like a boxer as she spoke, "in the Upper Southeastern Lower Middle Tennessee district."

Donna laughed.

They finished their tour of the house. Cindy took careful measurements of all the rooms. They stood by the back door, as Cindy was about to leave.

"I'd say it's a solid one-ten-five. Maybe one-fifteen if you want to hold out." She made another note. "If you just want to sell it quickly we can probably go with something under one hundred and it won't last more than a week."

"Really?" Donna's eyebrows rose. "That quickly?"

"You've been away too long, girl. Middleton's practically a suburb of Nashville now. We're moving uptown."

"It almost seems sacrilegious to sell this old house." Donna glanced around the kitchen. "I was eleven when we moved in here. I thought it was a palace compared to the little two-family place we were renting."

"It's none of my business, I know... but..." Cindy rolled her eyes, searching for the right words. "What's the hurry?"

Donna looked at the ceiling. "My father," she continued, shaking her head. "He left instructions in his will to get the house sold right away."

"How do you feel about that?"

"I don't know. He always seemed to know the right thing to do." Donna stared momentarily into the ether. "This is probably best."

"Maybe some young couple will buy it and raise a family."

"I hope so. This house needs to hear the sounds of little feet again."

"Well," Cindy said, opening the door to leave. "Here's my card. Just call me and let me know what you want to do."

"I will." Donna looked down at the card.

"Sure was good seeing you again." Cindy gave her a healthy hug.

"I'll get back with you on Monday."

"Bye, sweetie."

Cindy pulled the door closed behind her. Donna watched her walk away through the curtain on the back door. After a brief pause in the kitchen, she walked back to her bedroom. Once inside, she headed for the closet and opened the door. She was reaching for something high on a shelf when she was interrupted.

"Our room looks no different than when we lived here." A voice, *her voice*, startled Donna. She turned with a jolt to see Mai standing behind her, in the doorway.

"You scared me," Donna replied. "I thought the realtor had come back in for something."

Donna looked her up and down. Mai was wearing a simple cotton dress, tied at the waist.

"Why would you be meeting with a realtor?"

"I am selling the house."

"I see," Mai said, moving to position herself in front of Donna. "Why waste time?"

"What's that supposed to mean?"

"He left everything to you." Mai stepped closer. "The sooner you sell this house, the sooner you will have your money. *His* money."

"I don't need the money."

"Oh, yes, I forgot," Mai said. "You are so successful. What is a mere hundred thousand dollars to someone like you?"

Donna turned and walked back into the living room. Mai was right on her heels.

"Leave me alone," Donna said, her fingers rubbing her forehead. "I don't want you here."

"This is my home, too." Mai slowly approached Donna, who had stopped in the middle of the living room. "You can sell this house, but you will not be rid of me."

"What do you want?" Donna asked, looking up at the lovely woman before her, her voice sounding desperate.

"I want what you want."

The two women stood, staring at each other. Donna finally blinked and looked down at the big easy chair, at the stack of journals she had brought with her.

"You said I would not find what I was looking for in there." Donna pointed at the books.

"I said you would not learn the truth until you are ready to face it," Mai corrected her. She took a step closer and spoke in a much more benevolent tone. "And you will not find all that you seek in there. The rest you will only get from me. You need me to face the truth about what we did."

The room was growing warmer as the furnace labored away, pumping waves of hot air into the house. Donna slipped off her coat and collapsed into the easy chair, the journals brushing against her hip as she sat down.

"Why would you help me?"

"In spite of what you think," Mai replied. "I am not your enemy."

"Nor are you my friend."

Mai nodded in concession. "We seek the same thing and need each other to get it."

"What if I don't help you?"

"Only through helping me will you help yourself."

"What if I don't want to help myself?"

Mai's tone became more ominous, once again. She took yet another step, stopping directly in front of Donna. "We both know you are well beyond that point." She knelt before her. Donna looked up, meeting her eyes. They were cool and emotionless. "It is no longer a question of *if* you will face the truth," Mai added. "But, when."

"I don't know where to start," Donna said.

"At the beginning," Mai replied, pointing at the journals. "Your questions will not be answered by reading entries at random."

A sharp pain shot through Donna's head, causing it to jerk suddenly.

"We had better begin soon," Mai added. "We have little time."

Donna glanced down at the stack of leather-bound books. Reaching down to her side, she grabbed the topmost journal: the one written in nineteen sixty-eight. She gave Mai a nervous look before opening it. The first entry was made on January 21st. Donna began reading a few words of the entry before looking up to an empty room.

January 21st, 1968

I don't even know why I'm doing this. I've never kept a journal before and I don't know what good keeping one will do me now.

We're only a few days away from the cease-fire that's supposed to begin on the Tet celebration. I've only been over here a few months now and I could use a rest. We've been pretty lucky, though. Some of the guys coming back from up north tell us that they're getting the shit kicked out of them up there. A buddy of mine said Khe Sanh was the worst of it. I'm glad now that I didn't join the Marines.

It was foggy this morning. Just like it is every morning. Duffy found another snake in his bag. This time he had the good sense to shake it out before getting inside. He still limps from the nasty bite he got last time.

He was lucky. I can still hear the Sergeant from the In-Processing briefing – "Gentlemen, there are 297 species of snakes in Southeast Asia. Exactly 2 are non-poisonous."

Chapter Five

Sticky red clay tugged at the bottom of Mai's bare feet as she walked the narrow path into the tiny hillside village. Fighting for traction on the slick mud, she quickened her stride, trying to keep pace with her mother.

Rivulets of thick red water meandered down the pathway, sluggishly skirting small rocks and downed limbs along the way. The rains that had been steady all morning had subsided, leaving only random droplets from the heavy jungle canopy falling in intermittent waves through slivers of muted sunlight.

It was late January in the central highlands of Viet Nam. Mai, her mother Lien, and her baby brother had just walked back from Khe Sanh village, where they had traded spent artillery casings for a few yards of cloth. Once a year they would gather together their small cache of brass and other metal objects they had scavenged from the battle-weary land and head into town. With just a few more days before the Tet celebration, they felt once again blessed to be carrying back with them a few extra rations of rice.

Mai approached her village with a sense of excitement. Soon she would have a new set of clothes. Every year her mother would somehow manage to secure enough cloth to make them just in time for *Banh Tet*. Aside from her clothes, the only thing Mai possessed was a small brass bracelet. Engraved with local Bru tribal markings, it had been made from the same kind of brass casing she and her mother had just carried to town. One of the elder tribesmen, from a nearby village had given it to her as a rare gesture of friendship between a Bru and a Viet.

In the small settlement, old women wearing cone-shaped hats sat near smoldering fires, their teeth blackened from years of chewing betel nuts. Young children, naked from the waist down, chased each other around on the soggy ground. Nearby, two old men sat together on a log, water dripping from their woven grass hats. They smoked cigarettes and stared in resolute silence at the motley trio passing before them. One of them nodded as Mai walked by.

Their sagging hooch was one of a dozen tucked together into a mountain pass just a few kilometers from the US Marine base at Khe Sanh. The roofs were made of thick layers of loosely bound elephant grass, providing a formidable barrier to the heavy incessant rains. The side sections, made of coarse grasses and palm fronds, had been bound together into heavy mats, woven into neat criss-cross patterns to provide extra strength against the occasional stiff winds that howled through the steep mountain terrain. The frame, visible from the outside, consisted of heavy bamboo anchors with smaller bamboo cross pieces. A covered porch, with a ladder for access, spanned the front of the small hut. The whole structure was held aloft about a meter off the ground.

The recent rain had soaked through their weathered clothes, leaving Mai feeling naked in the steamy, mid-afternoon warmth. The determined five-year-old held tightly to the hand of her three-year-old brother. They climbed a steep incline and paused before their crudely fashioned hut.

Mai scurried up the short ladder after her mother, a young woman of Bru and Vietnamese descent. At twenty-three years old, Lien had a slight build, jet-black hair, and penetrating brown eyes.

"Watch your brother while I prepare our meal," her mother said to her in Vietnamese.

Mai's brother Hung, the 'mischievous monkey,' as his mother referred to him, climbed the ladder onto the porch and disappeared into the hut, his naked little bottom the last thing Mai saw as he vanished.

Shrieks of laughter wafted out from the hut as Mai turned to see where her brother had gone. She barely noticed the blur of two gray objects flying past her head, followed shortly by her little brother toddling by on his way to the ladder.

Mai sat with her feet dangling off the porch, watching Hung scamper after his newfound treasures.

"Give me those!" Lien was suddenly kneeling next to Mai. "That is our dinner, Hung!"

The young boy squealed with delight, bending down to pick up the two, very large dead rats by their tails.

"Don't make me come down there!" Lien shook a cooking spoon at the boy while stifling her laughter.

Hung stomped his feet. Thick red water splashed in all directions. With the intensity of an Olympic hammer thrower, the boy swung the rats, one after the other, by their tails and released them into the sultry tropical air.

Mai heard the grasses overhead rustle as the first one struck the roof. It rolled off and landed with a splat near the bottom of the ladder. The other rat sailed past Mai and her mother and landed somewhere behind them, just as a loud explosion shook the ground and pierced the quiet of the peaceful village.

Mai looked at Lien, searching her face for reassurance. She found none, only the surprised look of a mother who hadn't yet had time to panic.

A heartbeat later, the hut next to them exploded into splinters, the debris and shock wave sweeping them both off the porch. They landed near Hung, who had also been knocked off his feet.

Lien was shouting something to Mai, but Mai could not hear her, the ringing in her ears still too loud. She fought to stand, only to have another nearby blast send her tumbling, as if shoved from behind, down the embankment.

Mai felt the cool smoothness of the soft, wet clay sliding against her face as she skidded, head first along the ground. She never heard the explosion, only a noise sounding more like a hammer striking a large piece of steel.

From the ground, Mai could hear the muffled sound of heavy gunfire drawing closer. High above, the familiar high-pitched whine of the fighter jets streaked across the sky. Soon the napalm drums would come tumbling down and light up the jungle with huge fireballs. In the distance the punctuating thuds of artillery cannons interrupted the steady chatter of machine gun fire. Still face down in the slippery red mud, Mai cowered in the muck, crying out for her mother.

A series of mortar and artillery rounds pounded the earth nearby, shaking the ground like a giant stomping his feet in anger. Mai twisted in the mud and fought to stand up. The next round landed a little closer, sending her sprawling near a clump of bamboo. Thick smoke began encircling her.

Another shell hit close by. Mai felt a flash of heat on her back. The ground shook so hard that she was lifted up by the concussion. Wet dirt and chunks of wood rained down on her moist skin. Amidst the terror she felt a familiar sensation: the softness of her mother's hand on her back.

Mai, still lying face down on the ground like her mother had taught her, turned her head and looked up. Lien Nguyen hovered over her, shielding her with her body, her baby brother cradled in her arms.

"We must leave!" her mother shouted in Mai's ear over the roar of the bombardment. "The soldiers are coming!"

Mai glanced up, once again, at her mother. Lien was straining to see in all directions while trying to cover her children with her body.

"Come!" Lien said, lifting Mai up by her arm.

They ran through the mud to a clump of heavy brush at the edge of their settlement. Just as they were burying themselves into the branches and leaves, a patrol of North Vietnamese soldiers emerged from the wet jungle.

They watched in horror as the men, dressed in their black uniforms, dragged men, women, and children from their huts and lined them up in the village common. Lien cowered close to Mai, wrapping her hand over the young girl's eyes as shot after shot echoed through the rugged hillsides. In less than a minute the shooting stopped. They lay trembling in the brush, afraid to move. Mai stared from between her mother's fingers at a small puddle, just a few feet away. Its contents, runoff from the village above, gradually turned a deeper red hue.

High above, invisible through the dense jungle canopy, a jet roared past. Lien's eyes widened at the first signs of the rumbling. The soldiers looked skyward and then began dispersing in all directions at the menacing sound of the jet fighter.

Amidst the confusion, Lien seized her opportunity. With Hung held fast in her right arm, she grabbed Mai's hand and bolted through the thick undergrowth. Heavy explosions rocked the ground as they ran, the heat from the blasts clutching at them as they went.

It was only a few seconds after they had taken flight when a huge fireball rolled up into the sky where their village had been. Mai tried not to hear them, but she could not shut out the screams emanating from where their village had once stood. She finally put her hands over her ears as she ran, blocking out the agony of those who were burning alive in the wake of the napalm strike.

They kept running until the screaming subsided.

Exhausted, they finally stopped. Lien pulled her babies close to her and hugged them for what seemed to Mai an eternity. Hung was screaming at the top of his lungs. Mai, with tears streaming from her terror-filled eyes, could not stop shaking.

They had stopped in a small clearing that looked like it had once been used for an artillery emplacement. A few survivors from their village were already waiting there. One by one, stragglers began to emerge from the smoking jungle. Dazed, confused, and in shock, many were burned and bloody. Those who were able helped the injured and stunned find a place to rest.

Still more injured wandered into the clearing. One young woman collapsed face down in the matted grass, a large shard of bamboo sticking out of her back. She heaved one last time and went still. An old man, badly burned, fell to his knees. He listed to his side, writhing in pain, his skin still smoldering.

After a few minutes the last of the survivors emerged from the jungle into the small clearing. In all, there were twenty-five or thirty of them huddled together, stunned, many injured, wondering what to do next.

Lien pulled away from her children. Mai took her brother from her arms. "We must go to the base," Lien said to the dazed refugees scattered amidst the clearing. "They will help us there."

Faced with no other option, they walked off together toward Khe Sanh.

Shortly after starting down the rough-cut, dirt road, an old woman with a gaping belly wound collapsed on the side of the road. One of the men went to her, looked up at the others and shook his head. He glanced back at her for a fleeting moment as he rejoined the group.

During the next hour four more injured villagers succumbed to their wounds along the rut-filled roadway, each one left where they had fallen. When they reached Khe Sanh, the remaining refugees who could still walk under their own power were nearly ready to drop from helping those who could not.

The village was a vast collection of small buildings constructed from anything the Marine firebase had discarded. Ramshackle shanties, made from plywood scraps, corrugated metal, canvas, and plastic sheets lined unpaved streets running with fetid water, open sewage, and muddy runoff from the surrounding hills.

The streets themselves, empty of vehicular traffic, were filled with villagers dressed in little more than rags, peasant farmers, beggars, soldiers, parked military vehicles and various domesticated animals such as oxen, pigs, and even the occasional elephant.

"Wait here," her mother said to Mai. "Stay with your brother."

Mai stood in the mud, clutching her three-year-old brother's hand, watching her mother disappear into a single-story building constructed mainly of haphazardly arranged plywood pieces and sections of corrugated metal. The boy began crying as he saw Lien enter the shanty. He tugged wildly against Mai's grasp, trying to join her.

"No!" Mai yanked back against the toddler. "You cannot go in there!"

But the boy persisted. Exasperated, Mai picked him up and held him around his waist. His dangling feet nearly touched the ground and his head was almost even with that of his five-year-old sister.

"*Me!*" The boy continued wriggling. "Mommy!"

"Hung," Mai shook him in her grasp. "Stop it, now!"

Lien reappeared through a narrow opening in the front

of the dilapidated store. Wearing a frown, she strode across the street toward them, reaching out with an open hand as she approached.

"Come," her mother commanded. "We have not enough money for food." She clutched a small sack in one hand. "There is help at the base."

"Where will we sleep tonight?" Mai asked, afraid of the answer.

"We will do the best we can, Mai." Lien cast her an uncertain glance before turning toward the Marine base.

Mai, Hung, and their mother were the first to reach the base gate. It was no more than a red and white horizontal wooden pole that could be raised and lowered to let people and vehicles pass. It sat next to a small guard shack.

"Stop," an ARVN soldier yelled in his native tongue. "You must go back. This is a restricted area."

"Our village was bombed," Lien answered. "We need help. Many are injured."

The little man looked them up and down, suspiciously.

"We are full," he barked at them. "Come back tomorrow."

Before Lien could answer, another man stepped out from the guard shack. He was much larger than the Vietnamese soldier, his uniform slightly different. He looked beyond her, down the road at the rag-tag group of villagers limping and shuffling toward them. The big man leaned in to say something in the smaller man's ear. The little man nodded.

"You will go with him," the Vietnamese soldier said, pointing to the American soldier, already walking swiftly toward the interior of the base.

Lien nodded to the guard and the three of them scurried to catch up with the Caucasian soldier. They hurried past tidy rows of drab green tents. Further ahead were a series of low buildings with tan-colored walls and corrugated metal roofs. In the distance Mai could see a collection of huge airplanes lined up on a runway.

After a short walk they came upon a work detail of soldiers and civilians filling and stacking sandbags around several wide trenches. The huge man stopped them and motioned for one of the civilian workers to join them. He said something in a language Mai did not understand.

"You fill bags," the middle-aged Vietnamese man said to them. He motioned toward the trenches where he had been laboring. "You get food."

When they had finished for the day, they were given food and shown to a place where they could sleep for the night. Exhausted and aching, Mai laid her head down next to Lien's on the first pillow upon which she had ever slept.

"Momma?" Mai asked, looking around at the inside of the huge canvas draped overhead. "Is this where will we live now?"

Lien stroked Mai's hair and answered softly, "I don't know."

Mai was silent for a moment, her thoughts racing, her fears mounting. "If we have to leave here," she continued, her eyes searching her mother's face, "will we starve?"

Smiling, Lien took Mai's chin in her hand. "Heaven made the elephant, Mai." She nodded off into the distance. "Heaven will make the grass."

Mai looked down, puzzled. "I don't understand," she finally said.

"Has God not already provided for us?"

Mai looked up, the languishing dusk barely illuminating her mother's benevolent eyes. "Until now," she said, finally.

"We are alive, Mai." Lien took her hand and pulled her tight. "As long as we are, he will provide."

Mai's thoughts turned back to her village, where the

people she had once known as neighbors had perished so
suddenly just hours before. Were they somehow exempt
from God's protection? Had they done something so wrong
that they should be killed?

In the fading light she drifted off to sleep while the
steady drone of the huge cargo planes faded into the heavy
tropical night.

*   *   *

Mai lay cuddled against her mother in the cool, pre-
dawn stillness when she first heard the familiar sound of
incoming mortar rounds pounding the earth outside their
makeshift canvas shelter. She looked up, the faint, first light
outlining her mother's silhouette against a gun-barrel blue
sky.

"Mai!" her mother screamed. "Mai, where is your
brother?" Lien sat up in the Army issue cot, her head turning in all directions.

Mai looked around, afraid to answer. She hopped down
off the cot and weaved a path through the other refugees,
who were stirring at the sound of the nearby blasts.

"I have him," Mai replied, as she returned to her mother, her little fingers wrapped tightly around the younger
boy's wrist.

Several of the American soldiers were running towards
them. Some of them were frightening to look at: their skin was
black and they were so big. Mai grabbed for her mother as the
men approached. Lien scooped Hung up off the ground.

When the soldiers arrived they began yelling things in a
strange language. Her mother clung to the toddler cradled in
her arms. Two of the men reached out for her. Lien pulled
back, crying, trembling. Mai curled closer and tighter to her
mother. The largest of the men began screaming even louder at them as two rounds exploded nearby.

Mai never saw the explosion that sent her flying backward. The only recollection she would have was a sudden, deafening thud and then blackness. She had landed upside down in a trench; several dislodged sand bags had come to rest on top of her, plunging her into total darkness. Sand was pouring through a rip in one of the bags onto her face.

She tried to right herself but the bags were too heavy. In the silent blackness that was now threatening her with certain suffocation, she could only feel the ground thump with each mortar round that pummeled the area. Mai tried turning her head, only to find more burlap and sand blocking her breath. Panic began to seize her as she fought for air.

Above the surface of the bags showers of fresh dirt were landing on her stomach and legs. Hundreds of miniature feet scurried over her skin, tiny, sharp nails biting into the soft flesh of her arms and chest. Large nests of rats, dislodged from between the sandbags by the blasts, scurried for cover over Mai's trembling body.

Her little lungs, desperate for air, ached and burned under the heavy bags. As her senses were fading she felt a huge hand wrap itself around her ankle. With one mighty heave she was ripped from her would-be tomb. The heavy fabric and the rough earth scraped against her face as she was excavated from the sandy pit.

Mai drew in a heavy gasp, all the while trying to see this person who had plucked her from death's grasp. Still upside down, dangling from one ankle, she saw the dusty face of the huge man who had saved her.

Several rounds hit nearby. Mai and her rescuer fell into the trench. Seconds later, they were joined by several more men, all jumping into the long ditch and shouting at one another.

A round exploded near the edge of the trench. One of the men fell forward, next to Mai. His left arm had been severed at the elbow. More men came running. Two of them helped the injured man to his feet and scurried off with him.

Two men picked her mother up off the ground and carried her away in another direction. The last man scooped Mai up in his arms and slung her over his shoulder. Her stomach and chest slammed repeatedly against his bony upper torso as he sprinted with her across the compound to another trench.

A mortar round exploded just a few yards away. Mud and chunks of clay covered everyone in the trench. The air, foul with the smell of spent munitions, stung her nose. She began coughing and one of the men dressed in green offered her his handkerchief. Mai extended a tentative hand and took the dull green cloth. She held it to her mouth and breathed in. The strange-looking man smiled at her. Mai turned away.

"What is your name?" a slight Vietnamese soldier, crouched among the many men, asked her.

Mai did not answer. Her stomach lurched in spasms of terror, making speech an abstract concept.

"Where is your family?"

Mai looked around, but did not see them anywhere.

One of the men in green started yelling something to the young Viet soldier. He nodded and turned toward Mai.

"Come with me."

"No!" Mai reached for a piece of wood that had been driven into the ground nearby. "I want my mother!"

A huge man came forward, grabbing her around the waist. Her grip on the stake was easily torn free and she was quickly on her way out of the filthy trench.

The shelling stopped. Men scrambled in all directions; some carrying other men, some with bundles of strange objects. Overhead the silver jet planes screamed across the sky. As they banked in the distance, Mai saw the drums tumbling toward the earth. In an instant the horizon lit up in a bright orange mushroom. She stared into the conflagration knowing that anyone close to the impact site was dying horribly at that moment. Even at five years old, Mai had come to know the many faces of death in war.

After a brief respite the shelling started again, this time with greater fury. Mai huddled with a small group of refugees in another ditch, where she waited for several hours while the base was pounded with hundreds of additional mortar rounds.

Sometime around mid-morning Mai heard a ground-shaking rumble. She stood up and peeked over the side of the trench to see a huge fireball billowing upward through a thick shroud of black smoke in the center of the base.

The fire spread quickly and soon there were additional eruptions. Mai ducked for cover as streaks of fire shot from the heavy smoke. Loud explosions ripped into the morning air as stockpiles of munitions detonated in the firestorm.

The air was thick with the smell of burning oil, exploded ordinance, and choking red dust kicked up from the blasts. Amidst the rumbling from the enormous flames, the thunderous explosions, and the roar of the jet fighters overhead, Mai strained to hear her mother's voice through the surreal chorus of screaming women and children.

Mai squinted to see through the thick smoke, but could only make out the occasional green blur of a soldier running by. Without warning she felt a pair of hands lifting her off the ground. She tried to break free but his grip held and she was hoisted into his huge arms; the young soldier offering her a crooked smile.

While she squirmed, he carried her across the base to the runway where hundreds of villagers huddled in groups along the ground in front of the giant cargo planes.

After they arrived, one of the men in green approached.

He motioned to someone unseen within the aircraft and the end of the airplane seemed to open its mouth. Many of the civilians, who had been herded together, were hurried onto the aircraft. The huge rear door slowly closed behind them, the last few inches culminated in a resounding bang as the giant metal cargo ramp seated into place.

Mai sat on the smooth metal floor with her back against the fuselage amidst all the crying babies and frantic mothers. She desperately searched the faces of the women on the plane hoping to see her own mother. As she stood to inspect another part of the plane, a man yelled something at her and motioned for her to sit.

The plane began to shake and vibrate. Mai heard a rumbling from just outside the aircraft. Her heart raced as the plane jolted forward. Within minutes she was clinging to a nearby metal post as she felt herself being pulled to one side. She tried sitting up but could only lean against the cool, hard side of the airplane. The plane tipped sharply, sending many of the children tumbling toward the back of the aircraft.

Still trembling, Mai somehow pulled herself up and looked out a small window on the side of the plane. Nothing in her young life could have prepared her for what she saw next. She stood with her mouth agape looking at the burning, rain-soaked, moonlike landscape of Khe Sanh as it sank slowly away into the murky depths of the low-lying cloud cover.

Chapter Six

The ride to Kingsport took less than two hours. Donna stared out the window at the rugged mountain landscape as they cruised north along Interstate Eighty-One. Brad took the I-181 exit and they were soon winding down the narrow pass into the small northeastern Tennessee city.

Donna turned from her window and looked straight ahead. Stretching out before them was the seemingly end-less expanse of a nearby chemical plant. Small wisps of steam rose lazily into the chilly autumn air from dozens of large brick buildings; each one festooned with its own set of tanks, steam pipes, and rooftop chillers. Connecting the buildings were miles of piping, bundled together into metal-lic umbilical cords captured by racks of girders and cross pieces.

"Ever been in there?" Brad said, pointing toward the sprawling complex of buildings.

"Only once," she replied. "I was still a co-op then."

"I'll bet you could have fun in there, huh?"

"No doubt," she said, turning to him with a loving smile.

"I could just see you working in there," he said, a smirk forming. "You'd have all these pipes and wires running everywhere. Big-ass pots of some gooey stuff bubbling and boiling over."

She laughed at the image.

"The evil Doctor Donna's laboratory," he offered. "I don't even want to know what crazy stuff you'd do in a place like that."

"I would only use my powers for good deeds," she replied. "I would create the perfect spring roll."

They exited the highway onto an access road that ran along the perimeter of the massive complex. Near the main entrance they turned left and drove through a commercial district.

"You seem to be in a good mood today," Brad said.

"As opposed to how I normally am?" Donna glanced at him sideways and smiled.

"Always the wise-ass."

Brad looked up at his rear-view mirror while pulling into the parking lot of a small grocery store.

"What the hell do they want?" he said, slipping into a parking space near the sidewalk.

Donna turned to look out the back window. Behind them a police cruiser was following them into the lot, its roof-mounted lights flashing. The patrol car pulled to a stop behind them. The two officers within waited for nearly a minute before approaching the car.

"How long have they been following us?" she asked looking out the back window.

"Long enough." He jammed the stick shift into park while still staring into the mirror.

"Did you renew the tags?"

"Yeah, I thought I did…" Brad's face contracted while he glanced down at the dashboard. "Sure, we renewed your car the next month and we said how we might as well just wait and do 'em both together."

A slender officer appeared and leaned into Brad's window, his blonde brush cut sparkling in the sun. Brad reached for a switch on his door and his window slid open.

"May I see your drivers license please, sir?"

Brad reached into his back pocket and pulled out his wallet while giving Donna a disgusted smirk. After slipping his drivers license out, he handed it to the young policeman.

He inspected Brad's license for several seconds before pulling on the exterior door handle. "Would you please step out of the car, Mister D'Amato?"

Donna heard her own door handle pull up. She turned to see a young black cop motioning to her. "Ma'am," he began, swinging the door open. "Would you please step out and come with me?"

"Ah, come on guys," Brad said, rising to his full height in front of the skinny cop. He stood a full head and stocky shoulders above the young man. "Nothin' better to do on Thanksgiving than hassle us?"

"Mister D'Amato," the officer replied. "This will go a lot easier if you'll just—"

"What will go easier?" Brad shot back. "What's this all about?"

"Step over this way, Ma'am." The other officer gently grabbed Donna's arm. "If you would, please."

"Brad," Donna said, shifting glances between the hand on her elbow and Brad. "What is going on? Why are they doing this?" She offered no resistance, following her captor to the back of the car.

"I have no clue, Donna," Brad replied over his shoulder across the top of the car.

"What'd I do?" Brad said to the young policeman guiding him to the front of the vehicle. "I wanna know what this is about." He stopped short and yanked his arm away.

The officer ran a considerate glance up and down Brad's large frame before reaching for the mike clipped to his lapel. "Central, unit twelve requesting backup at the Crossroads Market on Jefferson.".

"Oh, for Christ's sake." Brad rolled his eyes and looked off to his left. "You don't need backup. I'm not gonna give you any trouble."

Donna watched the whole event from the back end of the car, wondering what terrible mistake had been made. Surely, someone would discover the error: a misspelled name, the wrong tag number, maybe even a description close to their own.

The two officers stood flanking Brad for a moment, their hands resting on their weapons holstered at their belts.

"Sir, I need you to turn around and put your hands behind your head for me, please."

"Come on!" Brad threw up his hands in protest. "You gotta be kidding me! This is bullshit!"

At that moment three cruisers, lights flashing, sped into the lot. Six more officers evacuated their vehicles and quickly surrounded Brad with batons drawn.

Donna started toward him, but was held back by the officer. Brad's eyes met hers as she heard the identifying click of the handcuffs being placed around his thick wrists. As if in parade formation, the seven cops escorted their prisoner toward the back of the car. They stopped in front of her; Brad stood with his head down.

"Are you all right, ma'am?" the skinny cop with the buzz cut asked. "He didn't hurt you, did he?"

Donna glanced around the small mob. A few of them were smacking their batons into their palms and sneering at Brad.

"No!" She shook her head. "You have the wrong man. He has done nothing to hurt me!"

Skinny pulled a note pad from his shirt pocket.

"No?" he said, flipping it open. "How about romantic involvement without any sincere gesture of commitment?"

The words fell like a deck of cards thrown into the air.

"What?" Donna answered, her nose crinkled in confusion.

"Uh, huh," the cop continued. "Keeping a beautiful young woman guessing about her long term options for an undefined period of time." He flipped a page. "And," he elbowed Brad in the gut for good measure. "Negligence in the first degree by taking the chance that you might get away from him before he can make an honest women out of you."

Donna's hands were already over her mouth when one of the officers unlocked the handcuffs. Several of the cops pretended to force Brad to his knees with their batons. As he settled to the pavement, he reached into his jacket and produced a ring box.

"I know it's only been a short time since your father passed," Brad said, looking down at the ring box. "But, he made me promise I'd do this right away." He looked up and smiled. "Besides, these guys threatened me with bodily harm if I didn't do this properly," Brad continued, opening the box. Inside was a simple golden ring set with a tastefully-sized diamond.

Brad shuffled closer, the group around him pulled back, slipping their batons back into their belts. He reached for her hand.

"Donna," he began, his voice cracking ever so slightly. "I don't know why I haven't done this before now, but I swear it's been on my mind since the minute we met." He inched closer, walking on his knees. "Before I met you, my life was in the tank. You're the best thing that's ever happened to me and I want you all to myself."

She wiped away the tears streaming from her eyes.

"So," he continued, sliding the ring onto her finger. "Will you be my wife?"

Donna tried to speak, but the words would not come.

The best she could do was a vigorous nod. She grabbed him by his jacket and pulled him upward, throwing her arms around him as he stood. "Yes," she finally managed. "Yes. I will be your wife." She buried her face into his shoulder and clung to him as if he would vaporize in her grasp.

The small crowd around them began clapping. Some of the men were slapping Brad on the back and offering their congratulations.

"You had this all planned."

"Ya think?"

"I can't believe this." Donna looked down at the ring.

"I was gonna wait until we got to my parents' house," Brad said, pulling her close. "But, I wouldn't know what to do if you said no."

"You all scared the *hell* out of me!" Donna finally pulled away amidst the laughter of the constabulary cast. "You big oaf!" She playfully slapped Brad on the arm. "How do you know these people?"

"We moved down here while I was in high school," he answered, escorting her back into the car. "Played football with most of these guys. We got to be good friends." He opened her door and helped her into her seat.

"Congratulations, Brad," one of them said, giving him the thumbs up. "You're a lucky man."

Skinny walked up to Brad and shook his hand. "Congratulations."

The policemen waved at them both as they loaded into their cars. As they were pulling away, one of them called after them. "Hey, if it don't work out, I'm available!"

"Get your own girl, buddy," Brad called back to him. "Thanks, guys!" He yelled as they waved and sped away.

After hopping into the driver's side, Brad pulled the car back onto the four-lane boulevard. They drove for a few blocks before turning from the main drag onto a residential street in an older, working-class section of town. The houses were wood-framed, small, and close together. He parked across the street from his parents' home, a two-story colonial with a porch, a dark blue Ford pickup truck parked in the driveway. The shutters on the upstairs windows needed painting. He shifted into park, turned off the engine and sat for a moment in thought.

"What do I need to know about your family?" Donna asked, while inspecting her new ring. She held her hand at arms length, her fingers splayed along the dashboard.

"Ma's pretty cool," Brad began, looking at Donna. "Loves to cook." He smiled. "My sister, Gina." His eyes drifted to a point in front of the car. "She's…" Brad's eyes rolled upward, momentarily. "Not shy about expressing her opinions."

"I see." Donna's lips pursed into a smile as she nodded slowly. "What about your father?"

"Pops?" Brad's eyebrows rose. "Yeah, Pops. He's in a class by himself." He glanced away, at the house. "He's a good guy. You'll be okay. He's just not…real big on charm." He squinted and looked sideways at the roof. "He's not exactly what you'd call a Dale Carnegie grad." Brad looked at her straight away. "Know what I mean?"

Donna's heart kicked up a notch and her palms moistened slightly as Brad opened his door. It was time. Why it had taken so long to meet them, she didn't know. There was always an excuse: always somewhere else to be, something to do. She stood on wobbly legs casting Brad an uncertain look. Why was this so scary? An oblique and ominous thought lurked just beyond her consciousness.

"Come on," Brad said, reaching for her hand in the middle of the street. "We'll go 'round back to the kitchen."

They walked up the driveway, past the pickup to a back entrance. Through the back door window Donna could see a tall, big-boned woman wearing an apron. Her hair, brown with a red tint, was pulled back into a bun. Standing over a stove, she was stirring something in a pot. Brad turned the doorknob.

"Heinrich!" His mother said, laying down the spoon and throwing her hands wide. She stretched her arms around her son, pulling herself up onto her tiptoes to kiss his cheek. "So nice you could visit your old mother."

"Sorry, Ma." His apologetic tone bordered on sarcasm. "Been busy with work, ya know?"

The kitchen was small with plain white cabinets, some of the doors ajar from a few too many coats of paint. A simple kitchen sink, beneath a window, was already piled with dishes. The stove, ancient and bulky, labored away across the room, the pots and pans atop bright red burners, puffing steam like a miniature version of the massive plant they had passed along the way. The wallpaper was typical seventies, rows of beige baskets separated by some rope-like pattern.

"Has been too long." His mother shook a finger in his face. "You should call more."

"Hey, Ma," Brad tried to interject, motioning toward Donna. "Got someone—"

"Oh, the sauce!" His mother turned abruptly toward the stove where thick red liquid was bubbling from a large covered pan.

Donna watched, amazed at the swiftness of the big woman. The kitchen filled with the smell of spaghetti sauce as she lifted the cover from the pan.

"Ma," Brad made another attempt to get her attention. "This is—"

"Wha'jyasay?" A voice bellowed from the den, just off the kitchen. "Somebody here? Who ya talkin' to?"

"Your son!" She gave the pan a vigorous stir. "Or maybe you don't remember him. He does not play the football any-

more." She set the spoon down. "This burner..." she muttered. "If your father would spend half as much time..." She
cranked down the knob and wiped her hands on her apron.

"Hey, Ma?" he waited a second before continuing.
"This is—"

"So much time with the football he could be fixing." His
mother shook her finger, again. "No?"

"Absolutely." Brad said.

"Well," his mother said, slapping her hands at her sides
and looking at Donna as if she hadn't yet noticed her.
"Aren't you going to introduce your friend?"

"Ma." Brad rolled his eyes and threw up his hands.
"I've only been trying to—"

"Ah, hush, hush." His mother waved him off, while
walking toward Donna. "Hello," she said. "I am Elena.
Slave to the football." She offered her hand.

"This is Donna, Ma," Brad added, quickly. "She's
gonna be your daughter-in-law."

Elena's face lit up. "Well," she added, beaming at them
both while taking up Donna's left hand. She pulled the ring
close, giving an approving nod. "We make it a hug, then."
She wrapped her stout arms around Donna and squeezed.
"A big one."

Donna hugged her in return. "It's very nice to meet you,
Missus D'Amato."

"Elena, please." Elena's expression suddenly turned
solemn. She turned to Brad. "Your father..." Her eyes went
wide for a moment.

His father's voice, cheering from the den, broke the
silence. "Hey Brad, come here, you gotta see this replay!"

"It'll be all right, Ma." Brad placed reassuring hands on
Elena's arms. "I'd better get in there before he blows a gas-
ket."

Brad disappeared through the doorway to the den. The

two men whooped it up in the adjacent room, out of sight from the kitchen.

"I wish I understood the attraction," Donna said. "They seem to have so much fun watching that game."

"Ah, let them have their fun." She handed Donna a wooden spoon. "Stir the sauce. Don't let it burn to the bottom."

"Smells good."

"Johnny," Elena offered. "His mother's recipe." She reached for the oregano. "She came from the '*Old Country*' is how she used to say."

"And where are you from?"

"Leipzig," Elena answered. "You know it?"

"Northern Poland. Along the sea."

Another round of cheers from the den raised the roof.

Elena stretched to reach a serving platter on a top shelf. "You were not born in this country either," she offered, pausing to glance at Donna over an outstretched arm. "Were you?"

The question carried enough weight at the moment to send Donna reeling. While she struggled with at least a dozen ways to avoid answering, she was caught in the sights of Elena's probing eyes. Her reply slipped past her lips before she could stop it.

"No." Donna's eyes shot downward momentarily.

Elena had pulled the platter down from the cupboard. She stood across the kitchen holding it to her chest like a breastplate of armor. Her expression bore the burden of some untold secret: an anxious look suffused with dread. She blessed herself and muttered something in Polish.

"What is it?" Donna asked, taking a step closer while instinctively glancing toward the den doorway.

"Johnny will not understand," Elena said to no one in particular.

"Understand what?"

Elena did not answer. The steam rising from the sink, as she poured the pirogues into a strainer, lifted errant locks of her brown hair as it billowed up from the pan. After a thorough rinsing with hot water she poured them onto the huge platter. Another mushroom cloud of steam climbed to the ceiling as she removed the top of the double boiler.

"Have I done something to offend you?" Donna searched Elena's face for a clue. Her heart began a slow descent.

Elena turned, facing her, as if to answer. She dumped the green beans from the boiler into a bowl in silence.

"That was some finish, eh Brad?" His father's voice carried from the den. She heard the TV go silent. Her heart suddenly raced.

Donna saw Brad emerge from the den, looking over his shoulder.

"I don't know how in the hell he ever held onto that ball," Brad replied to his father.

"Flypaper," a voice called to him, still in the den. "They use flypaper on them gloves, I tell ya."

The kitchen floor vibrated with the dull thumps coming from the den. It wasn't until Johnny appeared in the doorway that the source of the sound became evident.

He was an inch or two shorter than Elena, stocky yet muscular. His dark hair was graying near the temples, his face dark with a permanent five-o'clock shadow. Johnny looked after his son with a wide smile, his hand reaching out for Brad's shoulder.

"Well, it wasn't exactly an ass kickin', but we'll take it just the same," Johnny said, dragging a leg while sticking his cane into the floor with angry authority.

The smile left his face as he turned his head to look at Donna. His once cordial expression quickly turned to one of surprise and then just as quickly to anger.

"Who the hell are you?"

Donna felt her stomach drop, the void space it left quickly filled with adrenaline. Their eyes met for an instant. As if by some mystical force, she felt his hatred, his fear.

"What is *she* doing in my house?"

Johnny glanced at Brad and then at Elena, holding her gaze for a few seconds before hobbling back into the den. In the silence that followed they could hear only the steady thud of his cane smacking the floor followed by the shuffle of his trailing foot against the hardwood. They stood in the kitchen as the sound trailed off, echoing down a hallway. It stopped just as a door slammed.

"What the hell was that all about?" Brad's eyebrows were raised halfway over his head. He started after his father but his mother grabbed his arm.

"Leave him be."

Donna saw compassion in Elena's eyes that only a mother and a wife could possess.

"I should leave," Donna said, avoiding eye contact.

"No!" Brad spun around, his finger extended. "This is bullshit!"

"He will need time," Elena said, placing a hand on Brad's arm.

"He's had time." Brad shook her hand away. "How much time does he need?"

Elena looked down at the floor, slowly shaking her head. "Some wounds never heal."

Donna's mind raced; a jumble of memories flooding her head, catching her off guard. She felt a low boil of nausea slowly rising up from her bowels.

"I need to go now." Donna looked desperately at the side door, wanting to lunge for the knob and take flight.

"No," Elena said, gently taking her by the arm. "You will stay. Eat. I have made so much food."

"I'm really not hungry anymore." Donna looked at Brad for help, but the reassuring look of support was not forthcoming.

"I don't believe this." Brad motioned with an open hand toward the path his father had taken in retreat. "I'm being run out of my own house."

"No one is running you out." Elena was gently guiding them both toward the dining room. "He just needs time to accept this."

"Accept what?" Brad's face was flushed. "What is she, some kind of disease?" He motioned toward Donna with a flip of his hand. "What's the recovery time for racism?"

"Your father is a good man, Heinrich." Elena pulled Donna along as she ushered them into the dining room. Drawing a high-back chair from the weathered oak table, she motioned for them to sit. "If he wants to sulk, let him. We will eat our dinner."

Elena left the room. Brad looked over at Donna, an 'I'm sorry' smile stretched across his lips.

"I really want to leave," Donna said, glancing around the table at the simple china place settings, wondering which seat belonged to Johnny: Which seat was his throne.

Brad reached for her hand. "If that's what you really want, we'll go." He squeezed it gently, his eyes asking her to understand. "But, it'll break her heart if we leave now."

It'll break her heart? Donna sat among the empty place settings and thought about broken hearts. *What about my heart?* Why was she always the one having to hold it together? Why couldn't she just once run away screaming and let someone else clean up the mess?

The side entrance to the kitchen opened and a woman's voice called out to Elena. "Hey, Ma," followed by the sound of paper bags hitting the kitchen table. "Sorry I'm late. It was slow coming out of Charlotte and the road over the mountains was down to one lane."

"Oh, great," Brad blurted, letting his head fall into his outstretched hands. "That's all we need right now."

"What?" Donna's eyebrows contracted while she glanced back and forth between Brad and the doorway to the kitchen.

"Gina's here."

"Come," Elena said, still out in the kitchen. "Come meet your new sister-in-law."

"Sister-in-law?" Gina replied, still unseen. "You're joking, right?"

"Your brother gave her a ring."

Elena was the first through the doorway, followed by a very pretty woman in her late twenties. Her slightly curly, shoulder-length hair was dark and pulled into a ponytail. She was big, like her mother, but more slender and girlish. Gina was still conversing with her mother as she entered the dining room.

"I couldn't find the mustard you like so I had to get another—" Gina pulled her eyes from the jar she was holding and locked eyes with Donna for the first time. "Holy shit…" She stood staring for several seconds before glancing around the room. "Guess who's coming to dinner?"

"Gina!" Brad started to stand. "Jesus, could you be any more insensitive?"

Gina pushed him back down into his chair. "Shut up." She reached out a sturdy hand to Donna. "I'm Gina. Lard Ass's little sister. Welcome to the family."

"I am Donna," she replied, accepting Gina's warm hand; smiling at Gina. "Thank you."

Gina smirked. "Or, as we refer to it, 'dysfunction junction'."

Elena left for the kitchen once again.

"So," Gina continued. "Did Pops blow a fuse?" She nodded toward Donna while glancing sideways at Brad.

"He blew the main, this time," Brad replied. "Stormed off into his room. Haven't seen him since."

Gina took off her coat and sat next to Donna. Pulling her chair close, she leaned in to her. "Don't let him get to you. He's okay. He just has his moments."

Out in the kitchen a heavy wooden spoon struck a pan. The smell of spaghetti sauce wafted into the room. Donna's stomach turned as Elena came into the dining room with a steaming bowl in each hand.

Outside, they could hear the unmistakable sound of an engine starting. A moment later the pickup truck was backing out of the driveway.

"We'll eat without him." Elena set the bowls on the table. "If he can be stubborn he can also be hungry." She cast them all a benevolent look.

Brad raised his hand. "Ma, look, maybe I should—"

"Eat."

Chapter Seven

It was late afternoon when Johnny decided he'd had enough. After trolling slowly through the streets of Kingsport for two hours, he pulled his truck alongside the curb just a few blocks from downtown. His ass was sore and his leg was throbbing like hell. He turned the key and sat motionless, staring at the deserted streets, thinking that anyone with any sense was home eating Thanksgiving dinner with their family. Afterward, they would rush to their dens, recline in their favorite chairs and watch real men play the only game God ever personally sanctioned.

He concluded for the moment that having sense was overrated.

Downtown Kingsport looked more like an old neighborhood from up north than a city center. Most of the buildings were small commercial structures built before World War II. Much of the newer development in town had been along Stone Drive, a few miles away. There were no tinted glass restaurants with fancy chromed trim. Only a small collection of one and two-story brick buildings crammed together between the steep valley slopes of the small Appalachian city.

The Riverside Saloon served as Johnny's second home. Its century-old brick exterior and shorted neon Bud Ice Lite sign in the window beckoned him like an old pair of worn slippers. Johnny climbed out of his full-sized pickup, hopped onto the cracked sidewalk, and hobbled through the shadows cast by the waning sunlight along the half-block distance to the one-story bar.

He paused for a moment in front of a thick, lime green hardwood door, the remnants of several handbills still stapled to the grainy surface. Johnny braced one hand against the rough brick of the recessed entranceway and pulled open the heavy door. Inside, the usual cast of barflies awaited his arrival. Almost in unison, gray-haired heads turned his way. Several sets of watery eyes squinted against the light from the open door intruding on the dark intimacy of the cave-like watering hole.

To his right, the long bar ran the length of the wall. Its dark wooden surface, rounded and shiny on the leading edge was home to a handful of tired old men. They sat on their barstools in threadbare clothes moored to the bar like weather-beaten fishing boats tied to an abandoned dock. A gaunt old man with a hunched over back leaned against the bar, talking with one of his patrons. His face, scored with deep-set wrinkles, sagged slightly around his jawbone. A freshly lit cigarette dangled precariously from the corner of his crooked mouth.

"Whataya know, Johnny?" Hank the barkeep said, raising his graying head.

"I know I need a shot," Johnny replied, limping over to the bar, his cane thumping along the floor as he went. "Hell, make it two."

The oversized shot glass full of Jim Beam was already waiting for Johnny before he reached his favorite stool. At the far end of the room, through a blue haze of cigarette smoke, two figures in faded jeans huddled near a pool table. The subtle snap of the balls colliding filled the silence of Johnny's second home: this morgue for living souls.

Johnny climbed into his usual seat. He took a healthy

chug of his bourbon and turned to see who else was pitiful enough to be there on Thanksgiving. Two seats down Dusty Baker turned and nodded. Johnny wondered how it was possible that he could always have a three-day beard. He had never seen Dusty clean-shaven. Nor had he ever seen him with a full beard. Johnny had long ago concluded that his heavy growth of silver must have somehow been forever stunted at its current length.

Stretch Cummings and Mickey Brightbill occupied their usual seats, staring blankly at the television set mounted over the bar. Old Pete Willis was nodding off in the corner, the brim of his Red Man cap pulled down, covering his eyes, his old body propped up by the walls and the truss he had worn since his hernia two years ago.

As Johnny turned back to his Jim Beam he saw Scooch Henry turn the corner from the restrooms. Tall and lanky, Scooch was in his late fifties with graying hair that was thinning near the crown of his head. He smiled as he approached; his yellowing teeth suddenly beamed in contrast with his nearly jet black skin.

"Johnny," Scooch blurted. "What brings your sorry ass in here on Thanksgiving day?" He motioned with one of his huge hands toward the floor in front of him.

"Can't a guy just go out for a drink without getting the third degree?" Johnny reached for a menu that was leaning against a bottle of ketchup on the bar. "What's on special, Hank?" he said to the bartender while turning back to the bar.

"Turkey samwich," Hank replied, the cigarette tip dancing up and down in rhythm with his words. "Or maybe I should whip up some lasagna."

"Hey, go fuck yourself, Hank." Johnny swiped his fingers under his chin at the bartender. "When you're done, make me a samwich." Johnny turned his head, suddenly in thought. Then he smiled. "And that better be mayo on that samwich," Johnny called after Hank, who was retrieving a wet rag from the other end of the bar.

Scooch sidled up beside Johnny and sat on the stool next to him. "Have a fight with the missus?" he asked, motioning to Hank to draw him a beer.

"Since when is that any of your business?"

Hank poured a draft beer and set it on the bar in front of Scooch before heading into the kitchen to make Johnny's sandwich. Scooch nodded vaguely at Johnny's question and sat silently sipping his beer, staring ahead at the bar back.

"For the record," Johnny offered, waving his hand in Scooch's direction but never actually looking at him. "No. I did not have a fight with Elena."

"Uh, huh," Scooch drawled, still looking straight ahead. He took another long sip of his beer.

"Scooch. You got a daughter, right?"

"That's right," Scooch answered, nodding. "Lives with her mother in Roanoke."

"She ever bring home a white man?"

"She better not." Scooch turned to face Johnny, who had also turned himself to face Scooch. "Is that why you in here? Your daughter seein' a black man?"

"Aw fuck no." Johnny smirked and shook his head. "I could almost handle that."

Johnny sat staring ahead for a while, sipping his Jim Beam while Scooch quietly drank his beer and scarfed down pretzels from the brown bowl in front of him on the bar.

"Here ya go." Hank returned and set a plate in front of Johnny. The freshly cut turkey was piled high between two slices of whole wheat bread.

"Turkey on Thanksgiving," Johnny mused while scooping up the sandwich. "What a concept, huh Hank?" He took a healthy bite and chewed madly. "Beats the shit outta' pirogues," he added, his words garbled.

"Anything would," Hank shot over his shoulder, walking away.

"It's Brad," Johnny blurted between heavy chewing. "My son."

Scooch pulled back slightly, a confused scowl came over his face. "Your son bring home a black man?" He stared down at the bar and shook his head. "Damn, Johnny. I didn't know he was gay."

"Shut up," Johnny said. "He's not gay, ya moron."

Johnny watched his friend Scooch laughing to himself.

"Fuck you." Johnny took another bite of his sandwich.

"So, your boy brought home a sister. Is that what this is about?"

Johnny finished chewing and swallowed. He turned to Scooch and looked him in the eye. "He's marrying a fucking slope."

"Damn." The smile left Scooch's face. He looked down, "Sorry, man."

"Don't be sorry." Johnny reached out and patted his big friend on the arm. "You can't help it if you're an asshole."

"What're ya gonna do about it?"

"What?" Johnny's eyebrows rose. "You being an asshole?"

"No, fool. About your son and his woman."

"Do?" Johnny turned away, staring blankly at the bar. "What the hell *can* I do?" He downed the last of his double shot and tapped the empty glass on the bar. "I thought I raised him better than that, ya know?"

At the far end of the room Hank's head popped up, hearing the shot glass striking the wooden bar.

"Hit me again, Hank." Johnny raised the glass momentarily.

"Seems to me you gotta take control of the situation." Scooch took another sip of his beer. "A man's gotta establish the proper protocol for his family."

Johnny reared back, a little surprised that his friend even knew the word 'protocol'. "Yeah?" Johnny, once again, glanced up at Scooch. "And what if he don't listen and he marries her anyway? Then what?"

"He's either with you, or against you on this, Johnny. Ain't no middle ground."

"So what are ya saying?" Johnny motioned with his fingers toward some unseen figure before him. "It's either her or me?"

"What kind of a son brings home a little hooch momma when he knows how his old man feels about that?" Scooch turned in his seat and pointed a long finger at Johnny. "That's disrespect, right there, Johnny. That boy done shit all over your world, man. Everything we went through. You getting' all fucked up with your leg over there." Scooch pointed down at Johnny's crippled limb. "That don't mean shit to him if he can do that."

Hank arrived with a bottle and refilled Johnny's shot glass.

Johnny sat quietly, contemplating his friend's words. His thoughts floated back through time to a tiny house in an Italian neighborhood on Syracuse's north side. Another Johnny stood on trembling legs, about to introduce his new girlfriend. Papa stared up from the table, over the outstretched newspaper, his dark eyes fixed on the young Polish woman standing before him.

But, that was different, he thought. The Poles hadn't been shooting at Papa. Besides, Elena could almost pass for an Italian girl, until she opened her mouth. And, wasn't that the point? Women should keep their mouths shut anyway, right?

Johnny took another sip of his bourbon. It flowed from his lips down to the pit of his stomach, the burn fading to a calming warmth. Setting the glass on the bar, he stared quietly into the remaining amber liquid. "Maybe you're right, Scooch," he said, folding his hands on the bar.

"You damn right, I'm right." Scooch thumped the bar with a clenched fist.

"It's bad enough those people got better treatment than we did, for Christ's sake." Johnny raised a hand and let it fall back to the bar. "We got veterans living on the street while we're payin' for these people to live in nice cushy apartments."

"Tell it," Scooch chimed in.

"I moved us down here when they started takin' over the old neighborhood." Johnny's movements became more animated. "They were everywhere," he added, waving a hand. "I thought I was back in Nam. We were overrun with 'em."

"Your son know why you moved down here?"

"Yeah. He knows damn well, why." Johnny turned away and nodded. "I can't fucking believe this."

"Take a stand, Johnny." Scooch Henry leaned closer. "You take a stand right now." Scooch poked the bar with his long index finger for emphasis. "Or you'll regret it for the rest of your miserable life. Pretty soon she'll be coming over for *all* the holidays... Then what?" He chuckled, as if suddenly struck by an irony. "Grandbabies?"

Johnny's head snapped around, his eyes wide.

"See, man." Scooch pointed, again, at Johnny. "This some serious shit, right here. You want little D'Amato grandbaby gooks runnin' all 'round your goddamn house?"

"Not on my watch." Johnny grabbed up his shot glass and downed the rest of its contents in one gulp. As the burning slug ran down his throat he glanced down the bar to see Hank looking back at him, slowly shaking his head.

*   *   *

"You could have warned me about your father." Donna was sitting in the passenger seat with her arms folded across her chest as Brad got in the car and closed the door. The sparkle of her shiny new diamond caught her eye as she stared at the floor of the car. She wondered how a day that had started out so perfectly could have turned out so bad.

"I don't know what to say." Brad extended his hand, palm up.

"Not much *to* say."

"Donna," Brad replied, turning the key. "I had no idea that was coming. I knew he had some issues with…" He paused, as if choosing his words carefully. "Your people. But, I never—"

"My *people*?" Donna shook her head and stared in near disbelief as she spoke the words. She would have found the hackneyed phrase amusing if it hadn't carried so much weight at that moment. "So, you knew he was a racist and yet you brought me up here anyway?"

"Yes." Brad nodded while glancing over his shoulder out the window. "You got me," he added, patting his chest. "I brought you up here, proposed to you in front of half the police force in town just so I could embarrass and humiliate you in front of my family." He set his jaw; the muscles on the side of his face tighten. "Now you know the real me. I'm just a shit head."

"I didn't say that."

They pulled onto the main street and were soon on their way toward the interstate.

Brad drew in a long breath and sighed. "Pop's not a racist."

"No?" Donna shook her head and looked away and then back again at Brad. "So what do you call a man who hates another person because of their race?"

"Confused." Brad shifted in his seat, still looking at the

road. "Angry." His lips puckered, as if contemplating a new facet of his father's behavior. "Scared."

"Scared?" Donna turned and absently stared out the window. "Of what?"

"Hell, I don't know," Brad said. There was a brief silence. Donna felt the car accelerate as they entered the onramp to the interstate. "Everyone's afraid of something."

Donna knew all about being afraid. For most people the source was external: a threatening person, a wild animal, or even something as exotic as an erupting volcano. But, her biggest fears did not come from without. They came, instead, from that place in her mind where thoughts and memories were locked away in hopes that they would someday fade safely into obscurity.

But her demons were merely biding their time, growing stronger each day; awaiting the moment when they would be unleashed to wreak untold havoc. She closed her eyes and unconsciously shook her head, fighting off the images lurking like insatiable ghouls around the fringes of her psyche. For an instant, she felt the service forty-five jumping violently in her tiny hands.

"I hate the thought of scaring anyone," Donna blurted.

"Who said anything about you scaring anyone?"

"Never mind." Donna turned toward Brad. "I'm concerned about your father's influence over you. He'll try to come between us, you know?"

"Let him try."

"He'll want you to choose." Donna cocked her head, leaning toward Brad. "Me, or him."

Brad looked down at her ring. "I think I've already made my choice."

Donna placed her hand on top of Brad's, resting on the console. "I'm sorry," she said. "I've had a lifetime of this and I'm not sure how much more I can take."

"What do you mean? A lifetime of what?"

"Another time." Donna's head dropped. "I still owe you a conversation."

"Yeah," Brad said, nodding his agreement. "You do."

"Soon," she offered, giving his hand a loving squeeze. "Very soon."

"Pop's just gonna have to get over it or we won't come up here any more."

"Having you in my life has been a blessing." Donna looked up at Brad and smiled. "I was hoping that might include your family, too."

"I was hoping things would go better." Brad glanced down at her hand. "I'm really sorry." He lifted his hand and fondled the ring on her finger. "Of all the days…"

Donna lifted his hand to her lips and gently kissed it. "I love you."

"Yeah?" he said, giving her a lopsided grin. "Even though I'm a shit head?"

Two hours later they arrived at Donna's house. She turned the key and entered the foyer and Brad started to follow her through the front door.

"Where do you think you're going," she said, turning to block his way. "You have your own home."

"Aren't we supposed to celebrate our engagement?" he asked, sliding his hand up under her shirt and caressing her back.

Donna smiled and kissed him tenderly on the lips. "Celebrate?" She wrinkled her face in mock confusion. "I think the word is celibate." Donna slid her shapely thigh between Brad's legs. "Now that we're engaged," she continued in a teasing tone, "you have to wait for our wedding night."

Brad slid his powerful hand down her back and under the waistline of her panties, firmly rubbing the soft skin of her buttocks. "Whatever you say," he said just before their lips met in a lingering, passionate kiss.

Donna slipped her foot behind the door and kicked it closed.

*   *   *

Donna's eyes popped open. She stared through the darkness at the big red numbers on the alarm next to the bed. It was 3:13. Rolling over and wrapping a delicate arm around Brad, she closed her eyes in hopes that his rhythmic breathing would lull her back to sleep. By 3:45 she knew it was hopeless. Careful not to rouse Brad, she slipped from beneath the covers and pulled on her robe.

She stood next to the bed for a moment and watched him sleep while thinking what a difference a few hours can make in a person's life. While she had fully understood the implications of being in love, the concept of marriage had brought the equation to a new quantum level. Did she have what it takes to be a good wife? Could she make him happy? Was she ready to spend the rest of her life with this man?

A moment later her thoughts flashed to another man who had also been sleeping. A young soldier, unaware he was being watched, slept peacefully before her. Donna closed her eyes and shook her head, purging the image.

She grabbed one of the journals as she left the room on her way downstairs.

Curled on the couch in the den under a blanket, Donna turned to a book-marked page and continued reading where she had left off just a few days prior.

January 31st, 1968

All hell broke loose today. What was supposed to be a ceasefire turned into an all out assault by the enemy. We got reports today of massive attacks in all the major cities. Chatter on the radio net said some of the worst fighting was around Hue.

I pray I never see another day like today. We encountered literal human waves of soldiers trying to overrun our position. Many of them didn't even have weapons or charged our perimeter wrapped in explosives. I have never seen so many dead bodies. I never dreamed I would ever fire upon unarmed men. May God forgive me.

So much for the cease-fire.

Chapter Eight

Mai sat among the bewildered passengers in the huge transport plane. The air had grown cooler since taking off. While it was not as cool as nighttime, she still felt a slight chill. Their time in the air lasted longer than a walk to the next village but not as long as the trek to Khe Sanh. Time was somewhat irrelevant to someone who didn't own a watch.

The drone of the engines changed pitch. Mai felt the lumbering cargo plane slowing in mid-air as it began descending. She put a finger into each ear and wiggled them vigorously, trying to relieve the building pressure. A young airman tapped her shoulder and handed her a piece of gum. He made exaggerated motions, showing her how to chew it. Shortly after, Mai felt a strange sensation, as if she were suddenly lighter. The discomfort in her ears began to ease while the air around her became warmer.

The plane jerked heavily upon landing. The engines roared and she felt herself being somehow pulled toward the front of the plane. She grabbed a nearby strap and held tightly while children tumbled around her amidst the thundering turbines and screaming babies.

In about the time it usually took Mai to eat dinner, the shaking subsided and the engines ramped lazily to a stop. Everyone in the plane glanced around with uncertain stares. Startled faces turned suddenly as the huge cargo ramp in the back of the plane began opening. Glaring shafts of bright sunlight invaded the relatively dim interior, blinding Mai for several seconds.

As the opening in the plane grew larger and her eyes adjusted to the light, Mai gradually became aware that something was wrong. She turned her head in all directions while deplaning with the rest of the refugees. As much as she wanted them to be there, the jagged mountains that had stood like silent guardians over her village were nowhere to be found. Her little heart quickened at the sight of several multi-storied buildings off in the distance. Her world had, somehow, suddenly changed.

Mai was swept along with the current of slow-moving refugees, able to see only the slender backs of the young mothers and older children in front of her. After walking for a short distance they were instructed to gather together near the edge of the tarmac. Mai scanned their faces, desperately hoping to see her mother.

Frantic women ran between small groups of huddled children in search of their own lost sons and daughters. Young ones cried and babies screamed as more frightened and confused refugees arrived in a steady flow from the large transports.

An Army jeep skidded to a halt a few yards from the crowd. Several soldiers jumped from the rear of the vehicle onto the paved ground. An ARVN captain climbed out of the front seat and began barking orders in Vietnamese at the crowd while pointing at the buses that were arriving from the runway. Many of the women and children who had been reunited were ushered onto the buses and taken away. As the crowd thinned, the numbers of adults dwindled to only a few frantic and trembling women.

"Where is my baby?" one of them cried out to a young South Vietnamese soldier. "I can't find her anywhere!" She grabbed him by his shirt and shook him while tears poured down her face.

"Where is your mother?"

Mai turned toward a man's voice, a young ARVN soldier. She felt his hand gently gripping her shoulder.

"I don't know," she replied, the words nearly caught in her throat. "They got lost."

"Wait here," the soldier commanded in her native tongue. "Go with the others when the bus arrives."

Mai shrank back into the throng, her eyes filling with tears. She turned to look at the large group of children milling around her, crying, shaking, and reaching for each other as another huge cargo plane rolled toward them.

But, this airplane turned in another direction; its cargo of soldiers and large crates were quickly unloaded. With each passing moment Mai feared she would never again see her mother or Hung. After a long wait, a bus pulled up in front of the remaining children. The young soldier was back, lifting her by her arm.

"Now," he said to her. "Go with the others."

"No!" Mai tried breaking free. "My mother is lost! I have to find her!"

A middle-aged Vietnamese man in western style clothes approached. He wrapped his arms around her and took her from the soldier, who quickly disappeared into the crowd. Before she knew what was happening, she was inside the bus. The man who was holding her plunked her down in one of the many rows of seats.

"Stay here," he said to her, leaning close to her face.

In a few moments the bus started moving. Mai's heart sank as the runway, and any hope of finding her mother, faded from her sight.

The ride took her into the biggest city Mai had ever seen. The streets were wide and smooth, the buildings shiny, uniform, and large. Traffic clogged the busy streets lined with palm trees. The commotion filled her ears with more different sounds than she had ever heard in Khe Sanh. In what seemed like an endless ride through a boundless city, Mai found herself staring out the open windows at the marvels of this modern metropolis.

They drove past more houses than she had ever seen: Huge white houses, with glass windows, tile roofs and leafy trees rising out of closely cut grasses. Planted in many of the neatly manicured yards were slender bamboo shafts, stripped of their leaves save for a small tuft at the top. Small strips of red paper, hanging from the poles, fluttered in the hot breeze.

The streets were filled with cars, bicycles, and scooters moving quickly along in a noisy procession. Colorful banners and clusters of balloons spanned storefronts and commercial buildings. Flowers of every kind, colors like a rainbow, covered the medians and grassy parkways. This strange and new city had prepared well for the *Tet* celebration.

People walking along the paths next to the wide streets wore clothes she had scarcely ever seen. The young women wore vibrant garments with floral patterns. The young men wore tight-fitting pants that flared at the bottom.

Mai gazed out the windshield of the bus, her eyes wide as they entered onto a long bridge over the Perfume River. Tiny sampans floated lazily along the current. Cramped, ramshackle houses crouched together on the far bank, held aloft over the water by skinny poles embedded in the soft mush of the murky bottom.

At the far end of the bridge Mai saw a rounded opening through a great stone wall. The bus was momentarily plunged into darkness as they passed into the maw of the massive stone beast. Emerging on the other side was like

stepping back in time two centuries. A few blocks distant a
great palace loomed over the tops of the closely packed
two-story buildings. Its ornate rooflines reflected the
Chinese influence amongst the French provincial architecture. Curved tiles lined steep roofs atop lavishly decorated
red and yellow exterior walls. Hand-carved dragons lined
the peaks of the rooflines. Around the perimeter, cylindrical
columns held sturdy awnings in place along the spacious
exterior promenade.

Farther into the old city the houses and buildings grew
closer together. Many were made from cut stone with thick
block or concrete walls running in front of them along the
tree-lined sidewalks. The streets narrowed and the bus
slowed to negotiate the pedestrian-filled thoroughfares.

They pulled to a stop in front of a light-colored stone
building with tall spires that narrowed at the top. The towers attached were the tallest things she had ever seen. On the
tops of the towers, and at the peak of the roof in between,
Mai saw the same symbol she had seen on a chain around
the neck of the man who had grabbed her from the soldier:
two straight pieces crossing each other. She remembered
seeing that same symbol on the tiny Catholic Church in Khe
Sanh.

Mai followed the rest of the children off the bus and into
a large room just inside the church. Inside, they were led to
a long wooden bench. It was the last in a long line of such
benches running the length of the huge room. At the front of
the room Mai saw something that sent her heart surging.
She swallowed hard and instinctively reached for her mother. She, instead, grabbed the arm of an older child seated
next to her.

The girl, about thirteen, shook her arm away and glared
at Mai.

"*Bui doi,*" she said, turning her head away in disgust.

Mai drew back her hand and cowered. Her eyes were, once again, drawn to the front of the room to the image of a bearded white man hanging from two pieces of wood brought together in the same fashion as the symbols outside the building. She stared at the grotesque image. His hands and feet were bloody, his face drawn and anguished. *Is this why they brought us here? Momma, where are you?*

Her mind raced, taking her back to the tiny village that had erupted in flames just hours before. Even with her eyes covered, Mai knew what fate had awaited the people she had left behind. Had the same people who attacked her village taken her prisoner? Were they preparing something equally horrific for her?

She stood up to run. A sturdy hand gripped her arm, nearly lifting her off the ground. "Where do you think you're going, little one?"

Mai looked up to see a Vietnamese man looking down at her, the same man she had seen at the airstrip. His eyes squinted with his smile, forming fine lines at the corners. His full head of black hair was neatly combed and parted. The black robe he now wore concealed his body all the way to the tops of his shiny black shoes.

"I'm going to find my mother," Mai said, looking him up and down while breaking free of his weakening grasp. She stalked toward the door, glancing over her shoulder just once to see if the man was in pursuit.

"Maybe I can help you find her," she heard his voice call from behind.

Mai stopped, contemplating his words. She turned to him. "You don't even know what she looks like."

The priest's hearty laugh echoed throughout the large room, causing several of the children to crane their necks in search of the source. "You have a point," he said, raising his hand, his index finger extended toward the ceiling.

"Perhaps together we can find her."

"Who are you?" She stepped back slowly.

"I am Father Nam," he replied.

She should have bolted. But there was something in his expression that stopped her. It might have been the sincerity in his eyes. Maybe it was his smile, exposing his straight white teeth.

"You are not my father."

The man offered a benevolent nod. "Where is your father?"

Mai did not answer, but only looked at him and shrugged.

"Do you know where you are?"

She thought about his question for a few moments and slowly shook her head.

"You are in Hue City."

Mai stood looking at the man in the black robe trying to understand the relevance. She had heard some of the adults mention the name on occasion, but to her it was just another far off place she would never get to see. She stared at Father Nam, his body framed in the distance by the figure hanging in the front of the room. He turned to see what held her transfixed.

"Does that frighten you?" he asked, taking a cautious step closer.

Mai nodded, alternating glances between the figure and the slowly approaching man in black.

"He's a good friend of mine," he continued, inching closer. "And he loves children."

"What's wrong with him?"

The man turned, once again toward the tormented figure. "Some people hurt him," he said, turning back toward her. "But, he's all better now."

"Why did they hurt him?"

"Are you hungry?" The man reached toward her.

Mai took another step backward, staring at his out-stretched hand. After a few moments she nodded vacantly.

"Come." He took a step closer, grasping Mai's hand. "I'll tell you more while we eat."

After feasting on a bowl of rice and fish, Father Nam led her upstairs and into a room filled with beds similar to the one she had slept on at the base in Khe Sanh. It was growing dark and Mai's eyes were heavy. Several women, some of whom were Caucasian with colorful round eyes, brought her fresh white clothes and a large cloth for her bed. One of them, dressed in the same kind of black robe as the man, took her to a tiny bathroom and washed her with warm water and sweet smelling soap. Her skin tingled afterward in a way she had never before felt.

A short time later, Mai curled into a ball within the soft clean fabric on her bed. Barely able to keep her eyes open, she pulled the sheet close to her and thought of her mother and Hung. Mai lay in her bed, trembling; the warm patches of wetness on her pillow the last thing she was aware of as she drifted to sleep.

*   *   *

"Give it to me," the boy said to her. He was perhaps seven or eight. A deep scar ran from his left eye to his ear. "It's mine."

"You already had a piece!" Mai raised a hand and slapped at the boy, landing only a glancing blow on his arm. In her other hand she held a small piece of *Banh Chung*, a square piece of sticky rice cake traditional to *Tet*, the Vietnamese New Year.

Within seconds she was being pulled back away from the boy. "Now, now. Let's not hit people, Mai," a stern voice admonished her from behind. She knew in an instant it was Father Nam.

Nearly a week had passed since she had arrived. There was still no sign of her mother or her brother. With each passing day her hopes of ever seeing them faded a little more.

Father Nam reached over to the small table covered with trays of holiday treats. From a large platter he produced a piece of *mut*, a sweet candied fruit.

"I want to talk to you about something, Mai," he said, offering her the treat.

She took the *mut* and stared at the priest. "Have you found my mother yet?" Mai looked at him with hope-filled eyes.

"There was no one at the base with a baby boy," he said, kneeling next to her. "But, the men at the base have been talking to a woman who has lost a little girl." He motioned with his head and offered her a wink. "She's waiting downstairs."

Mai's face lit up. "My mother is here?" She grabbed his hand and pulled him quickly along toward the stairs.

"I didn't say that, Mai," he replied, reaching for the railing while they approached the stairwell. "It might not be—"

His words were interrupted by Mai's high-pitched squeal. She let go of his hand and raced down the rest of the steps, calling for her mother.

"*Mẹ!*" The word echoed throughout the veranda. "Momma!"

A slender woman with her back to Mai had been waiting in front of an open doorway in an outdoor corridor, her hair and light clothing soaked from the heavy rain. She turned when she heard her daughter's voice. Lien's face contorted in jubilant agony as Mai bounded across the tiles, squealing with joy. They crashed together, the force of their embrace sending them to the ground.

"I thought I had lost you," Lien struggled to speak

through choking sobs. She gripped Mai's head in her splayed fingers and kissed her head repeatedly.

Mai fell silent, clinging to her mother as if she would once again vanish should she let go. "What about Hung?" Mai finally said.

Lien's eyes closed, her grip on Mai tightened. Mai felt the warmth of her mother's tears against her neck. No words were spoken; only the slow shaking of her head back and forth against Mai's shoulder; her wet hair and clothing smelling like the rain.

"We'll find him, momma," Mai said, reaching up to stroke her mother's hair. "Just like I found you."

Lien pulled away and smiled through a tear-streaked face. She nodded, her sad eyes betraying her doubt.

"You are welcome to stay here," Father Nam offered. "We could use some help," he looked over his shoulder toward the dormitory. "You could use a place to live."

"Can we stay here?" Mai looked up at Father Nam and then at Lien. "Please? We can look for Hung."

Lien held Mai at arms length and looked up at the priest. Mai glanced at him as well. He returned a sad, yet benevolent smile. Lien nodded, shaking loose fresh tears. They streaked down her face in heavy tracks.

Lien was taken to the dormitory. There she bathed and was given fresh clothes, bed linen and a meal. Later that evening, Mai sat with her mother, curled together in the soft bed among the many orphans getting ready for the *Tet* festivities.

"Why is everyone so happy?" Mai asked Lien. In the background the others were hanging banners, lighting candles and playing music.

Her mother was combing her long black hair. She paused in mid-stroke and looked down at Mai. "It is our most joyous time, Mai," Lien said, her face fixed and somber. She set the brush down on the bed. "It is the beginning of the new year. We honor our ancestors and hope for a happy and prosperous year ahead. We celebrate our family and life with a fresh start."

Mai's thoughts turned to the events of the last week. Her Buddhist upbringing taught her that to live is to suffer. She wondered if she was a good Buddhist and if God was pleased. If life was suffering, Mai was living it to the fullest.

Mai thought about her brother, the 'mischievous monkey', looked deeply into her mother's eyes and said to her, "I miss Hung."

Lien's head dropped, she raised her hand to her face, cupping her mouth. Her eyes narrowed, her body shook. She wrapped her arms around Mai and pulled her close. They lay against the wall on their bed, holding each other while the rest of the room joined in the revelry surrounding the impending holiday celebration.

At the stroke of midnight there was a great commotion from outside. In spite of a monsoon rain, the sounds of fireworks split the air. Heavy gongs rang out from crowded balconies throughout the walled city. Inside the bustling dorm, people scurried around, cheerfully greeting one another, clasping hands and offering best wishes for the New Year. Mai and her mother greeted the arrival of *Tet* alone from a remote corner of the room.

Shortly after midnight, Mai and her mother fell asleep, exhausted after a long day.

Wrapped in the safety of her mother's arms Mai drifted off to a serene dreamscape, where her mother and brother walked along a tranquil tree-lined river. Flowers rose on giant stems high overhead, dropping endless streams of candied fruits and jellied rice cakes. Hung was toddling ahead of them, his naked little bottom darting back and forth among the pretty flowers.

The sky went suddenly dark and the roll of thunder

grew louder in the distance. Candied fruit falling from the huge flowers turned to snakes that slithered along the ground and started chasing Hung. The little boy screamed as one after the other, snakes began wrapping around his tiny body. Bright flashes broke the darkness; claps of thunder shook the ground.

Mai bolted up in the bed to the sounds of chaos. Brilliant bursts lit up the night sky outside the window. The building shook with a thunderous explosion. Broken glass showered the beds. Lien pulled Mai to the floor, where they cowered together amidst the frantic screaming of the orphaned children.

A shaft of light pierced the darkness as three nuns burst through the door. They set about trying to calm the children only to have their efforts thwarted by the light's sudden extinguishing. A luminous flash preceded a violent rumbling by only a heartbeat. In the next instant, a blast ripped a hole in the ceiling along the opposite wall. Mai and her mother clung to each other on the floor pelted by splinters of wood, chunks of stone, and shards of metal.

Chapter Nine

Johnny awoke to the familiar aroma of frying bacon. He was lying on the sofa in the den, trying to gather the energy to rise from his stupor. Just before drifting back to sleep he was jarred by the sound of a skillet landing noisily on a burner. It clanged heavily against the old range-top. Soon after, the morning quiet was once again split by the rapid rhythm of a fork churning scrambled eggs in a glass bowl. He opened his eyes, still heavy from his bender the night before. Sitting up, he glanced over the back of the couch to see Elena through the doorway, pouring the contents of the mixing bowl into a frying pan. It hissed and crackled as the runny mixture made contact with the hot metal.

"So you are not dead after all," Elena said to Johnny as he entered the kitchen. She was standing at the stove, stirring the eggs in the pan, a red and white apron tied around her waist.

"Don't start." He hobbled toward the coffeepot, shifting his cane to his left hand while reaching to open an upper cupboard door.

Elena stood silently with her back to Johnny, staring down at the eggs.

"The smell of bacon makes me sick when I'm hung over," he offered, pouring himself a cup of coffee, his stomach protesting the olfactory overload.

"I know," Elena countered, dropping a handful of fresh

strips into the skillet. Grease spattered out from the pan as she turned to him, her stern look devoid of any sympathy. "You smell like a gin mill. Like smoke and liquor."

With unsteady movements Johnny settled into a chair at the kitchen table. He sipped his coffee without reply.

Elena placed two slices of bread into the toaster and jammed the lever down hard. Johnny stared straight ahead and took another sip of his coffee. An agonizing minute passed in silence before the toast popped up. She abruptly snatched the pieces from the toaster and hastily slathered them with a thick coating of butter. In what seemed like one smooth motion, she spooned a healthy portion of eggs and placed three slices of bacon onto a plate and set it before him.

"I'm not hungry."

Even before the words had left his lips, Elena had grabbed up the plate, emptied its contents into the trash and tossed it into the sink. It crashed amidst the other dishes.

"Where were you last night?" she demanded, turning from the sink. "I almost called the police to search for your body."

"Out." Johnny stared back at her for a moment before glancing away.

"You should have called."

"I didn't know I needed your permission."

Elena took a step toward him. "You should be ashamed."

For an instant Johnny wondered if she might be right. It had been many years since he had taken flight from his troubles, seeking refuge in a bottle of bourbon. While not clinically diagnosed as an alcoholic, some 'Ivy League Doogie Howser' had dubbed Johnny an alcohol abuser. He hadn't been drunk in years. His thoughts flashed to Donna's image as the bile churned in his stomach.

Johnny glanced, once again, at his wife: the same woman who had stood by him through the tough years. So many nights of passing out on the sofa, puking on the front lawn, and even standing before judges accepting his sentences for everything from public intoxication to drunk driving.

He recognized the familiar look. On the surface it was anger. But, Johnny knew better. Deep down, it was fear.

"That's why I slept on the couch," he said, his voice uncharacteristically weak. "I thought I'd save you the trouble of kicking me out of the bedroom."

"You owe your son an apology."

"No," he replied, his voice flat and certain. "I don't."

"What kind of way was that to greet your new daughter-in—"

"No!" Johnny pointed at Elena. "She is not my daughter." He glared at her in silence for a moment. "And, she never will be. You got that?"

Elena's lips pursed, her face reddened. She turned toward the sink and reached for the dish soap.

"Those people are animals," he continued. "You don't know anything about them." Johnny raised his mug and took a drink of his coffee, waiting for some reaction from Elena.

"Oh, thank God." A desperate voice came from the kitchen doorway. "Ma, you're a saint. You know that?" Gina, still in her pajamas and robe, dragged her slipper-clad feet toward the coffee maker. They swiped the linoleum as she shuffled across the kitchen. "I knew I smelled your coffee."

"Happy to be of service," Elena replied, still engaged in her dishwashing. She was seemingly trying to scrub the black off a cast iron skillet with a piece of steel wool.

"What time did you get in, Pop?" Gina poured coffee

into a large mug, turned toward Johnny and took a sip. "Your truck was still gone when I got in at two."

"I don't know." Johnny was suddenly wishing he had kept his mouth shut about not being hungry. "Not much after that, I guess."

"You drove home?" Elena spun around, her hands covered with soapsuds.

"No, I did not drive home." Johnny's glances darted back and forth from Elena's accusing stare to Gina's semi-comatose gaze. "I got a ride."

"From who?" Elena demanded. "Who gave you a ride?"

"I don't remember."

It had been a long time since he had seen her look at him the way she was now. Not since the night she was rousted from sleep at four o'clock in the morning to come down to the jail and bail him out.

"But, you remembered how to get drunk, eh?" She raised a soapy hand into the air.

Johnny turned toward Gina, wondering what had kept her out until two. He stared at her, thinking how grown up she looked all of a sudden. Where those wrinkles at the corners of her eyes?

Gina turned suddenly, as if aware she was being observed.

"Pop?" she said, setting her mug on the table and leaning in to him. "You all right?"

He looked away. "Yeah," he replied, weakly waving a hand. "I'm fine."

"Brad told me about the meltdown yesterday."

"It's none of your business."

Gina picked up her mug and took a long sip of coffee. "She's a really nice person, Pop. You should get to know—"

"I don't think so." Johnny cast her an icy stare. "And I don't need you telling me what I should do."

"She's marrying your son, for God's sake," Gina countered. "What're you gonna do, shun her from your life for the next twenty years?"

"If I have to." Johnny raised his eyebrows and set down his coffee cup. "You think she's so nice, huh? Those people can make you believe they like you. They work along-side you in the daytime and they're back at night to cut your throat."

Gina rolled her eyes. "Pop, come on. That was, what," she looked up at the ceiling momentarily, "thirty-some years ago? She was a freakin' kid."

"It don't matter." He shook his head. "It's who they are. They have no loyalties to anyone. They'd sell their own mothers for a dollar. And a lot of them did." Johnny pointed at Gina. "You didn't see the things I seen over there. You don't know how ruthless those people are. I seen things your lily white liberal ass couldn't even conceive of."

"Johnny!" Elena piped up from the counter. "Watch your language in this house. You are not at the bar with your loudmouth—"

"Yeah, yeah…" He patted the air with his fingers. "Gina. You don't know anything about this. You kids have never faced anything tough. If you had, you'd have a different attitude toward people."

"No, I wouldn't," Gina responded. She stared back at her father with conviction. "I'd never make a person pay for another person's offense."

"Spoken like a true bleeding heart liberal that's lived a sheltered life."

"So, I need to fight in a war before I can have an opinion?"

"About this?" Johnny raised his chin and gave one stiff nod. "Yes."

"Is this where we get the 'Jane Fonda, that rotten commie-hippie-traitor-bitch speech'?"

Elena stopped her scrubbing and turned around.

Johnny glared at Gina for a moment and said, "You know you are never to say that name in this house."

They were silent for a long moment before Gina spoke, softly. "You're going to have to deal with this, Pop." She took a deep breath. "Brad loves her and they're getting married."

"She's not coming back into my house." Johnny looked straight at Gina and then at Elena. "Not as long as I'm alive."

Gina looked at Elena. "Well," she said. "It's kinda chilly in here all of a sudden. I think I'll take a shower and get dressed."

Elena turned and began rinsing the sink. Johnny stared off into the distance, beyond the walls, into some undefined oblivion. Neither one answered her.

"Right." Gina set her mug on the kitchen table. "I'm meeting a friend for brunch, Pop. You need a ride to pick up your truck? I can drop you off somewhere."

Johnny nodded, vacantly. "Sure," he muttered, almost imperceptibly. "Why not."

"I'll be ready in an hour," she said, pausing in the doorway. "That okay?"

"Yeah," he answered, studying the bottom of his cup. "Fine. An hour. I'll be ready."

Gina offered her father one last look before turning and walking down the hallway.

Several minutes passed before Elena broke the silence.

"You were dreaming again, last night," she said, drying her hands on a dishtowel.

Johnny flinched and felt his gut tighten at the mention of his dreams. He straightened in his chair. "Do I need your permission for that, too?"

Elena untied her apron, folded it neatly and placed it on the counter next to the dishtowel. She joined Johnny at the table, reaching for his hand as she sat down across from him.

"You were dreaming about the dogs."

Johnny's heart rate quickened. For a moment he thought of denying it. But, he knew she could not be fooled. After thirty-eight years together, there was little she didn't know about him. For now, his avoidance strategy was one of silence.

"Weren't you?" She continued with her interrogation while gently squeezing his hand.

"So what if I was?" He pulled his hand away. "It's just a dream. A stupid dream about some yapping dogs."

The image of a small pack of angry dogs appeared in his mind. They snarled and snapped at him while pulling desperately against the chains hooked to their collars. Their frenzied barking grew louder until Johnny could scarcely stand it. He shook his head.

Elena remained silent until Johnny could not resist her gaze. "We should talk to Father Pete," she said, as their eyes locked.

"I don't need a priest." He folded his arms across his chest. "I need her to be gone." He poked the tabletop with his index finger. "I haven't had that dream in ten years, maybe more. She shows up and I'm right back in the shitter again." Johnny pointed an accusing finger at his wife. "And you want me to make like it's okay her coming in my house? You know what those people did to me. I hate 'em. I hate 'em all," he said, waving his hand in sharp movements.

Elena's eyes began swelling with wetness. "Then, I don't know what to do for you." She shook her head slowly. "I can't go through this again." She rose from the table. "I can't do it."

$*$ $*$ $*$

"Play time's over," Nurse Betty announced from the hallway. "Nap time for the little ones before dinner."

Collective groans of disappointment rose up from the children gathered in the playroom on the pediatrics floor. Toys and stuffed animals littered the bright green carpet. Circus clowns and dancing bears graced the walls of the large play area. The décor of the room was the only sanctuary from the institutional tile floors, tile walls, and tile ceilings in the rest of the hospital. About the only thing that wasn't tile was the mauve wallpaper on the lower half of the walls, below the bumper pads along the endless corridors.

"You are amazing," the short, pear-shaped nurse said to Donna from the doorway. She had a pouting little face that peeked out from beneath fuzzy red hair and a pair of blue, horn-rimmed glasses. "Some of the best psychologists in Knoxville have tried with her and gotten nowhere."

Donna sat in a rocking chair holding a small child amidst the small throng of children filing out of the large room. Dressed in pajamas and small hospital-issued gowns, many of the little patients bore the outward signs of their particular maladies. Some were bandaged, or encumbered by casts. Some sat in wheelchairs while others were bald and sallow-faced.

In her arms Donna cradled a sleeping five-year-old girl. The victim of a series of brutal sexual assaults, the little tawny-haired child had not spoken or allowed anyone to touch her since she arrived at the University of Tennessee Medical Center nearly one week prior.

"She is very frightened," Donna said, gently stroking the top of the girl's head. "She is worried that someone will hurt her again."

"She spoke to you?" The nurse took a step forward, her mouth dropping open.

Donna nodded and smiled.

"Praise the Lord," the nurse said. "You have a gift, I've never seen anyone who cares so much for children."

The little girl stirred in her embrace. Her tiny arms tightened around Donna's neck while trying to snuggle closer.

"I used to know a frightened little girl like this," Donna said. "Someone helped her when she needed it most."

"You have any kids?"

Donna shook her head slowly, a sudden sadness sweeping over her.

"Do you ever think about having some of your own, someday?"

"All the time." Donna pulled the girl closer, kissing the top of her head.

"Bless her little heart," the nurse said, inching closer and touching the girl on the shoulder. "It's nap time for the little ones."

"I'd like to stay a little longer, if I may," Donna replied, gently rocking in the big chair.

"You stay as long as you like. We're happy to have all the help we can get here." Nurse Betty walked to the doorway as the children were filing out of the room. "Jenny's in room two-twenty-four. You can just lay her down in her bed when you go."

Donna sat with the girl for another twenty minutes before taking her to her room. She laid the sleeping girl down for her nap and stood over her bed wondering how anyone could hurt a child. But, she knew all too well about hurt and those who could inflict it upon others. A pang of sorrow rippled through her as she watched the sleeping child, safe for the moment from her demons. Donna remembered a time from her own past when even sleep offered her no refuge.

It was mid-afternoon and there was still plenty of time

to indulge in the busiest shopping day of the year. She stopped at the nurse's station on her way to the parking garage.

"Thank you, so much," a pretty blonde nurse said to her from behind the counter. "The kids really love having you visit with them."

"I do it for selfish reasons," Donna answered, smiling.

The blonde nurse smiled at her. "See you on Tuesday, then?"

"Right after work," Donna replied. "But, I'll be about an hour later than usual. I've got a late afternoon meeting with some stuffed shirts from the Pentagon."

"Well, if you ever get tired of building bombs up there at the labs," the nurse called after her as Donna entered the stairwell. "You can come to work with us."

Donna took the stairs to the main floor and followed the walkways to the parking garage. After taking the elevator to the third level, she walked to her silver Lexus. As she approached the car, she felt as if the floor of the garage was tilting to one side. She stopped next to the vehicle, steadying herself against it for a moment. Shaking her head, she pressed the remote door control and slid behind the wheel.

The traffic on Interstate Forty was heavy for a Friday afternoon. She surmised it was due to the post-Thanksgiving day shoppers. The steering wheel felt strangely removed from her fingers; the surrounding cars on the freeway seemed distant somehow. After driving no more than ten minutes, Donna could not remember where she was going. It was only instinct that led her to exit Interstate Forty and take the Pellissippi Parkway onramp heading north to Oak Ridge.

She had gone only two miles on the parkway when a sharp pain shot through her skull. Jerking her head as it assailed her, Donna momentarily lost sight of the road. A blaring horn jolted her attention back onto her lane. Another wave seized her, this time causing her to close her eyes. When she opened them her heart surged at the sight of a bridge abutment racing toward her at sixty miles an hour.

Donna tried to turn the wheel, but her arms and hands would not respond. Her foot would not move to the brake. For a few, agonizing seconds she could only watch as the menacing concrete monster grew larger in her windshield. The last thing she saw was the hood crumpling just before the soft fabric of the airbag exploded into her face.

*   *   *

She awoke to a steady beeping just beyond the grasp of her ability to understand what it was. With her eyes closed, her only reference was the rhythmic cadence, somehow strangely familiar. With great effort she managed to open her eyes just enough to see a dim red light splitting the darkness from her right. While straining to look toward the source, her head throbbed in pain as the red LED lights on the monitor near the bed came into view. Still trying to focus, she glanced slowly around the room, aware that even the slightest movements were painful. Catching a glimpse of a figure among the shadows, Donna managed, "What happened?"

"What do you think happened?" A woman's voice came from the darkness in the corner of the room. "You could have killed someone. You shouldn't be driving."

Donna tried to respond, but could not. From out of the blackness Mai came into view next to the bed, a dim red hue casting subtle shadows over one side of her pretty face.

"So," Mai continued. "Where is this man who claims to love you so much?"

Still groggy and unsure of her status, Donna grappled with the question. Where was Brad? What time was it? How long had she been there? She looked around the room for a clock.

"Now you know," Mai said, placing her hand on the top of Donna's head. "Since our mother died, all we really have is each other." She ran a gentle hand over Donna's hair. "We're all we've ever had and I will be with you until we see her again."

Donna strained to speak, but could not make a sound; her head suddenly filled with memories of Lien. She could only watch as Mai turned and left the room, before drifting off to sleep.

When she awoke the next morning, Brad was sitting next to her bed asleep in a chair. He stirred in his seat as she struggled to move: the rustling of the covers making faint sounds in the stillness of the room.

"Donna," Brad exclaimed while sitting quickly upright. He reached for her hand, grasping it in his strong fingers. "God, I was worried sick you wouldn't wake up." He edged closer, kissing her hand and then her forehead. "I was over at Mack and Eileen's when I found out. Becky Edinger tracked me down at around seven."

She, once again, tried to speak. Brad looked on with a pity-filled gaze as she struggled to move her lips.

"Baby, don't try to talk right now." He placed a finger on her lips. "The doctor will be here in a little while. We'll know more then. Just relax. It's gonna be okay."

When the doctor arrived a short time later, they were still holding hands.

"Good morning," he said, entering the room. He was a little man with dark skin and thinning black hair. "I am Doctor Pathakar, a resident neurologist."

Brad rose and shook his hand. "I'm Brad D'Amato. Donna's fiancé."

"Nice to meet you," the doctor replied in a heavy southern Asian accent. He advanced toward the bed, looked down and smiled. "How are you doing?" he asked, pulling a small penlight from the pocket of his white coat. He clicked the end and shone the light into Donna's eyes.

She flinched and turned her head away, a searing pain just behind her eyes.

"Still very sensitive to light," Doctor Pathakar continued, still looking intently into her eyes. "Your pupils should begin responding soon." He clicked the penlight off and stuffed it into his coat pocket. "Can you speak, yet?" the doctor asked.

Donna glanced at Brad, then back at the doctor and slowly shook her head.

"Any news, doc?" Brad said, taking his seat.

"I have some preliminary test results that I would like to review with you." The doctor pulled a sheet of paper from a large manila envelope and drew closer to Brad and Donna. Pointing at the colorful images, he continued. "This is an enhanced image of your brain," he said, leaning over the bed for Donna to see. He pointed with a pen to a region in the center of the page. "The ischemic attack—"

"Doc," Brad interrupted. He closed his eyes and smiled. "I'm a roofer." He nodded toward Donna. "She's the Ph.D. But, she can't talk right now. So, if we're gonna communicate, we need to cut out the buzz words."

The doctor glanced at Donna for a moment before nodding in understanding. "I'm afraid the news is not good," he offered, his tone devoid of condescension. "Your fiancé suffered a mild stroke, from which she will very likely fully recover."

Brad tightened his grip on her hand.

"So," Brad said. "What exactly does that mean?" He looked at Donna and then at the doctor. "You said she'll recover. Right?"

"It may take a few days before she shows significant improvement."

"So, what's the problem?" Brad cast a hopeful look at them both.

"I'm afraid the situation is much more serious than the stroke alone." The doctor paused while he collected his thoughts, as if conveying bad news was not in his nature.

"What do you mean?" Brad straightened in his chair. "How bad is it?"

"As you can see, the blood vessel in this region," he made a small circle with his pen around a bulbous portion within the image, "is grossly enlarged." Doctor Pathakar slid the paper into the envelope and engaged them both with a somber expression. "The aneurysm is very large."

"Aneurysm?" Brad glanced quickly around the room. "Jesus," he said, shaking his head. "Can't you fix it? Operate, or something?"

Doctor Pathakar was silent for a moment. He looked straight at Donna before looking at Brad. "I'm very sorry, but it is inoperable."

"So, what are you saying here, doc?" Brad's voice was almost in a whisper.

"The enlarged vessel will eventually rupture." The two men fell silent. Brad looked down at the floor. "When that happens, she will most surely not survive."

Brad sat holding Donna's hand, stunned for the moment. She felt his fingers tighten around hers. Their eyes met. There was a sadness there that she had never seen in him before.

In a weak voice Brad asked, "How long?"

"I wish I could say," Doctor Pathakar answered. "With an aneurysm of this size, it could occur at any moment." He took a deep breath before continuing. "With the proper rest and medication, it might be weeks, perhaps even months."

The doctor's words hit Brad like fists. Donna watched as the hulking man beside her turned her way and buried his face in her shoulder. At that moment she would have done anything to wrap her arms around him but all she could do was lay helplessly in the bed while Brad squeezed her lovingly. Donna felt the wetness of tears on her temples, not sure if they were Brad's or her own.

"I'm very sorry," the doctor said while backing toward the door. "I'll arrange for you to have a follow-up visit in my office in about a week." With that said, he turned and left the room.

Chapter Ten

"The damn phone's been ringing off the hook." Brad appeared in Donna's bedroom doorway with a cordless phone in his hand. Wearing a pair of sweat pants and a long-sleeve T-shirt, he was badly in need of a shave. "I never knew you had so many friends," he said, stepping into the room, his silhouette nearly blocking the doorway. "Hell, I don't even know half the people who've called."

Donna smiled. She was reclining in her bed with her head propped up on two pillows. In her lap lay her father's journals. She had been reading one of them when Brad came up the stairs.

"You've got," he paused, looking down at a piece of paper he carried in his other hand. Turning it over, he nodded his head faintly as he silently counted. "Fifteen messages from this morning alone," he said, looking up at her, his eyebrows raised.

It had been a little over a week since the accident. Just released from the hospital earlier that day, she was still sore from the wreck. With her injuries on the mend, she had regained much of her movement and speech. But, even with the progress she was making, Donna could not help thinking about the ominous message the doctor had so unceremoniously delivered.

Donna had been there when another doctor had told her father about his cancer. The news had hit her hard, but it wasn't until hearing her own death sentence that she under-stood the weight of such a disclosure. The news had sent her sprawling like the shock wave from a heavy blast. She could still feel the rumbling.

Her days were filled with anger and frustration and her nights were equally restless, the darkness taking control of the part of her that could not understand why this was hap-pening. She fought it as best she could, but her will was quickly fading. There were even times when she saw the dark humor in surviving the ravages of a war only to suc-cumb to a tiny clot of coagulated blood produced by her own body.

"Call," she began, her words labored and deliberate. "To work...I need." She closed her eyes and grimaced in frustration knowing that she was coming across like a two-year-old child. Donna tried again, determined to get it right. "I need work...to...call." She slammed her open hand down on the journal in her lap.

"Baby, take it easy." Brad rushed to her side. He sat on the bed and tried to put his arms around her.

Donna pushed him away.

Brad persisted, eventually harnessing her flailing arms.

Donna struggled only half-heartedly before conceding the fight and then covering her face with her hands. She sat on the bed wanting to flee the scene. But she knew there would be nowhere to run, even if she could. Was this how she would spend her remaining days? A woman with an IQ of one hundred and eighty relegated to communicating in broken sentences, grunts, and jerky hand gestures?

"It's okay," he said, cradling her. "I know what you meant." He kissed the top of her head. "I know you so well that we don't need—"

The phone rang in his hand. Brad sighed and threw the phone on the bed. "I'm gonna let the machine get it." It rang twice more before the faint sound of Donna's recorded voice wafted up from the kitchen.

She noticed his bloodshot eyes. For the last few days Brad had been juggling the housework, talking with doctors, and fielding dozens of calls from concerned friends and neighbors. His business could run for a while without him. They had a healthy backlog and his crew could handle just about anything. Just the same, he was awake at all hours cutting checks for his employees and preparing quotes to keep new work coming in. All the while making sure Donna was comfortable and resting well.

"You…need rest," she said, reaching with a shaky hand for his whiskered face.

He met her hand with his own, holding it against his cheek, his three-day beard feeling prickly against the back of her hand. "I'll be all right. You just concentrate on getting yourself back together." Brad smiled at her. "I miss my little wise-ass girl."

"Work," she said, again. "Call to them…me to…not—"

Brad patted her on the arm. "It's handled. Don't worry about it. They know. Remember?" He turned toward the front wall, motioning toward the many flower arrangements sitting beneath the window. "There's a lot more downstairs."

"I'm sorry," she said, gently smacking her palm against her forehead.

"Nothing to be sorry about." He stroked her hair. "That skinny doc said you'd have some memory lapses for a while." He kissed her head again. "Doesn't bother me. I'm just glad you're here with me."

"For now."

The comment stunned them both. It had escaped from her lips before she could call it back. Brad exhaled heavily and slowly shook his head. He looked away.

They sat in silence for a long moment. A jet rumbled high overhead outside.

Donna suddenly became aware that her pajama tops had been pulled away from her left shoulder during their tussle. She reached across her chest to adjust her top when her movement was arrested by the gentle grip of Brad's thick fingers.

"You don't have to hide it from me," he said, guiding her hand away from the soft cloth of her pajama top.

"It's so ugly," she replied, turning her head away from him in shame.

"There's nothing ugly about you, Donna." He unbuttoned the top button and pulled the fabric farther away from her shoulder, revealing a jagged round scar about the size of a quarter. Radiating from the disfigured flesh were two lines of suture scars extending another inch in each direction, looking like miniature pink railroad tracks on her otherwise flawless skin.

She turned her head, not wanting to see it. Brad leaned across her body in the bed. Her hands instinctively rose to clasp the back of his head while she felt his lips gently kissing her shoulder.

"You always know…" she began, holding his head against her chest. "What…to do."

Donna could feel wetness where Brad's head lay against her. She stroked his hair while they lay together on the bed. Her mind drifted far away to a time when the only comfort she had ever known was suddenly torn away from her. At the time, she didn't know it was coming. For Brad, it would be different. He would have to wait for the day when his comfort would be gone, watching her end advance like the steady march of an invading army of darkness, but never knowing when they will attack.

She kissed his head.

"There's a mountain of food downstairs." Brad abruptly sat upright and motioned toward the doorway and the stairway, just beyond. "Most of it's from the church." He turned his head away from her and ran his sleeve across his face. "I had to take some of it over to the Cleveland's to freeze it."

Donna nodded while staring at the flowers across the room.

"Mom said she'd come down and help out while you recover."

She was jarred from her trance. "No," she said, shaking her head weakly. "Father...won't...like."

"To hell with him." He turned to her, looking her in the eye. "To hell with him."

"Must...respect..." Donna strained with each word. "He...is...father."

"He sure doesn't act like it." Brad stood up. "What about my respect?" he asked, his fingers landing on his sternum. "Why does he have to be such a jerk?" he continued, pacing the floor. "I wonder how he feels now. I'm sure my mother's told him what happened." He stopped pacing for a moment. Looking momentarily at the ceiling, Brad chuckled. "The bastard's probably happy about it."

Donna sat motionless staring up at him while trying not to believe anyone capable of such thoughts. But, she knew better, having personally witnessed far worse throughout her lifetime. She offered no rebuttal.

*   *   *

A week later Brad was back to work. Elena had moved in for a few days, allowing Brad to address some important issues with his roofing business. Donna had made remarkable progress and was out of bed for brief periods of time. Able to converse in nearly complete sentences, the frustration of not being able to communicate had eased somewhat for her.

"Your color looks good today," Elena said to Donna while pouring her a glass of orange juice. They were sitting at the kitchen table about to eat breakfast. Donna had showered, dressed herself, and traversed the stairs on her own.

"I am feeling much...good." She took the glass of orange juice from Elena. "Thank you for coming to..." she paused, struggling for the next word, "down to stay with me."

"Is all right." Elena smiled and patted Donna on the arm. "You won't need me much longer." She poured herself a cup of coffee. "You are getting stronger. Soon, you will be good as new," she concluded, slapping the table with her open hand for emphasis.

Donna tried not to stare at Elena. Did she not know what the doctor had told them? Had Brad told her everything? She bit into her bagel. Across the table Elena looked as if she had something to say, occasionally making eye contact and then looking away or taking a sip of her coffee.

"I want you to come for Christmas," Elena finally said. She set her mug down afterward and stared expectantly at Donna.

"Oh," Donna stammered for a moment. "I...no." Shaking her head, she looked away. "No...sorry. I don't...can't do that."

"It will be better," Elena continued, reaching again for Donna's arm. "You will see."

"Your husband," Donna replied, her words a little slow in coming. "He made clear...it clear to...how he me about...feels." She shook her head and started again. "He said—"

"I know what he said," Elena countered, setting her hands on the table. Her expression was suddenly stern. "He is a fool, sometimes. A good man, but a fool." She took a deep breath before continuing. "The war," she cast a glance to one side. "It took something from him." Elena turned to Donna. "He is angry and doesn't know what to do."

"He hates me."

"He hates how you make him feel." Elena cradled her coffee mug in her hands. "He hates the things he remembers when he sees you." She stared into the cup for a moment before continuing. "He hates being angry."

"I don't know…" Donna felt a hint of nausea in her gut.

"He is too proud to admit he was wrong," Elena replied. Fine wrinkles framed her green-hazel eyes as she smiled at Donna. "If you don't make the effort, there will never be peace between you." Elena reached for her hand. "I know him. He is upset with himself, but he can't say this."

Donna processed the new information, filtering out the bias, allowing for a statistically significant margin of error, and adding a ten-percent safety factor. What if Elena was wrong? She could be setting herself up for more abuse. Was it worth it? After all, she had only a limited number of days left. Was this how she wanted to spend one of them?

"We were going to Florida for Christmas," Donna finally said.

"You can go to Florida anytime." Elena stared intently at Donna. "This is our most important family day for us. I want you to be part of it. You are family, now."

"Have you talked to…with Brad about this?"

"He knows, yes." Elena closed her eyes and nodded slowly. When she opened them, she continued. "He said it would be up to you." She motioned with an open hand toward Donna. "He will do whatever you decide."

"What about Gina?"

"Gina likes you." Elena laughed and glanced up at the ceiling. "She does not like the other girls Brad has brought home. But, you she likes." She picked up her mug and took a sip of coffee. "That is saying something. Yes?" She paused a moment before continuing. "Gina wants you to come."

"Brad's father?" Donna engaged Elena with a tentative stare, as if half expecting him to appear from behind the cupboards by the mere mentioning of his name.

"I have told him, yes." The smile once again vanished from Elena's face. "He made his threats. His big speech." She motioned in an arc with her hand. "He has told me he will not be there already." She hit the table. "Ah! He will be there and he will behave himself." Elena raised her hand, the index finger pointing skyward. "Johnny knows when he wears the pants and when the pants wear him."

Donna laughed at the analogy. She had seen some of his father in Brad. The stubborn streak followed by the proud sulking. Sometimes days would pass without conversation, only to end in a conciliatory roll in the hay, the incident never brought up. Apologies were few and far between. But, she had grown to recognize his outward signs and acts of contrition. Maybe Johnny was the same way. Maybe the incident would simply pass into the past and never be mentioned again.

"Brad and I talk...will talk about it." Donna searched for a sign of understanding in Elena's expression. "Okay?"

"Good. You talk about it." Elena nodded. "Then, you come anyway."

They finished breakfast. Donna had been up for almost three hours and was feeling tired from so much activity that morning. Elena helped her to the couch in the den and covered her with a blanket.

"Can I get you something?" Elena asked, pulling the blanket snug over Donna's feet.

"On my bed," Donna answered, weakly pointing up to

her room. "There are some books. Journals. Would you please bring them down?"

In less than a minute Elena had returned with the leather books. She inspected one of them before handing them to Donna.

"These are yours?" Elena said, pointing to the journals. "You wrote them?"

"My father's," Donna replied, setting all but one of the books on the floor next to the couch. "They begin when he arrived in Viet Nam. They end...after he returned to...here...The US."

"Did you discuss, much?" Elena motioned at the journal in Donna's hands. "Did you talk about the war with your father?"

Donna shook her head while staring down at the journal. "We never did."

"Johnny has dreams," Elena said, glancing toward baskets of flowers piled in the corner. "About the dogs."

"My father had dreams, too."

"Did he drink?"

"When we first..." Donna stopped short of saying what was coming next. "He quit after a while."

Elena stood next to the couch staring down at Donna. There was benevolence in her eyes that Donna could not readily place. Elena broke the silence.

"Do you have dreams?" Elena blurted.

Taken aback by the question, Donna could only offer a few rapid blinks of her eyelids. She stared at the wall for a moment hoping the conversation would end with her silence.

"You have much you are hiding," Elena offered. "Much pain. Many bad memories."

Donna could only look up at her future mother-in-law in stifled amazement.

"Is in your eyes," Elena said, moving toward the kitchen. She stopped in the doorway and turned to Donna. "You and Johnny," she said, pausing a moment before continuing. "You are not so different. No?"

Elena turned and disappeared into the kitchen.

Donna stared after her for several seconds before glancing down at the journal in her hands. She opened it to a book-marked page and began reading.

February 5th, 1968,

This has been the longest week of my life. We can't keep enough helicopters in the air to carry off the wounded to the hospital ship offshore. I heard the colonel and the major talking today about the situation in Hue. It's a real mess up there, they said. Word coming back is that North Vietnamese death squads are pulling people out of their homes and shooting them in the streets. They're killing women and children and old people alike. I'm resolved more than ever to help these people win their freedom.

Chapter Eleven

"We need Mai's help," Father Nam said to Lien, who was huddled with Mai amidst the remains of the church sanctuary. "I've made a tunnel to the kitchen but I can't get past the door." The priest pointed to the pile of rubble that used to be the back wall of the old stone church.

The siege had raged for five days; the intense fighting faded with the setting sun, only to return with renewed vigor at dawn. For the last thirty-eight hours, the ancient city of Hue had weathered the constant shelling from the US navy ships parked just a few miles off shore. One of the artillery shells had hit close enough to the three story dormitory section to cause its collapse. The devastating impact of the naval artillery was accompanied by the deep basso *whump* of the mortars and the staccato reports from small arms fire combined in a macabre symphony of devastation.

Lien reached for Mai. "What do you want her to do?" she asked, closing her arms around her daughter. Mai felt her mother's grip tighten as the priest approached.

"We need the bags of rice from the pantry," he offered, squatting before them. "The older children will not fit through the opening I have made." Father Nam reached out his hand and cupped Mai's chin. "The younger children are too small to tear open the bags and carry the rice."

In the days since the attacks on the city began, the church had received nearly three hundred people seeking

refuge from the siege. Father Nam, and the five nuns, did their best to stretch what food they had left. Without access to their rice stores, the children who had survived the collapse would now surely face starvation.

With Lien close behind, Father Nam led Mai to a small opening in the wreckage. He knelt beside her and grasped her arms. "Don't be scared," he began. "I'll be right behind you."

Mai peered into the dark makeshift tunnel, wondering what monsters laid in wait for her. She cast her mother an uncertain look. Lien smiled back and nodded, but the worried look on her face offered Mai little reassurance.

"It's okay," the priest said after a long silence. "I'm right here." He plucked her into his arms and placed her, feet first, through the opening. "Thinking about it will only make it harder. We need you, Mai. We need you to be a big girl."

Mai slipped from his arms and stood on unsteady legs among the bricks and broken concrete. She turned and looked at the priest, a little frightened at the look of concern on his face. She knew that this was not a game.

"Are you ready?" he asked, giving her a slight nod.

Mai looked down and nodded in return.

"Let's go," he replied, straining to squeeze his middle-aged body through the small gap.

They crawled on hands-and-knees most of the way through the jagged timbers, chunks of rock, and twisted metal. The passage grew darker the farther they went.

"Here," Father Nam said. Mai felt something nudge her hip. "Take this. It will help you see the way." She reached back and took the flashlight from his hands. Already turned on, the bright beam illuminated the way. Grotesque creatures, emerging from the newly created shadows cast by the jagged pieces of debris jutting into their path, seemed to claw at them as they slunk through the wreckage.

They reached the outline of a doorway. Father Nam grabbed her arm. "I can't go any farther," he said between heavy breaths. "But, I will talk you through. Just do what I tell you and you'll be fine."

Mai wiggled through the small space beyond the doorway. It opened into a cramped chamber lined with splintered timbers, broken glass, and shattered concrete. Overhead, wires dangled like vines. Near the far end of the chamber, she saw another doorway.

"Many people are counting on you," Father Nam urged from the opening.

Mai shined the light into the debris, inspecting the pathway she would take. "I'm scared."

"You can do this," he replied. "I'll be right here."

She let his words settle for a moment before venturing forward. Just as she was about to move, a horrible stench wafted her way, causing her to retreat toward the priest. It was a smell she knew all too well.

"Oh," Mai said, turning her head away from the foul odor. "It stinks in here." She shined the light back toward the doorway through which she had just come.

Father Nam's face was bathed in the bright light. He squinted against it and nodded. "I know, Mai," he said. His voice was gentle and reassuring. "Breath through your mouth."

When she turned back toward the other doorway the light shined briefly on the source of the odor. She recoiled at the sight. About an arm's length away, two small legs stuck out from between the layers of rubble. Both feet had been sheered off at the ankles, exposing the tissue beneath. Scores of maggots writhed together in the gray flesh between the skin and bone. She covered her mouth and retched, suddenly becoming aware of the steady chorus of flies buzzing around the rotting flesh.

"You must get into the pantry," Father Nam coaxed from the opening. "We need to get the rice from there. We have many to feed and no food." Mai was still bent over, trying not to breathe in the stench. "Can you do that for us?"

She slowly straightened, and coming to her full height, turned to the priest and nodded. "I'll try," she answered. "It smells so bad in here."

Carefully following the priest's instructions, she located the pantry and dragged several large bags of rice from the small room. With a knife that Father Nam had tossed to her, she cut the bags open and scooped smaller portions into bowls he had also passed to her through the small opening. During a rest break, one of the nuns cut a strip of cloth from a bed sheet and soaked it in wet soap. She tied it over Mai's nose and mouth, allowing her to remain in the small chamber without having to endure the smell.

It took over an hour, and the help of several of the nuns and older children, to form a relay and pass most of the rice from the pantry. After the last load, Father Nam reached through the opening and pulled Mai through. When she emerged, Mai was met with Lien's outstretched arms.

"I'm so proud of you," she whispered into Mai's ear. "Tonight we will all eat because of you."

And, so they did. For the first time in days, the people taking refuge in the church slept on full stomachs. Later that night, Mai lay with her mother on the cold stone floor of the sanctuary, staring at the stars through a gaping hole in the ceiling. Outside, the distant sound of automatic gunfire echoed throughout the old city. Mai closed her eyes, feeling the sudden burn of a trace amount of teargas floating in on the night breeze. From some unidentifiable direction they heard a woman scream. Her agony was abruptly ended with the single report of a weapon.

Mai nuzzled closer to her mother. Half asleep, Lien

stirred and unconsciously pulled her little girl close. They fell asleep amidst the backdrop of gunfire and mortar shells exploding in the distance, happy that the battle was elsewhere for the moment.

Early the next morning Mai and Lien awoke to the sound of automatic weapons. They sat up quickly to see several North Vietnamese soldiers, with red stars on their caps and wearing dingy gray-brown uniforms, pouring through the front doorway. One of the soldiers ran to the center of the sanctuary, raised his weapon, and fired several shots into the ceiling.

Women and children screamed while the men among them tried to shield them with their bodies and arms.

"Everyone outside!" the soldier shouted. The stunned masses just stared at the man, too terrified to move a muscle until he screamed, *"Bây giờ!"* and fired another volley over their heads. Glass from the stained glass windows showered the room as he strafed the walls.

From where she was crouched in the church, Mai could hear the faint sound of vehicles approaching. Soon after, more soldiers rushed into the badly damaged old church, shouting and pulling people to their feet. Three of the men walked among the hundreds of people huddled on the floor and singled out a family of five at the far end of the sanctuary. One of the men grabbed the woman Mai thought to be the mother of the family. He pulled her to her feet by her hair and screamed into her ear.

"You are traitor!" The young soldier twisted the jet-black bundle of hair in his hand. "Now, you will die like one!"

A man, who was probably the woman's husband, stood to defend her. He had taken no more than a step or two toward the soldier holding her when one of the other soldiers quickly raised a handgun to the man's head and pulled the trigger. The woman screamed as the man collapsed before her, blood and brain matter spattered her white *áu dài* from a gaping wound in the side of his head.

Mai felt the softness of her mother's arms envelop her. The gentle tug of her mother's hands gliding across her face concealed the scene from Mai's eyes, now wide with fear.

"Don't watch, Mai," Lien whispered to her. "Don't look."

The three small children with the captive woman began crying. Mai could hear the woman's panic through her sobs. "No!" she pleaded, just before another shot echoed through the old church. Mai's heart raced as she heard several people scrambling for cover on the floor. Hearing the sounds of gunstocks slapping against the soldiers' palms, Mai knew the men had just brought their weapons into the firing position in response to the movements.

The woman's screams trailed off at the sound of hands slamming against flesh. Once more, she wailed as another shot split the commotion within the sanctuary. "Why?" the woman asked, her voice muffled and slurred.

"You are a traitor to the people," a voice answered. Another shot silenced the last of her crying children.

Mai lay trembling in her mother's arms while the woman's agonizing sobs filled the church. Lien pulled herself close, laying her head over Mai's. One last shot put an end to the woman's nightmare. Her body landed with a thump against the stone floor in the ensuing silence.

"Everyone outside!" One of the soldiers yelled in Vietnamese. He appeared to be the leader of the group. "Move!" he screamed, punctuating his command with another volley of machine gun fire.

Mai and Lien followed Father Nam and the rest of the frightened refugees outside. She took one last look at the crucifix at the front of the church before going out the door.

Father Nam had told her the story of Jesus on the cross. Why would someone worship such a man? He couldn't help himself then and he wasn't helping anyone now.

The previous night's rain left a thick layer of fog covering Hue. The sun, barely above the horizon, had not yet burned through the mist. It was still too early for the shelling to start: Not until the sky was clear, not for hours.

There was still enough light to see the devastation the city had endured. Mai looked in shock at the debris-filled streets. The tidy homes and storefronts had been blown away, their contents spilling onto the streets like disemboweled hogs.

"You," the soldier said, aiming his gun at the priest. "Come here."

Father Nam complied, glancing back at the five nuns standing with a group of orphans as he approached the soldiers.

"And you," the leader added, motioning for the nuns. "All of you. Come." He pointed at them and then gestured for them to follow the priest. When they had joined Father Nam in the middle of the cluttered street, the leader said, "You are charged with treason against the People of Viet Nam. You will now be executed for your crimes."

Cries of protest spread quickly throughout the large group of mostly women, children and the elderly gathered in the narrow street.

"Silence!" the leader screamed, stifling the crowd.

Two soldiers stepped forward and pulled back the levers of their weapons. The priest and the five nuns stood in a line, their eyes closed, making the sign of the cross when the bursts of gunfire split the heavy air. Lien, caught off guard, had not been quick enough to shield Mai's eyes from the tragic event unfolding just a few feet away. Mai watched in stunned terror as the six figures, cloaked in black, crumpled onto the pavement.

From behind them the soldiers began pushing and then shoving members of the group out into the street. A short, balding man with glasses was next. The soldier next to him slammed the stock of his gun against the man's head, sending his glasses skidding into the rubble. Another soldier raised his weapon and fired a single shot into the man's forehead.

Right afterward, a young woman was forced to stand in the small stream of blood flowing freely from the balding man's head wound. As she was turning to say something to someone in the crowd, she was nearly cut in two by a burst of automatic gunfire.

From the edge of the large group, a few of the younger people tried making a break to safety. When the soldiers saw them running they opened fire on them as they fled. While the hundreds of captives looked helplessly on, the soldiers cut down five more with ruthless precision.

A moment passed. The street became silent in the wake of the incident.

"The rest of you will follow along," the young commander instructed. "Anyone trying to run will be killed."

They filed out of the city in a doublewide line that stretched for a block or more. In all, there were nearly four hundred of them in the procession. Mai recognized the smell she had encountered in the rubble, growing more familiar with each day. As if on cue, heads periodically bobbed ahead of Lien and Mai as the people stepped over large beams, fallen utility poles and some of the hundreds of dead lying in the streets.

When they had reached the edge of the ancient, walled city, one of the soldiers raised his hand. "We wait here," he shouted. "Sit down." He motioned for the crowd to be seated where they stood.

After several minutes, two young soldiers approached.

The man in charge leaned in to them as they whispered into his ear. The commander turned and looked out over the people squatting in the street. He nodded and glanced at his watch.

The two young soldiers opened the gates in the city wall. The commander nodded to his men, who quickly rousted the people to their feet with the butts of their rifles. In less than a minute they were once again on the march.

Mai struggled to keep up with the pace. The heavy rains had subsided and the sun was beginning to bake the ground through the vanishing mist. The trail they followed wound first through fields of rice before plunging into the dense jungle surrounding the old city.

"Listen to me," Lien said to Mai under her breath. Her mother's grip tightened on her tiny hand. "You must do exactly as I say." She paused, holding a tree branch aside for Mai. Lien grabbed Mai by her arm as she continued walking and looked deeply into her eyes. "Do you understand?"

Mai nodded at her mother, a hint of panic creeping into her thoughts. Mai didn't know where they were going or why. She only recognized the look of concern on her mother's face.

"Where are we going?" Mai asked, her voice carrying ahead up the trail.

"Silence!" a soldier screamed from somewhere ahead.

Lien shot Mai an urgent look and put a finger to her lips. She shook her head, a clear sign to Mai to make no further outbursts.

The path narrowed. Moving through the dense undergrowth became even more difficult and the line of people stretched as their progress slowed.

"Mai," Lien said quietly, the branches swiping at their bodies masked the sound of her whispers. "I need you to be a big girl right now." The leaves rustled against their clothing as they squeezed through the narrow trail. "Just like when you got the rice for us. Can you do that?"

"Yes, momma," Mai replied, trying to keep the low hanging branches from slapping her face.

"We will stop soon," Lien continued. "When we do, I want you to do something."

"What?" Mai braced a hand on a log that had fallen across the trail.

Lien scooped Mai up in her arms. "Can you count to one hundred?" she asked, carrying her along the path.

"*Một, hai, ba—*"

"Good," Lien cut her off. "Not now, Mai. When I tell you." The procession slowed. Lien strained to see what awaited them along the trail. She turned to Mai and knelt beside her. "When I tell you to, you run in the direction I am pointing." Lien took Mai's chin in her hand. "Do you understand?"

"Yes, momma."

"You take one hundred steps and stop. Hide in the jungle. You stay there and don't move or make a noise until I come for you."

Mai's little heart started beating harder. She realized her mother was doing her best to hide the terror they were both feeling. A tear rolled from Lien's eye and ran down her cheek.

"You must not call out for me," she continued. "Do you understand? No matter what." She shook Mai for an answer. "Promise me."

"I promise." Mai thought she felt her mother trembling. "When will you come for me?"

"I don't know, Mai," Lien whispered into her ear. "It may be a long time. You must not move no matter what." With a quick glance up the trail she continued. "If I don't come for you by morning…" Mai felt Lien's arms squeezing her tightly. "If I don't come for you, find another church. Do you understand?"

Mai stared into her mother's eyes, not sure why she was so frightened. Maybe it was the way she felt her mother trembling or the way Lien's false smile failed in its reassuring efforts. From up the trail she felt an unexplainable and ominous tremor propagating like the waves from an earthquake. It carried an emerging terror, unspeakable and, as yet for a child, undefined.

The trail opened up into a clearing next to a wide creek. Most of the people were already crowded together next to the water when Lien and Mai approached. Their progress slowed as the people began bunching together in the open area. Lien set Mai down and cast nervous glances around the unfolding scene. The soldiers herded everyone toward the water. Mai looked up at her mother, suddenly frightened by the furrows forming in her forehead. Murmurs of confusion began permeating the crowd. Mai noticed her mother's breathing growing more rapid as the people pressed together along the water's edge. What were they doing? *Why have they brought us here?*

Billows of realization began resonating among the wide-eyed faces. What began as a subtle stirring, grew to a series of panic-stricken faces and turning heads. The chatter rose to new levels as many of the hostages realized that the soldiers were lining up in formation.

A woman screamed. Heads turned. Soldiers moved shoulder to shoulder. Babies cried, instinctively aware that their mothers were in distress. The commander's hand made a slight motion. A dozen Chinese-made assault rifles came to bear. Chaos ensued.

"Now, Mai!" Lien turned to her daughter. "Run," she said, pointing behind Mai. "One hundred steps and hide." Lien spun Mai around and pushed her away into the thick green of the jungle. "Go!" was the last thing Mai heard before the thunderous reports of the AK-47s and the screams of the people trying to flee the clearing drowned out the sounds of the jungle.

Mai ran as fast as she could through the tangle of branches and tufts of heavy grass. Twelve, thirteen, fourteen, she counted to herself as she struggled against the jungle. Something rough scraped her face. Twenty, twenty-one... She tripped over a fallen tree. Her shin burned from the impact, but she scrambled to her feet and kept running. Behind her, the obscene chatter of the assault rifles rocked the quiet of the peaceful forest. Thirty-seven, thirty-eight... The shooting trailed off. Mai could hear a few isolated screams and the anguished cries of the wounded. Fifty-eight, fifty-nine, sixty... Single gunshots and short bursts of gunfire stifled the screams. Mai heard one lone woman's plea for mercy answered by the last crack of a weapon. Eighty-six, eighty-seven... Her foot sank into deep mud. She struggled free and continued running. Ninety-five, ninety-six...

Mai stopped, breathless. Sweat poured down her little face. Her hair was matted against her scalp. She had stopped in the middle of a swampy area, thick with low-lying cover. Thirsty and out of breath in the stifling heat, Mai found a thick clump of bamboo and crawled within its enveloping confines. In the distance she heard a voice order the soldiers' to search for survivors. She curled tightly and kept low, scanning the brush and listening for her mother.

Time dragged on and the urge to search for her mother became almost unbearable. Several times she almost left the safety of her hiding place in hopes of reuniting with Lien. Each time, it had been a random noise or the faint sound of what she thought was a man's voice that had stopped her.

Hours passed and there was still no sign of Lien. Mai's

exposed skin was a mass of mosquito bites. They itched and burned where she had been scratching them. She felt something on her leg. Looking down, she saw a huge black spider creeping along her skin near her knee. Bugs of every kind scurried over her hands and feet and up into her clothes. Nearly delirious from the heat and humidity, Mai scarcely noticed the bright green snake slowly winding through the stalks. It wasn't until it had brought itself nearly face to face with Mai that she noticed the venomous bamboo viper.

Resisting every instinct to run, Mai somehow willed herself to remain perfectly still while the snake flashed its hideous forked tongue at her. Seemingly satisfied that Mai was not a threat, the snake eventually moved on.

Sometime after noon, Mai fell asleep from exhaustion. She awakened a short time later to the sound of a snapping twig. Her little heart hammered violently at the site of a pair of sandled feet tromping nearby. The figure passed close enough to rustle the bamboo stalks that served as her blind. Another man joined the first, approaching from the opposite side of the clump of brush. They stood together for a moment before walking away.

As darkness approached, Mai began to worry that her mother was not coming. How long would she have to wait? What if she never came? With the encroaching shadows came the dark thoughts that Lien had not survived the massacre. Mai slowly crept from her hiding place. Careful not to make a sound, she continued in cautious movements. In spite of her efforts, her extrication from the hammock proved to be quite noisy. She froze in mid-movement when she heard something rustling through the brush just a few feet away. Mai continued making her way through the jungle, engaged in a cat-and-mouse game with an unseen player.

After a few minutes, Mai lost track of the sound in the

undergrowth. She stared into the densely packed branches, their form growing more grotesque in the waning light. Around her, the chorus of crickets, frogs, peepers, and unseen jungle creatures grew louder as night set in. Her breathing grew heavy as she realized she had no idea where to go or what to do. Mai's fear began turning to anger toward Lien for abandoning her in this strange place. She turned to continue on her way - to where she had no idea - when she felt a hand clasp her mouth.

"Make no sound," her mother's voice whispered into her ear from behind. "Some of them are still around us."

Mai turned and slid into the awaiting embrace of her mother's arms. With both of them soaked in sweat, Mai did not notice the blood on Lien's clothing in the diminishing light of dusk.

"Momma," Mai said, seeing the hole and the large, dark red stain on the side of her mother's peasant garment. "You have blood."

Lien offered a weak nod, her eyes halfway closed. "I know, Mai." She groaned as she pulled herself to her feet, gripping a sapling to help herself stand. "I will be all right. We must find our way out of here before dark."

Mai tried to offer her mother support, taking her hand and wrapping her tiny arm around her mother's hips. "I'll take care of you."

Darkness set in as they emerged from the jungle into a large clearing of rice paddies. Lien dropped down onto the levee that surrounded the watery fields and motioned for Mai to sit next to her. After a long moment of rest, Lien pulled Mai close.

"You must never mention what you saw to anyone," Lien admonished. "Ever." She looked Mai in the eyes. "Do you understand?"

Mai nodded, but she didn't understand at all.

"No one must ever know that we survived," Lien continued. "We must leave here and never come back."

"Why, momma?"

"We are not safe, here." Lien held her ribs and rolled onto her side. "We'll sleep now," she said, her eyes barely open. "Tomorrow, we must travel south." She took a few labored breaths. "Far away from Hue."

Her mother fell silent.

Mai lifted Lien's arm and wrapped it around her as she snuggled close.

Chapter Twelve

"Sorry, we're late, Ma," Brad announced as he and Donna entered through the kitchen door to his parent's house.

"Ah," Elena replied, turning from her workstation at the stove. "You are not late. The food is just now cooking." She set a large wooden spoon down and approached with outstretched arms. "Merry Christmas." Elena hugged Brad and turned to Donna. "Thank you for coming," she whispered into Donna's ear while gently hugging her future daughter-in-law.

"Merry Christmas, Elena," Donna answered. "We brought you something." She held out a basket full of cans, jars, and boxes. Tied to the handle was a big red bow. "Brad said you had trouble finding these items in the local stores, so we sent away for them."

Elena took the basket, inspecting the contents. "Oh, I don't believe it!" she exclaimed, her open hand pressed against her chest. "Where did you find these?" She plucked a colorful can with bright red lettering from the wicker. "Has been years since I have had these."

"Whad'ja get, Ma?" Gina chimed in, rising from the kitchen table.

"Salscesony," Elena responded, turning the can to show the label.

Gina's face contracted in revulsion. "Oh, jeez," she

offered, turning her head away, yet still staring at the can as if driving by a bad car wreck. "People move to this country so they don't have to eat that kind of stuff anymore."

"You should try," Elena countered. "I will open for dinner." She moved to the other side of the kitchen and set the basket on the counter and rummaged through a drawer.

"Let's hope she can't find the can opener," Gina said, glancing over her shoulder at her mother. "Merry Christmas, fat ass," she said to Brad, giving him a hug.

"Yeah," Brad answered, reciprocating the hug. "Same to you, mattress back."

"Brad!" Donna added, slapping his big arm.

"Oh, it's okay," Gina said, wrapping her arms around Donna. "We're Yankees. The greater the insult, the more you like the person. It's our little code."

Donna glanced sideways at Brad. "So, when he calls me a stubborn little…" she leaned in close and lowered her voice, "…bitch. He's really using a term of endearment?" She smiled.

Gina laughed.

"Now, you know I only mean that in the nicest possible way." Brad pulled Donna close and kissed her cheek.

"Of course," Donna answered, nodding, her eyebrows drawn together.

"So, how have you been?" Gina asked Donna. "You look great for someone who went ten rounds with a bridge abutment."

Donna glanced at Brad. In an instant she realized that none of them knew. He hadn't told them. Was it out of denial, or perhaps respect for her privacy? For a moment, Donna languished in her thoughts trying to decide if she was upset with him or not.

"I'm doing well, I guess," Donna said. "I've been back to work part time. After the first, I think I'll try it again full time."

"Brad said you blacked out, or something."

"Yes." Donna waited for Brad to jump in. He stood looking straight ahead at his mother pulling the lid off the can of
headcheese. "We're still trying to determine what that was
about." There was a sudden absence in her tone.

"Come," Elena blurted from the other end of the room.
"Try some." She held out a plate full of crackers along side a
truncated, self-supported cylinder of yellowish-gray chunks
suspended in a viscous, translucent jell. Alongside it on the
plate was a thick green paste that smelled like old socks.

"Oh, no." Gina waved her mother off, shaking her head
vigorously. "God, Ma. Your gonna make me sick."

"Heinrich, you try." She poked the plate at Brad. "Take
some kapuska. Just a thank you portion."

Brad lowered his nose to the plate and took a shallow
whiff. "Oh, Jesus," he waved a hand in front of his face and
coughed.

Without comment, Donna reached out and took a cracker
between her thumb and forefinger, scooped a portion and
popped it into her mouth. Brad and Gina stared with wide
eyes while she chewed. After swallowing, she took a breath
and said, "Tastes like river rat."

"You see," Elena said, once again poking the plate at
them. "Is good. No?" She looked expectantly at Donna.

"Not as good as your pirogues. But, not bad," Donna
replied.

"Speaking of food," Brad said, tipping his head back and
nodding toward the oven. "What's for dinner?"

"I have pork roast and butternut squash," Elena said.

"Apple pie for dessert," Gina added. "Grandma's recipe."

"With the crushed macadamias and brown sugar sprin-
kled over the top?" Brad asked.

"Oh yeah," Gina answered. "Makes my ass bigger just
thinking about it."

Donna laughed.

Brad joined in, shaking his head and chuckling at his sister's self-deprecating remark. Their levity was interrupted by the steady beat of Johnny's cane thumping the floor. The smile left their faces. Donna braced for another scene.

"What's everybody laughing at?" Johnny said, entering the kitchen from the den.

"Nothing, Pop," Brad said, walking toward his father. "Merry Christmas." He shook his hand.

"Yeah, yeah," Johnny replied, smiling. "Merry Christmas."

"Merry Christmas, Mister D'Amato," Donna said from across the room.

Johnny turned toward Donna but would not look directly at her, the slight smile on his face disappeared. He nodded in her direction and said, "Yeah, Merry Christmas." He glanced around the kitchen at the expectant stares. "Hope you're feeling better after the accident." Johnny looked away, as if his reserves of tolerance were about to run out.

"I'm doing well," Donna answered. "Thank you."

"How's the roofing business going, these days?" Johnny turned away from Donna. "Been keeping busy?"

Brad shot Donna an understanding look before answering. "It's been pretty steady," he said. "It always slows down a little this time of year."

"I see the college over in Johnson City is looking to replace the roof on one of the main buildings." Johnny leaned against the counter. "You puttin' in a bid?"

Brad shook his head. "No thanks," he answered, smiling. "I've had my fill of institutional work. Biggest pain in the ass you'll ever find." He turned and opened the refrigerator. "Donna?" he called across the small kitchen. "Diet Coke?"

"Sure," she replied, taking a step closer.

Brad pulled two cans from the refrigerator. He handed

one to Donna and pulled open the other. "I'm not doing any more government work. Not after the fiasco at the Labs." He took a sip of his soda. "I'll tell ya, right now the best work going is over in Nashville. They can't find enough contractors to build the houses going up right now."

"I wouldn't give you ten cents for the whole damn city," Johnny offered, frowning. "The place is a mess. Traffic's a nightmare." He nodded toward the refrigerator. "Hey, grab me another beer, will ya?"

Elena turned and cast Johnny a supervisory look.

Donna approached Elena, who was removing the pork roast from the oven. "Can I help with anything?"

Elena's face was flushed from the heat wafting out from the oven. She set the roast on top of the stove and closed the oven door. "You and Gina can carry food to the dining room while Johnny carves the roast. Yes?" She turned from the counter and plunked a basket of warm rolls into Donna's hands, their sweet smell prompting her stomach to growl in anticipation.

"Wow," Gina said to Donna as they entered the dining room. "She put you to work on your second visit. Ma must really like you."

"I hope so," Donna answered. "We had a nice time visiting when she came down to stay with me."

"Pops is behaving himself so far today." Gina set a large bowl full of butternut squash on the table. "He's still not looking at you, but at least he can be in the same room."

"It's a bit awkward."

"Hell, it's a lot awkward," Gina corrected. "I think he's trying, though."

"Then, I will try as well."

After the roast was carved and the table set, Elena called the family to order at the dinner table. "Who will say the grace?" she asked, doing a visual survey of the faces in the room.

"Don't look at me," Brad said. "I suck at it."

"Yeah," Gina piped in. "Me, too. What about you, Pop?" she said, casting her father a sarcastic smile.

"Let's just eat," Johnny replied. "Before it gets cold."

"Hush, hush." Elena slapped Johnny's hand away from the plate of roast pork. "We say the grace, first." She looked in Donna's direction. "Would you like to say?"

Donna sat at the end of the table. Johnny was seated at the opposite end, facing her. Their eyes met for the first time. "I would be honored," she answered, reaching for the hands of those to her right and left.

"Father in heaven," she began. "Bless this meal you have so generously provided for the nourishment of our bodies. Thank you for your gift of family today. We pray for those who have no one to be with. Please comfort those who have unmet needs and help those who seek to find you. Thank you for this day we celebrate the birth of your son and our savior Jesus Christ. Through him we pray. Amen." She gently squeezed the hands she held.

"That was very nice," Elena said. "You have gift for prayer."

"I just speak from my heart," Donna answered, blushing slightly. "That's all."

"Can we eat now?" Johnny held the bowl of squash in his hands. "Would that be all right?"

"Yes. Yes." Elena waved her hand over the table. "Eat. Everybody eat."

The table came alive. Spoons clanked as generous helpings of squash, corn, salad, and ambrosia were plopped onto their plates.

"So," Gina said, scooping a helping of corn from a bowl. "What church will you guys get married in?"

Donna and Brad looked at each other, suddenly realizing that the thought had never crossed their minds. Brad hesitated for a moment before saying, "I guess we'll get married in Oak Ridge at the church we go to now."

"Which church is that?" Johnny asked, a piece of bread poised in his fingers a few inches from his mouth.

"Well," Brad began, his voice tentative. "We go to a Methodist church right now."

"What was that?" Gina said, her tone sarcastic. She cupped her hand to her ear. "Was that the sound of a can of worms opening up?" The room grew quiet. "Why, yes," Gina continued with her theatrics. "That was a can of—"

"Gina!" Elena said.

"Sorry, Ma," Gina replied. "Being a former Catholic is like being a reformed smoker." She shoved a fork full of squash into her mouth.

"And what is wrong with the Catholic Church?" Johnny asked. His glance bounced back and forth between Gina and Brad.

"Nothing, Pops," Brad answered, glancing quickly at Donna. "I'm just not that fussy about where I go to church."

"Obviously," Johnny shot back.

Brad shrugged. "Donna likes her church, so we go there."

Johnny's bloodshot eyes met Donna's once again. Strike two.

"What's the matter?" Johnny suddenly spoke to Donna. "No Buddhist temples in Oak Ridge?"

"Johnny!" Elena admonished. "You apologize."

"No, Elena, it's okay," Donna said. Looking at Johnny, she added, "I was once a Buddhist."

"You what?" Brad turned and stared at Donna. "You were a Buddhist?"

"Yes." Donna nodded at Brad. "When I was a little girl." She smiled and engaged Johnny for round three. "I suppose, technically, I was also a Catholic…for a week."

"So," Gina piped in. "You're in the club, then."

"The club?" Donna turned toward Gina.

"Recovering Catholics," Gina delivered in monotone. "It's like AA, but with a *lot* more guilt."

"If anything," Donna replied. "I'm a recovering Baptist." She cut a piece of meat and stabbed it with her fork. "A neighbor invited us to his church one Sunday and we ended up attending for almost a year."

"What happened?" Elena asked. "Why did you stop going?"

Donna set her fork on the table and looked down. Vivid memories of a stocky preacher with big hands suddenly appeared upon the intricate woven pattern of the linen tablecloth. Drops of perspiration fell from his balding head, an index finger protruding from a clenched fist pointed heavenward.

From her pew, she could see the heads turning to steal a glance at the little half-breed, war orphan with her baby-killing stepfather. Even at nine-years-old, barely able to see over the top of the pew in front of her, she could feel the chill of their stares. In the front of the sanctuary, the preacher was raising the roof with his sermon about love and togetherness. Beneath him, in the neatly arranged trenches of the spiritual killing fields, the combatants were forming their battle lines.

Donna groped for the answer that would incite the least reaction. "Some of the members were a little uncomfortable with our being there."

"Buddhist?" Brad repeated, his face still contorted in confusion.

"I was very young," Donna replied to Brad. "I remember very little about it."

"What did you expect, Brad?" Johnny added, his words starting to slur. "Those people have all kinds of crazy beliefs." He shifted his gaze from Brad to Donna. "Isn't that right?"

Donna swallowed hard, sensing a slow burn starting in her gut. Taking a deep breath before answering, she finally said, "The culture of Southeast Asia is quite different than some, yes."

"Maybe that's why they're still squatting in the mud for their food and living in grass huts." Johnny's eyes narrowed. "Funny how the countries that don't believe in the Bible seem to be the poorest and most screwed up."

With the names of several South and Central American countries on the tip of her tongue, Donna made no reply.

"The Catholic Church is the only true Christian religion," Johnny continued. "What's it say in the Apostle's Creed? Huh? It don't say 'The Holy Methodist Church', or 'The Holy Baptist Church'. It says, 'The Holy Catholic Church'." He slapped the table for emphasis.

"Pop," Gina interjected. "There's much more to it than that. That prayer—"

"Your people don't value human life," Johnny continued, pointing at Donna, as if Gina was not even in the room.

"Hey, come on Pop," Brad said, tipping his hand over the table. "Take it easy. This is my future wife you're talking—"

"They get that from their religion. They're taught to accept suffering as God's will." He poked the table with his stubby index finger. "No sense of human decency."

Brad started to rise from his seat. "Pop," he said, his voice carrying a slight edge. "This is starting to get a little personal."

Johnny raised his eyebrows and looked at Donna. "Am I wrong?"

Even as the words were leaving his lips, Donna's thoughts turned to some of the young mother's and wives she had seen cradling their dead children and husbands; their faces grotesquely twisted in anguish. She thought of her own losses and the value she had placed on them. Religion was an abstract concept. The beliefs that accompanied each were more than the words written by ancient scribes: Each person's reality dictated the depth of their own convictions. The reality of holding your dead child in your arms cut through any dictum about noble suffering. The trauma of laying a loved one to rest tied each one of us more closely than any words in a sacred book.

"The culture I am from," Donna said, walking carefully through Johnny's minefield, "is different in many ways from this one. But to say that we don't value life is not true."

"Oh, really?" Johnny set his fork down and leaned on one elbow while pointing at Donna. "You call using women and children as walking weapons respect for life?"

"We don't have to listen to this," Brad said, leaning to make eye contact with Donna.

"Were there not atrocities committed by Americans, as well?" Donna felt her composure slipping away. She saw Brad in her peripheral vision but did not engage him. "Perhaps it was not the people involved as much as the circumstances that drove them to act as they did."

Johnny's stare became more menacing. "There's a difference between doing what you have to do, to survive and premeditated murder." Brad, Elena, and Gina grew silent, watching and listening to the unfolding debate the way children watch their parents argue. "It's no different than those bastard Iraqis…" Johnny's voice trailed off, his eyes grew distant. He took another long swig of beer. "We should just bomb them all back to the stone ages and be done with it."

"That's right." Gina finally broke in. "Just kill everybody. Right, Pop?"

"Turn that whole country into one giant sheet of glass."

Johnny moved his hand in an even swath over the table, as if running it over a smooth surface. "Nobody'd even miss 'em."

"What about the innocent people?" Brad asked his father. "You'd just kill all of them, too?"

"You find me an innocent Iraqi and I'd let 'em live." Johnny pointed his fork at Brad. "They're just like the Vietnamese and everyone else east of Italy, not an innocent one among them. Any of 'em." He paused to stab a piece of pork and stuffed it into his mouth. "Bomb the hell out of 'em, I say."

"Oh, yeah," Gina weighed in. "The Italians." She nodded her head in exaggerated movements, her lips puckered. "Fine examples of real humanitarians, those Romans were. Yes, indeed."

"They civilized the known world," Johnny countered.

"They slaughtered countless numbers of people to expand their empire," Gina said.

"The difference was that they didn't kill their own." Johnny nodded in Donna's direction. "These people... hell, they kill their own, for Christ's sake."

"Johnny!" Elena admonished him once more.

"I seem to recall another country with a similar tradition." Donna's voice carried an edge that caused Johnny to glance in her direction.

"What tradition is that?" Johnny said, cocking his head.

"Killing their own," Donna replied. "Or, perhaps my recollection of nineteenth century American history is somewhat distorted."

"That was different," Johnny answered. "There was a cause involved." Johnny looked at Brad while gesturing toward Donna. "See that? They twist things around like that."

"I think we'll be leaving now," Brad announced. He

started to rise from the table but Elena gripped his arm, stopping him.

"Please," Elena said to Brad, her eyes pleading. "Sit down. We have talked about this long enough."

"Pop," Gina said, her tone growing more impatient. "What are you doing? Where are you going with this?"

Donna felt her heart rate increase. Brad reached for her hand, but she pulled it away. She took another deep breath.

"What about the children?" Gina asked. "You would bomb them, too?"

"Little Iraqis grow up to be big Iraqis," Johnny replied. "That's the mistake we made in Viet Nam. We tried to be too nice. We bowed to the pressure from those rat-bastard liberals and we didn't get the job done right. We shoulda' bombed the sh—"

"Johnny!" Elena cautioned again. She offered him a cold stare.

"Come on, Pop," Gina said, her face growing red. "You make it sound like we should've just wiped everyone out."

"If we'd have bombed those people silly right from the start we'd have won the war in two years," he held up two fingers, ironically poised like a peace sign from the sixties. "As it was, we were too concerned about," he made quotation marks in the air in front of him, "collateral damage.

"And," Johnny continued, as if rolling down a verbal hill out of control. "As far as those kids are concerned," he paused to take a breath. "I seen them do things you wouldn't believe. They weren't even human."

"That's enough!" Brad shook his head in rapid movements. "I don't believe this. Do you hear yourself? Do you understand what you just said about her?" he added, motioning with his hand at Donna.

Donna could feel the heat building on her face. Her hands clenched the napkin in her lap beneath the table.

"I'm sure you know what I'm talking about." Johnny looked directly at Donna, somehow feeding off her growing anger. "Don't you?" When Donna offered no answer, he upped the stakes. "What's the matter? Nothing to say about that? Maybe you were one of them."

"Johnny!" Elena grabbed for his arm. "Stop it. You stop it, now!"

Donna sat staring at Johnny, her gut boiling. *Where do you keep your ear collection?* She started to respond, but caught herself. It was bad enough that she was letting him under her skin. She was not going to give him the satisfaction of disgracing herself in his home. A sliver of pain gripped her head for an instant. Flinching at the discomfort, she looked away momentarily. When she brought her attention back to Johnny he was getting up from the table.

"Whatever we may have done. Any of us," Donna said in a weak tone, her head down. "We did out of desperation." Her mind wandered to a place a million light years away as she spoke the words. She sat in her chair, oblivious to all but Johnny.

Johnny turned to her, letting himself settle back into his chair. He remained silent.

"You knew you would leave one day," she continued, glancing up at Johnny. "From the time I was born until the time I left my country, all I ever knew was war. My mother would sometimes speak of a place where there was peace: A place called America. But, I never dreamed I would ever see it. For us, there was no escape. No hope of leaving."

Donna scanned the faces in the room, all of them staring at her except for Johnny, who was now staring out the window. "Yes, suffering was all we knew. And, death was almost a certainty. For many, a relief."

"You wanna talk about death?" Johnny turned to her. "How about fifty-eight thousand of our boys killed over there trying to save your people?"

"Mister D'Amato," Donna replied, her tone steady. "I would never minimize the sacrifice your country made in an effort to help mine. But, we suffered losses as well. Unimaginable by American standards." She let her eyes drop for a moment. "More than six million dead." Donna looked up. "And every life had value."

Johnny engaged her with his stare. "Yeah," he finally said. "The poor little victim." His eyes narrowed. "You might fool these people here," he continued, pointing to the others around the table. "But, you don't fool me. You didn't get through that over there, by being a victim."

"We were all victims, Mister D'Amato."

Johnny smirked and pushed himself up from the table. "You do what you want, Brad," his father said, rising to his feet. "But, I'd get to know this one better before I married her." Johnny hobbled toward the kitchen door. "She's hiding something," he said over his shoulder as he disappeared into the kitchen. "I can tell from the way she looks at me." He walked away through the kitchen and down the hallway, slamming a door a few seconds later.

"Goddamn it!" Brad pounded his fist on the table. "If he wasn't my old man, I'd kick his ass!"

"I might kick his ass, anyway," Gina said. "What a bigoted bastard."

"Heinrich!" Elena said, glaring at her son. "Gina!" She turned to her daughter. "You will not talk that way—"

"Jesus, Ma!" Brad countered. "He just ambushed her for no reason."

"Practically called her an animal to her face," Gina followed up, motioning with an upturned hand toward Donna. "What the hell was that all about?"

"I will talk with him," Elena said, her eyes closing slowly. She turned to Donna. "This is my fault," she continued, her hand on her chest. "I am sorry for this."

Donna sat staring silently ahead at the empty seat Johnny had occupied. The image of a sleeping soldier came to mind. He laid before her in the darkness, half covered by a lightweight, olive green sheet. She flinched as the same familiar, haunting image flashed through her mind. She remained silent for a long moment, thinking that she might vomit. Johnny's verbal attack had been unprovoked. It might even have been cruel. But, through all of her anger, she could not deny one simple truth. In spite of his motives or intentions, his words had stung not from the unkindness from which they were born, but by the fact that they harbored some truth.

Chapter Thirteen

March 23rd, 1972

Turner came through, just like he said he would. My discharge papers arrived today with a notice that the adoption paperwork was waiting for me in the embassy in Saigon. It rained like hell again, today. I hope that's not a bad omen. I've seen a lot of action here over the last six years and I can honestly say that I have never been as scared as I am right now.

I haven't seen her in days. I've got 72 hours to get to Saigon and through the out-processing center. God only knows where she is. I'm hoping she was taken to one of the orphanages in town.

So much to do. Good Lord, I'm a father.

"Major Roberts?" A young army corporal stuck his head into the command and control tent at the encampment outside of Da Nang. "Colonel Schipley wants you front-and-center immediately, sir."

Jack Roberts looked up from the reconnaissance report on the large table. "What now?" he asked, letting his eyes come back into focus after studying the 3-D photogrametric images through a set of stereoscopic glasses. They focused on the wiry, red haired, corporal. "Is he in a good mood?"

"No, sir," the corporal replied. He shook his close-cropped head as he answered. "I'm wearing my chain mail skivvies today, sir."

"Tell him I'm AWOL." Jack eyed his watch, wondering if he could manage to get lost for the rest of the day.

"I'd love to help you out, sir," the corporal replied. "But, Colonel Schipley—"

"At ease," Jack continued, smiling. "It was just a joke. Tell him I'll be right there."

"Yes, sir." The young soldier nodded once and darted away.

Jack took one more look at the photos and wondered what useless mission the colonel had waiting for him. Not *another* two-week stretch with *another* hapless ARVN platoon. The last one he hooked up with was wiped out in two days. Maybe this time he wouldn't have to call for air support while hoping the pilot wasn't hung over, or worse.

With any luck it would be a simple ass-and-trash mission. A short chopper ride to drop off some grunts or supplies to one of the firebases. Sure, that's it. A quick out and back. Home by dinnertime. Yeah, right. The leather soles of his combat boots clicked against the perforated steel planking as he wound his way through the camp to the HQ tent.

"Major," Colonel Schipley began, sitting tall in his chair, looking over his desk at Jack as if he enjoyed the authority that came with his rank. Keeping Jack standing at attention in front of his desk, he had not offered Jack a chair or even allowed him to stand at ease. "Your discharge papers arrived today." The colonel said no more, only offering a cool stare.

Jack stared back thinking Schipley was born thirty years too late and in the wrong country. He had frequently wondered how many of his ancestors had donned Nazi uniforms. Today Jack would not be yielding any ground in what would be the last power skirmish he would have with the tyrant he had served under for the last year. "Yes, sir," he replied, only because he had to.

"You broke the chain of command, major," Schipley continued, leaning closer. "You went over my head for this, and I don't like it."

"If you'll recall, sir," Jack replied, his voice even. For the first time since he had been under Schipley's command, Jack felt suddenly in control. "I came to you with my request—"

"Request?" Schipley rose from his seat, a vein bulging in his neck. "It was not a request, major. You presented me with an unacceptable scenario that included one of my officers resigning his commission in the midst of a goddamn war. Major, I do not look fondly on that and will not condone such conduct."

"My reasons were sound." Jack took a deep breath, keeping in mind that he needed only endure this last conversation and he was free. "I think I've more than met my commitment to my—"

"You are not the only soldier in this army with connections in high places." Schipley cast Jack a menacing smile. "I want you packed up and out of my camp in seventy-two hours or I'll slow-walk your orders for the next six months. Do I make myself clear, major?"

"Very clear, sir," Jack replied, choking down the bile rising in his throat. "Is there anything else...sir?" He nodded with emphasis.

Colonel Schipley glanced down at a large manila envelope on his desk. "Report to out-processing." He flipped the envelope at Jack. "You have adoption papers waiting at the Embassy in Saigon. Be there within seventy-two hours with your..." a disgusted look formed on his face, "adoptee."

They stood in silence for a moment, the colonel still staring at Jack.

"Will that be all, sir?" Jack finally said.

"Dismissed."

Jack saluted. "It's been a pleasure serving with you, sir."

Cecil Schipley didn't move and refused to return Jack's salute. "Get the fuck out of here," was all he said before turning away.

"Yes, sir, Colonel Schipley...sir," Jack replied, reaching for the envelope on the desk. He grabbed it up and walked quickly away thinking that a laxative might do the colonel a great deal of good.

It was mid-morning when Jack went to his tent, not knowing what to do next. He sat on his cot and opened the packet. Inside were his discharge orders and a note from Turner.

Jack,

It took some arm-twisting, but I got it done. You ruffled some feathers, for sure. Watch your back around Schipley. You also have to promise never to work for those stupid pricks at the State Department!

I've had some time to think about this. You've always been like a son to me. (The son I know I'll never have.) While I don't like what you are doing, I respect why you are doing it. It's your life. It's your choice. I wish you only the best. Remember, you always have a friend.

Good luck,
Turner

What now? He had three days to find a nameless orphan child in a city of half a million and get her to Saigon. After packing his footlocker with the items he didn't want to travel with, and shipping it off to Saigon, Jack quickly showered and slipped into his only pair of clean fatigues. Within an hour he was riding in a jeep into Da Nang with another major.

After dropping off the major at a restaurant, Jack asked the driver, "What have you got planned while he's in there?"

The corporal glanced nervously around, as if giving the wrong answer might put him at risk. "Major said to pick him up in two hours, sir. Thought I might see some of the sights." The young man's eyes momentarily tracked the backside of a young Vietnamese woman walking past.

"How about you save your money and help me out for a while?"

The corporal gave Jack a suspicious look. "What'd ya have in mind, sir?"

"It's unofficial business, corporal," Jack explained, pulling a pencil and a piece of paper from his shirt pocket. "I just need to visit a few orphanages."

"Orphanages, sir?"

"Yes. That's right." The young driver squirmed in his seat at Jack's sudden cool stare. "Is that a problem, corporal?"

"Oh, no sir," the corporal replied. He stomped on the clutch and jammed the jeep into first gear. "Where to?"

Jack sat back in his seat and sighed. "I wish I knew." He glanced around at the busy street and thought for a moment. "Let's find a Catholic Church. They'll know where to send us."

After asking several pedestrians - in exchanges that combined Jack's broken Vietnamese with their broken English - they were able to locate a Catholic Church. It was very large with a small orphanage attached.

"We have received three wounded children within the last two weeks," the priest said to Jack. "The fighting in the surrounding areas has been very heavy lately." The elderly priest looked down and shook his head. "Sister Rose would know if any of the girls had a shoulder wound. Come. We'll go see her."

Sister Rose was of no further help except that Jack was able to acquire the names and locations of most of the orphanages in Da Nang from her. Jack checked his watch as he slid into the passenger seat of the Jeep. They had ninety minutes before meeting the major. Reaching behind the driver's seat, Jack found and opened a dark green canvas map case. He pulled out a map of Da Nang and a Bic pen wedged into a strap on the flap. Dividing the city into a grid, Jack plotted the locations of each church and orphanage that Sister Rose had given him. While riding to the closest orphanage, Jack made a mental note to find the phone numbers for each and call ahead. Taking a second look at the list, Jack knew further visits to town would likely be in order.

The next stop yielded the same results. "No," a kindly nun said, shaking her head. "I am sorry. No one like that here."

On their fifth stop, Jack's hopes were lifted. "Yes," a lay worker, a Caucasian woman in her early forties replied with a French accent. "Tien is nine. She was brought to us a week ago from an Army hospital with a shoulder wound."

"Can I see her?" Jack asked; half-hoping it wouldn't be her.

"Of course." She motioned momentarily with her head before leading him down a hallway. "This way."

They passed an open area where many of the children were playing or sitting watching the other children play. Jack shook his head imperceptibly at the devastation before him. There was not one child in the room without a missing limb, eye patch, or other remembrance of the conflict tearing the beautiful country apart. One little boy was pulling himself along the floor with his hands, his legs missing just below his waist. In one corner, a little girl sat silently, both eyes covered with bandages. Two boys kicked a rubber ball at each other, one of them missing both hands. Sadness enveloped him like a heavy shroud. He had seventy-two hours to find her. Jack didn't know how, but he just knew he had to.

"This is the part of war most people never see," the woman said to him. "They are the *bui doi*," she continued. "The leftovers."

Jack awoke from his daze, suddenly aware that he had stopped and was staring into the play area. Many of the faces bore the familiar look of children with mixed race parents.

When they reached a room at the end of the hallway, she motioned for Jack to look inside. He paused, unsure if he could make the leap. One look into the doorway and he was committed. If he left now, he would never know. He could always tell himself that there was a good chance that it wasn't her. His feet shuffled involuntarily toward the doorway. The inside of the room, crammed with beds, came gradually into view as he approached. Before he could draw back, he saw a tiny head on a pillow. She was sleeping, her face turned away from him. His heart thumped faster as he crossed the room. Leaning over the sleeping girl, he felt an unexplained relief when the face he saw was not that of the little waif he had seen so many times in camp.

He shook his head and glanced back at the woman. "It's not her."

The next day Jack arranged to be picked up by a local cyclo operator. They traversed the narrow streets of the port city seeking out every church, orphanage, and hospital they could find. Each one held a hundred tragic stories. Jack's spirits sank, as each place he looked yielded no results. The day ended at dusk, the cyclo driver dropping him at the entrance to the Tent City.

                              *   *   *

On the morning of his last day in-country, Jack Roberts changed his plan. Standing at the roadside looking at the rickety cyclo coming to pick him up, he decided that his chances of finding the girl would be greatly enhanced if his mode of transport were not limited to six miles-per-hour. When the motorized rickshaw arrived, he handed the thin man a small wad of *baht* and sent him on his way. A few minutes later he was walking into the motor pool.

"I need a jeep," Jack said to the Motor Sergeant.

"Yes sir," the young NCO answered. He was a stocky black sergeant, no more than twenty. "Should have one available early this afternoon. Just sign the—"

"Sergeant," Jack glanced at the young soldier's nametag, "Washington. I need a jeep now. Not this afternoon." He met the clerk's eyes with a fixed stare.

"I'm sorry, sir. I've got two in the queue, and they're both taken."

"Ah ha," Jack replied, his heart sinking. "I see."

"Got one going out in an hour with General Taggart and one going out to Colonel Schipley in about—"

"Sergeant," Jack said, pointing to the row of jeeps nearby. "All of these jeeps have been signed out?"

The clerk's face twisted in confusion as he looked down at the clipboard. "Sorry, major. Got a full schedule today."

Jack looked at the young soldier and nodded his understanding. "I'll be right back," he said, walking away remembering the Class Six Store across the street. Within fifteen minutes he returned carrying a case of Jack Daniels.

"What's the schedule look like now?" Jack set the case down on a nearby desk.

The sergeant glanced at the box and then at his clipboard, his mouth widened into a shit-eating grin. "Well, whadda ya know. Captain Russell's ride just threw a rod," he offered, crossing out a name with a single stroke of a pencil. "You know how it is, Sir. These jeeps break down at the most unexpected times."

"Are we in business?"

"Just like Proctor and Gamble, sir."

"Which one?" Jack looked in both directions at the long line of jeeps.

"Take your pick."

"Give Captain Russell my condolences," Jack said, climbing into the closest jeep. He turned the key and throttled the engine. Plumes of dust shot from beneath the tires as he raced from the dirt parking area, the sergeant pulling a bottle from the case in his wake.

On his fourth stop, at a small orphanage in a dirty suburb of Da Nang, he encountered a slight woman with a firm grip.

"We have many children who might fit that description," she said to him as she released his hand. "What do you want with a child?" Her blue eyes traversed his body from head to toe before holding him in their suspicious gaze.

"She's coming home with me," he explained. "I'm adopting her."

"We can have a look. Follow me, please."

Jack knew the routine. They walked through play areas populated by children missing arms, legs, and other body parts. They turned a corner into an interior courtyard. Jack quickly scanned the faces of each child, all the while wondering if he would recognize her if he saw her. After all, he had only been close to her once and it was dark. She was covered in blood. Her face was contorted in pain. What if he was mistaken?

Then he saw her, sitting on a bench staring blankly into her own private world. It was the face he had seen staring up at him from the elephant grass only a few weeks prior. He approached and gazed into the same young girl's eyes that had held him captive for an eternity while they waited for the Medivac chopper to arrive.

"That's her," he said, pointing at Mai without emotion.

At that moment another nun joined them. She was much older than the first. The two nuns exchanged glances and nodded before turning to Jack, wearing suspicious looks.

"I see," the young nun said. "Then you have the adoption papers, I assume."

Jack took a deep breath, studying her face peeking out from her habit. She must be French, he decided. Even covered from head to toe in her black robe, Jack could tell she had a fit body and youthful curves. What would a knockout like her be doing in a convent? The thought quickly evaporated.

"The papers are in Saigon. At the Embassy."

She smiled at Jack. "We cannot release her to you without the paperwork."

"Well, I can't get the paperwork without her," he replied, pointing at Mai.

"Then, I'm afraid you will have to make other arrangements."

Jack knew why he was getting the stonewall treatment. It wasn't unusual for pimps and opportunistic flesh peddlers to be out looking for future talent. Orphans were easy prey, especially the *bui doi*. He nodded silently and knelt next to Mai. He whispered into her ear, so the nun could not hear, "I'll get you out of here. I swear it. You're going someplace where you'll have a good life."

Mai sat motionless, still staring straight ahead without expression.

"If you don't have the adoption papers with you, I think

your visit here is over. Please come back when you have them."

"Oh, yes ma'am," Jack said to the nun, but still looking at Mai. "I'll be back. You can absolutely count on that."

It was dusk when Jack returned to the base. Stashing the jeep in some remote corner of the compound, he slipped into camp and began packing his gear for the trip home. He had spent his adult life traveling light. Everything he owned could be stuffed into a small footlocker and a duffel bag. With his possessions packed, Jack reported to out-processing.

The clerk carefully checked over all the paperwork, took possession of all critical military hardware and devices. Jack turned in his field gear: night vision goggles, backpack, M-16 rifle, grenade launcher, and field binoculars.

"Where's your forty-five, sir?" the clerk asked him.

"Combat loss."

The clerk nodded, offering a knowing smile. "Combat loss," he replied, scrawling something on one of the forms strewn on the desktop.

Jack emerged from the small wooden building that housed the administrative offices, his discharge papers in his hands. *What have I done?* He stood on the dusty street wanting to run away. Leave her where she belonged. After all, this was her country, her home. What right did he have to take her? Maybe she wasn't an orphan and he would be taking away the only chance she would ever have to be reunited with—. *Stop it!* The rationalizations were falling like the rain coming in from coast.

Before leaving for town, Jack hauled his duffel bag to a ramshackle building near the airstrip. "Need you to baby sit my things for a few hours," Jack said to the slight Vietnamese man behind the bar.

"Going somewhere, Mister Jack?" the barkeep said, setting down a glass he had been wiping clean.

Jack nodded and smiled at his friend. "Going home, Nip." He set his bag down on top of the locker. "I'm going home."

"Nip very sad to hear this, Mister Jack." The small, middle-aged man bowed his head. "I will miss you when you are gone home."

"Something I've gotta do first, though," Jack continued while slipping into one of the stools at the bar. "I need a ride."

Nip leaned closer, nodding in understanding. "I get Mister Larry. You wait here, please." In less than a minute, he returned with a sandy haired man with a five-day beard and a greasy blonde ponytail. He was tall, with thick, tattooed arms sticking out from his tee shirt advertising a Kansas City Harley-Davidson dealership.

"You need a ride?" the man said, his accent clearly middle American.

"To Saigon," Jack replied, shifting in the barstool. "For two."

"Hell," Larry continued. "You're a major. Just tell one of them jockeys to give you a ride."

"This is not an official operation. If you know what I mean." Jack lowered his voice. "I need your help to get someone out of here."

"I might be able to help." Larry's face turned solemn. "It's gonna cost you."

"I've been saving my allowance." Jack glanced toward the door and back at Larry. "How much?"

"Two hundred." Larry took a long drag on his cigarette. "American."

"Set it up." Jack reached into his shirt and produced a wad of bills. "I need a driver tonight, too. How much?"

"What for?"

"Personnel extraction."

"Hell, I'll do that just for the excitement."

Later that night Jack led Larry to the place where he had stashed the jeep. It was approaching dawn as they drove into the featureless port city.

"Park here," Jack said to Larry, about a block away from the orphanage. "Keep the engine running. I'll be back in a few minutes."

Jack hopped from the still-running jeep and glanced around the quiet residential streets before slipping into the shadows along the sidewalk. He approached the orphanage and turned down the alley behind the brick structure. Standing in the alley, Jack calculated her position based on his recollection of his visit. Having made his best guess, he began climbing a run of two-inch conduit attached to the building.

When he was alongside the open window on the second floor, he swung away from the metal pipe and grabbed the ledge. His boots landed with a thud against the bricks. Making as little noise as possible, he leaned through the window and slowly lowered himself onto the floor. As he stood, he surveyed the contents of the small room. In the dim, pre-dawn light he could see right away that he had chosen the wrong room. It was filled with cribs and sleeping babies.

With one quick poke of his head into the hallway, Jack determined that there was no one around to see him. He walked softly to the next room, where the subject of his mission lay quietly sleeping along with a dozen other children. Without a moment's hesitation, Jack scooped the sleeping child into his arms. She immediately awoke but remained silent, offering only an indifferent stare. He spun around to make his exit. To his surprise, there stood the elderly nun who had confronted him just hours before.

"Stop!" she bellowed with enough volume to raise the long-dead ancestors of the sleeping children. "Help!" The nun made a feeble attempt to stop Jack as he brushed by her.

In a full run, Jack dodged awakened children and nuns alike. He even caught a glimpse of the pretty young French nun just as she was wrapping a robe around her slender body. He smiled at her as he passed.

Slowed by the care he had to exercise carrying a young girl down a flight of steps, he was quickly set upon by the elderly nun wielding a broom. He carefully traversed each step while enduring the blows to his back and legs being doled out by the determined old woman. By the time he had bounded down the last of the stairs to the first floor, Jack could hear several distinct sets of footsteps in pursuit. The front door offered him little resistance as he leaned in and buried his shoulder like an open field runner with the football. In no time he was on the sidewalk racing for Larry and the familiar army-green jeep.

"Go!" Jack yelled to Larry, climbing the back bumper and falling into the back of the jeep. "Go, go, go!"

To Jack's utter shock, the old GP vehicle actually spun its tires on the dry pavement as they drove away.

The first traces of dawn were beginning to illuminate the ground fog as they drove onto the base. Larry pulled the jeep in front of his bar and Jack hopped out, ran inside, and emerged a scant few seconds later with his duffel bag. With a groan, Jack heaved the heavy sack into the jeep. He hopped into the back in one bound.

"Head for the runway," Jack yelled over the rumble of the old engine.

In a few short minutes they were rolling to a stop next to one of the several dozen Hueys lining the makeshift runway. As they approached, a figure emerged from beneath the helicopter, flanked by two other men in flight suits.

"When's the next run to Saigon?" Jack shouted to one of the men.

The man looked up, wiping his hands with a rag. He was older than most Huey pilots and to Jack's surprise his hair was slightly grayed. His face bore the weathered look of a man who had seen too many missions.

"Who wants to know?" the pilot replied. He stood up straight and leaned against the craft with his arms folded across his chest.

"Major John Roberts," Jack replied, climbing down from the jeep. "I need a ride to Saigon." He pulled his bag from the back.

"Saddle up," the pilot answered. "Taking off in five minutes." He held up his hand, extending all five fingers.

At that moment, Jack reached for Mai, picking her up and pulling her into his arms over the top of the jeep.

"Oh, now hold on there," the pilot protested, spotting Mai. "You can ride." He pointed at Mai. "She can't. No civilians. Army regs."

Larry slid from the jeep. "I thought we had this all arranged?"

"You didn't say nothing about no kids."

"Come on, Bert," Larry protested. "What's the difference?"

"The difference?" Bert smiled. "How 'bout another hundred? That's the difference."

Jack turned and cast Larry an accusing look. "You greedy bastard."

"Jack," Larry replied, taking a step closer to the chopper. "I swear. I had nothing to do with this."

"You're off my Christmas card list," Jack said to Larry as he was reaching into his shirt pocket. "Here," he said to Bert, handing him another hundred dollars. "If we're going, we need to get in the air."

"What's the hurry," Bert responded. "Late for a wedding?"

"More like a date." Jack stood looking at Bert, Mai lying motionless in his arms.

"Okay." Bert reached for Jack's bag. "Let's get going, then." He hoisted the heavy load onto the chopper deck. The crew chief grabbed it up and secured it with a bungee chord. Bert patted his co-pilot on the back and trotted around to the other side of the chopper and climbed into the pilot's seat.

Jack handed Mai to Larry while he climbed into the chopper bay. Once inside, he took the girl from Larry's outstretched arms.

"Thank you," Jack said to Larry, while fastening Mai into a shoulder harness. He sat next to her and strapped on his own harness and reached for Larry's hand as Bert started the rotors in motion. "If you're ever in town," he shouted over the high-pitched whine of the engines. "Don't look me up."

"I love you, too," Larry shouted. "Good luck!"

Jack waved goodbye to his friend, knowing he would never see him again. In his heart, he wished him well and a ripple of sorrow gripped him as they rose into the heavy morning air. A few seconds later, Larry dissolved into the mist, his arms still waving.

Jack turned to Mai, whose eyes were wide, remembering that the last time she had seen the inside of a Huey, she had been badly wounded, probably frightened out of her mind. Looking down at her with a shaky smile, his hand reached tentatively for hers. Finally, in one awkward surge, his fingers found the soft, warm flesh of her fingers. Filled with uncertainty, he sat holding her hand, nodding and staring vacantly ahead at the cockpit.

*   *   *

It was still early morning when they landed at Tan Sanh Nut. Bert helped Jack haul his belongings into the terminal before shaking Jack's hand.

"Thanks for the ride," Jack said. "Even though you fucked me on the fare."

"Man's gotta make a living," Bert replied. "Even in this shit hole."

"Well, anyway," Jack said, scooping Mai into his arms. "Thanks."

"You bet." Bert smiled at Mai and rubbed her knee. "Take good care of her."

It was mid-morning by the time they reached the embassy.

"Sir," the fastidious little lieutenant said to Jack while turning pages in his file. "Your instructions were to be here within seventy-two hours. I'm afraid you're almost ten hours—"

"From when?" Jack replied, offering a hard look.

"Well, the paperwork I have indicates—"

"Lieutenant?" Jack leaned across the desk. "Can you honestly say that you give a rat's ass what time I check out of here?"

"But, sir. Your orders were—"

"Son," Jack continued, his patience beginning to erode. "I've been here six years. I'm tired. I've been up all night. My ass hurts from a long chopper ride and my shoulders ache where a crazy nun beat me with a stick." Jack took in a long breath. "I'm leaving here. Are we going to ruminate over a few hours or can we just get on with this?"

The anal lieutenant with the slicked-back hair rocked back and forth in his chair. "I was only trying to be thorough…" He reached for another file. "No need to get all huffy about it." He opened the file and pulled out a form. "Name?"

"Roberts," Jack responded. "John, S."

The young lieutenant looked up from the paper, one of his eyebrows raised. "Yes, sir. I know your name." He paused, his lips curling in one corner of his mouth. "I meant, the girl. What's *her* name?"

For the first time since he had made the decision to take her home, Jack realized just how much he didn't know about this child he would now call his daughter. With one simple question, a snot-nosed lieutenant had brought his venture into focus with such clarity that the sudden imagery took his breath away like a punch to his solar plexus. He turned to Mai, groping for the words: any words.

"Sir?"

The word crashed into him like a runaway tanker truck, jarring him from his trance.

"Her name?" the young clerk asked, again. "What's the child's name. I need it for the forms."

"Right. The forms." He stared at the lieutenant for a moment before, once again, turning to look at Mai. His thoughts turned to an aunt he had known briefly as a child. She had been like a mother to him when his own had grown distant, probably from all the nights spent alone. Too soon, like always, his father was on the move and his aunt was soon just a fond memory. She sent a few letters, but they eventually stopped. He never saw her again, but he never forgot the way she filled some of the void left in his heart. In an instant, her name flashed into his mind.

"Donna," he said, with conviction. "Donna Christine Roberts."

Chapter Fourteen

Jack Roberts rolled to a stop at the first of three traffic lights in Middleton, Tennessee. With Donna seated next to him in the front seat of the dark green sixty-eight Chevy Impala, they waited for the signal to change, resting momentarily in the shadow of the old courthouse.

Behind the massive pillars, the shades on many of the dust-streaked windows had been pulled halfway down, looking like sets of weary eyes staring out from between forbidding rows of prison bars. Charcoal-colored streaks of neglect traversed the Roman columns and chunks of concrete had flaked away from the outside surface of the old building. Cracks in the mortar between the thick stone left noticeable gaps in the blocks that made up the exterior. Two carved stone lions guarded the bottom of the steps, one on each side leading up to the entrance. Their faces were weathered and one lion's nose was missing. Their eyes looked tired, as if resigned to their fate as impotent sentinels of this once great hall of justice.

On the top of the building, where the bright sky met the dull gray sloping fascia of the roofline, hung two flaccid pieces of cloth drooping in the still, morning air; one the American flag, the other the Confederate. A well-dressed man, carrying a brief case climbed the dozen or so steps from street level, opened one of the heavy wooden doors and went inside the building.

The light changed.

"It ain't much to look at," Jack said to Donna as they picked up speed. "But, it beats the hell out of Da Nang."

Donna sat, motionless in the front seat, staring out the window. She made no reply.

Jack glanced out his window at the town wondering what kind of life awaited them in Middleton. There had been no hero's welcome, no parades. He was just one of a half-million soldiers coming home to a country tired of hearing about them. One of the enlisted men he met in out-processing told him about some of his friends who had actually been spit on as they came home. *What the hell have I done?*

They rolled along Main Street, passing the town square on their right. It was tree-lined and took up the entire block, complete with the requisite gazebo and statue of a forgotten Civil War general. The statue was covered with bird droppings and the tip of his raised sword had broken off. Some of the latticework along the base of the gazebo had been pulled away, giving it the look of a face with missing teeth. Much of the green paint had peeled away from the rotting wood of the park benches. In the center of the square stood a great fountain, choked with weeds and looking as if it hadn't spouted water for twenty years.

"I'm thinking we might try it here for a while," he continued, half to Donna and half to himself. "We need to get you registered for school and find a place to live."

They had landed in Los Angeles only three days before. Donna sat staring blankly into space the entire trip from Saigon. The Army outplacement office helped Jack find a job at a plastics plant in Tennessee and arranged for him to meet with the plant manager as soon as he arrived in town. A phone call placed from the embassy also yielded Jack a deal on a used car. The car was waiting for them at the

Nashville airport courtesy of one of Jack's friends who had gone home a few months prior. Their flight arrived after midnight so Jack and Donna spent the night at a hotel in Nashville.

It was late morning and there was scarcely a person in sight. Many of the stores in the business district were vacant; their windows boarded up, broken, or smeared over with a milky coating of white shoe polish. The few stores that were still open looked as though they might soon meet a similar fate.

Jack eased the Chevy to a stop at the next light. Glancing to his right, he looked through the open door to Sandy's Coffee Cup. Inside, a sprinkle of people hunched over the counter, smoking cigarettes between sips of coffee. While Jack could not hear their conversations, their expressions telegraphed their state of mind. He'd seen that same look before in Da Nang. It was the look of despair.

Suddenly aware of Donna's presence, the old man sitting closest to the door turned his head in her direction. His face told the story of a hard life, deep lines intersecting along the sides of his eyes, cheeks pulled inward, leaving large hollows in his whiskered face. He stared at her absently while raising a gnarled hand and took a long drag from his cigarette. He held her gaze for a few seconds before blowing out the smoke and turning away.

About a mile past the center of town they pulled into the campus of the Middleton schools. Closest to the road was the elementary school, where hordes of shrieking children swarmed over dilapidated playground equipment. Rows of swings swayed back and forth like rusty pendulums out of synch; their gray rolled steel frames the only thing keeping the children earth-bound. The monkey bars sagged and shifted with the weight of the children moving across their rungs. Behind the elementary school was the heavy brick bastion of education that was Middleton Junior and Senior High School. It stood like a promontory against the backdrop of rugged hills of the southern Middle Tennessee countryside. Jack parked in front of the sturdy edifice and they climbed the hand-hewn granite steps leading to the front door. Once inside, they followed the signs to the district office.

They entered through an oversized door into an office with twelve-foot ceilings. In fact, Jack had noticed that the entire building was built like a fortress, a New Deal project from the thirties, no doubt. The doors and window trim were made of fine, dark hardwoods. The floors were marble, the windows large and ornate. The exterior walls were two feet thick, comprised of heavy cement blocks and a double layer of rust colored bricks. The windowsills were finely cut slabs of polished marble.

A breeze filled the office with the heady aroma of spring, a sweet blend of honeysuckle, pear blossoms and the scent of dogwood. A Merle Haggard song played almost imperceptibly in the background from an old radio perched on a shelf across the room. On the corner of a desk rested a brown nameplate. Embossed in white, were the letters MAVIS. A wall calendar, advertising a local real estate office, hung on a partition next to her desk. Each past day had been crossed out with a blue pen. It was Tax Day – April 15th, 1972. Jack remembered he hadn't filed yet.

The translucent window in the office door rattled loudly as it slammed shut. The Venetian blinds, clattering in the cross-flow created by the open door, settled back to rest as it closed.

"My goodness," said a startled, half-conscious secretary sitting behind a large desk, filing her nails. "You about gave me heart failure."

Jack looked back at the door and then again at the

woman, "I'm really sorry about that. It just got away from me."

"Oh, that happens to a lot of people," Mavis replied, putting her nail file away as she stood up. "We keep the windows open when it gets warm like this. The breeze catches the door sometimes."

Jack estimated her to be in her early fifties. She wore too much makeup and not enough clothes. Her pile of bleached blonde hair clashed with her white cotton dress, cut just low enough to reveal a deep crevasse between her generously endowed breasts. Obviously a bombshell in her day, her figure was still fairly trim, although her real estate had shifted somewhat over the years.

Mavis put her hands on her hips and blew a strand of misplaced hair away from her face with a sudden puff. She looked as if she had forgotten why she had come over. "My word it's stuffy in here." She took in a long breath. "What can I do for ya?"

"I need to see about getting my..." Jack paused, the words he knew he should say momentarily caught in his throat, "...daughter registered for school." The words echoed in his head. As many times as he had rehearsed it in his mind, the phrase still sounded alien and awkward.

Mavis looked over the counter at Donna, eyebrows raised. "This," she said, pointing, "is your daughter?"

"Yes," he replied, wondering for the moment if either of them believed it for a second. "Her name is Donna. I'd like to register her for school."

"Mister Martin approves all transfer requests," she said, pulling the nail file from her pocket. She began filing the nail on her left index finger, her eyes slightly crossed as she focused on the digit held just beyond the point of her nose. With her tongue lodged between her slightly pursed lips, she drew in her face in what could have passed for an expression of concentration. "Fill out these forms," she added, reaching under the counter. She produced a small sheaf of papers without even looking. "Bring them back with proof of residency and Mister Martin will make the evaluation."

"How long will it take him?" Jack took the papers and stuffed them into his back pocket. "I start my new job on Monday."

"It's really just a formality," she replied. "Just come on back with her transcript from her old school, get a physical from the county health department, and your proof of address."

"Physical?" Jack's head began spinning. "Transcript?"

Mavis stopped filing and looked at Jack the way a mother looks at a child who has just asked a stupid question. "Y'all are new in town, ain't ya?"

Jack glanced away momentarily. "Yes, ma'am." His eyes dropped down to look at the top of Donna's head and then back up at Mavis. "We are."

"You a G.I?" she asked, her expression softening. "Just back from the war?"

"Yes, ma'am."

Mavis once again slid the nail file into her pocket and pulled a sheet of blank paper from beneath the counter. She pulled at her dress, stuck with sweat to her chest while casting a benevolent look at Donna before she started writing. When she finished, she handed the paper to Jack.

"Here's directions to the clinic," she said, pointing at the neatly written text. "There's the phone number. Did y'all find you a place to live?"

"No, we just—"

"Mavis," Principal Ed Martin interrupted, emerging from his office. "I need these files sent over to—" His directive was cut short as he caught sight of Jack and Donna standing next to the counter. "Well, what have we here?" he asked, a smile slowly supplanting the shocked look he was wearing.

"This is Mister Roberts and his daughter, Donna," Mavis supplied. "She's going to be starting with us next fall."

"Is that so?" Ed Martin extended a tentative hand. He was six-feet-two inches tall and would still be considered obese even if he lost a hundred pounds. His dark brown double-knit pants barely stretched around his sloping belly. Yellow sweat stains ringed the armpits on his white, short-sleeved shirt. His chubby cheeks were red and flushed all the way down to the tip of his bulbous nose.

"Actually," Jack said, shaking Ed Martin's hand. "I was hoping to enroll her for the last few weeks of this year. Get her used to the idea of school before next term."

"I see," Ed Martin withdrew his hand and took a long look at Donna before continuing. "Well, you see, Mister Roberts, there are factors to consider when placing a child. We first have to evaluate them for certain...deficiencies." He took a deep breath. "You see—"

"Deficiencies?"

"Yes, sir. That's right." Ed Martin smiled and patted Donna on the head. "My goodness," he said, raising his eyebrows. "She is a well-behaved child." They all looked at Donna who stood motionless and silent, disconnected from the proceedings. Ed Martin leaned in toward Jack. "Does she talk?"

"She's...been through a lot." Jack placed a hand on her shoulder. "I'm working on that."

"What grade is she in?" Ed Martin asked.

Jack shuffled his feet while looking away before locking eyes with the principal. "She's never been to school, as far as I know."

"Yes, well," Ed Martin continued. "Maybe a Special Ed program might be in order. Why don't you fill out the paperwork and bring her back. We'll do an evaluation and see where it goes." He extended his hand again. "Nice meeting you Mister Roberts."

"Sure," Jack replied, again shaking his hand. "Likewise." Jack withdrew his hand, feeling like he should wash it for some reason. He couldn't place it at the moment, but something bothered him about Ed Martin. Jack watched him waddle away.

"I put the name and address of somebody with a place for rent," Mavis added. She glanced at Donna for a second before turning toward her desk. "Keep it handy. Just in case you can't find anything else."

"Got a paper in the car." Jack motioned with his head toward the door. "Must be a dozen or so ads in there. Why would I have a problem?"

"I'm not saying you will," she shot back, taking her seat at her desk. "Just keep it handy."

Jack glanced down at the note before taking Donna's hand and leading her toward the door. He paused before leaving. Turning to Mavis, he said, "Thanks. I appreciate it."

"See ya in a couple days," she offered without looking up.

He stared at her for a moment before turning the doorknob and pushing open the massive oak door.

"Let's find us a place to live," Jack said to Donna, perusing the classified section of the small town paper. He shifted into drive and they rolled out of the school parking lot and headed back into town.

Their first stop was in a quiet residential neighborhood. The ad said the apartment was a two-bedroom located on the second floor.

"Hello, ma'am," Jack said, as the door to the big Victorian home swung open. He smiled at the smartly dressed, gray-haired woman standing in the doorway. "We're here about the apartment."

The woman smiled back. Her eyes wandered down to Jack's side, where Donna stood. Her smile vanished. "I'm sorry," she said, stepping back into the doorway. "It's rented." She abruptly closed the door.

"Well, there's some tough luck for ya," he joked. "Guess she hasn't had her fiber yet today."

The next ad took them to a brick duplex near the edge of town. A big-bellied man with a three-day beard answered his knock. Jack noticed the man wore a black patch over his left eye.

"You'd be 'bout the last two I'd ever rent to," he said, just before slamming the door.

"I'm beginning to see a pattern emerge here," Jack quipped. For the first time, Donna moved her otherwise vacant gaze to meet his eyes. "You think so, too. Huh?" he said to her, wondering how much she understood.

The rest of the day went the same way. At one point, Jack thought he had made a deal. He had left Donna in the car, down the block. But, the landlord had spotted her and run him off.

"Eat your hamburger," Jack said to Donna while pointing at her food. They were sitting in Sandy's Coffee Cup in downtown Middleton. The intermittent stares from the other patrons were almost palpable, their comments just loud enough for Jack to hear.

Donna sat nibbling at her burger.

Jack reached into his pocket and retrieved the note Mavis had written. He stared at the address, wondering why she would have given it to him. The waitress brought the check and left it on the table without saying a word. Jack glanced over the counter from their booth to see the cook staring out at them from the kitchen. His face was expressionless, yet somehow menacing.

"You can finish that in the car," he said to her while scooping up the sandwich. He left a five-dollar bill on the table and they left.

It was getting dark by the time they found the address on the note. They were a few miles outside of town, in a run-down settlement next to the river. The single story houses were close together. Many of them slumped badly or were unpainted. A group of black boys played basketball under a streetlight. The goal had no net and was nailed to the telephone pole.

The porch heaved as he stepped onto it. Jack double-checked the note against the numbers hanging near the door. He looked at Donna and shrugged before knocking.

"What 'chu want?" came from inside the screen door. Jack squinted to see who it was. The voice was female, but in the dim light and through the screen he couldn't distinguish any features.

"I'm here about the apartment?"

The sound she made was a mixture of amusement and disgust. "You've got the wrong place. No apartment for rent, here."

"Yeah, okay," Jack replied, feeling almost relieved. "Right. Sorry to bother you." He turned to leave.

"Who told you we had one?" her voice called after him. The door opened. A lovely black woman, about thirty years old, emerged from the dilapidated house.

"Mavis," Jack replied, foolishly holding the note in the air. "I met her at the school. She said if we couldn't find anyplace—"

"How do you know Mavis?" she asked, noticing Donna for the first time. She reached inside the door and turned on the porch light.

"I don't know her," he answered, taking a step back onto the porch. "Like I said, we met at the school."

"Uh, huh…" The woman stared at Donna for a long moment. "Wouldn't nobody else rent you a place. Right?"

"Yes, that's right."

"They don't want no one looking like her livin' in their house." She planted her hands on her hips. "'Specially with some GI coming here taking all the good jobs away."

"Those thoughts occurred to me, yes."

"Otherwise," she glanced away for an instant before engaging Jack with an accusing stare. "You wouldn't be here." She paused for another moment. "Ain't that right?"

Jack looked her square in the eyes. "This would not have been my first choice."

"An honest man." She extended her hand. "I like that." She put her hand gently beneath Donna's chin. "My name's Wanda. What's yours?"

"She doesn't say too much," Jack offered. "Truth is, she doesn't say anything at all."

"Poor child. Is she deaf, or something?"

Jack shook his head. "She's had it pretty rough. Might be a while before she opens up." He held the note up. "So, what about it? You got a place to rent?"

"Two bedrooms. We share a bath and the kitchen. No overnight guests. No pets. No smoking. Park on the street. You get your own food. Do your own laundry. Utilities included. One-hundred and fifty a month. First and last month's rent in advance."

"The Army had fewer rules."

"We get all kinds here. Best to get some things straight from the start."

"I can only afford a hundred a month."

"I guess you'll be staying somewhere else, then."

Jack ran a hand over his closely cropped hair. "Okay…

A hundred-and-fifty a month, then. You drive a hard bargain."

"Shoot," she let out a grunt. "If Daddy'd been here, you'd be paying two-hundred a month."

"Well, thanks. I appreciate the place to stay."

"I ain't doin' this for you." Wanda glanced at Donna. "Can't have no little girl living on the streets. Besides, you ain't seen the place yet." She nodded toward their car parked in front. "When you wanna move in?"

"Tonight too soon?"

"I'll make the beds." Wanda turned and let the door swing shut behind her. "But, only this once," she called out through the screen door as she disappeared into the recesses of the run-down house.

Chapter Fifteen

"Bill," the heavy-set, gray-haired receptionist at the Graybill Plastics plant spoke into the intercom. The lobby walls were mid-nineteen sixties vintage, covered with dark paneling, the floors tiled in green. "You have a visitor." She cast a blank stare through a pair of horn-rimmed glasses at the console.

"Who is it?" came the reply, blaring from the speaker.

"Name?" She tossed an expectant glance up at Jack.

"Jack Roberts," he replied, smiling. The smell of melting plastics, detectable from at least a mile away from the plant, hung heavy in the air. "I'm here to get—"

"Says his name is Jack Roberts," she cut him off and looked away, as if his presence and that of the rest of the world filled her with contempt.

"Oh, right. Send him up, Sally."

Without looking up from the desk, Sally pointed with a pencil toward a door at the far end of the lobby. "Through that door. Up the stairs. Turn left. First door on the right." She turned and began typing.

Jack walked to the plain wooden door. Before turning the knob, he turned and said, "Thank you, Sally."

"Yup," was all she replied, never looking up at him.

As he opened the door, the dull hum that had permeated the wood was transformed into a cacophonous roar of machinery. Sprawling before him in neatly arranged rows were eighty-eight injection-molding machines, each one whining and hissing at a hundred and twenty decibels. The stench of molten polymer nearly took Jack's breath away. For an instant the strong smell triggered memories of war. It brought to mind the pungent odor that lingered in the aftermath of a napalm strike: The acrid smell of spent gunpowder: The putrid stench of death.

"Jack," Bill Walters said, rising from his chair behind a gray metal desk. "What brings you in here? You don't start until Monday?" He motioned toward a chair in front of his desk as he shook Jack's' hand. "Have a seat."

"Thanks." Jack sat down. "I really appreciate having this job. I wanted to thank you for taking me on like this. You know I don't have any experience—"

"Oh, hell," Bill cut him off. "The owner of this place," he pointed toward the back wall, "Mister Graybill, was a veteran himself. He likes to set aside a certain number of jobs for you G.I.s."

"I see." Jack shifted in his chair. "Well, like I said. It means a lot to me."

"Think nothin' of it."

"Thought I'd stop by and find out what I'm gonna be doing here."

Bill smiled and waved a hand at him. "Well, now, don't worry about that. There's plenty of time for training. You'll do fine." Bill kicked up his feet on the desk. His custom-made snakeskin boots landed with a thud.

Jack noticed Bill's boots had what looked like Texas Ranger badges harnessed by leather straps along the sides.

"Just the same," Jack countered. "I like being prepared. I was wondering if you might have some materials I can take home with me over the weekend so I can get familiar with what I'll be doing as..." He looked away and smiled. "I don't even remember what the hell my job title is."

"Maintenance Supervisor," Bill replied. "Jack, you'll have a staff. All good men. You really won't have to do much of anything, really." He leaned forward and lowered his voice. "Hell, let the niggers do most of it. That's what they're here for." He laughed.

"Just the same." Jack ran his hand over his chin. "I don't like looking foolish on my first day. Not in front of my—" Jack was about to say "men", but caught himself. "Direct reports. I'm just funny that way."

Bill sighed and rubbed the back of his neck. "Well, all right. This don't have to be so much work. This could be a pretty easy job, if you know how to work it. Those boys out on the floor know pretty much what to do. All you got to do is tell 'em to go fix stuff and they'll do the rest. Even if they are a bunch of nig—"

"Yeah," Jack cut him off. "So you said." He smiled at Bill while considering what it would be like working for him. Thoughts of Colonel Schipley crept into Jack's head. "I can't tell you how much I appreciate you getting me this job, Bill. I mean that." Jack leaned forward. "But, I can't work that way. Now, I don't know a darn thing about molding machines. But, I damn sure will come Monday morning."

Bill cast Jack a wary look from behind the desk. At the end of a short silence, he slapped his knees and stood. "Well, I don't guess I can hardly argue with that," he offered, turning toward a file drawer. "These ought to keep you busy." He pulled a thick folder and a rolled up set of drawings from the drawer. "Here's all the schematics and the O & M manual. Have at it." He plunked the heavy bundle on the desk. "Just try not to make the rest of us look bad." He offered a look that suggested he was only half kidding.

Later that night, Jack sat in a rocking chair on the sloping porch of his new home. In his lap lay a set of mechanical drawings, an exploded rendering of the hydraulic system of an injection-molding machine. Spread out around him, on the porch floor, were more drawings and various pages from the three-ringed manual. It was after dark. Donna was asleep in her bed.

"You work awfully hard for someone hasn't even started his job yet." Wanda, wearing a light sleeveless cotton dress, opened the door and slid into the rocker next to Jack.

He looked up from the drawings. Wanda's hair was still wet and she smelled like soap. Jack stole a glance at her legs, and neck. Her dark skin, still moist, reflecting the faint porch light reminded him how long it had been since he had been with a woman.

"Just trying to be ready for Monday morning," he replied, smiling.

"You always this prepared?"

He looked away and laughed. "Is that what you think?" he replied, turning to engage her. "At least I have you fooled."

"You're in Daddy's chair."

Jack caught Wanda running her eyes from his head to toe and back again. He started to gather up the papers. "Sorry. I'll move."

"It's okay," she said, reaching to stop him. They both stared at her hand on his arm for a moment before she continued. "He's gone to bed." She withdrew her hand, clasping it momentarily in her other.

"Having fun at my expense?"

"I can do worse." She turned away. "You're awfully polite for a white man."

"One of my many flaws," he replied. "Give me a couple weeks. I'll have you spitting nails."

Wanda flattened her dress against her stomach. They sat

in awkward silence for a few minutes. She rocked in her chair while Jack returned to his drawings.

"I know we barely know each other," Jack finally said. He met Wanda's eyes as she turned to him. "But, I need your help,"

"You need *my* help?" She tapped her chest with her fingertips. Her eyebrows rose.

Jack took in a deep breath and exhaled slowly. "I start my job on Monday," he began. "I have no one to watch Donna."

"So much for having it all together."

"I need to find someone." He folded the drawings in his lap. "Fast. Can you help me?"

"Why should I?"

Jack studied her face. She sat, poised in her chair. There was a certain kindness in her eyes that told him she would understand. "Because you can't help yourself." He held her gaze, perhaps longer than he intended. "Because I need you to help me."

"How much you paying?"

"I don't know. What's the going rate for something like that?"

"Most folks charging thirty dollars a week."

"She'll be in school most of the day."

"Not during the summer."

"Thirty dollars a week during the summer." Jack stroked his chin. "Ten during the school year."

"Thirty during the summer and twenty during school." Wanda stared, sullen-faced at Jack.

"Meals included."

"Lunch."

"You know somebody who'll do it?"

"Yeah," Wanda said. "Me."

"You work. How you gonna—"

"My boss wants me on second shift anyway." She waved her hand as she turned away. "Daddy can watch her after four."

Jack nodded and sighed. He suddenly felt a hundred pounds lighter. "You're turning out to be the answer to my prayers."

"Like I said," she countered. "I ain't doing this for you. It's just opportunity. Nothing more to it than that."

"Whatever it is," Jack said, rising with his bundle of papers. "I'm grateful." He paused in the doorway, the screen door halfway open. "Thank you."

"Uh huh," Wanda replied, staring off down the street.

*   *   *

It was four thirty on a Thursday afternoon. Nearly three months had passed since Jack and Donna had taken up residence in their new home. Jack let the car door swing shut and walked slowly toward the porch where Marvin Wilkins sat with Donna on his lap.

"Evening, Mister Wilkins," Jack offered, climbing the three steps onto the porch.

"Evening, Mister Jack," Wanda's father replied in a booming, gravely voice. He was a big man. With his huge hands wrapped around the ends of the armrests, Marvin looked at Jack with his big, yellowed eyes. "You look tired."

"How kind of you to notice." Jack set his lunch box down and sat in the vacant chair next to Marvin. "Has she been talking your ear off?" Jack asked, smiling. In the time they had been together, Donna had yet to utter her first sound.

"Oh, now. Give her time." Marvin wrapped his knuckles gently against Jack's forearm. "She'll come out of it when she's ready," Marvin answered. "She's a very bright little girl."

"How do you know that?" Jack leaned forward, his eyes narrowed.

"She don't have to talk for me to know." Marvin touched his index finger to his temple and said, "A body can just tell. The same way a body knows when a dog is smart. That dog don't have to talk for me to know he's smart."

Jack's mouth twisted as he shrugged. "Maybe you're right." He watched Donna closely. She turned to him, as if she knew he was observing her. Their eyes met and Jack could feel her intensity.

"Same thing I noticed with my Wanda." Marvin twisted himself in his chair to make eye contact with Donna. "There's a spark in there. I know there is."

"The school says she's retarded." Jack stretched out his legs. "The principal had her tested and thinks she has to be in some special education classes come next fall. I have to find her a tutor. If she can learn English, maybe they'll let her start in the first grade. Mister Martin said he doesn't think she'll be able to do it."

"Ed Martin?" Marvin said, his tone turning serious. "That cracker wouldn't know an intelligent child if he tripped over her. Whatever problems this little girl got, being retarded ain't one of 'em." He slid Donna off his lap. "Go on inside the house, now." He pointed to the door. "Go on."

Donna stared ahead without expression for a moment before going into the house.

"She's having a complete physical tomorrow," Jack offered, still checking to make sure Donna had left. "The people at the clinic said she checked out okay for school. But, thought she should see a doctor." Jack replayed the conversation in his head. The nurse at the clinic had only listened to her heart, taken her blood pressure, and checked her for lice.

Just before leaving Viet Nam, she was given all of the inoculations she needed. Her wounds were healing without complications. *Why did she need to see a doctor?* All the nurse would say was that she discovered some 'abnormalities', and granted provisional admission to the school pending a complete physical.

"I know it ain't none of my business," Marvin said to Jack, his jowls shaking with the turning of his head. "But, how did you—"

"How did I manage to end up with her?" Jack interrupted.

Marvin's lips curled into a smile, revealing his large teeth. "You gotta admit," he began. "Not too many single men takin' in orphan girls these days."

Jack drew in a deep breath and stared into the street for a moment before answering. "I grew up an Army brat; always moving from one post to another." Jack turned toward Marvin and leaned back in his chair. "As soon as we'd get settled in somewhere, Dad would get orders and off we'd go again." He thought for a moment and breathed a tired sigh. "You know, Marvin, I've been around the world three times, lived on sixteen Army posts in seven countries, and I have no place to call home." Jack chuckled under his breath. "Until three months ago, I never knew any different."

Marvin's eyes narrowed as he leaned his head back, listening intently.

"Almost got married once. A real nice girl from Saigon." Jack looked away as a pang of sorrow washed over him. "I'll probably rot in hell for what I put her through." He stared into the abyss for a brief moment before continuing. "Anyway. Donna used to hang around the camp, bumming food. One morning, we got hit real bad. Craziest shit storm I'd ever seen. I looked up and there she was, walking through the firefight with a sack tied to her back." Jack paused for a moment. "Sometimes the NVA filled the sack with explosives. Most of the time it was just dirt." Jack stopped, shaking his head to clear the unwanted image. "We couldn't take the chance. We had to shoot them. We'd try to wound them, but sometimes..." He cleared his throat. "Anyway... When I got to her, she just laid there staring up at me. I guess it was right then, that I realized it was over. I'd given all I could give and there wasn't one ounce of fight left in me."

"She made you see that?"

"Not directly." Jack slowly shook his head.

The creaking of the screen door interrupted their conversation.

"What 'chu doin' home?" Wanda asked, slipping onto the porch from inside the house.

"I'm supposed to be home," Jack replied, standing. "Why are you home?"

"Don't work at the plant no more." She accepted the chair Jack had vacated and sat down. "Got tired of their sorry ass politics and slave wages and told them I ain't takin' it no more. Find somebody else to scrape their nasty, slimy crud off those damn machines." She punctuated her last comment with a quick flick of her wrist.

"You got another job?" Jack asked, his eyes wide.

"Got a part time job down at the grocery store. I'm starting classes at the college over in Murfreesboro in the fall."

"What college?" Jack's eyebrows contracted into a pensive ripple. "MTSU?"

"That's right." Wanda gave a quick nod. "Gonna get my business degree."

"Good for you." Jack smiled at Wanda. "I'm sure you'll do well. Marvin tells me you're very smart."

"Oh, he did, huh?" Wanda gave her father's leg a playful shove. "I ain't even started classes yet and already you got the pressure on."

"I guess I'd better get myself some iced tea," Marvin said, standing slowly from the rocker. "She's all yours, Jack. Keep your guard up, now."

"I'll do that," Jack replied, gently patting Marvin on the lower back as he ambled by into the house. "But, I think she could take me in a fair fight."

"Oh, I know she could." Marvin let the screen door slam shut behind him.

Jack and Wanda sat in awkward silence for a minute before Jack finally said, "Fourth of July Parade's next week."

"Same time, every year." She turned and cast him a blank stare. "Funny how that works, huh?"

Jack picked up his lunch box and set it on his lap. "I was thinking about taking Donna."

"She'd probably like that." Wanda took a drink from the ice water she had brought with her onto the porch.

"Yeah." Jack flipped the latch open and closed on his lunch box.

"Do you have to do that?" Wanda asked, pointing at Jack's fingers flipping the latch.

"Huh?" Jack glanced down at the lunch box, unaware that he had been fidgeting. "Oh. Sorry." He set the lunch box down and let his hands come to rest on the arms of the chair. "I think Donna would like it if you came with us." Jack cleared his throat and looked away. "She's grown pretty fond of you over the last few weeks."

Jack turned toward Wanda, catching her gaze.

"Maybe," she replied. "I'll think about it."

"I know it would make her happy."

*   *   *

"Mister Roberts," the slender nurse with curly hair beckoned Jack from the opposite end of the waiting room.

"Would you come with me, please?" Even though they were in a clinic, Jack noticed that her tone was a little bit less friendly than he had expected, even from an overworked government employee. "The doctor would like to see you."

Jack set the magazine down he had been reading and rose to his feet. "Is she all right?" he asked, crossing the large room, a dozen heads turning to look at him. "What's wrong?"

"Doctor Reznik will explain," the nurse offered, holding the plain wooden door open for him. "They're right down the hall. Just follow me, please."

The nurse led Jack down a narrow hallway where they entered a tiny exam room. Donna was curled into a ball at one end of the exam table. The doctor rose from his small three-legged stool to greet him.

"I'm Doctor Reznik," he said, offering an insincere handshake. He was in his early thirties with an athletic body and hairy arms. "I need to ask you a few questions about your relationship with the child."

"Her name is Donna." Jack held the young doctor in an icy stare. "And I don't like the tone of this already." He stepped next to the table and put his arm around his daughter. "What's the problem?"

The doctor and nurse exchanged wary glances.

"How long have you lived with the..." Doctor Reznik caught himself. "How long have you lived with Donna?"

Jack leaned down and kissed Donna's head before turning to the doctor. He took a deep breath while clenching his fists for a moment. "I brought her back with me about three months ago." A sick feeling began seeping into his gut. It started as a tiny nebulous point of angst and gradually, insidiously grew into a full-grown knot as he started connecting the unspeakable dots. His head tipped back and his eyes narrowed while his knees weakened and his gut tightened. "What the hell is this about?"

"Mister Roberts," the doctor said, seemingly unfazed by Jack's posturing. "How long have you known her?"

Jack looked off to his left in thought. "I don't know," he began, staring at an eye chart on the wall. "Six months. Maybe eight." He turned his head toward them once again. "Listen, Doc, either you tell me what the hell is going on—"

"We found some scarring," the doctor interrupted.

"Scarring?" Jack stepped back to Donna's side. "I know. She's got a bullet wound on her shoulder," he pointed at Donna's shoulder, "and another one on her leg. Right he—"

"We know about those, Mister Roberts." Doctor Reznik looked down momentarily before he continued. "We found some deep scars along the uterus."

Jack was no doctor, but he understood where this was going.

"Are you telling me she was raped?"

The room fell silent for a moment before the doctor spoke. He took a deep breath and exhaled slowly. "She would have been lucky had it simply been a rape." Doctor Reznik sat on his tiny three-legged stool. For the first time, his expression turned from one of indignation to what could have passed for simple compassion. "Some one, or some persons, violated her with something jagged." He looked away, blinking his eyes rapidly. After a moment he continued. "I've never seen anyone mutilated like that."

Jack glanced at the nurse. Her eyes were filled with tears. He looked down at Donna. "Jesus," he said, wrapping his arms around her. "No wonder she won't talk."

"I suspect that she must have ended up getting some decent medical care at some point," the doctor said. "Someone did some pretty nice repair work in there. Probably saved her life."

Jack's mind raced. "She got taken to a hospital ship, off shore. I know that much." His tone was vacant. "They drafted a bunch of Harvard types for that duty. Probably got some top shelf care out there." He searched himself for the courage to ask what he knew would have to be asked. "What about children?"

Doctor Reznik simply looked at Jack and slowly shook his head. "I'm sorry."

"Can she go to school?" Jack was staring at the floor at nothing in particular.

"Sure," Doctor Reznik replied. "She's in otherwise good health."

On the way home Donna sat in the front passenger seat, staring straight ahead. The breeze from the open window blew her auburn hair around her face as they drove.

"Oh, the stories I'd bet you could tell us if you could talk," he said to her as they rolled to a stop in the center of town. "I might not be Wanda, but I can listen good like she can. If you ever want to get some of this out..." His voice trailed off.

They drove in silence the rest of the way home. Jack parked along the dusty road and turned to her. "What did they do to you, Donna?"

Donna blinked and turned her head toward Jack, holding him in her gaze.

Chapter Sixteen

Jack felt Donna flinch as the cymbals crashed together. She clung to him as if her very life hung in the balance in the wake of the ungodly clamor. In the street, a few feet away, a small sea of blue and white uniforms kept step with the music, their high, white hats bobbing up and down in unison with the cadence of the march. Donna watched intently from the sidewalk as the last of the Middleton marching band walked proudly past her position.

Next in the procession was a shiny red convertible. The driver, a brown-haired man, wore a white sports jacket, sunglasses, and a straw fedora. In the back, sitting on the trunk deck with her feet on the back seat, was a beautiful young blonde-haired woman. Her long hair fell down around her sequined blue dress and white gloves covered her slender arms, all the way up to her elbows. Her face was lit up in a smile while her hand pivoted back and forth at the wrist in a seemingly perpetual wave. The car stopped briefly in front of the courthouse before moving on behind the marching band.

Jack knelt beside Donna, studying her profile and wondering what was going on inside her head. Were so many *strange* people gathered in one place making her nervous? It suddenly occurred to him that Donna had probably never seen anything like it in her life. To Jack it was a Fourth of July parade just like any other. The car styles had changed, along with the skirt lengths. But, in most respects it was much like the events he recalled from his boyhood.

Out in the street, another marching band passed by in rigid formation. Donna covered her ears. Jack suddenly viewed the procession in a new way, trying to imagine what it must look like through Donna's eyes.

How would all of this look to her? Jack tried to purge his mind of his own experiences and view the unfolding events as he imagined Donna might see them. *How would she describe it to someone if she could?* He imagined her telling a playmate how some of the people in the street were blowing into shiny pieces of formed metal while others were banging wooden sticks on round buckets or throwing long silver sticks high into the air. A few of the larger people were completely engulfed by a mass of gold tubing wrapped around them. It gradually expanded from their mouths and ultimately formed a huge funnel shaped opening over their heads. They were blowing into the small end and producing sounds much like oxen farts from the other.

Jack smiled at the imagery.

Donna inspected the people lining the streets, as far as one could see in both directions. Jack wondered what she thought of them. Were the people wearing the funny clothes and making strange noises performing a punishment for whatever wrongdoing they had done? Why else would anyone subject oneself to such public humiliation? Jack chuckled. He was beginning to like these little revelatory moments. Maybe having a daughter wasn't such a scary thing after all.

In spite of the near triple-digit temperatures, Jack could feel the cool stares from the crowd. He tried not to let it bother him, but it seemed like every time he glanced in a new direction, he caught a glimpse of another good Christian citizen of Middleton boring a hole through the two of them.

"Come on," Jack said to Donna over the din of the marching band. "Let's find a better place to watch." He tugged at her hand and guided her through the bustling throngs. While turning to pick her up, Jack was jolted by a body moving quickly through the crowd. The lean, thin-faced man had collided with Jack and nearly knocked him and Donna to the ground. He remained expressionless as he glanced, quickly at Jack, then down at Donna and then, off into the crowd.

"Got a lotta' nerve bringing that little slope here today," the man said just loud enough to be heard, and to no one in particular as he passed within arms reach and back into the masses. Jack looked down at the top of the little head nestled in his rib cage. Maybe it was coincidence, but at that moment she looked up. Her expression bore a look of understanding along with a sense of burden, as if traversing that fine line between guilt and responsibility. Jack glanced back at the man, who had already disappeared into the crowd in front of the Town Square.

"Ah, screw him," he said, lifting her into his arms.

It was just after eleven o'clock. Not quite lunch time yet, but the smell of barbecued ribs and pecan pie wafting from the far end of the Town Square was making him hungry. The parade would end soon and maybe he could interest Donna in something to eat. They might even see Wanda somewhere around town. She said she might show up. Not that it mattered to him, of course. But, Jack knew how much it would mean to Donna, and it might be nice for them to see each other.

Donna's grip on Jack's arm tightened as a small formation of men in olive green army uniforms approached. Jack felt her little hands grab more of his shirt. "What's the matter, Donna?"

He already knew the answer. To her, they were the

destroyers. The men who came when people were about to die. She hadn't seen any of them, and had lived in relative peace for the last few months. There had been no gunshots and no screams in the night. That was over, for now. But, they were back. Did she think they had come for her? Did she think that many more would come and the killing would soon start again?

Donna stared with wide eyes at the marching men in their neatly pressed, field uniforms.

Jack knelt beside her and nuzzled the side of her face, trying to offer her some assurance that she was safe. "Not to worry, Donna," he spoke softly into her ear. "No one's going to hurt you, ever again."

Jack went to that place in his mind where he kept the memories he could still look at with relative safety. It was in the pre-dawn hours on a day much like this one when she lay dying in the jungle near Da Nang. What must have been going through her mind? She turned to him and engaged him and for reasons he could not fathom, Jack found himself seeing the events of that night through her eyes.

He was suddenly looking up at the sky, through the wisps of elephant grass, the pale blue early morning sky suddenly interrupted by the silhouette of a helmet, much like the ones worn by the men in the street. Only, this one wasn't silver, and the face beneath it was that of the man to whom she now clung with such resolve.

Jack could feel her heart racing as the dirt-covered soldier hovered over her. He yelled something in a strange language, to somebody in the distance. A few moments later, another one of the men had joined him. He took a bundle of white cloth from a drab green satchel and placed it on her shoulder. The pain shot through her like a searing, hot knife inserted under her skin. She feared those men. They had killed everyone she ever loved, or who had ever loved her.

These men had shot her, and were now torturing her wounded body. Killing her slowly, and painfully. They had been there ever since she could remember, and as far as she knew, they always would be.

Jack watched the marching soldiers as they passed, wondering how Donna felt toward him. Did she fear him? Would she ever love him as her father? Were they American soldiers who had brutalized her? Was she living in constant fear, in a living nightmare, wondering when he would do the same? If so, why had she slipped the bracelet off her wrist, the only possession she had at the time, and given it to him as they loaded her onto the chopper?

"There you are!"

Donna and Jack both turned to see Wanda's smiling face.

"Hello Wanda." Jack did his best to shake the thoughts from his head. "Donna, look. Wanda's here."

Donna turned her head. She didn't smile, but slowly extended her hand to Wanda.

Wanda instantly melted as she engaged Donna's large, soulful eyes. "You look so pretty today, Donna. Just look at you in that nice sun dress!" She wrapped her arms around Donna, brushing against Jack in the process. "I just want to scoop you up and hug you all day long."

"Thank you, Wanda," Jack answered on Donna's behalf. "She actually picked that dress out herself. We drove into Nashville last week and went shopping at the new mall just off the interstate."

Wanda laughed. "Do you like to shop, Donna?"

Donna looked at Wanda sideways.

A small group of people walked by. None of them said hello, or even looked at them. From across the street, Jack could see people pointing at the three of them. They looked funny standing there with their big gawking eyes, covered mouths, and extended fingers. The pattern was always the same. The stare, then a whispered comment to the person next to them, followed by a giggle or a disgusted look. And why not whisper and stare? There they were: a nigger woman, a retarded gook, and a baby killer. What a trio.

The sadness Jack felt took precedent over the brave smile he offered. He wasn't sure what was more painful to him. Being told Donna was retarded, and accepting her silence as a defect, or knowing she was intelligent and that her reticence was borne out of her suffering. If there were ever a way he could take it from her he would. From the first moment he had seen her, slipping between the tents near the mess hall, he had fallen in love with her; the way a father loves his own child. Finding her, wounded and starving in the jungle was more than he could bear. In that instant, he knew she would never wander alone in a savage world again. Looking down on her trembling, blood-soaked body, Jack Roberts swore before God that he would take care of this child until the very last breath had left his body. A promise he would have made anyway, even if it had not been a bullet from his own gun that struck her down.

Jack turned at the sound of two men approaching from behind. They were loud, drunk, and pushing their way through the crowd. A grizzly man, shoving spectators out of his way, emerged from the throngs wearing a pair of dirty blue jean overalls and no shirt. His sweaty, armpit hair stuck together in a dark brown matte. Behind him followed another man sporting a pair of blue jeans and a wrinkled, plaid button down shirt. He was shorter, and considerably thinner than his colossal friend.

The skinny one reached out and flipped Donna's ponytail. "Hey, Earl. What we got here?" he said, then took another long pull from his beer bottle. "She must be lost. Nearest zoo is 'bout fifty miles, that way." He pointed with a wavering hand toward the rugged hills, surrounding the small town.

"What's your problem, farm boy?" It was Wanda who reacted first. Jack held his position, reassuring Donna with his hands firmly on her shoulders. No harm done, so far: Just a couple drunks with an attitude. Stay calm.

"I ain't got no problem, bitch." The little man scowled at Wanda and then glanced back at Earl for reassurance. "Looks like you're the one with the problem." He cracked a smile riddled with holes and brown teeth while pointing at Donna. "What's the matter, the animal shelter wouldn't take her?" The two men erupted into a fit of laughter.

Jack moved Donna out of his way and started toward the little man.

Wanda stepped in front of Jack. "It's not worth it," she said, holding his arm.

Jack saw the resolve in her face and relaxed. Donna stood staring at him from the nearby sidewalk.

The two men came down from their laughter-induced high and Jack decided to take the offensive. "You boys best move along," he said, his sinewy limbs like a loaded gun, cocked and ready to fire. By now, the crowd had pulled back and people were beginning to circle around them. Jack looked around at the human arena that had suddenly formed in the Town Square.

"Maybe you're the ones need to be movin' on," Earl said, sticking out his massive chest and tipping his pumpkin-like head back. His wide face had lost the mirthful look of a few moments prior. He took a few steps in Jack's direction. "That... *thing's* got no place here." He was pointing at Donna.

The view, from Jack's vantage point was quickly turning red. He was resisting the urge to flatten the fat slob with every fiber of his being. But like a sapling in a strong wind, there was only so much he could take. He clenched his fists and took a deep breath. It would be hard caring for a war orphan from the confines of a prison cell, and Jack knew it. One split second of relief from the agonizing impulse to level these two idiots could cost Donna more than anyone could calculate. Foster homes were the playgrounds for people like these guys. He had to keep his cool.

"My buddies didn't go off and get killed so these little gooks could come over here and live in my town." This time the big man took a menacing step toward Donna. His whiskered face grew red as he raised his voice over the sound of the next marching band, fast approaching the square. "You've disgraced every one of us! She's got no place, being here!"

Jack looked over at Donna. Her eyes darted back and forth between the gladiators and the people gathered for the fight. Most of them looked upon her with disgust. It appeared that as much as they found the two drunks offensive, they couldn't help agreeing with them. They said nothing, but offered their endorsements with the nodding of their heads and quick glances around to the person next to them for reinforcement. There was strength in numbers.

"She's got as much right to be here as anyone!" Wanda shouted with her hands on her hips. A vein in her neck bulged as she rose up on her toes in anger.

"You got your nigger fightin' for you now?" Earl shook with laughter as he glanced around him, working the crowd. "She needs to have her stinkin' little gook ass shipped back to that shit hole she come from. That's what she deserves!"

Wanda started for Earl, her steps deliberate and long. His skinny friend stepped up to meet her half way between Jack and the big man in the overalls.

"She didn't start that war, and she didn't ask to have her family—"

"Shut up." The little man shoved Wanda backwards onto the ground. She landed in a heap at Donna's feet.

Jack felt his adrenaline coursing along with his boiling blood as he looked back at Wanda. Her expression quickly changed from that of surprise to anger. He reached down and helped Wanda to her feet.

"Are you okay?" he asked.

"Yeah, I'm fine," she replied, brushing off her skirt while still glaring at the two rednecks.

Jack turned toward the skinny man. "You owe the lady an apology."

Skinny boy slowly worked his jaw a few times then spit a wad of tobacco juice onto Jack's shoes. "I don't apologize to no niggers." The defiance in his eyes begged Jack to take action.

Without another word, Jack took a deliberate step in his direction.

The big man stepped in between them and put his hands on his hips. "You'll have to go through me to get to him," Earl said just before he swung a huge fist at Jack's head.

With a graceful sweep of his hand, Jack deflected the blow and redirected the man's arm across his own body.

"Okay," was all Jack said before landing a staggering right hook to Earl's ribs, doubling him over. With another quick motion, Jack placed his left forearm under the man's chin and wrapped his right arm around the back of his neck, trapping his carotid arteries in a vee. The maneuver would cut off the blood flow to the brain; not enough to kill, but Earl would sleep like a baby for a while. The big man slumped lower and lower until, after a few seconds, he fell unconscious onto the grass. By that time, his flyweight partner was nowhere to be found. He had apparently slithered his way through the crowd and was probably halfway to Alabama by the time his big friend hit the ground.

Jack left the sleeping giant curled up on the grass and went to see if Wanda was hurt. She was sitting on the ground, holding Donna, who had knelt down beside her and wrapped her little arms around Wanda's neck. Wanda looked up at Jack, her face nuzzled against Donna's thick hair.

"I was wrong," Wanda offered with a smile.

"Wrong?" Jack shot her a puzzled look. "About what?"

"About not being worth it." Wanda pulled Donna close. "It really was worth it. You shoulda' popped him a good one right in the face." Wanda looked over at the motionless hulk, still at rest in the grass.

Jack chuckled. "He would've just laughed at me. Last place you wanna hit someone like him is in the head. It's a good way to break your hand."

Most of the onlookers seemed disappointed, like they had paid to see a ten round bout only to see their favorite fighter go down early in the first. Many kept looking at the heavy man, sleeping peacefully in the hot sun. A few shook their heads, then looked at Jack for a few seconds and slowly walked away in silence.

The Middleton High School Marching Band had once again stopped and played on the opposite side of the square while the commotion took place. They had since moved on and been replaced by shimmering pieces of fire and rescue equipment. Two big red pumper trucks rolled along the street in front of them. The firemen walking beside the rigs wore baggy pants with suspenders; bright yellow metallic hats shaded their eyes from the merciless sun. Their heavy jackets had been sidelined in favor of the warm weather uniform of choice: A blue cotton t-shirt with *Middleton Volunteer Fire Department* emblazoned on the back in white letters.

"Come on," Jack said while grabbing Wanda's arm and taking Donna by the hand.

"We're leaving?" Wanda protested, her face broadcasting her disapproval.

"Let's put some distance between us and Goliath, over there." Jack tried to lead them across the street, but fire trucks still blocked the way and some of the crowd that had gathered around them was still dissipating.

"The parade's almost over, anyway." Jack added. "Let's just leave now, and avoid more trouble." As much as he was looking forward to the ribs, corn on the cob and pecan pie, it would have to wait for another time.

"So, we leaving 'cuz of him?" Wanda stopped short. "That's what he wanted us to do." She crossed her arms. "You can run away, if you want. But I ain't going anywhere."

Jack was about to respond when he heard them coming. He had read about them in the paper. They would be the highlight of the parade. The children were especially looking forward to seeing them; he had heard them talking about it while they endured the rest of the parade just to see them, if for only a brief few seconds. Even the adults swelled with pride as they passed overhead. They were a symbol of might, security and a way of life that was protected by the best technology on the planet. To the people in the streets the approaching sight seemed to bring excitement and pride to their otherwise uneventful lives.

Jack turned to Donna as he felt her tiny hands grip his waist. While the rest of the crowd looked skyward in wide-eyed awe, there was one among them whose expression revealed her unimaginable terror. As their eyes met, Jack understood the source of her fright. The sound was unmistakable; the dull, low, rhythmic thumping of approaching army helicopters. It was the sound that signaled the onslaught of death and widespread destruction. It was the sound that was a prelude to terror. It was the sound that, so often, when it subsided left haunting screams of agony burned into their memories. As the beating of the rotor blades approached, Donna was seized by panic and broke from Jack's side and ran from the Town Square screaming warnings in Vietnamese.

Donna ran blindly into the street, right in front of the last pumper truck. The expected sound of the screeching tires and blasting air horn could not be heard above the deafening sound of the four Hueys coursing through the sky just a few feet overhead. As the choppers banked away and disappeared behind the rooftops, the sound of their rotors subsided and Jack and Wanda were able to once again hear Donna's screaming. They headed in the direction of her voice and were relieved to see her lying, unhurt in the street.

Wanda was the first to reach Donna, curled up in a ball in front of the huge fire truck. The driver had leaped from the vehicle and stood over Donna as Wanda arrived. Wanda fell to the street and wrapped the trembling girl in the safety of her arms. Donna was still screaming; tears of terror filled her eyes and rolled freely down her cheeks. Her slender body convulsed in spasms of abject fear as the people in the crowd looked on without pity at the spectacle before them.

"I think I might've hit her," the driver said, visibly shaken by the incident. He was a young man, barely out of his teens. His baby face was ashen and drawn into a look of genuine concern. A few of the other firemen had seen the girl bounce off the front of the truck and came running to offer their assistance.

"I think she's all right," Jack put his hand on the boy's shoulder. "You did a fine job of stopping that truck, son. Another man might have panicked." He knelt next to Donna and stroked her hair. "Thank you."

One of the older firefighters put his arm around the driver and patted him on the back. "And you thought you'd save your first life from a burning building."

The young driver laughed. A few of the other men from the truck patted him on the head and they moved away, toward the back of the truck. Jack helped Wanda and Donna to the steps of the courthouse, where Wanda continued offering her comfort while Donna kept her arms tightly wrapped around her. She had stopped crying, but was still trembling, probably more from the threat she perceived from the helicopters than the collision with the big red pumper truck.

Jack knelt next to them. Donna's head was buried in Wanda's shoulder. Donna looked up at Jack, as she became aware of him next to her. He abandoned his futile attempt to blink back the tears as Donna reached out to him. She wrapped her arms around his neck and fused her body onto his with an enveloping hug. Of the hundreds of people, who had just witnessed the events of the last few minutes, only three knew the significance. The fire truck slowly moved on while the crowd along Main Street dissipated. Another Fourth of July parade was in the history books, punctuated by the traditional fly-by of Hueys from the nearby military base. It would certainly be a memorable day. Not just for Jack, Wanda and Donna, but for all the residents of Middleton. It hadn't quite occurred to them yet, but... Donna could speak.

Chapter Seventeen

On Saturday morning, Jack and Donna were sitting on the porch after a late breakfast. It was early September and the last scorching gasps of summer had driven them from the non-air-conditioned house. Jack reclined in a rocker while Donna sat looking at the road just a few yards away.

In spite of having slept until after seven that morning, Jack's eyes drooped closed and he was soon dozing in the heat. It seemed to him like no more than an instant before he was startled awake by a truck bouncing noisily by. Jack's head jerked forward and his eyes popped open as he came around. His first conscious thought, after regaining his senses, was to look for Donna. He glanced down, expecting to see her still sitting on the porch steps. But, she was gone.

"Donna?" he yelled, looking up and down the road. His call had scarcely echoed back from the river bluffs when he spotted her, about fifty yards away. She was sitting next to a car by the roadside with a middle-aged couple under a nearby tree. Still a bit groggy from his snooze, he left the porch to meet Donna's new friends.

As Jack approached, he could see them huddled around something on the ground. Drawing nearer, it became apparent that the man and woman were playing chess. Seeing that Donna was safe, he hung back unnoticed and observed the unfolding scene.

"Really, Herbert," the woman said. "Must we continue?" She was slender with dark hair coiled into tight curls. Her white, horn-rimmed glasses halfway obscured a pleasant face framed by fine laugh lines and neatly plucked eyebrows. "You win every time."

"Margaret," Herbert protested. Even though he was seated, he appeared to be tall and slender, balding with dark hair on his hands. He, too, wore glasses: black horn-rimmed, fastened with an elastic strap around the back of his head. "You can't stop now. I think you're getting the hang of it."

"What I'm getting," Margaret replied, standing to brush the grass from her flowery cotton dress, "is tired of this game and waiting for the tow truck."

"It's on the way, Dear." Herbert was placing the chess pieces in formation on the board. "There's really nothing more we can do right now. So, we might as well just—" He turned toward Jack, suddenly aware of his approach. "Oh, hello."

"Morning," Jack offered, standing in the shade next to the trio. "Is she bothering you?" He nodded toward Donna.

"Not at all," Margaret answered. "In fact, Herbert was just about to play a game of chess with her."

"I was?" Herbert's nose crinkled underneath his glasses as he stood to shake hands with Jack. He glanced at Margaret to see her giving him a silent nod while looking sideways at Donna. "Oh, right. Yes. Yes I was about to do that, right after this game."

"I don't expect she'll be much of a match," Jack said, patting Donna's head.

"She's a child of few words. That's for certain." Herbert sat in the grass and finished arranging the chess pieces into position for a new game. "But, well behaved." He studied the board for a moment before moving his pawn forward two spaces. "And well mannered, too. Your move, Dear."

"I told you," Margaret replied with a dismissive wave. "I'm played out."

"What about you, sir?" Herbert glanced up at Jack. "Do you play?"

"Me? No." Jack shook his head. "Not me. Sorry."

"Well, then." Herbert turned slowly to Donna. "I guess it's just you and me, this time." He pointed at the board. "You've been watching. By now you must have discerned my strategies." He glanced up at Jack and Margaret with a smile. "Your move," he continued, turning to Donna.

To everyone's surprise, Donna reached for one of the opposing pawns and moved it into play. Jack, Margaret, and Herbert shared a laugh at Donna's expense while Herbert quickly moved another pawn.

"Go easy on the child, Herbert," Margaret said, fanning herself with a folded section of newspaper. "I won't tell anyone if you let her win."

Donna's next move came right on the heels of Herbert's. Jack watched in amusement as the two players exchanged moves, each one quickly sliding their players along the board. Herbert's jovial demeanor gradually turned more serious with each move, however. Donna sat expressionless, moving only her arm enough to position the game pieces.

In a flurry of movements, pawns, rooks, knights, and bishops were taken on both ends of the board. Jack looked on in astonishment that Donna could even know enough to move each piece in the proper way.

The pace suddenly slowed. Herbert sat with his hand cupping his chin, his eyes narrowed looking at the board.

"She wins in three moves," he said, still staring at the board.

"I'm proud of you, Herbert," Margaret said, patting his arm. "I would have expected your competitive instincts to crush the poor girl. Instead, you let her win. Good for you."

Herbert was silent for a long time, perhaps even for an entire minute. "I am the Greater Knoxville chess champion. Ranked nationally," he finally said.

"Yes, Dear," Margaret replied, glancing first at Jack and then at the back of Herbert's shiny head. "You're also known for your humility."

Herbert looked up at Jack. "Is this your daughter?"

Jack cleared his throat. "Yes." He shuffled his feet in awkward movements. "Yes, she is. Adopted. She's adopted."

Herbert removed his glasses and swiped his head with a white handkerchief. "Where did she learn to play chess like that?"

Jack let out a burst of breath that transformed itself into a chuckle. "I have no idea. Maybe one of the nuns taught her at the orphanage."

"Remarkable," Herbert said, staring into Donna's eyes.

"Maybe you should play her for real, then," Margaret piped in. "See how many moves she lasts with you."

Herbert slid his glasses back on and turned to his wife. "That would be a good idea, except for one minor flaw in your logic." He turned to look, once again at the board. "While I certainly didn't play my best game by any means, I didn't *let* her win."

"Oh, come now," Margaret protested, leaning over to glance at the chessboard. "Surely you don't think me that gullible."

Herbert looked first at Jack and then at his wife. "In the thirty-five years we have been married," he said, pushing his glasses up his sweaty nose. "Have you ever known me to be that charitable?"

Jack took a knee next to the board. "You're not kidding?" He pointed at the chess pieces. "She really knew what she was doing?"

Herbert's laugh was condescending. "Sir," he spoke in a deliberate pace. "I know twenty-year veterans of the game who could not match the skill I just witnessed."

Jack looked at Donna and shook his head. "I know she didn't learn it from me."

"Even if she had," Herbert replied. "It wouldn't account for her skill." He raised a hand. "No offense intended. But, you can't teach what I just saw."

Jack fell backward into a sitting position and laughed out loud. "Not bad for a retarded girl!" His body shook in comic relief, his anxieties somehow let loose in a fit of irony.

"Retarded?" Margaret replied, her back straightened, her eyes narrowed. "I should say not. By whose reckoning?"

"Her school principal." Jack had stopped laughing. "He won't let her into the school because he's made up his mind she's retarded and has to be in a Special Ed program."

"Is that so?" Margaret pulled herself closer to Donna. She looked deep into the girl's penetrating eyes while she spoke. "We'll just see about that."

"Margaret is a professor of education at UT Knoxville," Herbert said, with obvious pride. "You should let her test the girl. She could tell you if she should be in school or not."

"You can do that?" Jack asked, his head cocked to one side.

"At this point," Margaret replied, using Herbert's shoulder to get to her feet. "I would insist upon it."

*   *   *

A few short hours later, Jack was back on the porch. The Westlakes were on their way back to Knoxville with Jack's address and phone number in hand. Margaret had promised to return within the next few weeks to offer whatever assistance she could in getting Donna into Middleton Elementary School.

"You look like you hidin' something," Wanda offered, walking slowly from her car. "What are you looking all happy about?"

"You wouldn't believe me if I told you." Jack hiked his khakis up as he dropped into a rocker. He folded his hands across his stomach and laid his head back.

Wanda stepped to the rear of the chair and placed a hand on his neck. "Try me," she said, beginning to massage his shoulders.

Jack proceeded to tell her about the encounter with the Westlake's and the promise of another chance to resurrect Donna's school career.

"Margaret is going to contact Ed Martin and request another meeting with the district psychologist." The smile on his face nearly touched both ears. "Not only does she think Donna is not retarded. She thinks she might be very intelligent. Maybe your father was right."

Wanda grunted. "He usually is."

"She could really use a break right about now." Jack looked up into Wanda's eyes.

Wanda stopped massaging his shoulders and knelt next to him. "God's looking out for that child, Jack Roberts." She put her hand on his cheek. "You two got the Lord's blessings. I know it."

"It doesn't always feel that way."

"God didn't put the notion in your head to take this girl in so he could watch you fall down." She took up his hand in hers. "He'll provide. We all get what we need."

"She doesn't need this." He squeezed her hand. "Not one bit."

"He's on it," she said. "What we want and what we need

ain't always the same. Trust in God. He'll come through. You wait and see." She slid into the other chair next to him. "He let you weasel your sorry ass into my heart." Wanda turned and grunted. "Sure as *hell* didn't want or need that."

Jack cast his eyes upon her as she gently rocked. A slight breeze lifted a few strands of her curly dark hair away from her face. Her ebony skin glowed in the shade of the porch.

"How is it a beautiful woman like you isn't married?" Jack asked, his question surprising even him.

"Maybe I don't need a man in my life to make me feel complete."

"I see." Jack puckered his lips and nodded. "Been reading Cosmo?"

Wanda laughed. Jack liked making her laugh. The contrast it made with her otherwise solemn demeanor made him feel somewhat like a healer. He gazed, enraptured, at her shiny white teeth and the fine lines that formed at the corners of her eyes. With each passing day, she became more beautiful.

"I'm a liberated woman, Jack. Get used to it. There'll be more on the way."

"Hey, I'm all for it." He stretched his legs. "When you and your sisters are pulling off your bras, I'll be the one holding the lighter to the bonfire."

"I was engaged once." Wanda's smile evaporated. "Three years ago."

"What happened?"

"He always thought his lucky number was seven." She looked down at her hands folded in her lap. "'Til he got his draft card."

Jack sat staring at Wanda knowing how the story would end.

"Went into the army." Wanda's gaze drifted. "I got a few

letters from Fort Benning. A few weeks later he was over
there." She waved her hand in no particular direction. "He
wrote to me twice after that. Wasn't too much later, his
Momma come over here one day all crying and carrying
on." She looked down and shook her head; her eyes pressed
shut. "She had this piece of paper in her hand. I knew what
happened before she got halfway 'cross the yard. She didn't
have to say anything." Wanda nodded her head. Tears rolled
down her cheeks.

"I'm sorry." Jack's fingers found her hand.

Wanda turned to him, wiping the wetness from her face.
She sniffled. "Look at me. Crying like a damn baby 'bout
something happened three years ago." She wiped more tears
away. "And I thought I'd cried all that out of me."

"Whoever said 'Time heals all wounds'," Jack gently
stroked the back of her hand with his thumb, "was full of
shit."

Wanda smiled and nodded. "Why you always wearing
that bracelet?" she asked, staring down at Jack's wrist.

Jack raised his hand, bringing Wanda's with it. He gave
the bracelet a considerate look and then returned it to the
armrest. "Believe it or not, Donna gave this to me."

Wanda leaned closer for a better look. "Pretty," she said.
"What are all those marks on it for?"

"They're tribal markings. Each one of the Montignards
had their own."

"Montignards?"

"Mountain tribes: The native people who lived in the
Central Highlands. Kind of like the Indians here in the
states."

"Donna was one of these…Montignards?"

"I doubt it." Jack shook his head while his face contracted in bemusement. "That's the strange part about it.
She doesn't look like a 'Yard' and when I found her she was

quite a ways from the nearest tribe. But, she was wearing this." He shrugged.

"Maybe she found it."

"Maybe." Jack's expression grew more pensive. "It's possible someone gave it to her in the same way she gave it to me. For that reason, I never take it off. Ever."

"Not even at night?" Wanda offered him a menacing smile.

Jack offered a nervous laugh and then the smile left his face. "If she did come from the mountains, then giving this to me means that I am a part of her. Friends for life." His thoughts were of the bloody, frightened girl being loaded into the chopper bay. She lay motionless on the stretcher among the wounded grunts; her piercing stare transfixing Jack as the Huey slowly lifted off. At that moment, he didn't know if he would ever see her again. As the helicopter disappeared into the treetops, Jack pulled the ends apart and slipped the brass bracelet onto his wrist, where it had resided ever since.

Wanda released her hand and wrapped it through Jack's arm. "Maybe she'll tell you all about it, someday."

"I have no doubt that she will." Jack gently rubbed her arm. "No doubt whatsoever."

Chapter Eighteen

"Jack Roberts," Sally's shrill voice blared over the plant's public address system, punching through the heavy thuds and high-pitched whining of machinery like a rock crashing through a plate glass window. "Call on line two." The page ended with an unceremonious click.

"Oh, what now?" Jack muttered to himself, having scarcely recognized his own name being paged over the din of the noisy sweatshop. Dozens of injection molding machines littered the floor around him in the quaking old building: Each one resting on a heavy cast iron frame and spitting out new plastic parts every few seconds, adding to the deafening rumble that permeated the sullen-faced workers populating the production floor. The entire building resonated with the steady, rhythmic pounding of the massive metal pieces, each one coming together with two hundred tons of force.

Dressed in a grease-stained white tee shirt and dark khaki pants, Jack was lying on his back attempting to repair one of the presses.

"Jack, number two just blew a hose." A dumpy looking man with a wiry mustache approached holding a section of tubing. From inside the machine, Jack could see a hairy stomach peering out from between the buttons of a dark blue work shirt and the name *Luke* embroidered in white stitching just above the left pocket. The man hadn't shaved in days and from the way his thick black hair laid flat on his head, it may have been at least that long since he had showered.

"Okay, okay," Jack replied. "Hang on a minute." Sweat poured from Jack's face as he strained to turn a reluctant bolt with a large wrench. His arms bulged as he applied the last burst of torque that freed the stubborn part. It let go with a jolt.

Jack glanced up to see a group of four women, operators of the machinery idled by the breakdown, standing nearby watching the procedure. With regularity, each of them stole a look at his well-toned body half-swallowed by the huge machine.

"I think the heater controls on fourteen are down." Another man joined the small group next to the crippled press. He was a lanky black man in his mid twenties. His hair was thinning and he wore thick, wire-rimmed glasses.

"Why do you say that, Cedric?" Jack replied, pulling himself out from under the machine.

Cedric approached Jack with the confidence of a man who knew his job. "Starting to see some defects on the parts around the corners," he answered, as if his word was taken to heart in spite of his age and race. He stood straight and square, offering and receiving mutual respect from his superior.

Jack stepped back from the machine and turned toward the group of women. "Okay, ladies," he began, shouting to be heard above the clamor of the mold machines.

They stopped talking and offered him their full attention.

"Sorry to say, but break time's over." Jack held up the wrench and nodded toward the machine. "We've got wagon wheels to make and Santa's counting on us."

Each of the four women smiled, and glided slowly past him on their way back to their posts along the line.

"I've got some things need fixing at home," one of the women said as she slipped by.

"Are you this handy with other jobs?" another purred, offering a seductive smile as she brushed against him.

Jack smiled and rolled his eyes: One job down, twenty more to go.

A bead of sweat rolled from his face and onto his tee shirt.

"Okay, Luke." Jack turned while rubbing the grease from his hands with a soft rag. "What's wrong with number two?"

The machine Jack had just fixed began to operate. The sudden rush of noise was too loud for them to hear each other talk so Jack motioned for Luke and Cedric to step away.

"I think the hydraulic unit shit the bed." Luke held up the piece of tubing as he spoke. He stood with his mouth open awaiting a reply, exposing rows of crooked and missing teeth. His dull eyes fixed in a stare off to his left, as if he were not worthy of looking upon his boss's face.

Jack shook his head. "I told the field service guy the seals were going bad!"

Luke's eyes met Jack's and he nodded his acknowledgement. "I guess we're gonna have to find another hydraulic guy, huh?"

Jack ran his hand through his thick hair and looked at the ceiling while he contemplated their options. They stood amidst the ever-present smell of molten plastic, while the heat from the machinery poured over them like the hot breath of a panting dragon. It was like being back in the army, he thought. One screw up after another and there was no one to complain to and little satisfaction if you did. The roar of the machinery rivaled anything he had known on the battlefield. All around him motors rumbled, hoses hissed in sudden spurts of high pressure, gears ground together, and polished metal pieces slid against each other with bone-crushing force. For a few blissful moments he drifted off in his mind to the place where problems were solved: A mental laboratory where solutions were born like formulas for some miracle substance. After a brief time, he lowered his head and, again, looked straight at Luke.

"All right, I guess we'll have to—"

"Jack Roberts," Sally's grating, amplified voice pierced him once again. "Call on line two." After a brief pause she added. "Let's get the lead out, Roberts."

"I gotta see what the hell they want now." Jack threw down the rag he was using to clean his hands.

Cedric smirked and rolled his eyes.

Jack walked away, still barking instructions over his shoulder as he went. "I'll be right over after I see who the hell is on the phone."

On the way back to his office Jack walked past rows of large green mold machines, each attended by teams of young women who smiled and waved. All heads turned as he strolled past each workstation. At the far end of the production floor he climbed a stairway to a second level. His office was just to the right of the landing.

Wanda was sitting with her back to the door in front of his desk as he entered. She spun around and started to speak but Jack cut her off.

"Just give me a second. I gotta see what they want up front," he said, while not quite sure why Wanda was there.

He held the receiver to his ear and punched line two. "Yeah, Jack here," he said while letting his eyes embark on a visual journey over Wanda's shapely form.

Wanda turned to engage him with a sudden movement of her head, as if she sensed him looking at her.

Too late to escape detection, he averted his eyes, wondering if she had caught him staring.

"You have a visitor," came Sally's reply from the other end of the line.

"Yes, Sally." He paused. Glancing down at his desk, he noticed a new stack of work orders and shook his head. "She's in my office right now."

"She said she knew you and it was important, so I let her through." Sally's voice was flat.

"It's all right," Jack replied while smiling at Wanda. "Thanks, Sally."

"Yup." She disconnected.

Jack hung up the phone. There was a certain look of purpose about Wanda today that he couldn't quite identify. He stared at her for a moment, still without any notion why she was there.

"You ready?" she asked, her eyebrows rising in expectation. Her eyes traversed his frame from head to toe. "You going like that?"

Jack's face contracted in puzzlement while he shook his head. "Going where, like what?"

"You going to the school looking like that?" She extended an open hand. "Look at you, all greasy and nasty. You ain't riding in my car like that." Wanda's voice rose in protest.

Jack turned his hands over and inspected his greasy arms and fingers. A quick look at his clothes revealed more grease on his pants and shirt. "The school?"

"Yes, the school." Wanda leaned forward. "For Donna's testing. It's today. That college professor is meeting us there. Come on. We're gonna be late if you don't—"

"Oh, shit!" Jack's palm slapped his forehead. "That's today?" He pushed aside stacks of papers to review his desktop planner. "Oh, hell. I completely forgot about it."

"Never mind your sorry-ass excuses. Just wash that grease off and let's get over there before they start without us."

"Wanda, I'm up to my ass in alligators." He rifled through the stack of work orders, conducting a mental triage of the tasks at hand. "I've got eighty-eight mold machines to keep running and two hundred and fifty people to keep busy."

"You also got a daughter they trying to keep out of the schools, Jack." Wanda stood and pointed at the door. "Now, we're going down to that school and make sure that girl gets a fair shot."

She held his gaze for a long moment. Jack knew she was right.

"I'll change my shirt and wash up." He placed the work orders back down on the desk. "I think this place can run without me for—"

The phone rang.

Jack grabbed a pen and jotted a reminder on the note pad sitting on top of his desk. There were already four pages of items on his list. What was one more?

"You don't happen to have a spare hydraulic unit in your car do you?" he said to Wanda, his lips parting easily into a playful grin.

"Yeah, but you can't have it." Wanda smiled. The skin around her high cheekbones slid upward, compressing against her eyebrows, forming slight wrinkles where they met.

Jack finished writing the note. He threw his pen down and stood straight. "Okay, let's get going before anyone else—"

A short stocky black man covered in grease burst through the door.

"Blow back on number forty-four. It's an awful mess," he blurted. "Ma'am." He nodded at Wanda.

"How bad is it?" Jack questioned.

The young man was in his early twenties. His left forearm was missing. "It's pretty bad. Plastic's backed up for 'bout two feet along the barrel. Startin' to smoke some."

Jack looked at Wanda and then at his watch. "Tell Pete and Eddie to get the girls away from the press. That stuff'll outgass cyanide."

"I'm on it." He left in a rush.

Jack turned back toward Wanda. "I think we'd better sneak out now, or we'll never leave."

*   *   *

Ed Martin was already flirting with Doctor Westlake when Jack and Wanda arrived at the school.

"They don't make 'em like this any more, my dear." Margaret Westlake leaned away from his booming voice. Ed Martin motioned with his hand in a wide arc around the large office area. "Depression era make-work projects. Spared no expense and used only the finest materials. This place'll be here for five hun'erd years."

Ed Martin turned to greet Jack. "Well, here he is now." He extended his hand while never acknowledging Wanda, standing at Jack's side.

Jack shook hands; noticing Mavis's nod at Wanda behind Ed's back. "I'm sorry we're late. We had some last minute—"

"Think nothing of it," Ed Martin replied. "We're still waiting on the translator, anyway. I was just telling..." Ed Martin placed a hand flat against his chest. "May I call you Margaret?"

"Perhaps we should keep this on a purely prof—"

"I was just telling Margaret about the construction materials used in the—" He abruptly turned to face the door as they heard someone enter. "There she is. Come in." Ed Martin motioned toward the petite Asian woman.

"Hello." The woman reached out with a tiny hand, still

holding open the heavy door. "I am Ling. I am here to translate."

Mavis glanced momentarily at Ling before turning away, shaking her head.

"Yes, that's right," Ed Martin provided. "Come in. Come right in," he added, opening the door a little wider.

Ling glanced at Jack and then at Ed Martin. "Is she ready for me?"

Ed Martin looked up at the ceiling and then off to his left. "Well, now that depends on what you mean by ready."

"Depends?" Jack drew his eyebrows together. "On what?"

"Well, now I wanna go over what it is you plan to do with this child, Dr. Westfall." He folded his arms and stroked his chin.

"Westlake. We went over this on the phone last week."

"I know we discussed it, but I just wanna be sure about some things."

"What things?" Margaret set her briefcase on the counter.

Ed Martin craned his neck before leveling his eyes on Margaret. "I don't believe this child belongs in a classroom. And I don't believe that mainstreaming this girl is gonna do anyone any good."

"Mr. Martin, I'm here to do an eva—"

"She'll be a disruptive element in our school." His jovial demeanor had been replaced by one of distinct gravity. "I don't intend for some liberal-minded academic type to tell me how I gotta put the likes of her into my classrooms." His face was turning red.

"The likes of her?" Wanda said, just loud enough for Jack to hear. She took a step toward Ed Martin. Jack caught her arm and stopped her.

"Mr. Martin, no one is trying to—'

"Now, I agreed to let you come down here." Ed Martin

shook his finger in her face. "But I don't have to change the way I run my school because someone thinks they know better than me."

"I'm sure you don't."

Mavis handed Ed Martin a skeleton key. It had a paper tag attached to it with a string. The words, '*Special Ed*', were written on the tag.

"Well then, we can go see her if you like." He straightened his tie and wiped several beads of sweat from his expansive brow while extending his hand, its palm facing upward, toward the door.

Their footsteps echoed up and down the huge corridors as they walked. Along the high, arched ceilings of the vast hallways hung glass-trimmed chandeliers, gently swinging in the warm breezes blowing through the building. The walls were lined with off-white tiles to a height of about four feet. The rest were textured plaster that climbed to the top of the high, rounded ceiling of the hallways.

Jack glanced inside the classrooms through the clear glass windows as they passed each doorway. Within them he saw children, seated in neatly arranged rows, learning to read, write, do long division, spell, and multiply numbers. In one room children were learning about the fall of Rome. In the very next room others were discovering the workings of the brain. In yet another room a film projector flickered in the darkness. A production of Hamlet danced against the whitewashed interior of the sturdy old building.

"Few sights give me more pleasure than that of children learning," Ed Martin offered while passing one of the doorways.

"The pursuit of knowledge is neither a privilege nor a gift," Margaret replied.

"Beg your pardon." Ed Martin cocked his head toward Doctor Westlake as he walked.

"In our country, it is a right," Margaret Westlake shot back.

"No one should ever be denied that right. Not even the people who have the most trouble acquiring it. I have devoted my life to making sure that every child can exercise that right."

"That's why I've consented to let her sit in on a first grade class for a few days," Ed Martin responded. "But, by the looks of things, I don't believe this is the right place for this child."

"Yes, well," Margaret said, casting Ed Martin a wary look. "Let's just see how she does with a few tests I have devised that remove language as a possible barrier."

"I still think we're just wasting our time." He stopped in front of the stairwell and gestured for the group to go up the stairs.

Margaret smiled politely and motioned for him to go first. She started climbing the steps beside him.

"You mentioned that you don't want any disruptions from her," Jack called after Ed Martin. "Has that been a problem in the last few days?"

Ed Martin pulled a white handkerchief from his back pocket and wiped his forehead. "She's a distraction to the other students. She can't do the work, she doesn't understand what's going on and the other children shouldn't have to share their teacher with someone who's never gonna' learn anything."

"Has she been given an IQ test?" Margaret asked.

Ed Martin laughed. "Yes. At least, we tried to. The child can't even talk or understand a word being said to her."

"She may not speak English," Margaret Westlake said.

Ed Martin looked down on her with a condescending countenance. "My dear woman," he began. "We used an interpreter." He motioned toward the diminutive Asian woman accompanying them up the stairs. "It made no difference. The child just sat there and stared."

Jack's gaze followed Ed Martin up the stairs. The overstuffed principal of the Middleton Elementary School wheezed and puffed loudly as he struggled to climb the long flight. Ed Martin motioned for them all to stop as they reached the landing that was the mid-point of their ascent. Jack watched him fight for every breath and wondered how often he had tortured himself by attempting the journey to the second floor. After a few moments he caught his wind long enough to speak.

"We may not be university professors here Doctor Westfield." Ed Martin tipped his head back and looked down his nose at Margaret. "But we're not completely ignorant."

"I wasn't implying—"

"You didn't have to," Ed Martin said, reaching for the railing and taking the first steps up the next flight to the second floor. "We sent for an interpreter to translate, but we still got nowhere with her."

"How has she been a disruption?" Jack asked, unsure if he should grab Ed's arm and help him along or just pretend he didn't notice that the man was about to collapse from exhaustion. A strange thought suddenly struck Jack. If Ed did start falling over, could he keep him from rolling down the stairs? He stifled a chuckle while contemplating the imagery of his rotund form tumbling down the stairwell, arms flailing and legs kicking.

Ed Martin heaved his leg up and forward onto the second floor. "She keeps wandering off to the library," he said between heavy breaths. "We can't have her bothering the other children who are trying to learn."

"Maybe she's just curious," Jack replied.

Wanda followed the group, silent for the moment.

They turned a corner and began walking down a corridor that ended at two oak double doors, each with an exquisite mosaic of stained glass. Beneath the windows was a sign indicating that they were entering the Library. They walked between massive shelves of books, heading for the far end of the stack room where they stopped in front of a plain wooden door. Ed Martin inserted the key and opened it.   ·

As the door swung open they saw Donna, wearing a simple cotton sundress with a yellow and green floral pattern, seated at a large table surrounded by four wooden chairs. The lights were off, but a shaft of sunlight split the room from a slit in the curtain covering a large window. Jack noticed right away that the heat in the room rivaled that of the shop floor in the plant. Strands of Donna's auburn hair stuck to her face and forehead in wet clumps. The rest was pulled pack into a ponytail and secured by a piece of bright red cloth, tied into a bow. Her moistened skin was dark and smooth. It shined like the surface of a polished statue.

Jack watched as Margaret pulled a chair close to Donna. "Hello," she began. "My name is Margaret Westlake."

"*Nihou*," Ling injected. "*Wo jiao* Margaret Westlake."

If he had glanced at her just a split second later, Jack would not have seen the contempt in Donna's eyes when the interpreter began speaking. A smile flashed across his face as he realized his adopted daughter had been holding out. He could barely contain a laugh when it hit him that she had just been betrayed by her own intelligence. It was so subtle, yet so profound. A simple look of disgust; the barely perceptible tightening of the eyebrows together in a gesture of recognition had told Jack everything he needed to know about Donna Christine Roberts.

Margaret leaned close to Donna and whispered just loud enough for Jack and Donna to hear, "Do you remember me?"

Donna stared straight ahead; her eyes fixed on the opposite wall offering no acknowledgement.

Margaret leaned back. "What's your name?" she asked Donna.

"*Ni jiao shenme?*" the interpreter followed.

"Can we open a window?" Margaret motioned to Ed Martin. He complied only after giving her a quick look of indignation. With a heavy sigh, he hauled himself over to the window. Brightness filled the room as he pulled open the curtains. But the window refused to open in spite of all the grunting and heaving.

"You must be very hot in here. We're going to open the window and let some breeze in."

"Here, let me try," Jack said, pulling back the curtain and lifting the heavy window.

"May I ask you some questions?" Margaret opened her brief case and took out some file folders and put them on the table in front of her. "Would that be okay with you?" The interpreter translated, once again.

Donna offered no reaction.

"It's a shame really," Ed Martin said, pulling out a chair and sitting along the wall. "Poor child like this not having any ability to communicate or understand anybody... Tragic, just tragic."

"Why is she locked in this room like this?" Margaret asked.

"Like I said, she likes to wander." Ed moved his hand in a circular motion toward the door. "The librarian caught her a few times out in the library, lookin' at books and such."

Margaret glanced back at Ed Martin out of the corners of her eyes and then again at Donna.

"Donna, I'm going to ask you to do something for me. We're going to play a little game." Margaret produced a small cloth sack from her case and dumped the contents, several dozen dice-sized cubes, onto the table. "I'm going to do things with these blocks and I want you to follow my directions. Okay?"

She placed a block on the table and put two more blocks together right next to it.

"Okay, Donna. Here is one block." She pointed to it. "Then there are two blocks," she continued, pointing at the other two. "How many blocks will there be in the next group?"

For the first time since they entered the room, Jack noticed Donna's eyes breaking out of their vacant stare and locking onto Margaret's. *Such beautiful eyes.* Awash in green, blue, and brown, they were vivid and alive.

Donna reached out and picked up a block from the pile and set it beside the others. In the middle between the single blocks were the two that Margaret had placed there, one then two, then one.

"See what I mean?" Ed Martin shook his head. "Dumb as a fence post."

Jack glanced at Wanda; the muscles in her face tightening. She looked like a cat ready to pounce.

"I'm gonna knock this man into next week he don't stop talking 'bout her like that," Wanda whispered to Jack.

"Relax." Jack glanced first at Wanda, then at Margaret and then at the interpreter. "He might have pulled this off except for one thing."

"Pulled what off?" Wanda replied.

"I know what's going on." Jack smiled and nodded toward Donna. "And so does she."

"What in the *hell* are you talking about?" Wanda whispered, leaning close to Jack.

"Stay calm," he replied with a reassuring touch on her arm. "Just let this play out."

"Can you think of another answer for this?" Margaret asked, pointing at the small cubes.

After a short pause, Donna reached out and picked up another block and placed it on top of the one she laid down a few moments before.

Ed Martin let out a long, heavy sigh and put his foot up on another chair. "This is a complete waste of time," he said. "You came all the way down here to play blocks with a retarded girl. I could have saved you the trip Dr. Westfield."

After another brief pause Donna picked up two more blocks and placed them with the two she had stacked. There were now four in the group she had made. Then she reached out with both hands and pulled the rest of the blocks toward her, selecting eight of them and stacking them together in a fourth pile.

Ed Martin let out a hearty laugh. "How much more of this you wanna see? This child belongs in a home."

Wanda's arm flexed under Jack's hand.

Margaret studied the group of blocks. Her eyes met Donna's, in a long exchange. "What are you trying to tell me? What don't I see?"

Donna reached out and put two blocks into a fifth group. Then she took the remaining block and held it between her thumb and forefinger, displaying it for Margaret.

"What?" Margaret had become the student. "What are you showing me?"

"Oh, come on now..." Ed Martin grumbled from across the room. "You don't actually think she's trying to tell you something do you? Good Lord, I've seen 'bout everything now. Mavis is gonna just love this one."

Margaret continued staring at the five groups of blocks on the table and then at the one Donna held in her hand. "I don't get it. What is it?"

One, two, four, eight, two and a block. Jack stared at the formation on the table until he felt a chill ascend his spine in spite of the late morning heat. "Jesus," he blurted.

"What...what?" Ed Martin was startled from his near slumber.

"I see it," Margaret replied, gently taking the block from

Donna's delicate fingers. "One, two, four, eight, two and a cube. Is that what you want me to see? Is that it?"

Donna locked her gaze with Margaret's for a long few seconds before disconnecting and once again staring blankly off into space.

"It's a geometric progression," Margaret said, slowly turning the block in her hand.

Ed Martin sat up straight in his chair. "How in the world do you get that from a bunch of—"

"Shut up." Margaret turned and glared at Ed Martin. "Shut your miserable, sorry mouth."

"Now see here—"

"No." Margaret stood, pointing at him with her finger. "*You* see here!"

"I don't have to sit here and listen—"

"Yes," she moved closer, "you do. This girl is not retarded. She's not even a little bit slow. In fact, she's probably smarter than the two of us put together. Not that you add much to the score!"

"What are you talking about?" Wanda piped in, glancing from Margaret to Jack.

"I'm talking about this pattern." Margaret pointed at the blocks on the table. "One. Double it. Two. Double it again. Four. Double it again. Eight. Cube root of eight...Two. The block represented a cube. Math and vocabulary all in one answer. She was way ahead of both of us."

Ed Martin smiled and slumped in his chair. "I really don't think—"

"No," Margaret cut him off. "That much is apparent."

"Now, see here." Ed Martin stood, indignant.

Jack spun in his chair and stood to face Ed Martin. "I've had about enough out of you," he said, sticking a rigid finger into Ed's sternum.

"Yes, well…" Ed Martin stepped back, rubbing his chest. "What I meant was…"

"Just what the hell were you trying to pull here?" Jack advanced on Ed, his finger back in his chest.

"I have no idea what you mean," Ed replied. "And you would be wise to remove your finger from my person, sir."

Jack chuckled. "You might have gotten away with it, but you didn't count on one thing." He slowly lowered his finger. "I know enough Vietnamese to know that she wasn't speaking it." He nodded toward the interpreter.

"Vietnamese?" Ling replied. "I speak Chinese." She turned to Ed Martin. "You said I would translate Chinese."

Ed Martin stood staring like a child who had just been caught in a lie.

"You should be ashamed of the way you've handled this girl's case," Margaret said. "You're a disgrace to education."

"Really now, Margaret," Ed Martin replied.

"And it's Westlake…Doctor Westlake," she countered. "Not Westfield, Westgate or Westfall… It's Westlake. Got it?"

Chapter Nineteen

A week later, Donna was enrolled in school; placed into the first grade without the benefit of a tutor. It was up to Jack to provide the necessary supplemental education to catch her up to the rest of the children her age. As it turned out, that didn't take very long. Although she would still not speak, Donna did respond to instructions and breezed through her assignments with ease. By mid-October she had already mastered most the normal first grade curriculum for the first half of the year.

Ed Martin, while still against Donna's enrollment, acquiesced to her promotion to second grade in January. After his foiled attempt to influence Donna's evaluation by using a Chinese interpreter, the principal of Middleton Elementary School had maintained a fairly low profile where Donna was concerned. Jack's rigid index finger jammed into his chest may well have sealed the deal between the two men.

Or, so Jack thought.

Late one Saturday afternoon in early November, Jack, Wanda, and Donna drove into Middleton to pick up some groceries and exterior house paint.

"Daddy really appreciates you helping us paint the porch," Wanda said to Jack as they were getting out of his car.

"I figure I've spent enough time on it," Jack replied. "It's time for me to help keep it up."

"Let's get the groceries first," Wanda said, pointing toward the small store in the middle of town. "Sally leaves in ten minutes and she always gives Donna a cookie when we in there."

Jack nodded in agreement and the odd-lot trio made their way along the sidewalk among the turning heads and pointing fingers.

"Let's split up," Wanda said, tearing the short list of items in half. "I'll take Donna with me. We can meet at the check-out when we're done."

"Fine with me." Jack snapped up the torn piece of paper.

Even though he was in a small country grocery store, it seemed to Jack like he was searching for obscure commodities in a fifty-acre warehouse. A little self-conscious, Jack smiled at an elderly woman who was no doubt feeling great delight at the sight of the uninitiated young man stumbling his way through the store.

Where the hell is the flour? Jack scanned the signs hanging from the ceiling above each aisle. As he approached the end of one of them, he heard some women talking. There were three of them, young white mothers he recognized from Donna's class. They stood with their backs to him, their carts parked in a semi-circle.

Jack stopped and listened.

"Well," one of them, a slender brunette began. "I just don't see how she can just skip right over the rest of first grade like that."

"She's eight years old, for God's sake," another chimed in. She wore tight plaid pants and a green jacket. "I don't want a girl that age in with my Nancy."

"Emily's worried that oriental girl might try to get into Brownies," the third, a plump woman with glasses added.

"Oh, don't worry 'bout that Alice," the brunette said. "I've already got the end run going on that one. That'll never happen."

In light of the unfolding discussion, the best Jack could do was enjoy the shocked looks on their faces as he strolled past.

"Ladies," he said, tipping his head ever so slightly.

Jack eventually found the staples on his list and headed for the front of the store. He heard Wanda, unseen on the other side of the store shelves, talking with a man as he approached.

"You don't know nothin' about it," Wanda said, her tone sounding defensive.

"I know you living with that cracker and keepin' that little freak in your house," the male voice replied.

"It ain't like that," Wanda replied.

"That's what it look like to me."

Jack turned the corner to see a well-built young black man standing with his back to him, facing Wanda.

"What daddy and I do with our house is our own damn business." Wanda's eyes widened as she noticed Jack approaching.

"So," the young man replied. "You his bitch, then?"

"Everything okay, here?" Jack glanced down at Donna and then up at Wanda.

"Everything's just fine," the young man said, his eyes engaging Jack's with a cold stare. "I was just leavin'." He ran a glance up and down Jack's body before bumping him as he walked past. "Say hello to your ol' Uncle Tom for me," he said over his shoulder as he sauntered away.

"Nice guy." Jack motioned with his head toward the man.

Wanda made no reply, only stood staring at the doorway as the man left the store.

Murphy's Hardware was located on the ground floor of a two-story, white brick building in downtown Middleton. Rakes, shovels, hoes, and a host of garden tools spilled out from the doorway onto the sidewalk in both directions. Power saws, chain saws, and various other power tools sat displayed on miniature shelves behind large plate glass windows that flanked the entrance to the store.

Jack glanced around at the pedestrians, many of whom turned their heads and stared as the trio entered the store.

"Can I hep ya?" a flat voice addressed them from behind a long wooden counter at the back of the store. Two elderly men in Carhart overalls leaned against the counter drinking coffee.

"We need a few gallons of enamel paint," Jack replied, pulling a piece of paper from his flannel shirt. "Let's see," he added while unfolding the list. "Three gallons of floor enamel and two exterior."

"What color?" A skinny man with beady eyes rose up from a stool. His face was expressionless.

The man looked familiar. Jack tried to place him as he drew closer.

"Grey for the floor," Wanda said. "White for the posts and rails."

"I figured you'd want black and yeller." The man behind the counter narrowed his eyes while offering a disgusted look.

Wanda nudged Jack in the ribs and nodded at the man while holding Jack's gaze. "That's one of them guys from the parade," Wanda whispered as the counter clerk turned to retrieve a paint guide.

Before Jack could respond, another man appeared from the back room. He was big, wearing bib overalls and carrying several boxes of nails. He set the boxes on the counter.

"What time Bubba say he was comin' fer these?" The big man said to the counter clerk.

Jack recognized the man from the parade; the same man he had put to sleep in the park.

"We got customers, Earl," the skinny man offered with a nod.

Earl looked up. His expression changed from curiosity to recognition. "Well, lookey here, Boo," Earl said to his emaciated friend. "We're gonna have to be more careful 'bout keeping the trash outa' here from now on."

"Who you callin' trash?" Wanda stepped forward.

The two other patrons in the store turned and stared.

"Look," Jack said, stepping in front of Wanda. "We just need some paint. We don't want any trouble."

"Oh, you already got trouble," Earl replied, grabbing up a two foot section of hardwood railing from behind the counter. "I'm fixin' to finish what we started a while back. But, this time you ain't gonna be so lucky."

The two old men brushed Jack's sleeve on their way outside, the door slamming shut in their wake. Boo took a few tentative steps from behind the counter toward a long shelf of paint cans.

"Now, Earl," Boo began, still keeping his eye on Jack as he walked. "Maybe this ain't the best time to settle this." He cast his big friend a mischievous look. "There's plenty of time to do things in a proper way." The little man laughed.

Earl grinned and broke into laughter along with Boo. "Yeah, Boo," Earl said, setting the club down on the counter. "You're right. There's a time and a place for everything. That's what the good book says, don't it?"

"Don't you blaspheme Earl Conroy!" Wanda shot back. "How dare you?"

"You know this guy?" Jack asked Wanda, his hand motioning toward his hulking form.

"Everybody know him." Wanda turned her head in disgust.

Earl smiled at Wanda and made a kissing sound. "Aww..." he said. "Missed me Wanda?"

Jack turned to Wanda in disbelief. But, she would not return his look. She stared instead back at Earl, the muscles in her face taught with rage.

"We'll have to do that again, sometime," Earl continued. "A man can get hooked on that dark meat. Right, Boo?"

Wanda lunged. Jack caught her by the back of her coat and spun her around just as Earl took a swipe at them both. He found Donna's arm and pulled them all toward the door while watching Earl carefully.

"Another time, army man!" Earl called out to Jack as the door closed behind them. "Another time!"

"What was he talking about back there?" Jack asked, helping Donna into the back seat.

Wanda slid into the passenger seat without a word.

Jack slammed the door shut beside him. "What did he do to you?"

Wanda only sat staring straight ahead, the fury in her eyes yielding to the tears streaking down her face.

*   *   *

Two nights later Jack was awakened at just after three AM by the sound of breaking glass. He sat up and opened his eyes to see a bright orange glow reflected on the wall opposite the bed. Rising to look out the window, Jack saw several hooded men standing around a burning cross in the tiny front yard.

"Stay in the house," he said to Wanda and her father on his way out the front door.

"I got your back, son," Marvin Wilkins said to Jack, holding a shotgun in his huge weathered hands. "You be careful, Jack. These boys ain't here to pay a social call."

Jack paused a moment as Wanda's hand clasped his arm.

"Don't go out there." Her eyes pleaded with him. "They'll just make some noise and go away."

"They're not gonna go away or give up." Jack took her hand in his. "Better to end this right now." He glanced down to see Donna's big eyes staring up at him. "Stay with Wanda," he said to Donna, patting her head before stepping onto the porch.

Jack counted eight figures in the front yard, looking like oversized ghosts in their white sheets and pointed hoods. The blazing cross illuminated the scene with a bright orange hue. He felt the heat on his face as he crossed the small patch of grass toward the men. Most of the figures before him were nondescript, potbellied forms with jean-clad legs and badly scuffed shit-kickers sticking out the bottoms of their 'uniforms'. But one form caught his eye, bigger than the rest with a distinctive slump.

Ed Martin. Fuckin' bastard.

"Jack Roberts?" a voice called from beneath one of the hoods.

Jack spun to answer. "Yeah," he said, coming about. He caught the stare of a man whose voice he did not recognize, his eyes orange-red with the reflected flames. "What do you want?"

"We want you," the unidentified man replied, "and that little gook animal to find another town to live in. Far away from here."

"Is that so?" Jack answered. He took a step closer to the man. "And by whose authority would you be making such a request?"

The man took a step toward Jack, glancing at his accomplices first for apparent reassurance. "This is not open to debate," he said, standing with his hands behind his back.

Jack glanced back at the house before taking another step toward the man. "We like it here." He stopped within reach of the man. "No thank you. We're staying right here."

"You do that," the muffled voice replied. "Live with the niggers. Just keep that filthy animal out of our schools."

Jack turned slowly to look at Ed Martin. The sluggish oaf shuffled his feet and looked at the ground. Jack smiled and shook his head as he turned back toward the assumed leader. As he was coming about, he saw the man swinging at him with an axe handle. Another man might have acted on instinct and pulled back, into the path of the business end. Jack's years of hand-to-hand combat training and martial arts mastery prevailed. Jumping into the swinging arms, he cut off the strike and diverted its energy into a perfectly executed throw. Jack twisted the axe handle from the man's hands as the hapless Klansman was sent airborne across the yard, landing with an agonizing thud near the front porch.

Gripping the handle firmly, Jack turned to engage the next hooded man who was fast approaching from behind. Faking a swing to the head, he slid his hands apart and held it like a rifle at waist level. With one quick thrust, Jack jammed the handle into the gut of his assailant, dropping him to the ground.

Coming about for another round, Jack was stopped in his tracks by a loud blast. He turned his head to see a stocky figure holding a sawed-off, double-barrel shotgun. Smoke curled in a lazy billow from one of the barrels, which from Jack's vantage looked as big as two drainpipes.

"What you gonna do now, army man?" the big man said.

"Hello, Earl," Jack replied, slapping the axe handle into his palm. "Back for more, I see."

"You just drop that right there, army man," Earl demanded. "Nice and slow." He nodded toward a place to Jack's left. "Over there."

"Let's settle this right here," Jack said, tossing the handle at Earl's feet. "Right now, you chicken-shit coward." He stepped closer, advancing in the face of Earl's raised weapon.

"That's close enough," Earl protested, bringing the gun to bear on Jack's stomach.

"You think this scares me?" Jack said, stepping into the shotgun. It pressed against his hard stomach. "This ain't nothin'," he said in a low voice. "I've been in shit storms you wouldn't believe." He stared into the hood, meeting Earl's faltering gaze. "You got one shot, you fat fucking slob." Jack clenched his fists. "You better hope you kill me with it."

It was the adrenaline talking. Jack's heart was beating so fast he could hardly breathe. His peripheral vision was gone. The only thing that existed at that moment was the trembling redneck with a loaded shotgun aimed at his belly.

In that instant Jack sensed weakness in his opponent. He knew it was the point when Earl would be the most vulnerable, and at the same time the most dangerous because Earl had sensed it too. Before Earl's fear drove him to pull the trigger, Jack snatched the abbreviated barrels of the shotgun and twisted it away. The gun easily slipped from Earl's hand.

Earl tried to back away but Jack tripped him, grabbing Earl's throat as the big man hit the ground.

"You listen to me," Jack said through clenched teeth as he knelt beside him. "You listen good."

Earl nodded weakly, suddenly appearing like a scared infant in Jack's grasp.

"Those are my girls in there." Jack nodded toward the house. "I care about what happens to them." He grabbed a handful of sheet and twisted his knuckles into Earl's ribs.

Earl winced.

Jack glanced around. Several men helped the two men Jack had tussled with to their feet. They stood watching him, unsure what to do.

"Here's how it is," Jack continued. "Either one of them

is harmed in any way, I'm coming for you." He twisted his fist, raking his knuckles against Earl's already bruised ribs. "If Wanda trips on the stairs and breaks her ankle, I'm coming for you. If Donna gets a sliver in her hand, I'm coming for you. Am I making sense, here?"

Earl nodded, his eyes wide with understanding.

"My little girl so much as catches a cold and you better leave town for a week." Jack ground his fist hard.

Earl grunted in pain.

"And," Jack leaned in close, "I don't know what you did to Wanda, but I can guess." He released the sheet and grabbed a handful of Earl's balls and squeezed hard.

Earl screamed in protest.

Jack let go and waited for Earl to somewhat recover. "If you ever touch either of them in that way, I swear to God I will beat you to death with my bare hands."

"That's enough." The leader was back, probably from his truck. This time he held a revolver at Jack's head. "Get off him."

Jack felt the cool circle of steel against his temple and then the unmistakable sound of the hammer being cocked.

"I'd think twice about that," Marvin bellowed from the porch, accentuating his remark with a pump of his shotgun.

"You drop that gun, nigger," the leader said.

"I don't think so," Marvin replied, standing his ground.

"I'll kill him," the leader offered, nodding. "Sure as hell and damnation. I'll do it."

"Go ahead," Marvin answered. "Be the last thing you ever do," he said, taking aim at the man. "Now this has gone far enough, Billy Ray. You made your point and said your piece. Now how 'bout we call it a night 'fore somebody gets hurt?"

Jack let his eyes wander among the men standing around him. The events taking place seemed to unfold in slow motion, the sound of their voices fading and distant. Through the tension and commotion Jack's eyes met those of a man who stood a few feet back from the rest. He had remained silent throughout and had not jumped into the earlier fray. A quick scan revealed the reason why he looked so familiar. Jack stared at the pair of custom-made snakeskin boots, the stars captured by the silver rings on the sides shimmering in the firelight.

"This ain't over," Billy Ray, the leader said, pulling the revolver away from Jack's head. "Not by a long shot."

Before Jack could answer, the stillness of the night was shattered by a series of gunshots. While they were quite loud, they were not shotgun blasts.

Men in sheets scattered in all directions as dirt flew up in clods and shot after shot echoed off the nearby river bluffs into the night. Jack turned toward the house, from where the shots were being fired to see Donna standing on the porch. In her hand she held Jack's service forty-five, bright orange flames bursting forth with every shot, its polished chrome finish reflecting the single porch light.

Chapter Twenty

"It's a risky procedure," Doctor Haskins said. He was a handsome man with silver hair. Peering over the top of his wire-rimmed glasses, he continued. "I want you to understand that."

"But, there is a chance it could work?" Brad asked, leaning forward in his chair. "I mean," he looked at Donna and then at Doctor Haskins. "She could come out of this okay, right?"

Donna sat silently in the office. A set of bookshelves, overflowing with medical volumes framed the doctor's head as he sat back in his leather chair, his fingers steepled in front of his lips. On the wood-paneled walls hung a half-dozen diplomas and certificates from some of the most prestigious medical institutions in the country.

Their quest for Donna's treatment had brought them face to face with Vanderbilt University Medical Center's best neurologist. They had driven to Nashville the day before and spent the night in a nearby hotel.

Doctor Haskins removed his glasses and leaned forward on his elbows. His expression turned grave. "If you go through with this," he began, alternating glances between Brad and Donna. "There is a chance you will fully recover after the surgery."

"And if I don't fully recover?" Donna asked, already knowing most of the answers.

"The enlargement is in a tricky place." Doctor Haskins dropped his glance for an instant before continuing. "Doctor Graff may encounter difficulties and damage some brain tissue in the region." He took in a deep breath and momentarily looked at the ceiling. "You may experience speech difficulties, vision loss, impaired motor function, loss of cognitive—"

"But, she could pull through, okay…" Brad's expression took on the quality of a five-year-old desperate for good news about his pet dog after being hit by a car. "Right, Doc? I mean, this stuff doesn't have to happen. Right?"

"You need to understand what I'm saying," Doctor Haskins replied.

But, Donna already did. Her mind reeled at the prospects of staring blankly from her wheelchair with drool running from her chin.

"There is a better than even chance that she won't survive the surgery." The doctor paused a moment for Brad to take it in. "And if she does make it through, she may not be the person you know now."

Brad dropped his head into his hands.

Donna reached for him, placing a delicate hand on his back.

"If we decide to proceed," Donna said. "When can we begin?"

"I consulted with Doctor Graff this morning." Doctor Haskins slipped his glasses back on and checked his desk calendar. "He would like to schedule you next Thursday at the University of Pennsylvania Medical Center in Philadelphia. He's the best there is in this field. If anyone can do this, he can." Doctor Haskins then stood up, signaling the end of their consult. "Let Debbie know your decision. We can set it up from there. Good luck in whatever you decide." He offered his hand.

"We'll keep looking," Brad said, stabbing the lobby button on the elevator with his index finger. "We've only been to three doctors. There's plenty more out there." The door closed. "We're just getting started. Maybe we can go to Atlanta or Chicago." Brad spun and shot Donna an excited glance. "What about that place in Minnesota?" He snapped his fingers. "Something clinic…"

"Mayo," Donna replied, letting her eyes drift toward the floor. "Maybe we can try that."

"My cousin lives in Minneapolis. We can stay with her while we're there."

"The clinic is in Rochester." She looked at their reflections in the shiny surface of the elevator panel. "Two hours from there."

Two weeks prior they had sought a second opinion from a doctor in Knoxville. Today, they were in Nashville hoping for better news. No such luck. With an unwelcome resignation creeping into her thoughts, Donna fought the urge to cry. She watched Brad's reflection pacing the tiny floor thinking about what kind of wife she would have been; what kind of mother. She wanted so much to adopt a daughter. Would she posses even half the strength her mother had? Would her daughter have loved her as much as Donna loved her own mother? Donna would never know.

"Let's get something to eat," Brad offered, his voice flat.

"I'm really not hungry." Donna stared at her reflection. Her cheeks were hollow, her clothes a little baggy.

"Baby," Brad said, turning abruptly and taking her into his arms. "You need to eat. You skipped breakfast. I don't remember you eating much last night." He pulled her close. "You're wasting away. You need to stay strong." He kissed her forehead.

He was right. She had lost ten pounds in the last month, her lack of appetite a side effect of her condition.

The door opened and they walked across the lobby and out onto the Vanderbilt University campus.

"I have a surprise for you," Brad said, taking her by the elbow and gently guiding her across West End Avenue. "Last time I was down here I looked it up in the phone book and found where it was." They stepped onto the curb on the other side of the busy street. "I thought you might like a home-cooked meal."

Donna gave him a sideways glance. "What have you done?"

"Just go with the flow." Brad wrapped his big arm around her. In the face of her own demise it somehow offered her security knowing he was with her. She knew he could no more stop what was awaiting her any more than the doctors: Any number of doctors. But, for the moment she was happy just to feel his warmth and strength.

"Where are we going?" They had walked only a block away from West End.

"You'll see," Brad answered as they turned a corner. "There ya go," he said, raising an open hand toward a single story stucco building.

Donna looked up at the red and yellow sign over the door. It read *Ban Toi Vietnamese Restaurant*. She closed her eyes and smiled.

"You did this for me?" Donna said, slipping her arm into his.

Brad looked away and shrugged. "No big deal, really."

"That's why I love you," she said. "Everything is so effortless when it comes to us."

Once inside, they were seated and enjoyed healthy servings of *Chao tom* and *Gio lua* and the tastiest butter cake Donna had eaten in many years. For reasons she didn't question, Donna ate like a starving inmate. When they finished, Brad was standing at the counter near the door paying the check when Donna noticed an elderly Vietnamese woman staring at her.

"*Chào Bà,*" Donna offered. "Hello."

The old woman, her skin wrinkled into furrows on her brow, looked away in disgust. She mumbled, "*Bui doi,*" before disappearing into the kitchen.

Decades of hurt rushed forth. Donna reflexively looked down in shame.

"What did that old lady say to you?" Brad demanded while holding the door open.

"Nothing," she replied. "Just forget it." Donna turned away and wiped her eyes.

"Bullshit," he answered, turning her. "You're crying. What the hell did she say?"

"She called me *bui doi.*" She scanned the roofline of a nearby building. "Dust of life."

Brad laughed. "That's it? That's the big insult? Dust of life?"

Donna turned to him, fighting back the contempt for his lack of understanding. "It is one of the worst insults in our culture. It means lower than dirt. Worthless. A term specially reserved for mixed-race like me." Her thoughts were suddenly of Wanda and Marvin Wilkins. "Maybe you can relate better to another term. She basically called me a..." But, she could not say the word. "What some call blacks in this country."

Brad clenched his fists and turned toward the restaurant, looking as if he might actually storm into the building and beat the old woman senseless. "What the hell's her problem?"

"No culture is immune to prejudice." She gently took his arm and led him away. "She was taught to be that way. You will not change anything."

"Yeah?" Brad said, looking back as he walked away.

"She's damn lucky she's an old lady. Otherwise, I'd go back in there and kick her ass."

"She'd probably kick yours."

They walked west for a few blocks to Centennial Park. There they strolled along the paths beneath sprawling hardwood trees between small man-made ponds. In the center of the park stood an exact replica of the Parthenon in Athens as it looked before it was nearly leveled in 1687 by a Venetian cannonball lobbed from the Mediterranean Sea.

"Let's go inside," Brad suggested. "There's supposed to be a big-ass statue in there."

"Athena," Donna replied. "The goddess of war."

"I hear she's a babe."

"Let's find out."

They climbed a set of stairs and stopped at a small art gallery on the second floor before continuing on to a huge room lined with two tiers of massive columns nearly fifty feet high. The floor was an expanse of cut stone stretching up to a five-foot high marble base, upon which stood the forty-two foot statue of a beautiful woman clad in a white tunic. Staring straight ahead, she held a six-foot high statue of Nike, the winged goddess of victory, in the palm of her right hand. Her left hand supported a seventeen-foot shield and thirty-six foot spear. Her headdress, almost seven feet high, nearly touched the top of the ornate ceiling.

"Wow," Brad blurted, his mouth slightly agape. "She *is* a babe."

Donna's thoughts strayed back three decades to a place where Athena would have felt more at home. "Stunning."

"Strange how one so beautiful is associated with something so horrible," Brad said.

"Proving again that there really is nothing new under the sun."

"What do you mean?"

"Even back then, people were putting new faces on the ugliness trying to pass it off as something good. If someone so beautiful was on your side, how could you be wrong?" Donna started walking toward the statue. "Athena represented the civilized side of war." Images of ravaged villages and shattered lives raced through her mind. "It seems there were spin doctors even back in 400 BC."

They stood silently looking at the figure for several moments.

"I still want to marry you," Brad finally said. "I still want you to be my wife."

Donna turned to him. "What's the point?" She stood looking at him hoping he wouldn't disappoint her with his answer.

An elderly couple strolled by, nodding as they passed. Donna stared at them in sadness as they walked, arm in arm toward the massive statue. Part of her envied them for the long life they had apparently enjoyed together. Another part of her couldn't help despising them. Donna had been robbed of her childhood, cheated out of her pre-teen years and hustled so quickly through high school and college that there was no opportunity to savor the spoils of youth. As a young adult, her career had already blossomed and before she knew it she was in her mid-thirties and still single.

She stood before the only man she could ever imagine loving enough to marry and even that was being denied her. Yes, she envied them: for their long lives: for their strolls in the park in their old age: for just being together.

"The point?" Brad repeated. He broke away, glancing around the vast room. "I don't know," he continued, nodding toward a nearby bench. "I don't know how to explain without it sounding like you're some kind of trophy." Brad sat on the bench next to Donna. He took a deep breath before continuing. "Nothing's changed."

Donna let a burst of breath escape from her lips. "Nothing has changed?" She closed her eyes and shook her head. "I'm dying Brad. You have to face that. Our getting married will not change that."

Brad looked away. "I can't give in to that. If I do, it'll come true." Donna started to speak but he waved her off. "Don't," he said. "We can't give up. There's plenty more doctors we can see." He turned to her, engaging her with hope-filled eyes. "There's a cure out there somewhere. We just need to find it." Brad took her hand and kissed it. "Right?"

Donna stared into his eyes, the eyes of a child on Christmas Eve. "Sure," she replied, nodding and smiling. "We'll keep looking."

"Maybe this guy in Philly will give us a better shake." The smile suddenly left Brad's face as if he just discovered there really wasn't going to be a Santa Claus.

"You still have time to find someone who has a future."

Brad took in a deep breath. "Look at me."

Donna turned to him, her eyes filled with sadness.

"I'm Joe average," he began. "I swing a hammer on rooftops for a living. I'm not very good looking, I didn't finish my first year of college, and I'm not very smart."

"Yes, you are."

Brad shrugged off her comment. "I wake up every day scared to death that you'll come to your senses." He stroked the locks of hair resting on her shoulder. "You could have any guy you wanted and here you are with this guy who's the poster child for mediocrity."

"I don't see you that way."

"I know." He took her hand in his. "In every way you have made me feel like I'm important to you. Like I really matter."

"You do matter."

"Then, why wouldn't I want to get as much of that as I possibly could?" Brad slid his hand behind her neck, letting his fingers meander through the thick strands of her hair. "It's really very simple, Donna," he said, his tone even and serious. "It's all about me. I'm selfish and I'm crazy about you and I just want you to be my wife, for however long God allows. 'Cuz I love you like no man has ever loved a woman and I want to be with you for as long as I can."

Donna gazed into the eyes of her soul mate, feeling no trace of disappointment.

"When?" she asked.

"I'd do it today if we could," Brad answered. "All we need is a blood test and a judge."

So much for her big wedding, the big white dress, the bridesmaids, the church, and the walk down the aisle. But, then again, why should her wedding be any different than the rest of her life? There had been no rides on her daddy's shoulders. No Barbie dolls. No Sesame Street. No Captain Kangaroo. The closest thing she had had to a mother-daughter talk came from Wanda, who had agreed to pinch-hit for Jack when it came time to have "the talk".

"What's the matter?" Brad lifted her chin.

She shook her head. "Nothing."

"Donna," Brad countered, cupping her face in his big hands. "We don't have to—"

"It's supposed to be my turn," Donna interrupted, her tone grave. She pulled Brad's hands away from her face and turned away. "When is it going to be my turn?"

Brad slid his arms around her, hugging her from behind. She could feel his breath on her cheek as he closed around her. He did not answer. They sat together for a long moment.

"I don't want to die."

"I don't want you to."

They were silent for a while, Donna soaking Brad in.

"When I was a teenager," Donna continued. "I wondered what it would be like to have a mother." She rested a hand on Brad's arms, still wrapped around her chest. "I never had a Christmas morning with Santa. I was too old to believe by the time I arrived here."

"It's easy to think about the things we don't have," Brad said. "You could still be in Viet Nam."

He was right, again. As a girl, Donna had slipped through death's grasp on many occasions. In some ways, being brought to the US was a curse. Everyday there were reminders of the things she had missed; things she would never know.

There had been no first day of school pictures. No birthday parties, Santa, Easter Bunny or Tooth Fairy. She didn't hear bedtime stories, bake cookies with her mom, or play dolls with her girlfriends. Donna had missed it all. The war had not only cheated her of her childhood, it had also robbed her of her motherhood. Now a threat from within her own body would finally take her life and any hope of knowing the joy of raising her own family.

"Throughout my life," Donna began, a calm washing over her. "People have given themselves for me." She let her gaze drop to the floor. "My father gave up a promising career to bring me here. He was about to become a colonel and he tossed it aside for me. My mother…" Donna paused, the word caught in her throat. She looked away momentarily. "She gave everything she had for me to survive, including her life."

"What happened?" Brad slid closer, taking her hand. "How did she die?"

Donna dropped her head and began crying. "I can't talk about that now," she said, shaking her head.

Brad held her until she stopped crying.

"There were others along the way," Donna continued. "All helping me. I just wanted to give back. I can't have children. The North Vietnamese soldiers saw to that. But, I so much hoped to find a child, or children who needed someone to do for them what was done for me."

"You already have."

Donna looked at Brad and smiled.

"When I met you I was trying my best to destroy my life," Brad began, still holding her. "I drank too much, ran around too much," he continued, softly rubbing her back. "I was a mess. Then you came along. Just like that. One day you're just walking below and I kick a brush off the roof by accident. I have never done that in my life and haven't done it since." Brad paused a moment. "I sometimes think God sent you for me."

Donna laughed. "Give me a break." She looked at him and rolled her eyes, still wet with tears.

"It's true, Donna. Hell, I'm going to church now. I hardly drink at all any more. I give money to panhandlers, for God sake. All because of you."

"I wanted a family with you."

"And we will. We can still have that together." Brad pulled her close and kissed her head. "I want to marry you."

"I want to go home."

"Okay," Brad replied, starting to get up. "You wait here while I get the car."

"I mean I want to go home." Donna pulled away and looked him in the eye. "To my home, on our honeymoon. When I recover."

"Viet Nam?"

Donna simply nodded once.

Brad contemplated her request for a moment before answering, "You recover, and we'll go."

Brad and Donna left the Parthenon and walked the path

around Centennial Park before Brad left her near West End Avenue while he went for his car. While waiting for him to pick her up, she spotted two homeless men, one black and one white, slumped against a wall. They were laughing and trading hits on a bottle wrapped in a paper bag.

"Hey James," the white man said. "Look at the little hoochie momma!" he yelled, his eyes wide and crazed.

"Huuueey," James whaled before grabbing up the bag. "She's a pretty little thang, too." He raised the bottle and took a drink, the paper rustled against his gray whiskers. "How 'bout you come on over here and give us a little kiss," James continued and then made kissing sounds.

"I'm not sure my fiancé would understand that." Donna took a step toward the two men reclining in the grass. "What's your name?" she said to the white man. He was fair skinned with a heavy silver beard.

"Ronny," he replied, looking askance at James in apparent disbelief that Donna had even acknowledged them. "Ronny Markum." Ronny wore an old army jacket over a pair of badly worn jeans. His combat boots were worn through the soles.

"It's nice to meet you, Ronny," Donna continued, enjoying the surprised looks they both wore. "So, your friend is partial to Asian women?" Donna smiled at James.

"Ah, don't listen to him," Ronny answered. "He's got no manners where it comes to women."

"My name is Donna," she said, extending her hand. "Where are you from?"

Ronny stared at her hand as if it had been so long since someone had shaken his that he had forgotten what to do.

"Cleveland," Ronny answered, taking her hand and gently shaking it. "Cleveland, Ohio." He withdrew his hand and stared at it.

"And you?" She reached for James.

"Chicago," James answered. He shook her hand. She felt his warmth.

"Have you eaten today?" Donna asked, kneeling beside them.

"Yeah, we had the buffet down at the Marriott this morning," Ronny replied. The two men launched into a fit of laughter that ended with spasms of coughing.

"What's in the bag?" Donna asked, pointing.

"Nectar," James answered. He raised it to her. "Have a belt. It'll put hair on your chest."

They all laughed. Donna took up the bottle and took a swig and promptly coughed until her eyes watered.

Ronny and James laughed again while Donna recovered. "Is this what they drink in Chicago?" she finally managed.

"So, where you from little girl?" Ronny asked.

"Oak Ridge."

"I meant," Ronny's expression grew more serious. "Where ya from?" He nodded at her in a way she understood.

"A tiny village in the highlands," she said, handing James the bottle. "Near Khe Sanh."

"I thought so," Ronny said, sitting up and reaching for Donna's arm. He pulled her coat sleeve up to reveal a small brass bracelet on her wrist. "I thought I saw you wearing a 'Yard' bracelet. You a 'Yard?"

"My grandmother was Bru," Donna answered.

Ronny pulled up his own sleeve showing her a nearly identical bracelet on his own wrist. "I never take it off. Been on there since sixty-eight."

"Were you there?" Donna asked. "In Khe Sanh?"

Ronny nodded, his eyes suddenly looked sad. "Yeah, I was. Got there just before the siege. Stayed another four months."

Brad pulled up nearby in his Trans Am and turned, staring at the boisterous vagabonds. "You all right, Donna?" he said, his neck muscles taut.

"Zat yer man?" the black man said, nodding toward the car.

"That's him," Donna replied, rising to her feet.

Ronny leaned forward and squinted at Brad. "He's a big som' bitch," he said and then turned to his friend. "Might take us both to kick *his* ass." With that, they both erupted in laughter. Ronny grabbed the bottle and took a long hit.

"Hey, go easy on that," James said. "I ain't had but a couple swallows."

"You are the biggest liar I ever met," Ronny countered. "You been hitting this thing all morning."

Before Donna left, she produced two ten-dollar bills. "Please," she said while handing each one a bill. "Get something to eat."

James reached out with a trembling hand, his eyes watery and tired. "Bless you," he said, taking the bill. "Bless you."

*   *   *

A week later Brad and Donna were in Philadelphia, at the University of Pennsylvania medical center. Donna was lying on a stretcher in the surgical holding area waiting to be prepped for surgery. Brad stood by her side holding her hand. Neither of them spoke in the awkward moments before the nurse came to take Donna away.

"I've had a week to think about this and I still don't know what to say," Brad finally said. "Nothing seems like it's enough."

"They gave me a sedative to calm me before surgery," Donna replied. Her breathing was still somewhat labored in spite of the medication. "I want to tell you something before the drugs take me away."

"No," Brad began. "I know what you're going to say and I don't want to hear it. I won't listen to it." He shook his head.

"Listen to me," she countered, squeezing his hand. "We may not get a chance to—"

"No," Brad shot back, looking away. "I'm not—"

"Listen to me!" Donna jerked his hand and glared up at him. "This may be the last conversation we ever have."

Brad's head snapped to, giving Donna his undivided attention.

Donna took in a deep, unsteady breath. "I might not come out of this as the same person you know." She covered his hand with her other hand. "I may not come out of this at all."

"Donna," Brad tried to interrupt. "You're going to come through this—"

"Shut up and listen to me!" Donna almost sat upright. After a moment she settled back on the stretcher and took another deep breath. "In case I don't make it through," she continued, her eyes freezing Brad where he stood. "I want you to know that my time with you has been a blessing and I love you more than you could ever know."

"You're gonna make it," Brad answered. "You have to. I can't imagine my life without you."

"Other than my father," Donna went on. "No other man has ever made me this happy." Donna nodded. "Make someone else as happy as you have made me." She squeezed his hand. "Have children and be the kind of father I know you can be."

Brad looked down on her, tears welling in his eyes. "You better not leave me," he said, his voice trembling.

The two double doors swung open and a plump nurse in green scrubs walked into the staging area. "So, which one of you would be Donna C. Roberts?" the nurse cracked in a thick Irish brogue.

Brad looked in her direction and almost responded.

"She's the one who is scared out of her mind," Donna answered.

"Not to worry, darlin'," the nurse replied. "We do this kind of thing all the time." She set the chart on the stretcher. "By the way," the nurse continued. "I'm Rosemary. I'll be prepping you for surgery today." She ran her fingers through Donna's thick auburn hair that had been cropped to a three-inch length for the surgery. "We'll need to shave some of your hair, dear."

"It won't do me any good if we don't," Donna quipped.

"Always the wise-ass," Brad answered. He gazed down at her with a loving smile. "I kind of like the short hair look on you."

"Such a pretty lass," Rosemary said. "We'll have you up dancin' a jig in no time." She gave Donna a reassuring pat on the arm. "We need to get you ready, dear."

Brad shifted his glance from Donna to Rosemary as if he didn't know what to do next.

"I'm gonna take her into pre-op now," Rosemary said to Brad as she stepped to the foot of the stretcher. "You might as well get comfortable somewhere for a while."

A sudden panic seized Donna as she looked up at Brad.

Brad's face bore the look of distress they were both feeling. "I love you," he finally said, his voice trembling. "You come back to me."

"I will," Donna replied, memorizing every detail of Brad's face. "I will."

Brad let go of her hand.

Rosemary gave the stretcher a forceful shove and set it in motion toward a second set of automatic double doors. "You can wait in the surgical suite waiting area. Doctor Graff will meet you there when it's over in about four or five hours." Donna raised her head and watched Brad disappear behind the closing double doors wondering if she would ever see him again.

The sedative was starting to kick in. Donna barely noticed the sudden hum of the clippers. Her thoughts were of Brad and how much she wanted to see him again as Rosemary began shaving a large patch of her thick hair down to the bare scalp. Her head felt suddenly cool where the hair fell away.

"I know people who would just kill for hair like this," Rosemary offered.

"I had most of it cut off a few days ago," Donna answered. "I did donate it."

Rosemary smiled as she finished shaving the last of Donna's hair. "You're probably an organ donor, too. Aren't you?"

Donna smiled and nodded.

"We'll need to remove your jewelry," Rosemary said, holding Donna's left hand by the wrist.

"Oh, no. Please," Donna protested, pulling her arm away. "I can't take this off." She rubbed the bracelet on her wrist.

Rosemary clasped her hands together and pulled them close to her waist. "Darlin'," she began, sounding like a grandmother. "We have to remove the metal from your body." She looked down as if about to deliver bad news. "They'll be using an electric knife to cut into that noggin of yours and the current can jump around a bit." Rosemary placed a gentle hand on Donna's arm. "We don't want you to get burned now, would we?"

"Is there no other way?"

Rosemary smiled and picked up Donna's chart. "I'll make you a deal." She leaned close, pretending to conceal the details of the transaction from unseen onlookers. "We'll tape that bracelet to the chart and I will personally see that it's right back on your wrist as soon as you're wheeled out."

Donna remained silent, only offering a weak nod of acquiescence.

"Such a pretty bracelet, too," Rosemary said, slipping it from Donna's wrist and taping it to the chart. "A gift from a friend?"

"It's my most precious possession," Donna replied. "Will you hold it for me?"

Rosemary was frozen by the gravity of Donna's remark, her face reflecting her understanding. "I'll guard it with me life, I will. You have my word." She slipped it into her pocket before cupping Donna's cheek. "It's in good hands and so are you."

A short man with thick arms entered the room.

"This is Mark," Rosemary said to Donna. "He'll be the one givin' you the anesthesia today."

"Hello, Mark," Donna said.

"Mornin'," Mark replied, reaching into a nearby cabinet.

"What do you know about Doctor Graff?" Donna asked Rosemary.

"Doctor Graff is the most arrogant, self-centered, egotistical, rude, unfeeling person God ever sent forth upon the earth."

Mark smirked and pulled a syringe and a small bottle of clear liquid from the cabinet.

"But, if I were lying where you are," Rosemary continued. "There is no other mortal man I'd want working on me."

"You've worked with him a lot?"

Mark drew some of the liquid into the syringe and squeezed a few drops into the air.

"He's no humanitarian, dear." Rosemary nodded. "The man is no more concerned about you than the gum stickin' to the bottom of his shoe," she added, while Mark stuck the

needle into the IV tubing. "His only concern is with his suc-
cess ratio."

"You're not filling me with confidence."

"On the contrary!"

Mark injected the liquid into the IV.

"He never takes on a case unless he's sure he'll be successful. You wouldn't be here if this wasn't a sure thing."

Rosemary's voice grew more distant. The room began
to spin and fade away. "I'll see you afterward with your
bracelet. Now, you just relax and we'll do the rest."

Donna closed her eyes and began to pray; the image of
Brad's face etched into her thoughts. She felt a warm hand
grip her arm. "I'll say a rosary for you, darlin'," was the last
thing she heard before drifting off to sleep.

Chapter Twenty-One

Six months later it was finally Donna's turn. With her eyes fixed straight ahead, she walked down the aisle in her flowing white satin dress; two young girls followed behind holding the end of the long taffeta train. Two hundred of their friends and Brad's relatives sat watching her glide toward the altar, her face reflecting the joy she felt when she saw Brad awaiting her in the front of the church.

Her recovery had been nothing short of remarkable. Within a few weeks her speech had returned along with all but a few fine motor functions. She would still need some physical therapy for her left hand and her left eye closed slightly more than the right. Other than those minor changes, Donna Christine Roberts was as good as new.

She walked alone down the aisle holding a bouquet of white roses and baby's breath, savoring every joyful second while the pipe organ filled the church with Purcell's Trumpet Voluntary. With the smell of fresh flowers filling the sanctuary, she turned to see the expanse of people gathered to see her wed. Beaming faces- most of them tear-streaked–smiled back at her as she joined the love of her life at the front of the church.

Just before reaching the altar, Donna glanced at Elena sitting alone in the front pew. She returned Donna's smile, a mix of happiness and pain on her face. Her eyes bulged with tears.

"This is your day, Donna," Brad whispered to her. He took her hand in his as she took her position next to the bridesmaids.

And it was her day. No bride ever looked prettier, more in love, or happier just to be alive.

*   *   *

"Hit me, again," Johnny said to Hank while tipping his empty shot glass, his bloodshot eyes barely able to focus on the bartender's face just a few feet away.

"Maybe you oughta take it easy Johnny." Hank stood with his hands on his hips.

"Maybe you oughta fuck yourself."

Hank smiled. "If I could do that, I sure as hell wouldn't be here babysitting you shit-faced drunks every night."

"Yeah," Johnny answered, his head weaving. "I'll take it easy." He pointed at Hank. "That's a good idea. I'll do that. Now how 'bout another?"

"I meant, maybe you should stop now." Hank wiped his hands on his white, beer-stained apron. "As in, no more to drink." Hank picked an olive from beneath the bar and popped it into his mouth. "You been at it all day. What gives?"

Johnny's head shot up. Sitting upright at attention, he shook a shaky finger at Hank. "When I need your advice, I'll ask for it." He caught himself just before plummeting from the stool. "Right now, I don't need your opinion," Johnny slurred. "Right now what I need is a drink." His voice grew louder. "And I need it now!" Johnny slammed the shot glass on the bar.

"I'll make you a deal," Hank shot back. He leaned into the bar as he spoke. "You give me your truck keys and the next shot's on the house."

Johnny glanced up into Hank's sober eyes. "Hurts my

ass to drive that thing anyway," Johnny said while fishing his keys from his pants pocket and tossing them on the bar.

"I'll make it a double if you promise not to puke in my bar." Hank poured a double.

"I ain't no puker."

"That's not what I heard," a familiar voice called out to Johnny from his left.

Johnny turned to see Scooch sliding into the seat next to him.

"Ah, Christ," Johnny said, looking down and shaking his head. "That's all I need is you riding my ass now."

Scooch raised his hands and spread his long fingers in surrender. "What the hell did I do?"

"You were born." Johnny felt the room tipping; his stomach churned the caustic brew deep inside him. He eyed Hank who had walked to the other end of the bar to serve another drunk.

"How long you been here?" Scooch looked at his watch. "You pretty well juiced up for this time o' night."

"Go ahead and say it," Johnny continued as if he had not heard Scooch's question. "I told you so." He looked at Scooch with half-open eyes. "That's what you want to say, ain't it?"

"Man," Scooch bellowed. "I don't know what in the *hell* your talkin' 'bout, fool."

"They got married." Johnny took a drink of his bourbon.

"Who got married?" Scooch asked, his eyebrows contracting. "Your boy and that hooch momma?" He motioned for Hank to draw him a beer. "When this happen?"

"Today." Johnny shook his head slowly. "They're at the reception right now."

"Ah, hell, Johnny. That's a goddamned shame, man."

"That ain't the worst of it," Johnny added. "Guess where they're going on their honeymoon?"

Scooch shrugged.

"You won't believe it," Johnny continued with a dismissive wave of his hand. He paused for effect before unloading his burden. "They're going to fuckin' Nam! Can you even believe that shit?"

"I'll tell you what," Scooch said, taking a mug of beer from Hank. "If that was my boy, I'd disown his ass right quick." He took a long swallow of his beer and wiped his mouth with his sleeve. "I wouldn't stand for that, Johnny. Uh, uh. No sir. That boy'd be on my shit list with interest."

"He's never setting foot in my house again," Johnny added. "I can tell you that." He waved his arm for emphasis, knocking over his drink. With his eyes half closed, Johnny turned his gaze toward Hank, who was staring back at him and slowly shaking his head.

"Man, I thought you was gonna catch a break with her going in for that surgery." Scooch reached with his long arm in front of Johnny and pulled a bowl of pretzels toward him. "But, she pulled through."

"I wish she hadn't," Johnny replied, looking down at the bar. "I wish she was dead."

"Closing time," Hank called from the far end of the bar.

Scooch glanced at his watch amidst scattered calls of protest from around the barroom. "Closing time? Hell, it's only ten-thirty!"

"We're closed," Hank reaffirmed. He pulled a wastebasket from the floor and set it on the bar. "File your complaints right here".

"I don't know why I come in here," Scooch grumbled on his way to the door. "All I ever get is bullshit. Never know when the hell it's closing time. Can't remember the last time I had anything good to eat..." he continued right out the door.

Hank waited for the last of the patrons to file out, looking like a half-dozen cast members from *The Grapes of Wrath*. He turned off the neon light and flipped the sign in the window to read 'Closed'.

"How 'bout a cup of coffee, Johnny?" Hank asked while walking back to the bar.

"How 'bout not." Johnny picked up the overturned shot glass and held it up. "How 'bout you keep it coming?"

"'Fraid not Johnny. You're cut off. Sorry." Hank slipped behind the bar and raised the pot of coffee that had been simmering most of the day. "Thick as tar. Just how ya like it."

Johnny slid off the stool and attempted to walk to the door. His descent from his seat culminated in his knee colliding with the adjacent stool. He fell forward, knocking one barstool over and pushing another into the bar. His face hit the floor with a resounding thud.

With his face still burning from the impact, Johnny felt a pair of hands tugging him upward from under his arms. "Come on, you drunken slob," Hank said, lifting him to his knees. He helped Johnny the rest of the way to his feet and guided him to a nearby chair. "You stay there," Hank said, pointing at Johnny. "I'll get you a cup of coffee."

"I ain't drinking any goddamn coffee," Johnny protested, tapping his bloody lip with his fingertips.

"Fine," Hank answered. "Be a belligerent asshole. Have it your way. It's always your way, isn't it Johnny?"

Johnny looked up through unfocused eyes, his eyelids feeling like curtains of lead. "I have no fucking idea what you're saying."

"I'm talking about your son and daughter-in-law."

"What about 'em. It ain't none of your damn business." Johnny leaned forward, resting his head in his hands. "Stay the hell out of it." His voice was muffled behind his fingers.

"You think you're the only GI to come back with nightmares?" Hank took a seat at the bar. "You think you're the only guy to come back from Nam with baggage?"

Johnny lifted his head from his hands. "Where the fuck do you get off talking to me like this?" He tried to stand but lost his balance and fell back into his seat. "What the hell do you know about it? Huh?"

"I know plenty about it. I was there, Johnny."

Johnny stared at Hank for several seconds, taking in the information. "So, you were there. So what? You didn't see what I seen. You weren't where I was."

"We all left something over there." Hank walked over to the table where Johnny sat and took a seat. "And, we all brought something home. Some of us brought home more than others." He fixed Johnny with his stare. "What did you bring home, Johnny? What's got you so balled up you can't see your own son marry the woman he loves?"

Johnny slammed his hand on the table.

Hank never flinched.

"I swear," Johnny said, struggling to stand. "I'm gonna kick your ass so bad they'll be a week puttin' you back together."

Hank shoved Johnny back down into his chair with one effortless push to his chest. "Sit down. You listen to me you idiot."

Johnny sat with wide eyes fixed on Hank.

"The sooner you put this anger behind you, the sooner you get on living your life," Hank admonished. "You got a son who's a good man. You should be proud of him. He's got his own company and now he's found him a good woman."

"Ha!" Johnny shouted. "A good woman. She's a slope! Jesus, Hank. A fucking sl—"

"I heard you the first time." Hank drew closer, his eyes narrowed. He drew a wiry hand from his side and grabbed

Johnny by the collar. "That is the last time you will use that, or any similar term in my bar. Do we understand each other?" Hank tightened his grip, causing Johnny to cough for air.

"Yeah, yeah," Johnny said, rubbing his neck as Hank released him. "Okay. What's with you, anyway?"

"Let's just say your son and I have something in common."

Johnny drew a deep breath and looked Hank over head to toe.

"Your problem is not with Brad's wife," Hank asserted. He reached out, this time with a gentle hand to Johnny's chest. "Your problem is in here." Hank's hand landed softly on Johnny's forehead. "And here."

Johnny swiped at Hank's hand. "You don't know anything about it."

"I know it's tearing you up inside." Hank cocked his head. "I know you have nightmares. You think they'll stop, but they don't. You think you can drink them away, but they just keep coming back. Even after thirty years. You think if you can just avoid her you won't remember. But you still do." For the first time he smiled at Johnny. "How am I doing so far?"

Johnny sat motionless staring ahead into the haunting memories. They circled him like a pack of ghostly wolves, shifting shapes and evading every defense he put up. Inside he tried fending them off, pushing them away with his hands and kicking at them with his feet. But they kept circling, their numbers growing: one for every face: one for every voice crying out in anguish.

"I went to college on a baseball scholarship," Johnny said, turning to Hank. "I'll bet you didn't know that."

"No, Johnny," Hank replied, shaking his head. "I didn't know that."

"Starting shortstop." Johnny held out an open left hand. "Nothing got by this glove hand." He smiled and closed his eyes. "Never a game went by there wasn't a scout there watchin' me. I woulda played in the minors, maybe even the big leagues."

"What happened?"

"Elena got pregnant my junior year. Had to quit school and get a job when Brad was born." Johnny's smile evaporated. "Instead of the Yankees, it was Uncle Sam who called me up. You know the rest."

"That sucks."

"You remember your first hot LZ, Hank?"

Hank smiled. "Who doesn't?"

"I'll never forget my first firefight," Johnny began, his eyes glazed in a trance-like gaze. "The Huey dropped us off and it wasn't ten seconds and we were under fire. Benny Girafillo was with me that day. We went through boot camp together. Went to the same high school, we did. Played baseball together. We were city champs my senior year." He managed a faint, fleeting smile. "Dated his sister Margie for a while."

Hank sat back and listened.

"We got separated and we had to dig in. Spent the night out there." Johnny's breathing grew faster and heavier. "They never let up. It was one wave after the next. Jesus, they were right there. Right on top of us all night with the flares and the mortars. We never slept. God, I remember I was so tired. I just wanted to sleep.

"The next day, they came back for us. Eight Hueys. We were all grunts. They just picked us up and ran us back to camp." Johnny ran a hand through his hair. "All I could think about was hitting my bunk. Ya know? I made a bee-line," he motioned with his hand, "for my tent." Johnny stopped. He shook his head and looked away. "They just put them in a row in the camp. They were just pulling 'em off the choppers all wrapped up in their ponchos."

"I remember," Hank finally said, his voice low.

"Then, I saw him. Just lying there, in the line. Must have been ten, maybe twelve boys in it. And there was Benny, half covered up just staring up at me, dead. Just like that." Johnny closed his eyes and shook his head, as if trying to clear the memory from his alcohol-soaked brain.

Hank just stared, his expression broadcasting his understanding.

"He was my best friend," Johnny continued. "And I didn't feel nothin'. Like I didn't care or something."

"You were exhausted."

"A few days later," Johnny added, ignoring Hank's comment. "I couldn't stop crying." He puckered his lips and fought back the welling emotion. "I felt so guilty."

Hank nodded in acknowledgment. "For surviving?"

"That," Johnny answered. "And for not feeling more when I saw him there, dead." He sat staring at the bar with the same numbness that had swept over him thirty years before.

The two men sat in silence for a long time until Johnny spoke.

"Did you have dreams, Hank?" Johnny asked, never making eye contact.

"For a while." Hank shifted in his seat. "How 'bout you, Johnny?"

Johnny nodded, his thoughts turning to a hot afternoon in '67. "Yeah," he said in a quiet voice. "I dream about dogs." He looked at Hank.

"Dogs?" Hank's eyebrows narrowed as he leaned forward. "What dogs?"

Johnny took in a deep breath and looked at the ceiling, unsure if he could relive the memory. He stared at Hank for a long moment, wondering how much he would regret saying in the morning. With the encouragement the bourbon had provided, Johnny decided to take that first dangerous step into the past.

"I had sixty-two days left before I came back to the World," Johnny blurted. It was out before he realized it was he who was speaking. "We got dumped in an LZ about fifteen clicks from camp." Johnny shrugged. "Typical recon patrol. Simple in and out. Back home in time for happy hour.

"We're getting' ready to meet the Hueys and we run into 'em. Ah, Christ they were everywhere. We couldn't figure out where the fuck they come from. They just appeared like they come up out of the ground."

"They probably did," Hank offered.

"Yeah," Johnny agreed. "They probably did." He stopped for a breath. "Anyway, we can hear the choppers coming in and this whole shit storm is going on around us. I can still hear them A.K.s... kachink, kachink, kachink."

"You never forget that sound," Hank piped in. "Nothing like it anywhere."

"They radio to the pilots to come around from the east with some air support." Johnny made an arc with his hand simulating the path of the helicopters relative to their position.

"The first one comes around and I can see the door-gunner ready to open fire when this fifty-one-caliber opens up about twenty yards away." Johnny swiped his forehead. "We were almost on top of it and we never even saw it." He swallowed hard and took another deep breath. "That Huey looked like a pin cushion on the way down. That fifty-one almost cut it in half. I think those guys inside were all dead before it hit the ground."

Hank met Johnny's eyes for a brief moment before Johnny continued.

"The flight leader radioed down that they were backing off until we took out the machine gun. I could hear 'em getting' farther away." Johnny unconsciously made a waving motion with his hand. "Christ, they were overrunning us. Swarming everywhere. I had no fucking idea what I was shooting at. I was crouched behind a fallen tree just shooting my M-16 into the trees and shitting my pants.

"I looked over at this guy who was with me and he's just as scared as me. I looked over the top of the log and I can see the son-of-a-bitch with the fifty-one. He's just strafing the jungle. I see him swinging around our way and I duck down and turn to my buddy to tell him to get down."

Johnny stopped. His breathing grew heavy.

"I didn't even get the first word out and he takes two rounds right in the mouth. Pops his head off like a cork." Johnny closed his eyes momentarily. "He never fell over. He was just propped up like some mannequin at Sears. Just sittin' there with his head shot off. Just his lower jaw flopping from his neck.

"Then I get this rush of anger, ya know? Like I'm all of a sudden not scared any more and I'm just pissed off that this goo—" Johnny stopped himself, remembering Hank's deceptively strong grip and accompanying admonition. "This bastard was gonna punch my ticket with only two months left on my tour.

"So, I popped up with my weapon and I got him in my sights." Johnny raised his arms and mimicked the pose he had taken with his M-16. "I can see him. He's just a kid. Couldn't have been more than fifteen. Hell, I wasn't much older than that.

"I can see him, there. He's chained to the gun. They had him chained to the fucking gun so he's just fighting for his life, just like me. I can see his face. The guy was in a frenzy just firing everywhere." Johnny paused and let his eyes drop. "He was just trying to make it out of there alive. Just like me."

"That's all any of us were doing," Hank finally added.

"The CO was about twenty yards behind me, yelling at me to take him out." Johnny motioned with his thumb, extended like a hitchhiker's toward the room behind him. "I had the guy in my sights, but he was moving around and I didn't have a real clear shot. I was gonna have to just strafe him, but there were all these dogs in the way. All chained up in front of the sand bags and jumping and barking and pulling against the chains."

"What happened then?"

"I could hear the Hueys circling for another run," Johnny continued, his voice weak. "The CO just kept yelling for me to take 'em out. The goddamn NVA were circling and I couldn't get a clean shot." Johnny stared into the abyss of his darkest moment. "The choppers were coming in for a landing and I could see the guy swinging the machinegun around on them."

Johnny fell silent.

"What happened, Johnny?"

Johnny retreated into himself. For a moment the booze and the bar faded to black and in an instant he was back behind the fallen tree with his weapon drawn and trained on the young gunner, nearly a dozen yelping dogs darting and weaving against the chains in front of him.

"D'Amato," a voice shouted from behind in an eerie echo. "Take 'em out! Take 'em out, now or we're never gonna make it out of here!"

Johnny felt his finger pulling against the trigger and was surprised when the gun jumped in his hands, spitting rounds in rapid succession into the machinegun nest. The dogs squealed and cried as the rounds ripped through them, the chains pulled taught as they fell to the ground. The young NVA gunner slumped against the machinegun.

Johnny allowed himself to dwell in the scene for only a moment before pulling back through time to the safe haven of the Riverside Saloon. He looked at Hank, who was still awaiting an answer he would never get.

"A few days later I got hit in the leg." Johnny took a deep breath. "I come home and there's people protesting and marching. One woman spits on me when I'm getting off the bus. She fucking spits on me, Hank."

"Have you been to the Wall, Johnny?"

Johnny shook his head. "Not planning to either."

"It's healed a lot of wounds."

"My wounds are healed." Johnny glanced down at his leg.

"Sometimes the deepest wounds are the ones you can't see..." Hank glanced over Johnny's shoulder and stood.

"Johnny," Elena's voice called to him from near the front door. "We should go home now, yes?" Her expression told of a day filled with embarrassment at Johnny's absence.

"How long you been standing there?" Johnny asked her, hoping it had not been too long.

"Long enough," she replied. Her tone was cold. "Time to go home."

Johnny sniffed and looked at Hank for a moment before slapping his knees. "Guess I gotta go home now, Hank. The boss is here."

"Get some sleep," Hank said, wiping down the bar. "You're gonna be hurtin' tomorrow."

Chapter Twenty-Two

Donna and Brad began their journey to Ho Chi Minh City at the Nashville airport. From there, they flew to Los Angeles and boarded a Japan Airlines flight to Tokyo. After an overnight stay, they completed the last leg of their journey to the city Donna had once known as Saigon.

The city had changed in many ways since Donna had seen it as a child. Its population had swelled to over seven million and it looked as though every inhabitant was riding a motorized scooter along the busy, tree-lined streets. In some ways it was still the same. Hungry children still walked the streets begging handouts from disinterested strangers. Donna could see herself in the faces of each child.

Brightly colored signs advertising Coca-Cola, Pepsi, Honda, Sony and others became more prevalent as they approached the city center. Crowded shops lined the wide boulevards and bustling side streets. Donna even spotted a Hard Rock Café on the way in from the Tan Son Nhut airport.

"You said it would be hot," Brad said, climbing out of the twenty-year-old cab outside the Continental Hotel. "But I clearly had no concept of what you meant."

"Right now," Donna replied, running her fingers through her three-inch-long hair. "I am thankful for my new haircut."

"I always liked your hair the way it was," Brad answered. "But, I've gotta tell you, this new look is pretty sexy." He engaged her with a playful smile. "In fact, it's almost like you're somebody else."

"You like that?" Donna pinched his nipple and twisted.

"Ow!" Brad rubbed his breast and laughed. "You know what they say about variety."

"Yes, I do." Donna turned and walked toward the hotel entrance. "I have my own variety of things for you later," she said, walking away.

"Oh, baby," Brad replied, catching up with her near the front door.

And she did have much in store for him. After a long, relaxing bath in their spacious air-conditioned suite, Brad and Donna made love for most of the afternoon before collapsing in exhaustion and sleeping until well after dark.

"Where are we off to tomorrow?" Brad asked while they waited for their meals in the hotel restaurant. They sat among two-dozen elegantly appointed tables in a room that would rival anything found in Paris. Crystal chandeliers hung from the ornate recessed ceilings while Roman columns struck periodic poses among the upscale diners.

"We are flying to Vinh and then going by car to Dong Ha in Quang Tri province," Donna provided.

"Dong Ha?" Brad mimicked, his forehead furrowed. "Quang Tri?"

Donna smiled at his antics. "From there, we will be driven to Khe Sanh."

"What's in Khe Sanh?"

"I want to visit the prefecture where I was born." Donna tore a small piece of bread from the loaf on the table. "I am hoping they will have my birth records."

"For what?" Brad raised the glass of water in front of him and inspected it.

"It's safe to drink." Donna laughed. "It's bottled." She raised a finger. "Although, once we leave here, you will need to be careful."

A slim waiter in a white shirt brought their salads. He cast Donna a disgusted look.

"I want to find out when I was born," Donna said, watching him walk away.

Brad grabbed his fork and was about to dig into his salad. His eyebrows rose as he glanced up at his new bride. "You don't know when you were born?" He crinkled his nose and stabbed a forkful of lettuce. "Your birthday is May first."

Donna snorted in amusement. "My father picked that for me. He picked May Day because it represents new life in the old Anglo-Saxon cultures. I think it was because he rescued me from my miserable life."

"How could you not know when you were born? Your mother must have told you."

Donna smiled and cast a glance across the restaurant; fully aware that there was no way Brad could truly understand.

"When you live from one day to the next just trying to survive, things like birthdays become somewhat trivial." She stirred the dressing around in her salad. Her mood turned suddenly somber. "There are also many things that I don't remember. Maybe I don't want to. Some are quite painful."

Brad laid his fork down and looked around the restaurant and out into the hotel lobby. "This is a whole side of you I know nothing about," he said. "It's like there is this other person inside you that I don't even know. I can't even imagine what living here during the war must have been like."

"I don't want to dwell on it, Brad. I just have a few things to resolve."

"You know I'll do anything I can to help."

"I'd say you've already done enough." Donna blushed.

"Happy to help out any time." He pointed his fork at her. "And, there's plenty left where that came from."

"No doubt."

The next morning, after long delays, they flew to Vinh, picked up a driver and guide and drove to Dong Ha. It was nearing dusk when they found a ride to a nearby hotel. After a short trip, they pulled in front of a modest one-story block building located in the heart of the small city.

"Things may be a bit rustic from here," Donna announced to Brad. "This is the equivalent to the Hilton in this part of the country."

Brad looked out his window at the surrounding collection of modest buildings and dirt streets. He smiled at Donna and said, "We'll make it work."

Inside, Brad set their bags down on a tiny bed located in the center of their small room. A single light bulb hung from the ceiling. The bathroom, complete with a washbasin of fresh water, was just down the short hallway. "When I was a girl, living in the hills," Donna said, reminiscing. "I couldn't imagine such luxury as this." She glanced around the barren room.

Later that night, they located and hired another driver to take them to Khe Sanh the next day: a young man who spoke a few words of English.

Donna and Brad slept well that night in spite of the cramped conditions and the lumpy mattress. The next morning they tore into their supply of Pop Tarts and juice boxes before meeting their driver for the arduous trek down highway nine to Khe Sanh. They piled into the dust-covered Isuzu Trooper and began the four-hour trip. It was noon when they rolled into the rundown settlement near the Laotian border.

"Not much has changed," Donna said, looking out over the closely packed shanties and rickety shacks that comprised the outskirts of the frontier town. "This used to be the Marine base." She pointed out the window at an open expanse of red soil. There was no trace of the old base other than the bare spots along the path of the old runway. The rest of the site had been overgrown by a large coffee plantation.

Brad pursed his lips and nodded without a word.

"This is the last place I ever saw my little brother." Donna cast a wistful look at the old runway. "I have no idea if he's even alive anymore."

"I can't imagine, Donna." Brad reached for her hand. "I just can't."

The village of Khe Sanh was not much different than the way Donna remembered it so many years ago. It was still run-down and dirty. The houses and shops were the same collection of unpainted boards and corrugated sheet metal. The only difference, much to Donna's delight, was the generally better conditions the children seemed to enjoy over the way they lived thirty years before.

After a brief exchange over a badly wrinkled map, they were on their way out of town and into the rugged, misty foothills.

"So, this is the old neighborhood?" Brad asked, inspecting the small village.

They looked out over a small collection of huts and crudely made shacks along the base of a steep hillside.

"The original village was destroyed," Donna said, getting out of the vehicle. "But, this is where it stood."

There was very little she recognized. None of the faces looked familiar and she barely recalled where her old hut had once stood. Her worst fears were being validated, as she had not seen a single Bru tribesman since she arrived. Some reports from humanitarian agencies reported that the Bru were being systematically exterminated for aiding the US Army during the war.

Using what little she remembered of her childhood, Donna did her best to reconstruct the layout. After a few moments of reflection, she concluded that her childhood home had once stood about fifty feet from where they were standing.

"Over there," she said, pointing at a small hut near a clump of bamboo. "I think it was over there."

They walked slowly through the village, amidst the stares of the women and children going about their daily routines. Donna stopped in front of the grass-covered hooch, recalling a time when one, much like it, had been her home.

"They must have rebuilt using some of the same posts," she said, bending to point out the charred portion of some of the bamboo anchors. Donna stared at the tiny hut, her throat tightening as memories of her brother and mother washed over her. How she missed them, even after all this time. Even though they lived in abject poverty, Donna still had fond memories of falling asleep in her mother's arms, listening to Hung's faint snores as she drifted off to sleep.

Tears welled in Donna's eyes as she thought of her mother and how many women in her position would have simply abandoned their child. Donna had been conceived the night her mother was gang-raped by four soldiers. Donna's features were living proof that at least one of them was Caucasian. No one would bother to ask if Lien had given herself willingly or not. No one would care that she was forced. All they would see was the bastard child of the enemy; a *My lai*. It would have been easier to just walk away. But, she didn't, and it would take Donna thirty-five years to understand the sacrifice her mother had made for her.

Their next stop was at the Vietnamese equivalent of a town hall. The local Catholic Church had kept meticulous records of the births and deaths in the prefecture for the last fifty years. After a brief exchange in broken English and Vietnamese with an elderly man in the church office, Donna was able to communicate that she was looking for her birth record.

"This is all we have for your village," the little man said to her. He hoisted a thick book with a tan canvas cover onto a nearby table and left Donna and Brad to look through the record book.

Donna eagerly flipped through the pages, checking for familiar names and dates.

She stopped on a page near the middle of the book and stared. "This can't be right," she said, pointing at an entry.

"What's the problem?" Brad replied, leaning forward to have a look.

"Here," Donna tapped the entry with her fingertip. "This is my mother." Beneath her finger was the name Nguyen Binh Lien. She moved her finger across the page. "And, this is me." Donna pointed to another name, Nguyen Khanh Mai.

"It seems so strange to actually see it in print like that." Brad smiled and stared at her name on the page. "It's like you're two people in one."

Donna smiled and nodded her understanding: an understanding that Brad could never fathom. "Well, according to this," she continued. "Your new, dual personality wife is a year older than she thought."

"What?" Brad did a double take between Donna and the page.

"It's right there," she said, pointing. "February third, nineteen sixty-three." Donna slumped back into her chair. "I'm thirty-six."

Brad began laughing. "You old hag."

"I came here to better understand myself, but this is not what I had in mind."

Brad laughed some more and kissed Donna's head. "You're still the hottest woman I have ever met."

Donna smiled and shook her head in mock disgust. "That was the fastest year of my life. It went by," she snapped her fingers, "just like that."

"We have plenty left," Brad said, gently rubbing her arm.

"Yeah," Donna answered. "Plenty more."

Later that night they were back in Dong Ha, where they spent the night, before venturing on to Hue City the next day.

Their entry into Hue appeared to be as magical for Brad as it had been for Donna those many years ago. The ride across the Perfume River took them over the same bridge and through the same tunnel she had taken as a girl. Donna relished the look on Brad's face as they cleared the tunnel into the ancient, walled city.

"Wow," he proclaimed, his neck twisting in all directions trying to take everything in.

They drove past the towering Buddhist temple and stopped at the palace complex in the center of the city.

"You lived here?" Brad asked, climbing from the Trooper. "This is so cool."

"Well, not right *here*." Donna nodded toward the palace. "It is beautiful. But, I never got the chance to see it like this. I was only in Hue City for a week."

"A week?" Brad's eyes narrowed. "How come so short a time?"

"I was airlifted out of Khe Sanh during the siege there." Donna slipped her arm through Brad's as they walked around the palace. "They brought me here where they thought I would be safe." She smiled at the irony. "The Tet Offensive began a few days after I arrived."

"I'm sorry." Brad shook his head. "History wasn't my strong suit."

Donna let out a long breath. "Ten thousand people died in this city in a single week. Many of them dragged from their homes and shot dead in the streets."

"Ten thousand," Brad said, looking around at the cramped confines of the picturesque city. "Did you see any of it?"

Donna nodded and looked away. "Too much of it."

They spent the rest of the day strolling around the city.

"This is where I stayed while I was here." Donna nodded toward an empty lot across the street from where they stood.

"What'd you do?" Brad asked, half joking. "Camp out."

"There was a Catholic Church here," she said, while crossing the street toward the place where she had taken refuge. "It was leveled during the shelling and never rebuilt." Donna stared at the grassy patch, where she had been reunited with her mother; wishing for that same feeling she had felt when she saw Lien standing near the bottom of the stairs.

"Shelling?" Brad turned to her.

Donna nodded, smiling at Brad's naiveté. "US Navy ships out at sea." She pointed in the direction of the South China Sea, just a few miles away. "Between that and the air strikes, the city was hit pretty hard."

"God, Donna," Brad said, looking up and down the street. "I had no idea you went through any of this." He looked down and shook his head. "I'm so sorry. I feel like such an idiot for not knowing how bad your life was."

"At the time," she replied. "I didn't know how bad it was either." Donna smiled at Brad. "I didn't know anything else."

The next day they headed for Da Nang. The going was slow, even with the benefit of traveling down a main highway, the old route one. Just a few miles outside of the port city, Donna asked the driver to stop.

"Here," she said, pointing at the side of the road. "Yes, right here."

The driver pulled over. Donna was still very young the last time she had been there, but she remembered certain details quite well. She thought it was strange how she had blocked out entire months from her memory, yet she could recall even the tiniest details of events that had occurred almost thirty years prior. This was one of those occasions.

"What are we doing here?" Brad asked her. "Why are we stopping?"

"We're close," she answered. "I recognize the bend in the road and the old bridge." Donna climbed out of the car with Brad following close behind. She stood next to the road surveying the landscape. Her breathing grew heavier and her heart rate quickened. "Oh," she blurted, unaware she had made a sound until she heard her own voice.

"What?" Brad was quick to her side. "You okay? What's wrong?"

Donna cupped her forehead. "So much coming back to me." With the sun baking down on her, she suddenly felt light-headed.

"Baby, you should rest." Brad clasped her elbows and helped her to the Trooper where she sat on the running board, on the shady side of the vehicle. The driver uncapped a bottle of water and handed it to her.

"Thank you," Donna said, taking the water. "I'll be all right in a minute." She took a sip. "I don't know if I'm ready for this or not."

"Ready for what?" Brad asked.

Donna nodded toward the road. "My nightmares," she

said. "Some of them come from this place." She pointed at the curve in the road near the bridge. "And over there," she tossed her head toward the opposite side of the vehicle.

Brad ran a hand over his thinning hair and exhaled heavily. "Why are you doing this to yourself? Why are you putting yourself through this?"

Donna grappled with a reply. If she didn't fully understand it herself, how could she ever explain it to Brad?

"When I was very young," she began. "The American soldiers were kind to us. They all tried to help us when they could." Donna reached for Brad to help her stand. "But, over time, things changed. Some of them became less friendly."

"Were they mean to you?"

"Some were. Most were kind." She walked toward the road. "Toward the end of the war, the American troops took this road on their way south. My mother and I used to wait along the highway hoping to get some of the food they would throw from the trucks."

"That doesn't sound mean."

"That wasn't," Donna replied. "But, over time, the routine changed. The soldiers became a little less charitable and more intent on using us for their entertainment."

She stood by the curve in the road looking toward the bridge.

"I was standing right here among many children begging for the soldiers to toss some of their rations to us as they passed." Donna turned to glance up and down the stretch of highway. "The men started pelting us with cans. I felt one sail past my face and hit the boy standing next to me." She raised a hand just above her eyebrows. "It split his forehead wide open and he just collapsed at my feet."

"Maybe it was an accident."

"I looked up to see them laughing as they rode away."

Donna paused, looking down, her lips puckered. "A few trucks later, the men were throwing candy and gum into the road, luring the children away from the shoulder." She looked away and shook her head, the images starting to take hold. "One little boy ran out to grab a candy bar and the next truck in line just ran him over."

"Jesus," Brad said, shaking his head.

"No one stopped. He was still moving and I could see him looking around for someone to help him when the next truck hit him." She stared into the road. "After that, the trucks just swerved around his body." Donna paused for a moment, shaking her head. "All I can think about now is how there was no one to help him or cry for him. He died all alone in that road thinking that no one loved him." She looked at Brad. "That could have been me."

Without another word, Donna pulled a cardboard tube from the Trooper, turned and walked down a path into the brush.

"Where you going?" Brad was right behind her.

"To say goodbye." Donna kept walking, following nothing more than her instincts and a twenty-seven year old memory of events and surroundings. They walked for half a mile until coming upon the overgrown remnants of a village. Some of the half-razed block walls protruded from a heavy growth of vines and underbrush.

Donna stood in the center of the collection of bombed-out structures. "I thought I would have a meltdown when I got here," she said, turning her head to view the surroundings. "But, I feel strangely peaceful."

"What happened here?"

"I was eight." She pointed to a hill in the distance. "There was a camp over there. Some of the soldiers would meet local women for..."

"You don't have to do this, Donna."

"Yes," she said. "I do." Donna took a deep breath and looked around for a place to sit. She spotted a stump in the shade and whacked it with a stick before sitting on it.

"What'd you do that for?"

"To scare the snakes away."

Brad glanced around the ground near their feet. "Oh."

"My mother left the roadside before I did," Donna began. "She told me to wait some time before coming for her. She said she would be in this village.

"But, I was upset at seeing the boy killed so I left early and looked for her here." Donna motioned toward the rubble. "Back then, these buildings were intact and I began looking inside them for her." An irony swept over her and she smiled. "Well, I found her…"

Donna recalled the events as she recounted the story. She could hear her own words describing what followed, but in her mind she was that same distraught eight-year-old girl seeking her mother's comfort; a little girl named Mai.

It was that very same little girl who had peered into the vacant building to see Lien lying on her back with an American GI on top of her and her baby sister lying beside them in the dirt.

"I'll never forget the shame in her eyes as she saw me."

Brad just looked at her, saying nothing.

"At the time, I didn't know why she would do such a thing." Donna swatted at a few mosquitoes buzzing her face. "I didn't understand where the food we sometimes ate would suddenly come from. All I knew was that she kept me fed. I never questioned how. I never knew what she put herself through to keep us alive."

Brad looked up at the passing clouds and took a deep breath. "So, what did you do?"

"What did I do?" Donna repeated, shaking her head in shame. "I ran…to this very spot. To this tree trunk…And I screamed at her as loud as I could how much I hated her and how I wished she were dead."

After all the years, Donna finally understood the humiliation and emotional pain her mother must have endured for her children.

Brad's eyes grew wide. He stood before her in the heat looking unsure of his role.

"How's that for gratitude?" Donna added.

"Donna, you were just a little girl." Brad approached, his hand extended.

"I can never forget the look on her face when she saw me in the doorway." Donna wiped a tear away. "She was so hurt that I saw her like that. I know she never wanted me to know."

"She was only doing what she had to, Donna," Brad said, wrapping his arm around her and pulling her close.

"I know," she replied. "That's what hurts so bad. Why didn't I see that?" Donna held up her hand. "Why did I have to blame her?"

Brad did not respond.

"I don't know what happened next. Much of it is a blur." Donna's eyes fixed on a pile of toppled blocks. "Suddenly I was surrounded by soldiers rushing into the village and shooting at everything in sight." Donna gazed into the surrounding overgrowth as if viewing the events projected onto a screen. "I was so scared I just sat here on this stump and watched it happen."

Donna watched the images unfolding on the movie screen of her mind. Soldiers ran from building to building firing their automatic weapons. Chickens, goats, and various livestock scurried for cover along with the terrified residents as bullets strafed the ground. Through the chaos she could see her mother emerge from one of the block buildings, her baby sister held in her arms. Their eyes locked and Lien started toward her.

"My mother tried to come to me," Donna said, choking on every word. "Her only concern was for my safety." Tears welled in her eyes. "And I told her I hated her."

"It's okay, Donna," Brad said, wrapping her in his arms. "You were just a kid."

"That's as far as she got." Donna pointed to a place about ten yards away. Her stomach heaved in spasms of grief.

The scene played out before her as it had those many years before. Lien ran toward Mai clutching her baby daughter. As she approached, Lien's body jerked and she fell to her knees. She slowly lowered her eyes to look at the motionless child in her arms. The baby's head flopped to the side and a bright red stain grew larger on the cloth covering her back.

Lien coughed and a spattering of blood coated her lips. She stared at Mai, a look of complete resignation frozen on her face. Her mother had given everything she had to give and there was nothing left. She locked eyes with her only surviving child and tried to speak.

"Donna," Brad said. "Stop it. You don't have to do this."

"Yes, I do," she answered, nodding. Donna shook as she wept, the image of her mother's face burned into her memory.

Brad could only hold her tight as she continued.

"I wanted to say something, but I couldn't. I wanted to run to her but I was too frightened." Donna clung to Brad in a tight embrace. "Then she was gone…"

One last memory assaulted her with the cruelty of a marauding army. Mai had just hopped down to run to her mother when a rocket hit Lien in the chest. Mai was thrown backward onto the ground while Lien was all but vaporized where she knelt.

"I had no idea." Brad kissed her head. "I'm so sorry."

"I woke up a while later. An American soldier helped me clean up." Donna shivered. "He took me to a creek where I washed her remains off my body."

Brad pulled a handkerchief from his pocket and dabbed at Donna's cheeks.

"I never said goodbye to her," Donna said, looking up at Brad. "I had to come here and say goodbye." She took the handkerchief. "The last thing I said to her was how much I hated her."

"You were a kid. You were upset."

Donna straightened on her perch and took a deep breath. "I love you mother and I miss you." She wiped away the wetness from her cheeks and stood on wobbly legs. "It has taken me all these years," she continued, her voice shaky. "But I know you did what you did, so I could survive. And I want you to know how much I love you for that."

Donna pulled a single white rose from the tube she had carried from the Trooper. She knelt on one knee and placed it on the ground where her mother had died. "Until I see you again." She stood, took Brad's hand, and walked away.

Chapter Twenty-Three

"The grass needs cutting," Elena said to Johnny, stepping around his feet as he sat expressionless in his favorite chair. "It's almost up to my knees." She ran a white rag over a collection of Brad's football and Johnny's baseball trophies on a shelf above the television.

Two weeks had passed since the wedding and it was the most she had said to him since.

Johnny sat staring at an old World War II movie. The Japanese had hunkered down in some caves and the Marines were dumping shell after artillery shell on the mountainside trying to root them out. He'd seen the movie before, but it still captivated his attention. That was a man's war. You knew who the enemy was. They came at you themselves. Not like the Viet Cong, who used innocent people to do their dirty work for them.

"The mower's broke." Outside, the July sun baked the hard ground on a cloudless afternoon. "Besides," he added, feeling the need to provide more excuses. "It's too damned hot to mow the lawn."

"Then fix the faucet in the bathroom."

"I need a washer." Still staring at the TV, Johnny held up a hand as if holding the tiny rubber ring between his fingers. "I'm all out."

"Then go to the hardware store and get one."

"My truck needs a new belt. I'm afraid to drive it 'til I can change it."

Elena stepped in front of the television and turned it off.

"Hey," Johnny extended an open hand, palm up, toward the screen. "I was watching that."

"And now you are done watching." She froze him with a glare that only a wife can generate. Every husband knows it. It was the 'I've had enough' look and Elena had fine-tuned it until it burned through Johnny like a highly charged cobalt laser.

"What's eating you?" Deep down, he knew the answer. Elena was locked and loaded and Johnny was centered in her crosshairs.

"All you do is sit in this chair!" Elena gestured with an open hand at the overstuffed, threadbare recliner. "The grass needs cutting. The faucet is dripping." Elena pressed her thumb and forefinger together and mimicked a faucet dripping. "Drip, drip, drip." She swiped her face. "You don't shave for days."

Johnny unconsciously ran a hand over the stubble on his face.

"You said you would clean out the garage last week." She placed her hands on her hips. "My flowers still sit out by the sidewalk." Elena pointed to her right.

"I'll get to it," Johnny replied. "I'm waiting for—"

"For what?" Elena's face was turning red. "What do you wait for, eh? Elves to come in the middle of the night and do it for you?"

Johnny squirmed in his chair and was about to respond when Elena cut him off.

"That's all you do is wait." She paused for a moment, daring him to reply. "You wait for the weather to be just right. You wait for the grass to die. You wait for the sink to fix itself."

"I don't like mowing the lawn."

"And I don't like the dusting." She shook the rag at him. "But, I do it just the same."

"I said I'd get around to it."

"Just like you will get around to calling your son?" Elena drew blood. "Or, will you wait for him to call you?" She stepped closer. "This time," she added, shaking her finger. "John Anthony D'Amato, you go too far. He is back from the honeymoon and he has not called."

"That's fine with me."

"Oh?" Elena raised her eyebrows and tipped her head. "Well that is a good thing, because I don't think he will be calling you this time." She clapped her hands as if applauding a brilliant stage production. "Bravo, you have pushed him away." She stopped clapping and took a deep breath. "You drive a big wedge between you and now you are too stubborn to fix!"

Johnny let her words roll around in his head. Brad would be upset for a while, but he'd come around. Unless that little bitch wife of his turned him against his own father. *I wouldn't put anything past them slanty-eyed bastards.* He imagined Donna plotting and scheming ways to keep tension between them. *That's how they work.*

"Your daughter-in-law called me this morning," she added.

"She's not my daughter-in-law." Johnny's gut tightened.

Elena let the comment pass and sat on the edge of a nearby sofa. "Heinrich is taking her to Washington." She paused for a moment. "They asked us to go with them."

"Did you tell her, no?"

"You tell her, no." She pointed toward the kitchen. "I'll get the phone. You can call."

Johnny had to admit that he admired the way Elena maneuvered him about. But he wasn't biting on this one.

There was no way in hell he was going to call down there and give even the slightest impression that he was mending any fences. No, this time Brad had gone too far.

When Brad was sixteen, he had taken Johnny's car without permission and wrapped it around a telephone pole. A year later Johnny caught Brad taking money from his wallet. A year after that, just a few weeks before graduation, Brad was caught with the young student teacher in a closet at school. Later that year, Brad flunked out of college in his first semester.

It all paled next to what he had just done.

"I'm not going to Washington."

Elena stood up, her cheeks flushed. She spoke through gritting teeth. "Yes," she said, her eyes fixed on Johnny as if she were viewing him through the sights of a gun. "You are."

"No," he answered, sticking out his chin. "I'm not."

Elena stepped in like a well-trained boxer. Johnny felt the sting of her hand landing a solid slap to the side of his face, his ear ringing from the impact. Elena towered over Johnny, her hands balled into fists and planted firmly on her ample hips. "You *are* going."

Johnny leaned forward to exit the scene, but Elena pushed him back down into the chair. She stood over him, pointing. "You can run away from your life if you want to," she began. "You can hide in your chair in your den in your little house way down in the mountains. Yes?" She nodded and offered a false smile. "You can run away from your home up in New York. You can run away from your nightmares," her voice grew louder as she continued, "and your demons and your son and your daughter-in-law on their wedding day!" She stomped her foot and extended a clenched fist, her eyes obscured with tears, stopping just short of striking him in the face. She drew it back and blinked fresh tears from her eyes.

Johnny saw the veins bulging in her neck, her fists still clenched.

She raised her hand once again.

Johnny raised his own hands in defense.

Elena stopped short once again before striking. "You can turn away from all these things," she said, trembling with rage, her voice barely above a whisper. "But, you will not turn away from me."

Johnny looked up into her eyes. For the first time in their married life he felt as if she could really do it. He wondered why she hadn't already. *Why does she stay?*

"You are going with us," Elena finally said, her tone even, controlled. She took a deep breath. "We leave Saturday morning. Eight o'clock." She fixed him with an icy stare for a moment before turning away. "And, you will shave your face," she added, walking into the kitchen.

*   *   *

"I'm glad the new owners were so understanding," Donna said to Cindy Lewis as they walked out of the real estate offices. "It was nice of them to wait for me to recover."

"Oh, they're such nice people," Cindy replied. "And, they really wanted the house." She placed her hand on Donna's upper arm. "See, everything worked out."

Donna nodded in agreement.

"How are you doing?" Cindy asked. "You know, after the surgery and all."

"I'm doing okay." Donna stopped next to her new car, a white Grand Prix. Her Lexus had been totaled in the wreck. "Well enough to drive again."

"I'm so happy for you." Cindy cocked her head in a gesture of sincerity. "It was so good seeing you again." She hugged Donna. "That's a nice little nest egg for you and your husband." Cindy nodded at the check in Donna's hand, the proceeds from her fathers' house.

"One hundred and twelve thousand," Donna said, looking down at the check. "You know your business."

Cindy nodded and smiled as Donna slid into her car. "Bye, sweety," she called after Donna as she pulled out of the parking lot.

A short time later Donna pulled up to a modest brick ranch house in a residential section of Middleton. She walked to the front door and rang the doorbell.

"Mercy sakes," Wanda said as she opened the front door. "Come give me a hug, child!" She threw her arms wide and wrapped them around Donna's neck. "It's so good to see you. Come in." She held the door wide and motioned for Donna to pass.

Wanda led her to a small kitchen with plain yellow walls and a green plaid border. The cabinets were dark veneer, the floor cheap linoleum with green squares. "Have a seat," she said, waving toward a plain pine kitchen table and chairs. "I'll get us some sweet tea."

"How have you been, Wanda?" Donna took a seat at the table. "I'm so sorry I haven't been in touch more."

"Don't be silly, child." Wanda waved a hand in the air. "Girl, I was worried sick about you. Did you get the cards and flowers I sent?"

Donna smiled and nodded. "All of them. Thank you for thinking of me."

"You're 'bout all I *have* been thinking of." Wanda said while pouring the iced tea.

"You're so sweet, Wanda."

"Yeah, well," she added, turning toward the table with the two glasses of tea. "Just don't spread that around. I gotta reputation to maintain. Halloween's comin' soon."

Donna giggled at the remark. "My father always said you were the nicest pit bull he ever met."

Wanda set the glasses down and stuck her hands on her hips. "He said that?" she asked, cocking her head for comic relief. "He called me a pit bull, huh?"

Donna laughed out loud as Wanda took a seat at the table.

"Lord, how I miss that man," Wanda offered, her expression turning somber.

"I came here to give you something," Donna said, reaching for the manila envelope she had brought into the house with her. "My father left very explicit instructions."

Wanda's face contracted as she inspected the envelope. "What is it?"

"Open it and see."

Wanda reached over to the counter and grabbed her reading glasses, unfolded them and slid them on. Her dark fingers pulled the clasp open and slid the contents onto the table. She looked inside, making sure she had emptied it, before setting the envelope aside.

Donna watched Wanda's expression turn from puzzlement to joy as she read the note that Jack had written her before he died. Tears streaked down Wanda's cheeks as she finished.

"Just a few days before he died," Donna said, her lips trembling. "He told me that he only had one regret in his entire life." She smiled at Wanda before continuing. "He said that he had fought in battles that would have turned most men into jelly. He told me he had more courage than most men, but he always regretted not having the courage to marry you."

Donna reached out and slipped the paperclip from the note and pulled the check out from behind. "He loved you so much." She placed her hand over Wanda's. "And so do I.

You are like a mother to me." Donna nodded as she spoke. "And, that's why we wanted you to have this." She slid the check for one hundred and twelve thousand dollars in front of Wanda.

Wanda covered her mouth with her hand. "I can't take this."

"Yes," Donna said, gently squeezing Wanda's hand. "You can. It's in his will. We both wanted it that way."

Wanda sat at the tiny table and took it all in. Her eyes glazed as she stared at the note Jack had crafted months before.

"It wasn't all him," Wanda offered, picking up the check.

"What do you mean?" Donna cocked her head, her eyebrows contracted.

"I never knew I could ever feel that way about a white man." Wanda shook her head. "You gotta remember somethin', child. That was almost thirty years ago. Things was different back then."

"Remember who you're talking to," Donna quipped.

Wanda chuckled. "I suppose you're right. You know all about it, don't you?"

Donna nodded.

"I loved him," Wanda continued. "Lord, we had it bad for each other, too." She burst into laughter, a reminiscent look coming over her. "We was like a couple of teenagers sneakin' around trying not to get caught." She stared into the past, shaking her graying head. "Daddy almost did once."

"Wanda!" Donna's eyes widened.

"Oh, hush now," Wanda answered, giving Donna's hand a playful pat. "You're all grown up. Ain't nothin' new under the sun, now."

"It's just hard to think of my father that way."

"Not for me!" Wanda laughed.

Donna joined in. "So, why didn't you marry?"

Wanda took in a deep breath and looked into the corner of the room. "There was enough trouble just raising you in this little town," she said, looking back at Donna and shaking her head. "Middleton could eventually handle you being here. It might even have been able to handle a white man marrying a black woman. But," Wanda shook her head, "not both."

"Why didn't you move?" Donna asked. "Maybe somewhere that was more accepting?"

Wanda looked back at Donna with sad eyes. "It wouldn't have made any difference." She shook her head slowly. "One town's just like the next."

"How sad."

Wanda nodded in agreement. "We both wanted you to have the best chance in life." She smiled and took Donna's hand. "We didn't think that you would have that if we married." She shrugged. "So, we didn't."

Donna placed her other hand over Wanda's and gazed into the eyes of the woman who had shown her the way so many times and said, "I really wish you had."

*   *   *

"You did what?" Brad stared in disbelief at Donna.

"Yes, I invited them both," Donna replied. "Your mother agrees."

It was early morning and Donna sat eating her eggs while Brad paced the floor. He had sold his house a few months earlier when they decided that Donna's house was a better place for them to live.

Brad's hands shook up and down, his eyes closed, his head shaking in spasm-like movements. "But…he's. Why?" His hand landed hard against his forehead. "Do you not…? What…?"

Donna sat at the breakfast bar watching Brad's theatrics, laughing at his apoplectic reaction to her inviting Johnny and Elena to join them on their trip to DC. "Really, Brad. It's going to be okay. He *is* your father, after all."

His hands swirled around his shaking head as if he didn't know where to make them land. "I don't even know where to start with this." Brad finally gripped his skull with both hands, his frenzy subsiding for the moment. "Is this not the same man who snubbed you at Thanksgiving?"

Donna set her fork down and put her index finger to her lips. "Yes," she replied, nodding in mock affirmation. "I believe so."

"And is he not the same guy who practically called you a sub-human at Christmas?"

Donna inhaled deeply and looked up at the ceiling. "I'm pretty sure that's him."

Brad stared at Donna in disbelief. "You invited the guy who boycotted our wedding?"

She looked off to her left before turning to Brad. "Yeah," she replied, nodding. "I guess I did."

Brad held his hands in front of his face as if he was holding an invisible volleyball. "Are you freakin' nuts?" He dropped his hands to his sides. "Or, just crazy?"

"Come here." She motioned for him to join her at the bar.

Brad glanced to his right and exhaled before shuffling over to her.

She slid her arm around his waist. "Whatever problems your father has with me will not get any better if we don't get to know each other." Donna jockeyed her head to meet his shifting glance. "One of us has to be the grown-up." She pulled him into her, parting her thighs to let him slide against her. "We are a family now. Like the preacher said, for better or worse. We can either act like one, or not. Your call."

Brad alternated between craning his neck and bobbing his head while trying to avoid looking at her. "Would you do me a favor?" he finally said.

"Sure," she replied, her voice reserved, almost cautionary.

"Sometime in our life together," he said, his eyes coming to bear on hers. "Could you be wrong…just once?"

"We'll see," Donna said, offering a wicked grin.

Later that day, Brad left for the store to pick up some items for their trip. Donna sat curled on the sofa in the living room reading the final volume of Jack's journal. Engrossed in one of the pages, she barely noticed the sudden movement in the kitchen through the doorway. Donna stopped reading and set the book on the coffee table. She had just risen to her feet when a figure, in a white dress, appeared in the threshold.

"Mai," Donna blurted, her heart surging. "God, you scared me," she added, her hand flat against her chest. A moment later, Donna found her composure and her expression changed from fright to confusion. "I thought you were gone."

Mai smiled. She had lost all traces of her antagonistic persona. "Our journey is not yet over," she said to Donna, slowly advancing. "You still have one more dragon to slay." Mai stood across the coffee table with her hands at her sides. "And, time is not your friend."

"What about you, Mai?" Donna asked, sinking back into the sofa. She pulled the journal from the table as she sat down. "Are you my friend?"

Mai smiled and took a seat in the matching chair at the end of the table. "I have always been your friend." She melted Donna's apprehensions with a benevolent nod. "I have always been there for you. Until now, you have not been ready to accept that."

Donna picked at a corner of the journal with her finger-nail. "I'm really very happy now." She glanced up at Mai. "We don't need to do this. I've made my peace."

"With our mother," Mai answered. "Yes. That is true. But, you have not made peace with yourself."

Donna looked away and shook her head, her open hand stretched defensively in Mai's direction. "We're not going to do this," she said, pulling herself into a ball. "I'm happy now. I have a husband and a new life. Leave me alone. Let me enjoy it. It was so long ago…"

But, it was only a heartbeat away. Donna was no longer in her living room. Instead, she stood at the edge of a small firebase with a satchel strapped to her back. In the midst of a raging firefight, she could see the muzzle flashes and hear the bullets whiz past her head from the soldiers shooting in her direction from behind the sandbags that lined the perimeter.

She started walking toward the camp, the image of the younger children somewhere behind her held at gunpoint. The North Vietnamese officer had assured her that he would kill them all should she try to run away. He was the same officer who had captured her and forced her to disclose information about the base and its activities. He was the same officer who had stood by, expressionless while three soldiers brutally raped her with a rifle barrel.

"Why are you doing this?" Donna asked Mai. "Please," she pleaded. "I have put this all away."

"Not all of it." Mai leaned closer. "You have more to do."

Donna clasped her head in her hands and sunk further into the sofa. Her father's face gradually came into focus as she approached the stacked sandbags. She was close enough to see his eyes through the fixed sights of his M-16 taking aim at her.

"You never told him that you knew it was him," Mai said.

Donna shook her head, still clasped in her fingers. "No," was all she said.

"And you never told him it was you who spied on them and disclosed their movements and whereabouts."

Donna tried to turn away from the guilt and the shame, but the sofa cushions blocked her retreat. She had observed their routines and reported back to the NVA soldiers on many occasions, making their assaults that much more devastating. They had threatened her, starved her and deprived her of sleep before suddenly offering her food and rest. The brainwashing had been masterfully undertaken, yielding precision results.

"They made me believe it was the Americans who killed my mother," Donna responded. "I was so confused. I believed it was American soldiers who assaulted me. I believed them."

"You know better now," Mai said. "And you wish you had told our father, don't you?"

Donna could only nod her head in agreement. "I never told him I was sorry."

Mai stood as they heard Brad's car pulling into the garage. "The peace you seek awaits you, but you must have the courage to face what we did," she said, gliding into the kitchen. "Only then, will we be reconciled."

Brad opened the door leading to the garage from the kitchen as Mai vanished through the doorway.

Chapter Twenty-Four

"Is going well, so far. Yes?" Elena whispered to Donna across the back seat of the Grand Prix. Brad drove while a stoic Johnny rode shotgun.

"Johnny is so quiet," Donna said, leaning close to Elena. "How upset is he with me?"

"Only with himself," Elena replied. "Deep down, he is ashamed, but he is too stubborn to admit." She tapped her forehead with her fingertips. "Sometimes I just want to crack his thick skull."

After an awkward morning of travel, devoid of much conversation, they had stopped for lunch before driving the rest of the way into DC. In spite of having to stop every hour for Johnny to stretch his legs, they made good time in the light weekend traffic.

"Here we are," Brad announced, pulling into a parking space at the suburban Metrorail station. "Anyone have the slightest idea what we do now?"

Donna sat behind Brad, watching Johnny smirk at the notion that the trip hadn't been planned out to the very last detail.

"We'll figure it out when we get inside the station," Donna offered while climbing from the backseat, feeling just a little defensive about Johnny's attitude. Brad held the driver's seat forward as she exited the two-door vehicle.

"That's right," Elena joined in, no doubt sensing her opportunity to support her new daughter-in-law while breaking some of the tension that enshrouded the group like the remnants of an ice storm. "We are explorers on an adventure. Is part of the fun, no?"

Johnny remained silent, as he had for most of the trip, responding only when spoken to.

Once inside the station, Donna approached one of the six subway fare ticket machines standing side by side against the wall opposite the long row of turnstiles leading to the passenger platform. Each machine was nearly seven feet high and four feet wide, complete with an array of illuminated buttons alongside somewhat cryptic instructions.

"I have a Ph.D. in thermodynamics and I have no idea how to use this machine," Donna said, turning to Brad and laughing.

"Need some help?" a tall, slender black man asked. The close-cropped hair around his temples matched the dark gray uniform he wore, a Metrorail logo on the sleeve.

"Yes," Donna replied, turning toward the man. "Thank you. I was just trying to figure out how to buy our tickets."

"Takes some getting used to," the attendant offered. "You folks from out of town?"

"It's that obvious?" Donna replied, smiling.

"Let me guess," the man said with a smile, likely having had the same conversation at least a hundred times a day. "Heading for the Smithsonian?"

Donna nodded. "Yes, there and to the rest of the Mall."

"You'll need this, then." The man reached into a nearby kiosk and produced a folded map. "This has all the hours and exhibits listed for the Smithsonian and Mall events."

"Thank you," Donna replied, taking the map. "Now if we could only buy our tickets."

"No problem," the man said. "Slide your credit card right in here." He pointed to a card reader on the machine. "Now punch in your destination right here."

Donna carefully observed every step for future reference while Johnny looked disappointed that they were
about to clear their first hurdle with such ease.

After a short subway ride, they arrived at the
Smithsonian Metro stop. Donna felt her stomach tighten
with each step she took through the dimly lit station. She
tried ignoring it, but her anxiety only increased as they
walked beneath the arched concrete ceiling toward the stairs
leading them to daylight.

The Capitol building, nearly a mile in the distance
across the open grassy expanse of the National Mall, was
the first thing they saw as they climbed the last few steps
into the heavy, summer heat. Its white cast iron dome,
divided by pillars at the base and segmented by dozens of
ornate arched windows, shimmered in the mid-day sun.
High atop, supported by over eight million pounds of metal,
stood the bronze statue of freedom keeping her silent vigil
over the nation's capital.

"Magnificent," Elena said, stopping just beyond the
steps leading up from the station. "My poppa would be so
happy knowing I could see such a thing in my life." She
clasped her hands together and brought them to her lips.

Donna, too, was struck by the significance of the structure. For so many years it stood as a symbol of decency and
democracy in a world confused by greed, poverty, and igno-
rance. Many years before, decisions made in its chambers
had affected each one of their lives. In some ways it may
have brought Donna untold misery that she might not have
otherwise suffered. At the same time, she may not have survived at all without the presence and intervention of a
young army officer who had dared to care.

To the immediate right stood the red sandstone
Smithsonian Castle, looking like a postcard picture with its
spires standing tall against the cloudless blue sky. Across

the mall to their left, the Museums of American and Natural History stood beside each other like academic buildings flanking some Ivy League college quad. Behind them, the downtown buildings, many of their designs reflecting a French influence, rose to uniform heights in Parisian fashion.

"What should we do first?" Brad asked, glancing around at the Smithsonian buildings and then toward the Washington monument.

Johnny stood by himself, a few feet away, casting disinterested glances among the joggers, roller-bladers, and bicyclists crazy enough to be in motion in the stifling heat.

"I have a suggestion," Donna spoke up, fanning herself with the top of her shirt. "It is supposed to rain tomorrow." She unfolded the map the Metro guide had supplied as she continued. "Maybe we could see the outdoor sights today and save the museums for tomorrow when it might be raining."

"Is good idea," Elena agreed. "Heinrich. What about you?"

Brad shrugged. "I'm just along for the ride. Whatever you two want to do is fine with me."

"Johnny?" Elena turned to her husband. "What do you want to do?"

Johnny turned to Elena. His lips curled into a half-frown. "I don't care," he replied, shaking his head. "Do whatever you want." He started to turn away, but added, "I ain't waiting in any lines."

"No lines for Johnny," Elena said, nodding in false affirmation. "Good. We make a note of this. Maybe you can see things no one else wants to see." Craning her neck, she feigned a look at Donna's map. "Yes, there is good one for you, Johnny." Elena pointed at the map. "American Museum of Cranky Husbands."

Johnny shook his head and waved her off with a single swipe of his hand.

Donna stifled a laugh and looked across the street at the Washington Monument, closed for renovation. A wave of disappointment swept over her as images of a panoramic view of Washington from atop the monument faded from her thoughts.

"We can walk along the reflecting pool and see the Lincoln Memorial," Donna said, glancing down at her map. "I've always wanted to stand where Doctor King stood while he delivered his *'I have a dream'* speech."

Johnny's head came about at the mention of King's name. He shot Donna a quick glance from the corners of his eyes.

"Good," Elena said. "We'll go there." She glanced both ways along the Mall. "Which way to Lincoln Memorial?"

"This way," Johnny offered, pointing toward the monument.

Elena looked at Donna, her eyebrows raised and her lips curled downward.

They passed under the shadow of the Washington Monument, five hundred and fifty-five feet of white marble and granite rising to a pyramid shaped point high overhead. Donna strained her neck to see the top as they walked beneath.

"Wait here," Donna said, walking briskly away. "Let me take your picture in front of it."

Donna lined up the shot and snapped a picture of Brad, Elena, and a reluctant Johnny framed by the massive base of the stone monument.

"Hey, ma," Brad said to Elena. "How 'bout you take one of me and Donna?"

Elena walked back to where Donna had snapped her shot and pointed the camera. Johnny stepped to the side, as if unsure of what else to do.

After the photo session, Donna and Brad walked hand-in-hand along the tree-lined walkway toward the Lincoln Memorial with Johnny and Elena a few steps behind. Donna's chest grew tighter as they approached. A heavy feeling of nausea gripped her with each advancing step. In spite of the near tropical conditions, deep in her gut she could feel a shiver starting as the statue of Lincoln became visible between the massive columns.

Donna knew the Wall was there, but she would not look to her right at it as they passed. She turned to look at Johnny instead. He was staring straight ahead unaware of how close he was to the tapered cut stone that loomed just a few yards away.

They climbed the steps to the Lincoln Memorial, stopping halfway up. Donna turned and imagined looking out over two hundred and fifty thousand people gathered together in the name of human rights to hear one of the most gifted speakers of the twentieth century. She could hear his words echoing among the crowd.

When we let freedom ring, when we let it ring from every village and every hamlet, from every state and every city, we will be able to speed up that day when all of God's children, black men and white men, Jews and Gentiles, Protestants and Catholics, will be able to join hands and sing in the words of the old Negro spiritual, "Free at last! Free at last! Thank God Almighty, we are free at last!"

There was still the matter of Donna's freedom. In her purse back in the car, she carried the last volume of Jack's journal. She had completed it the night before, in the wake of Mai's ominous visit. From beyond the treetops that partially obscured the Wall from her view, a lone soldier's voice called out to her from the litany of engraved names.

From the top step she could see it: Four hundred and ninety-three feet of black granite bearing the names of each

American killed or missing in Viet Nam. It beckoned her with the same insistence she had felt from Jack's footlocker on the day of his funeral. Surrendering to the urge to look, Donna stood like a child at Lincoln's knee stealing glances in the direction of the long wall rising gradually out of the ground; her heart pounding as she contemplated what awaited her there.

"Ready?" Brad startled her.

Donna nodded, her breathing labored, her stomach in knots. She barely recalled anything about Lincoln or the monument as they descended the steps. Reaching the bottom, they turned to their left, passing a collection of makeshift booths manned by Viet Nam veterans in fatigues and combat boots. Some wore tee shirts bearing the emblems of their units while others bore the familiar black and white POW / MIA logo.

Johnny glanced around at the men and the POW / MIA bracelets they had displayed along with the other military regalia. A look that might have been panic flashed over Johnny's face as he realized where he was. He searched Elena's face and then for the first time in months, Johnny's eyes locked with Donna's in an exchange loaded with accusation and contempt.

Donna's stomach lurched. She fought the urge to vomit and took a deep breath. Reaching for Brad's hand, she walked past Johnny and down the long, brick pathway leading toward the 'Wall that heals.'

                          *   *   *

"I am *not* going down there," Johnny said to Elena, pointing after Brad and Donna walking hand-in-hand along the shady path. In his effort to divorce himself from the activities, Johnny had failed to take in his surroundings. Feeling ambushed, Johnny reacted the only way he knew how. "I don't know what you think you're pulling here, but I ain't going."

Elena turned to him. Taking his hand gently in hers, she said, "In a thousand years, I would never ask you to." She let go and backed away, starting to follow her son and daughter-in-law. "But, if you do," she added, still standing within arms reach. "You will not be alone." Elena turned and walked away.

Johnny watched Elena walk down the brick-lined path through the shade. He turned toward the booths and saw a handful of vets looking back at him, their faces somber, full of understanding. Without a word, one of them nodded, silently offering permission for Johnny to take those final frightening steps.

But, Johnny had other plans. In spite of the urgent and unseen force pulling him toward the path, he put his head down and started walking away.

"Semper Fi," another one of the vets, a stocky man with a bushy mustache, stepped into Johnny's way.

Johnny looked up into his eyes, a 'how did you know' look on his face.

"I can spot a brother a mile away." He gently placed his hand on Johnny's shoulder. "Fifth Marines. Happy Valley...Sixty-seven."

"I don't wanna talk about it," Johnny answered, looking away.

The man pulled back his hand and nodded. "That's cool." The two men were silent for a moment before the unnamed vet continued. "You're headin' the wrong way."

Johnny glanced down at the ground. "I can't," he said, scanning the sidewalk.

"Yeah," the man replied. He puckered his lips and nodded. "I put it off as long as I could, too." He took a deep

breath and folded his arms across his chest. "But, I did it
and was glad I did."

"I'm all right," Johnny said, not believing it for a
minute. "I just wanna leave now."

"Part of you wants to, though," the vet said. He waited
for Johnny to turn and look at him before continuing. "Am
I wrong?"

Johnny turned and glanced, once again down the pathway, his stomach churning, his head spinning. He tried taking a deep breath but it was cut short by the trembling in his
gut.

"I'm not ready," Johnny said, gripping his cane tight
and jabbing it into the sidewalk before turning to look at the
man. "I'll come back later... when I'm alone."

"You're never alone here, brother." He offered Johnny
another somber nod. "I'll go with you if you want."

"No thanks."

The man smiled and turned toward the booths. "I'll be
here," he said, walking away.

Johnny turned back toward Elena, who was still walking away. He watched her join Brad and Donna near a
pedestal covered with a glass shroud. His new daughter-in-
law appeared to be searching for something within the
pages of a book tucked beneath the glass. Johnny turned,
once again toward the rest of the vets manning the booths.
They were still looking back at him, their faces telegraph-
ing their brotherhood. For reasons Johnny would never
comprehend, he turned and followed his wife down the
pathway, the faint sound of his own heartbeat echoing
somewhere amidst the rumble of an advancing avalanche.

Chapter Twenty-Five

Reaching under the glass canopy, Donna paged through the book containing the more than 58,000 names etched into the black granite memorial. The information listed next to his entry directed her to panel 2W, a section near the middle bearing the names of those dead or missing between August '71 and April '72. She scribbled down the row number, turned to Brad and Elena, and moved on.

"You still haven't told me why you're here," Brad said to Donna, taking her hand in his and nodding at the piece of paper in her other hand. "Whose name are you looking for?"

Brad's voice was like an echo reverberating through a long tube. Donna knew he was there, but her thoughts carried her back to that early morning outside Da Nang nearly thirty-years before. After seeing her mother killed, she had been captured and brainwashed by an unscrupulous North Vietnamese officer. While still in a near fugue state after her subsequent brutal assault, she received her simple instructions and carried them out with detached precision.

"Donna?"

She heard Brad in the distance. Turning to him, she remained expressionless, still lost in her memories.

"Are you in there?" Brad asked, stepping in front of her and leaning to look into her eyes. "You didn't answer me."

"Heinrich," Elena said to Brad. She stepped close and laid her hand on his shoulder.

Donna turned her head to Elena, meeting her eyes. Elena gazed back at Donna for a moment before turning her attention once again to Brad.

"We let your new wife go ahead by herself now, yes?" Elena said to Brad, nodding with an understanding she could only have acquired through experience.

Brad turned to Elena. "Whadda ya talking about, ma?" Brad said, his face contracting in confusion. "Whatever she's doing here, I'm sure she wants me with her." He turned to Donna for validation, but she could only stare back in silence. "Right?" he asked, his eyes pleading with her to include him.

Donna swore she heard Brad's heart breaking as she took his hands in hers and slowly pushed them toward him. She looked at Elena, wondering how far a new mother-in-law's help extended.

"Some things," Elena piped in, taking Brad's hand and gently pulling him away. "Must be done alone." The smile she offered Donna harbored comprehension beyond normal bounds. "Come," she continued, glancing back at Johnny who was standing near the book of names. "We go to your father now."

Donna watched Brad and Elena walk away and join Johnny at the west end of the memorial.

The sun overhead reflected off the polished surface of the Wall, bouncing streaks of light onto the walkway. Along the path, middle-aged men stood next to, leaned against, and knelt in front of the tapered granite slabs. Along the base, small American flags, flowers, letters, stuffed animals, unit patches, medals, and other personal mementoes lay tucked against the dark stone, parting remembrances from family, friends and brothers in arms.

The Wall's height increased with each tentative step toward the apex. His name was near the center, almost halfway down the long slab of stone. Donna heard his voice echoing in the eerie distance of her memory.

"What are you doing here?" the fair-skinned soldier had said to her, rising from his slumber in the early morning hours. Mai was far from fluent, but she had picked up a functional command of English in the three years since she left Khe Sanh. "You must be lost." His hair was cut short, but it was clearly blonde. His silver dog tag hung from a metallic necklace against the bare skin of his hairless chest.

Mai had snuck in an hour earlier, using the usual tunnel under the sandbags along the perimeter. She hated the tunnels. They were full of huge black spiders, roaches the size of her fists, and rats. Of course, where there were rats, there were snakes looking to eat them. On that night, however, she didn't notice any of them. Nearly catatonic, Mai had slipped underground and crawled into the camp without a thought about her fears. At the time, she had none. At the time, she felt nothing.

Donna passed a young family gathered in front of a panel mid-way to the apex. The father was explaining to his young daughter that 'Pappy' had died a long time ago in a far away place. For a moment, the image of an old woman from her village clutching the lifeless body of her son swept into Donna's thoughts. She tried to imagine what a wall with six million names on it would look like: One entry for each of her countrymen killed.

A few steps away, a man sat in his wheelchair, leaning to touch a name on the Wall. He wore a yellow tee shirt with the Marine logo and the words *Semper Fidelis* silk-screened below. His long, gray hair was pulled into a ponytail. His gray mustache wrapped around his mouth and followed the lines of his jawbone back to his ears.

A few more steps and she stopped in front of panel 2W, row 105. Donna stared at his name, the same name Jack had entered into his journal, killed on the morning of February 11th, 1972 by an unknown assailant.

Donna stepped forward, within reach of the Wall. Raising her arm, she extended her hand and her fingers gently touched the etched letters. Their edges, precision-cut into the hard surface, felt clean and sharp. Running her fingers along the length of his name, the last haunting images of that morning focused clearly in her mind.

Her instructions had been simple.

As the young soldier rose to greet Mai, he reached for something on the trunk next to his bed. "Maybe you're hungry," he said, holding a chocolate candy bar out to her. "I won't tell anyone you're here," he whispered, holding a finger up to his lips.

Donna fell to her knees, her stomach heaving. She fought for her breath through anguished sobs, the letters on the Wall just inches away blurred by the tears streaming from her eyes. Her forehead landed against the cool surface, her fingertips still clutching at the letters of his name overhead. Donna heard her own painful cries as the memory of her darkest moment seized her thoughts like a raging beast.

Without emotion, Mai drew the US Army service forty-five the North Vietnamese officer had given her from behind her back and pointed it at Private First Class David Mark Bishop and pulled the trigger. The bullet struck him in the forehead, blowing away most of the top of his head.

Donna collapsed against the unyielding surface of the Wall, her hands covering her face, writhing in spasms of grief. "Forgive me," she said, barely able to speak through her sobbing. "Oh, God," she continued, her face wet with tears. "Please forgive me."

She heard the approaching tap of a cane, but did not make the connection: The steady, rhythmic beat followed by the familiar shuffle of shoe leather against pavement. Donna was about to turn toward the source when she was startled by the sudden grip of a hand on her shoulder.

                    *   *   *

Johnny stood near the registry, watching Elena and Brad approaching. "She doesn't belong here," he said to himself before they arrived. As they came within earshot, he poked his chin toward the opposite end of the memorial and said, "Where'd *she* go?"

"She wants to be alone for a while," Brad replied, avoiding eye contact.

Elena slipped her arm into Johnny's. "Are you ready to walk with us?"

Johnny gazed into Elena's loving eyes and in an instant remembered why he loved her so much. While he couldn't pinpoint it, there was a kindness and understanding there that was deeper than his ability to comprehend. It had sustained him throughout their years together and it sustained him now. He moved with her, taking a tentative step while clinging to her arm as a drowning man might clutch a floating limb in a swift current.

A few steps away, a man about Johnny's age leaned with one hand against the Wall; wiping tears from his eyes. Johnny stopped short at the sight. He felt Elena's soft hands embrace his arm in a reassuring squeeze before continuing.

The names and faces of several men in his unit raced through his mind as he drew closer to the apex. He saw Jimmy 'Stitch' Mitchell's grinning face. *Crazy bastard.* Jimmy could walk on his hands all the way across camp. He couldn't have weighed over a buck thirty. Johnny fought back a lump in his throat as he considered what a good father Jimmy might have been.

Then there was Michael Carter. The ladies' man: the best-looking guy in the unit. Johnny recalled lifting the stretcher off the chopper and looking down at Michael's mangled face, thinking how light he was without his legs. Maybe it was better that he died en route.

A few yards ahead, Johnny saw Donna slumped against the wall, her anguish echoing in the quiet of that sacred place. Without a conscious thought, he reflexively pulled away from Elena and started toward his daughter-in-law before realizing what he was doing and stopped in his tracks.

Brad started toward Donna, but Elena grabbed his arm. "No," she said to Brad. "Wait."

Johnny's incredulous glance bounced between Brad and Elena before he said, "Aren't you gonna...?" He shot a quick glance toward Donna and turned once again to Elena. "You just gonna leave her...?" Johnny licked his lips, his feet shifted in a nervous shuffle as he tried to decide what to do.

"Go to her, Johnny," Elena said, just above a whisper. She reached out and rubbed his upper arm. "It was your first instinct just now."

"I just..." Johnny waged the last of a losing mental battle against the inexplicable compulsion to assist her. "How do I...?" He heard his own words, yet they were as distant as the memories that came rushing back to him in waves.

"Go to her." Elena took a step and pulled Brad along with her. "You are only one who will understand." Johnny stared into his son's eyes as Elena led him away.

Johnny turned to see a man in a wheelchair wearing a yellow shirt moving toward Donna. He stopped, glancing at Johnny before he got to her. Johnny raised his hand, waving him off before sticking his cane hard against the walkway and taking the first step toward the Wall. The man backed away, nodding.

Seeing Donna slumped and sobbing against the granite, brought to mind a hundred similar scenes from his tour. There was always someone left to grieve after a firefight. So many times he had simply walked away, climbed into the chopper and put the suffering out of his mind.

When he touched her shoulder, Donna jumped and turned a terrified face. Her eyes were red and swollen, her cheeks streaked from her tears. She stared up at Johnny, the fear she felt toward him frozen in her expression.

Johnny extended his hand.

Donna's sobs subsided as she studied it, as if unsure of what to do.

Staring into Johnny's eyes, Donna took his hand. At the gentle contact of her soft fingers against the rough skin of his palms, Johnny realized it was the first time they had ever touched. He shook his head as he felt himself heading for the edge. His eyelids fluttered in a last line of defense.

"Did you know him," Johnny asked, helping Donna to her feet, his voice beginning to crack.

"No," Donna replied, shaking her head and trying to catch her breath between sniffles.

Johnny nodded, wondering what connection she had with anyone on the wall. "Your father?" He pulled a clean handkerchief from his back pocket and handed it to her.

"Thank you." Donna wiped her face. She took a deep breath before continuing. "I don't know who my father was."

"I figured he was a GI," Johnny said, recalling some of his buddies bragging about their encounters with the local 'hooch mommas'. "What about your mother?"

"My mother died when I was a young girl," she began. "Along with my baby sister."

Johnny pursed his lips and nodded. "Why did you come here?"

Donna glanced away for a moment before answering, inhaling deeply. "After my mother was killed, I was all alone. I was captured by the North Vietnamese." Her eyes glazed as she told him the story. "They raped and tortured me for days." Donna paused, letting a wave of anguish subside. "After a while I was so brainwashed and confused I didn't even know who I was."

Johnny could barely form words. "I didn't know." The corners of Johnny's mouth pulled downward as he spoke.

"One night," Donna continued. "They gave me a gun..." she added, her face contorted, her hands covering her face. "They made me do it..." She bowed her head and wept, her hands shaking, her body convulsing.

Johnny's hands, in involuntary movements, closed around her. Her slender body shook in his grasp, shedding the hurt and guilt in rhythmic surges.

In the darkest corner of Johnny's mind came the far away sound of barking dogs. He flinched at the sound, causing Donna to lift her head and pull away. He clasped his forehead as the vivid images of the chained dogs came into focus.

For a moment Johnny was back in the jungle, staring down the barrel of a turret-mounted machinegun. Its young gunner was swinging it around in wild arcs firing indiscriminately into the trees. Behind him, the captain was screaming at Johnny to fire on the nest. The circling helicopters were fast approaching and the NVA were swarming in waves.

"Take it out!" came the command from the rear. "Take it out!"

Johnny stared down into Donna's face; her mixed-race features the trigger for his most haunting nightmares. "I was just a kid when they drafted me," he said, pulling back from her. "Hell I don't think I shaved more than twice a week then."

Donna smiled at him through the pain.

"We were pinned down." He took a deep breath. "We couldn't get the choppers in to land on account of this machine gun nest." Johnny stared into the grain of the granite. "He already shot down one Huey and it was up to me to take him out."

Donna listened quietly as he told the story.

"He was just a kid," Johnny said, gesturing toward an unseen location. "They had all these dogs around him…. all chained up." He circled the front of his neck with his finger indicating where the chain was connected. "I couldn't get a good shot. So I had to strafe 'em all."

Johnny stared into the Wall as if it was a television screen. He'd seen the unfolding scene before but this time something was terribly wrong. His gut heaved. He lost his breath and his words caught in his throat. Johnny fought to speak, but no words would come. His stomach lurched in spasms while his eyes burned with the tears welling inside them. Stuttered breaths escaped between desperate gasps. Johnny reached out, steadying himself against the Wall, reflecting the ugly truth.

"What did I do?" he managed. Johnny brought his other hand up to his face. To his shock, it was wet. The shimmering surface of the Wall, obscured by his tears, projected a mental image in all of its cruel clarity.

Johnny stiffened, taking in a deep breath in one quick gasp. His eyes widened at the sight of the barking dogs straining against the chains as his finger squeezed the trigger. His body trembled as he relived the moment, the gun jumping repeatedly in his hands.

"Sweet Jesus," he said, trying to catch his breath. "What did I do?" Johnny turned his head to see Donna's eyes filling with tears, her hands cupped over her mouth. "They weren't dogs…" Johnny fought for every word, for every breath. "They were—"

"I know…" Donna put her fingers to Johnny's lips. "You don't have to say it," she said, slowly shaking her head. "They were *bui doi*. Just like me." She pulled her lips tight and closed her eyes. More tears slid down her cheeks. "I know…" Donna reached for him.

Johnny pulled her close, burying his face into the thick soft strands of her hair. He tried to purge the image of the children pulling against the chains; their faces twisted in terror. "What did I do?"

"What you had to," Donna answered. "The only thing you could do." She pulled away, wiping her face.

Johnny took a couple deep breaths and straightened himself. They both stood in the ensuing silence reflecting in the healing tranquility.

"My father's name was John," Donna finally said after a long moment.

Johnny swiped the wetness from his cheeks. "I thought you didn't know who he was."

"My adoptive father." Donna smiled. "People called him Jack."

"He was in Nam?"

Donna nodded. "A major in the army."

Johnny looked around, surveying the area for gawkers who might have seen him lose his composure. There were none, only the steady flow of people lost in their own journeys, each one passing by as if they were the only one there.

Donna held out her arm, turning her wrist to show her brass bracelet. "Do you know what this is?"

Johnny leaned close and nodded. "Yeah."

She examined it for a long moment before removing it. "I want you to have it," she said, holding the 'Yard' bracelet between her fingertips. "I gave it to my father once and I am giving it to you now."

Johnny's throat tightened, the tears came back to his eyes. "After the way I..." He shook his head. "I can't take this."

In the very next instant Johnny knew how badly he had hurt her. Donna's gaze faltered and it dropped to the ground, her head nodding. Tears dropped to the walkway, making dark spots on the bricks.

"No," Johnny reached for her hand. "No, it ain't like that." He lifted her chin. "I don't deserve it, is what I meant."

Donna slid the bracelet onto Johnny's wrist. "This means that we are bonded together. Friends for life." She looked into Johnny's eyes and smiled. "Family."

Johnny looked down at his wrist and contemplated her words. "Family." He nodded.

Donna took a deep breath and exhaled her relief. "We should go."

"Just one more stop," Johnny replied, pulling a slip of paper from his pocket. On it was written the name Bartholomew Benjamin Girafillo and the panel number 17E.

"I understand," Donna replied, looking down at the paper. "I'll leave you alone." She started walking away.

"Will you go with me?"

Donna stopped and turned to Johnny. "I'd be honored," came her reply.

Chapter Twenty-Six

"So what was your favorite part?" Traci, a perky blonde sitting at a patio table with a wine cooler asked Donna. She was one of the nurses that worked at the hospital where Donna volunteered. "Besides consummating the marriage, that is," she added, laughing and nudging her husband, a stocky man with wire-rimmed glasses and reddish hair.

"Oh, let's see," Donna replied, looking at the darkening sky. "I think the look on Brad's face when he saw the village where I grew up was worth the trip alone."

Most of the twenty or so guests gathered for Brad's thirty-third birthday party shared a laugh at his expense.

Johnny sat with Elena on the edge of the patio taking in the banter of good friends celebrating in the warmth of a late August evening. Unfettered by his anger or his fears, Johnny looked at Donna with new vision. No longer a reminder to him of the horrors of his past, Johnny could now see her exquisite beauty, the joy in her laughter, and the zeal for life she exhibited in everything she did. Even the way she smiled wrapped everyone around her in her warmth.

"What about you, Brad?" Kathy, Donna and Brad's neighbor, piped in. Big boned and freckle-faced, she was the image of the stereotypical farm girl. "What did you like best?"

Johnny knew all he needed to know about his son's marriage by the way Brad looked at his new wife. In kind, he knew all he needed to know about Donna by the way she looked back.

"You really can't tell from the pictures," Brad said, pointing at the small stack of photos on a nearby table. "But, that palace in…" He turned to Donna, awaiting her to plug in the name.

"Hue City," Donna provided, smiling.

"Yeah," Brad continued, nodding once at Donna. "That place was really cool."

"God, Donna," Susan, Brad's receptionist, chimed in. "What was it like to go back there after all this time?"

Donna turned to Johnny, the only other person present who could understand the true gravity of the question, and winked before she replied. Johnny smiled back thinking what a difference a month could make in a man's life and how lucky Brad was for finding a woman who rivaled his Elena for her compassion. Johnny's long nights of worrying about his boy were over.

"I found joy where there was joy," Donna answered. "And sorrow where there was sorrow." She shrugged and looked down at her intertwined fingers, silent for a moment. "Things were definitely better than I remember, but there were still so many children begging in the streets."

"How do you like your new job at the center?" Trish, another friend asked Donna.

"I love it," Donna answered. "Now I can work with children all the time."

"Brad told us you had a rude awakening over there," Traci said, waving a hand toward the western horizon.

Donna dropped her head and smiled. "Oh, yes. I would say I did." She paused for a moment more before lifting her head with a smile. "I found out I'm a year older than I thought," she added, rolling her eyes.

"Here's to you Missus Robinson," Patrick, Brad's slender employee said. "Must be Brad's got a thing for them older women."

"Rob that cradle, honey," Traci said, raising her bottle. "Good for you, girl. Don't pay him no mind." She waved a hand in Patrick's direction. "You got yourself a boy toy. What more could you want?"

"Two boy toys?" Donna shot back. "Oops," she quickly added, looking at Johnny and Elena. "Just kidding." Donna wrapped her arms around Brad and kissed his neck.

"Is all right," Elena responded. "I keep my other man at home in the closet."

Johnny felt Elena's lips pecking his cheek. "She's more woman than one man can handle anyway," Johnny said, tipping his head toward Elena. The astonished, younger guests turned and laughed at the remark.

"Johnny!" Elena slapped his arm.

"The guy comes in handy when I'm too tired," Johnny added. "Besides, he cleans the gutters and he's a Yankees fan, so what's not to like?"

The small group was still laughing when Donna stood up from her patio chair and walked toward the house.

"Do you need help with anything?" Elena called to her from across the back yard patio, starting to get out of her chair.

Donna waved her off with a single flip of her slender hand. "Oh, no thank you, Elena." She continued into the house, rubbing her temple. "I just need to take something," she added, letting the back door close behind her.

"Is she all right?" Elena asked Brad. "She looks pale."

"She's been having headaches, again," Brad replied, his smile vanishing.

"Has she been to the doctor?" Elena asked, concern on her face.

"Not yet," Brad answered, shaking his head. "She said she's going next week."

"I think I'll go in for a minute, too," Johnny said, pulling himself out of his seat with his cane. "These diet sodas make me pee worse than beer."

Johnny hobbled around outstretched feet and patio furniture on his way to the house. He climbed the three steps onto the back porch and pulled open the screen door, nodding at Donna on his way to the bathroom.

*   *   *

Donna stood at the kitchen sink, swallowing the second jell cap when she heard a familiar voice.

"Did you find it?" Mai asked, her words coming from the adjacent family room.

Donna froze at the sound of Mai's voice. She swallowed the last gulp of water before saying, "You have to stop scaring me like that." Donna set the glass in the sink and turned toward the family room.

"You haven't answered me," Mai continued. "Did you find it?"

"Did I find what?" Donna entered the family room, searching for the source of the voice.

"That which you sought." Mai was silent for a moment. "Was it worth the pain?"

Donna smiled and nodded, understanding the nature of the question. "Yes," she said. "We are at peace."

"Are we?" Mai replied.

"Yes." Donna was suddenly dizzy. A second later the room went dark. She heard the crash of her own body hitting the floor but didn't feel the impact. Fighting the urge to sleep, she hardly noticed that as she opened her eyes she was looking up at the ceiling.

"You are not yet at peace," Mai offered. "One more thing to do."

"You said you would leave me alone," Donna protested, straining to keep her eyes open. "No more visits."

"This isn't a visit," Mai continued, unseen. "I've come to take you home."

*   *   *

While using the bathroom off the kitchen, Johnny felt a heavy thud resonate up from the floor. Johnny had almost reached the back door, on his way outside to join the party, when he thought he heard Donna's voice coming from the next room.

He turned toward the sound, peering through the doorway into the family room.

"No," he blurted, knowing what was to follow. "No," he repeated, rushing into the room. "No."

Donna was lying on her back on the floor; her eyes still open, motionless.

Johnny knelt beside her, lifting her arm and searching for a pulse. "Don't you do this. Not now." He stood and bolted for the back door. "You hang on!" All heads on the patio turned toward Johnny as he shoved the door open. It slammed into the railing with a crash.

"Brad!" Johnny shouted over the voices.

Brad turned, looking at his father over the surrounding heads. A smile left his face as his eyes met Johnny's, a sudden comprehension setting in. Brad nearly knocked Traci over as he brushed past her on his way to the back porch. Johnny could only watch his son's approach while praying for a miracle.

*   *   *

Johnny's image suddenly blocked her view, a genuine

look of concern on his face. He muttered something unin-
telligible and beat a path to the door. Deep down, Donna
knew she was living the final moments of her life; the fear
she was feeling gradually waning, replaced by a profound
peace she could never before have imagined possible. Her
head was starting to spin, her vision fading as Brad burst
into the room with Johnny and Elena close behind.

Brad knelt beside her and lifted Donna into his arms.
Safe in his embrace, she felt herself drifting, the feeling
draining from her limbs. Behind Brad, Elena stood next to
Johnny, her hands over her mouth, crying. Johnny stood
helpless, his arms around Elena, staring in disbelief at the
woman he had just come to know. Blurred faces and muffled footsteps swarmed into the room from the kitchen.
Distant voices melted together into a far away chorus,
growing weaker.

As much as Donna wanted to say goodbye, it wasn't to
be. With Brad's gentle sobs echoing in her ears, she slipped
from this world into eternity. As if with a new set of eyes,
Donna saw the clarity of the universe, all of its secrets disclosed in a heartbeat, her life's purpose revealed. Engulfed
in the purity of a cleansing white light, Donna saw Lien,
smiling as she stood among an endless throng of young
children, holding a single white rose.

Chapter Twenty-Seven

"I killed her," Brad said, staring into space. "I know I did."

Johnny stood in his black suit with Brad next to Donna's open casket at the funeral home. Elena and Gina, in their black dresses, lingered close by.

"You know that's not true," Gina replied, rubbing Brad's left shoulder.

"I did." Brad nodded, his eyes pressed shut. "When I knocked her in the head with that brush, I killed her."

They had all endured two grueling days and sleepless nights of calling hours. The funeral director said he had never seen so many mourners. The short service that had just ended was standing-room-only, spilling out into the hallway. Outside, the funeral procession extended for blocks. The funeral home had to request extra police escorts and borrow extra flags from other homes to accommodate all the cars. Johnny had never felt more helpless in his life. Only a few days before, he had seen the joy on Brad's face. Today his son's new wife was gone and Brad was left in ruins and there wasn't a damn thing Johnny could do about it.

"You didn't kill her," Johnny said, reaching up to clasp the back of Brad's neck. "The doctor said it was something that was in there for a long time." He glanced at Elena, searching for her reassurance.

"Was meant to be, Heinrich," Elena said. "Was God's will."

"You gotta understand something, son," Johnny added, gently grabbing Brad's arm and turning him. "God only knows what kind of chemicals she was exposed to over there."

Brad reached down, gripping the side of the open casket with his big hands. He bowed his head; his body shook. "How do I just leave her here?" he said, turning to Johnny, his eyes swelling with tears. "Do I just walk away now and let them put her in the ground?" Tears rolled down his face.

Johnny glanced toward the door where the funeral director was waiting. "Yeah. We do," he said, nodding. "She's gone, Brad," Johnny continued, looking right into Brad's eyes. "We have to let her go now." He turned his head toward Elena; unable to imagine the day he might be standing in Brad's shoes.

Fresh tears slid down Brad's cheeks as he nodded his reluctant affirmation. He turned and bent down, giving Donna one last kiss on her cheek.

"Take him outside," Johnny said to Elena and Gina. "I'll be right there."

Johnny watched the three of them walking toward the doorway while the director approached.

"Give me a minute," Johnny said to him. "Please."

The man, dressed in a black suit, stopped short and offered a closed-lip smile. "Of course." He gestured toward the double doorway. "I'll be right outside."

"Yeah," Johnny said after him. "Thanks."

Johnny turned toward the casket and took a deep breath. Edging closer, he cleared his throat. "I ain't very good at this kinda thing," he began, placing his hands on the casket. "So, you might have to read between the lines a little."

He took another deep breath while thinking how beautiful she looked, even in death. "Me and God," he continued. "We're gonna have some words over this." Johnny clenched his fists. "I'm not ready to get into it with him right now, but he's gonna hear from me about this."

He looked away, fighting back a tear. "I was just getting to know you, too." Johnny lost the fight as the wetness slid from his eyes. "I think we woulda been good friends." He looked down at the brass bracelet on his wrist and laughed. "Friends for life, right?" he said, inside making a silent vow that he would never take it off.

Johnny reached into the pocket of the only suit jacket he owned and pulled out a service medal. "I brought you something," he said, holding the Purple Heart between his thumb and forefinger. "I figure you deserve this more than me."

He pinned it onto one of the folds of her dress.

"Don't worry about Brad, either," he said, backing away. "We'll take good care of him."

Johnny placed a gentle hand on hers before turning and walking away. When he reached the doorway he nodded at the funeral director, who quickly walked past Johnny and into the viewing room.

"You must be Johnny," an unfamiliar voice called to him from behind.

"Yeah," he replied. "Who are you?" He turned to see a black woman, about sixty years old, in a dark colored dress approaching.

"Wanda," she answered. "A friend of Donna's." She looked Johnny over head to toe. "She told me all about you."

Johnny looked down and shook his head. "I'm not proud of the way I've behaved." He glanced back at Donna, still visible in the casket. "I know how I must have hurt her."

"She was the sweetest girl I ever met," Wanda said. "And I have no idea what you're talking about."

Johnny looked up. "I thought you said she told you all about me?"

"She said your wife was right about you two."

"How's that?"

"You weren't so different after all."

"She said that, huh?"

"She did." Wanda nodded, then smiled. "She said you must be a good man to raise up a son like Brad."

Johnny squeezed his eyes shut for a moment, choking back his shame.

"That's one thing you didn't count on, huh?" Wanda laughed. "That girl was so full of love she couldn't say anything bad about anybody." The smile left her face. "No matter how much he deserved it."

Johnny thought back over the last year, wishing he could take back so many things. He had still not allowed himself to look at the wedding pictures. "How do I say I'm sorry when it's too late?"

"It ain't never too late." Wanda placed a consoling hand on his arm. "I'll see you at the cemetery." Wanda smiled and walked away.

Johnny took one last look over his shoulder at Donna. The director was just closing the lid on the casket. He turned and gazed out toward the parking lot through the large plate-glass windows at Elena and Gina, their arms wrapped around his grief-stricken son. Johnny wiped the wetness from his face, pushed open the door and walked toward his family huddled together in the late morning sunshine.

Nguyen Khanh Mai

February 3rd, 1963 — August, 28th 1999

Bạn tôi luôn

www.dustoflife.com

About the Author

Cameron Michaels has lived the kind of life that seldom attracts the attention of agents, publishers, or filmmakers. He's not a lawyer, astronaut, or secret agent. In fact, he grew up in Syracuse, New York in a very modest house in a very modest neighborhood. He's never been to prison, drug rehab, or even been divorced, for that matter. He smokes an occasional cigar with a good friend, usually chasing it with a pint of Guinness. He's been with the same girl now for going on twenty-six years. In fact, he's never been with anyone else. Couldn't imagine it. Once upon a time he was a Regents Scholar. He graduated from UCLA and has since held jobs as a janitor, garbage man, painter, insurance agent, industrial salesman, small business owner, and company vice-president. He is currently a large account executive with an international company. Active in his church and community, he has worked with rape and sexual abuse counseling and education, served as Pack Committee Chairman of a scout pack, committed himself to raising money for cancer research through the Relay For Life events, and is currently assisting homeless through his church through the Room In The Inn program. He currently resides near Nashville, Tennessee with his wife and three children.

author@cameronmichaels.net
www.dustoflife.com
www.cameronmichaels.net

Printed in the United States
1288500003B/43-153

9 780970 760036